George M. Barbour

Florida for Tourists, Invalids, and Settlers

George M. Barbour

Florida for Tourists, Invalids, and Settlers

ISBN/EAN: 9783337327842

Printed in Europe, USA, Canada, Australia, Japan

Cover: Foto ©Andreas Hilbeck / pixelio.de

More available books at **www.hansebooks.com**

FLORIDA

FOR

TOURISTS, INVALIDS, AND SETTLERS:

CONTAINING

PRACTICAL INFORMATION

REGARDING

CLIMATE, SOIL, AND PRODUCTIONS; CITIES, TOWNS, AND PEOPLE;
THE CULTURE OF THE ORANGE AND OTHER TROPICAL FRUITS;
FARMING AND GARDENING; SCENERY AND RESORTS;
SPORT; ROUTES OF TRAVEL, ETC., ETC.

GEORGE M. BARBOUR.

WITH MAP AND ILLUSTRATIONS.

REVISED EDITION.

NEW YORK:
D. APPLETON AND COMPANY,
1, 3, AND 5 BOND STREET.
1884.

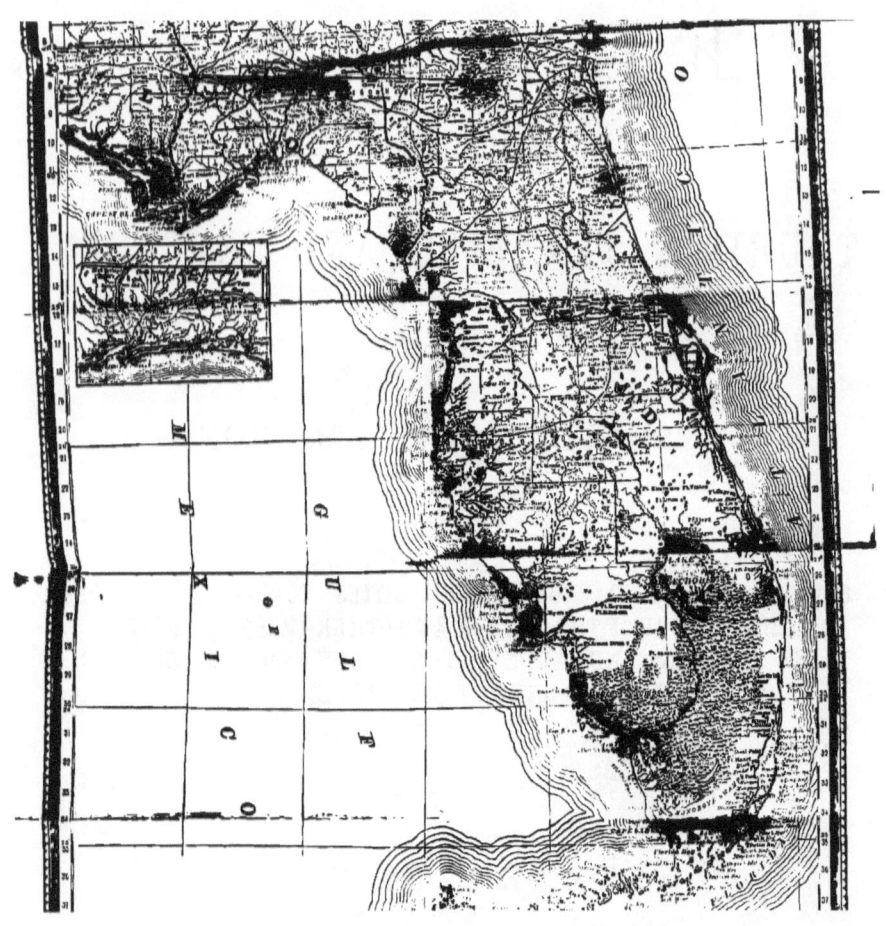

PREFACE.

The writer of the following pages first saw Florida in the month of January, 1880, when he accompanied General Grant on his tour through the State, as correspondent of the "Chicago Times." He had previously either traveled or resided in nearly every other portion of the country, East, West, and South; but his first impressions of the "Land of Flowers" were so favorable that, his special service as correspondent being over, he returned thither with the idea of making for himself a permanent home which should put an end to his wanderings. Since then he has enjoyed an extended experience in the State, engaged in a vocation requiring visits to all the more prominent places, and traveled over its immense territory under circumstances the most favorable for learning its real resources and observing the great variety of its productions.

Almost from the beginning, the importance of writing a book embodying the results of his observation and experience was urged upon him by the friends whom he made in the course of his travels; and his perusal of the multifarious inquiries addressed to the State Bureau of Immigration, at Jacksonville, convinced him that there is a real demand for an adequate and trustworthy descriptive work on Florida. With the exception of a few brief pamphlets, written for the most part in the interest of some land scheme or other speculative enterprise, there appears to be really no publication (except the Bureau of Immigration pamphlet) which answers practical questions in a practical manner; and even those books designed for transient visitors have been rendered wofully inadequate and antiquated by the progress that has been achieved during the past few years.

The present volume is the result of personal observation and study; and is written with a sincere desire to do justice to all parts of the State, and to describe accurately and with precision its real resources and advantages. It is written for Florida *entire*, and not in the interest of any corporation, speculative scheme, or special locality. Having no land to sell, and no personal interest of any kind to further, the author has found little difficulty in following Othello's injunction, "naught to extenuate, nor set down aught in malice."

Where so many have aided him with information and suggestions, the author feels that it is almost invidious to name only a few; yet he can not forbear thus explicitly acknowledging his obligations to the Hon.

Seth French, late Commissioner of the Bureau of Immigration; to Captain Samuel Fairbanks, Assistant Commissioner; and to Mr. William Bloxham, the present Governor of the State. Last, but not least, he would offer his acknowledgments to Mr. C. H. Jones, of Florida, who rendered him invaluable aid in the arrangement and revision of his work.

G. M. B.

September, 1881.

In this edition of this work the chapter on Routes (Chapter XXIII) has been entirely rewritten; and an Appendix has been added containing much important information brought down to the present date.

October, 1884.

CONTENTS.

8 *CONTENTS.*

LIST OF ILLUSTRATIONS.

FLORIDA.

CHAPTER I.

FLORIDA! What kind of a place is it? How does it look? What does it produce? What are the conditions of success there? How do the people live? How do they like it? These are a few of the multitude of questions that are eagerly showered upon a resident of this sunny, genial clime, when visiting the less favored regions of our country.

Those who ask them commonly suppose that they can be answered as compendiously and precisely as the some-what similar questions in a geographical text-book; but, unfortunately, this is not possible, and the numerous pages comprising the present volume are none too many to answer them in full. In fact, it is for the sole purpose of answering these and similar inquiries that I have written the following book; and I trust that, when he has finished it, the reader will acquit me of having made any larger demands upon his attention than was necessary to the accomplishment of this object. I might say, indeed, in response to the first question, that it is a delightful place; to the second, that it looks like a region perpetually breathed upon by airs from Araby the blest; and to the other, that it produces nearly everything, with less expenditure of labor than is the case in any other portion of the wide domain included within the United States. There are few, however, who will be satisfied any longer with such "glittering generalities"—a surfeit of them having already been dealt out by previous writers on the subject ; and my own aim has been to give as clearly and specifically as I can such information as may prove helpful to the three classes of readers to whom the book is addressed : the tourist who comes for amusement, sight-seeing, or sport ; the invalid who comes in search of that more genial climate which shall prolong his days in the land ; and, even more especially, the settler whose aim is to make himself a home under pleasanter and more promising conditions than those which he encounters on the stern soil or amid the harsh blasts of the northern sections of our country.

Florida has a history (as will be told in the chapter on that subject) that extends back to 1512, covering a period of nearly four hundred years ; yet in spite of this, and in spite, too, of its unequaled natural advantages, it has a smaller population, in proportion to its great size, than any other State in the Union, except, perhaps, Nevada and Colorado. A constantly rising tide of immigration is now flowing in, and there has been a surprising increase in the number of inhabitants during the past ten years; but some of the very choicest localities in the State are still in a state of nature, and there is room and verge enough for an additional million of busy and prosperous workers. For Florida is a very large State—one of the largest in the' Union—with an area of nearly sixty thousand square miles; and, in proportion to its size, it has as large an acreage of productive soil as any other, except the prairie States of the West. Many portions, no doubt, are ill adapted for what are commonly regarded as the great staples of the country ; but in the range and variety of its productions it is hardly equaled, and is certainly not surpassed, by any other section of equal area. (See Appendix, note 1.)

This fact in regard to Florida is usually overlooked by those who derive their ideas from the hasty conclusions of transient winter visitors. Each so-called "season" witnesses an influx of thousands of these visitors, in search of health or "on pleasure bent," usually wealthy, and equipped with more prejudices than their well-filled traveling-bags would contain. Their chief desire is to find an elegant hotel, having "all modern conveniences"; and, once established there, to secure some cozy nook on a broad veranda, where they may watch the fruits and flowers growing in the open air, breathe the soft, balmy air, and lazily enjoy all the luxury and delights of June in January. For recreation, they ride to the nearest orange-groves, or indulge in a moonlight sail, or, if a little more adventurous and "masculine," take a few quiet fishing-trips, or hunt quail and duck. Once, at least, during their stay, they make the "grand tour" by the regulation route—up the St. John's to Palatka, Enterprise, and Sanford, up the darkly-mysterious Ocklawaha (very few, on this excursion, even leaving the boat), then down the river again and over to St. Augustine, where the longest stay is apt to be made, as its many points of interest and its animated social life render St. Augustine peculiarly attractive to the average pleasure-seeker. This, in the great majority of instances, is the full extent of their study and observation of the characteristics and resources of Florida; and, such being the case, it can hardly be regarded as surprising that they should represent it as a pleasant enough place of resort in winter for invalids, but a hot, unwholesome region in summer, poor in soil, arid of aspect, the haunt of alligators, reptiles, and insects. (See Appendix, note 2.)

It need hardly be pointed out, however, that the true capabilities of a great State can not be dealt with adequately in this summary fashion ; and, as a matter of fact, Florida has a soil in which can be grown every variety of fruit, flower, garden-vegetable, field-crop, or forest product, that grows in any temperate or semi-tropical region of the world. Every one has heard of its fabulous yield of oranges, lemons, and the like ; and the stories told on this head are not always exaggerated. I have seen groves of orange-trees which produced from two hundred to four thousand dollars to the acre, and know of an acre of pine-apples that, within two years after the trees were cleared from its surface, yielded the owners (two bright young New York lads, by-the-way) eighteen hundred dollars. But these, and such as these, by no means exhaust the list of valuable products which Florida yields to the cultivator. I have seen fields of wheat ripening in January that produced twenty-eight bushels to the acre ; corn that produced in the same month seventy bushels to the acre ; sugar-cane that yielded one hundred and sixty dollars net profit to the acre ; common Irish potatoes producing two hundred bushels to the acre ; fields of rice that paid a net profit of two hundred dollars an acre ; and cassava that netted a hundred and fifty dollars per acre. Water-melons and garden-vegetables grow rapidly, attain great size, are of excellent quality, and, where convenient to city markets, or to lines of transportation, pay the producer from one hundred to one thousand dollars per acre. Of garden-vegetables three and even four crops are sometimes taken from the same tract within twelve months ; and of the entire list of strange or familiar farm and garden products, fruits, and flowers, you may, in a trip through the State, find growing in abundance. The largest peach-tree, undoubtedly, in America, is near Orange City, in Volusia County, with a spread of branches over seventy feet. (See Appendix, note 3.)

Nor is this all. I have seen bean-vines in their third

year bearing as vigorously as when first planted ; pears growing on vines ; peas growing on trees ; and plants growing on nothing at all—the latter being the common air-plants. Of live-stock, I have seen as large, fine, fat swine, and as neat cattle and sheep, as in Vermont, New York, or Illinois ; and they can be raised and kept in good condition at so small a cost that comparison with Northern-raised stock is absurd.

The climate of Florida in the winter months is simply delightful, and the summers are about as endurable as in most other portions of the United States. The summer of 1880 was said by all to be the hottest for many years, and the winter of 1880–'81 to be the coldest ; yet I can affirm from the sure basis of personal experience that they were both healthy and agreeable, even to a new-comer. It seems absolutely impossible that any human being, or any living creature able to move about, should really suffer from either cold or heat, or from hunger, in Florida. It is asserted (and meets with no dispute) that no case of starvation, of freezing, of sunstroke, or of hydrophobia, was ever known in the State ; and local epidemics have never been heard of.

Consider the terribly cold weather of the long, dreary winter season throughout the North ; the suffering it causes ; the many deaths among the poor, perishing for want of a little friendly warmth. Consider also the cases of sunstroke, the suffering and deaths caused directly or indirectly by the heat, in those same regions during the summer ; and the still more sorrowful cases of actual starvation for lack of the plainest food in many of the large cities. Then contemplate the advantages of this favored clime, where food—even such articles as are regarded as luxuries in other localities—may be had in abundance, for very little cost or labor, and where a genial temperature prevails at all seasons !

But there is one thing to be remembered in connection with all this—and it is forgotten oftener than would be supposed : even Florida is not the garden of Eden, and a man can not live even here like the lilies of the field, "which toil not, neither do they spin." Florida soil and climate can and will do a great deal ; but living without labor is not possible, and here as elsewhere the great law prevails, that in the sweat of his brow shall man eat his bread. The true advantage which Florida offers is, that by little labor can much comfort be enjoyed, and the better directed the labor the greater the comfort. To those who have but little capital (or none), and who are anxiously seeking for a home with all the comforts of life, I believe that this State offers the best chances of any in our country.

Finally, as a compendious answer to the many inquiries upon the subject that have come to my knowledge, I would say that a settler in Florida—whether he comes as a capitalist, as a farmer, or as a laborer—can live with more ease and personal comfort, can live more cheaply, can enjoy more genuine luxuries, can obtain a greater income from a smaller investment and by less labor, and can sooner secure a competency, than in any other accessible portion of North America.

CHAPTER II.

As I have already remarked, Florida is a very large State, containing nearly sixty thousand square miles (59,-268). From north to south it stretches 450 miles—from a temperate to a tropical clime. Washed along its entire eastern border by the equable waters of the Gulf Stream, which always pours its pure salt breezes over the peninsula, and by the tropically warm waters of the Gulf of Mexico on much of its western boundary, it possesses a variety of climate, soil, and products, such as can be found nowhere else save in Italy, which enjoys a similarity of geographical conditions.

Though its extreme length from the Perdido River to Cape Sable is about 700 miles, its average breadth is less than 90 miles, and in shape it is a long and narrow peninsula, extending southward into the Atlantic and pointing toward Cuba, Havana being only 110 miles from Key West. On the southeast it is separated from the Bahamas by the Straits of Florida. The peninsula proper terminates on the south in Cape Sable; but a remarkable chain of rocky islets, known as the Florida Keys, begins at Cape Florida on the eastern shore, extends southwestward nearly 200 miles, and ends in the cluster of sand-heaped rocks called the Tortugas, from the great number of turtles formerly frequenting them. South of the bank on which the Keys rise, and separated from them by a navigable channel, is the narrow and dangerous coral ridge known as the Flor-

ida Reef. The entire State is comprised between latitude
24° 30′ and 31° north, and longitude 80° and 87° 45′ west.

LIGHTHOUSE ON FLORIDA KEYS.

In the aggregate Florida possesses a coast-line of more
than 1,150 miles, but on this long stretch of seaboard there
are only a few good harbors. The principal on the Atlantic coast are St. Augustine, Fernandina, Port Orange, and
Jacksonville (on the St. John's River); those on the Gulf
coast are Pensacola, Appalachicola, St. Mark's, Cedar Keys,

Tampa, Charlotte Harbor, and Key West. The latter is
one of the most important naval stations of the republic,
owing to its commanding situation at the entrance of the
most frequented passage into the Gulf of Mexico. The
chief rivers are the St. John's, which furnishes nearly 1,000
miles of water navigation; the Indian River, a long, narrow lagoon on the eastern coast; the Ocklawaha, the Appa-

A HAMMOCK.

lachicola, the Ocklockonnee, the Perdido, the Suwanee,
and the St. Mary's. The Withlacoochee, which discharges

its waters into the Gulf, is an important stream, as are also Peace Creek, which falls into Charlotte Harbor, and the Caloosahatchie, which empties into the Gulf still farther south. Kissimmee River, connecting several of the smaller lakes with Lake Okechobee, is also a navigable stream.

The surface of the State is generally level, the greatest elevation being but little more than 500 feet above the sea, and this being attained in only a few places. The lands are classified as high-hammock, low-hammock, savanna, swamp, and pine. The hammocks vary from a few acres to thousands of acres in extent, and are found in all parts of the peninsula. They are usually covered with a dense growth of red, live, and water oak, magnolia, gum, hickory, and dogwood; and when cleared they afford a soil of almost inexhaustible fertility. The savannas are rich alluvial tracts on the margins of streams, or lying in detached areas, yielding largely, but requiring ditching and diking in ordinary seasons. Except in the hammocks, the soil is generally sandy and apt to be poor. Numerous lakes dot the surface of the interior, the largest being Lake Okechobee, which is said to cover an area of more than 650 square miles. Perhaps the most remarkable geographical feature of the State is the immense tract of marsh or lake filled with islands, in the southern part of the peninsula, called the Everglades (by the Indians "grass-water"). It is about 60 miles long by 60 broad, covering most of the territory south of Lake Okechobee, and is impassable during the rainy reason, from July to October. The islands with which its surface is studded vary from one fourth of an acre to hundreds of acres in extent, and are usually entangled in dense thickets of shrubbery or vines. The water of the lake is from one to six feet deep, and the bottom is covered with a growth of rank grass which, rising above the surface, gives it the deceptive appearance of a boundless prairie. Another noteworthy feature of Florida are the subterranean streams which undermine the rotten-limestone formation, creating numerous cavities in the ground that are locally known as "sinks." These are inverted conical hollows, or tunnels, varying in extent from a few yards to several acres, at the bottom of which running water often appears.

The foregoing is a rapid summary of the geographical or cyclopedic descriptions that are usually given of Florida, and it is as accurate, perhaps, as such sweeping generalizations can be expected to be; yet when taken too literally these descriptions are not only inadequate, but misleading. For the truth is, that there are three kinds of Florida—three Floridas, so to speak—each distinct in soil, climate, and productions; and it is because of this that the people of other sections, as they read about the State in short newspaper sketches, or in pamphlets published in the interests of some special locality, are apt to draw erroneous inferences. For instance, the winter of 1880–'81 was exceptionally severe everywhere, making itself felt even in Florida; and the Northern and foreign reader, learning that fruits were destroyed, garden-crops hopelessly ruined, oranges frozen on the trees by thousands, in fact that cold and frost played havoc in Florida as well as elsewhere, doubtless came to the conclusion that it was not much of a tropical State after all. Well, these things happened, just as reported. The frost came, and immense damage was done, and much loss inflicted. Yet the fact is that the section thus visited included but a small portion of the State —only the northern and a portion of middle Florida. A large portion of the State was not—and never is—visited by frosts that kill. So that, while the reports were true, they were not the whole truth, and there were many districts to which they did not apply at all.

The three natural divisions under which Florida must be described, if it is to be described accurately, may be classified as the Northern or Temperate, the Semi-tropical, and the Tropical.

Northern Florida, especially the western section of it, in soil, productions, and general appearance, closely resembles regions much farther north. It is a land of live-stock, of corn, wheat, cotton, cane, jute, rice, ramie, potatoes, apples, grapes, peaches, figs, in fact all the products of fields, forests, and gardens of a northern clime, with a few of the hardier of southern products. The tropical banana, pineapple, etc., do not grow there, nor the orange or lemon, as a crop for profit. Its soil is excellent; its surface is rolling and hilly, with grand forests, rocks, springs, and streams; and the roads are firm and good. It is not tropical, but is very picturesque and home-like, and, to the Northern visitor, is the most agreeable portion of the State. Better live-stock, or crops, can not be produced in the world, in greater abundance, or with less expense and labor, than grow here; but they are *not tropical crops.* Such is Northern Florida, where frosts and "cold snaps" are not only possible, but frequently occur.

Middle Florida is that portion of the State lying between the twenty-eighth and thirtieth parallels, and may be termed Semi-tropical Florida. It is the region where many of the products of both the temperate and the tropical climes may be found growing side by side; where the orange, lemon, fig, guava, citron, grape, and all garden-vegetables, may be found growing, for profit, in the open air, all the year round. It is where cotton, cane, rice, and all field-crops pay best, and where wheat, corn, and live-stock are noticeably less productive than a little farther north. The soil here is mostly of a sandy character, and begins to have the characteristic appearance of a tropical soil; while the surface is generally flat and uninteresting, with occasional slightly rolling tracts. There are but few streams or lakes, except in the central portion—known to the residents as the Orange Lake region—where there are several quite large-sized lakes, which are of very attractive appearance. (See Appendix, note 4.)

Large orange-groves are found growing in all parts of this region, and thousands of trees are being set out yearly. Hundreds of the settlers there—especially along the line of the Transit Railroad (that runs from Fernandina to Cedar Keys) and its branches—in the vicinity of Starke, Waldo, Gainesville, and of Ocala and Leesburg, are engaged in raising vegetables of all kinds for the Northern markets. Thousands of crates of green peas, tomatoes, beans, cucumbers, onions, cabbages, cauliflower, spinach, celery, lettuce, beets, etc., and car-loads of watermelons, are gathered and shipped to all points North in January, February, March, and April. It is an industry that has, in a few years, grown to great proportions, and, when the season is at all favorable, repays those engaged handsomely. In many cases profits of several hundreds of dollars (upward of a thousand dollars are known of in several cases) have been made in a single season, from an acre or but little more, of some special crop, that fortunately ripened and reached the market at the right moment. Strawberries here grow abundantly, and with proper care and culture yield immense crops, repaying wonderful profits. I know of several cases where the clear profit, netted from about an acre, was almost fabulous. This is rapidly becoming a leading crop or industry of the State.

Semi-tropical Florida, while not very attractive in scenery, probably produces the greatest variety of marketable and profitable crops of any region in our country. Although the hardier field-crops of the North, such as wheat, corn, etc., and the more delicate fruit-products of the extreme South, like the banana, pineapple, etc., do not grow well in this region, yet the variety of the vegetable

2

kingdom, including the hardiest of the Southern and the
tenderest of the Northern crops, is so great that the land
will always produce paying crops in one form or another.
As transportation facilities increase, the opportunities and
advantages will multiply ; for the crops of this region
are grown in that season, and are of that kind, that they
must be at once placed in the hands of the consumer.

Without entering into a lengthy description of its
climate or physical features, I may say that it is a healthy
region, and that game and fish are plentiful. There is but
one unpleasant feature to mar its numerous advantages :
it is liable to frosts. They may come any winter—and
may not in a dozen years—but a visit, when it comes, is
very apt to destroy your hopes of profit for that season.
Of oranges and such fruits, in this semi-tropical belt, the
farther south the better ; every mile north is a step toward
greater risk. You can not get too far south—that is, if
you find good soil—but you can easily get too far north,
even for semi-tropical products.

South Florida comprises all that region of mainland
and innumerable keys or islands, great and small, lying
south of the twenty-eighth parallel, and is the really, truly
tropical Florida—the Italy, the Spain, the Egypt, of the
United States. In this region frosts rarely come, and
every fruit, flower, shrub, plant, or product, that grows in
any tropical region of the world grows, or can be grown,
here. Either on its Atlantic, breezy, rocky coast ; its hot,
torrid, south end shores, or its balmy Gulf coast, or within
its vast interior—the famous Everglades region—in all
these prolific, tropical soils can something of profit be
grown ; though, of course, the farther south the more
surely can the really tropical products be counted upon.
It is the region of the pineapple, banana, cocoanut, guava,
sugar-apple, bread-fruit, sugar-cane, almond, fig, olive, and
all the innumerable list of tropical fruits.

The great Everglades region includes much of the mainland of this part of the State. It is not a swampy region, but is a flat, prairie country very much like Illinois, only this is covered with clear, pure water for thousands of square miles, from three to thirty inches deep, and studded with islands that have a dense growth of palmetto, cypress, pine, bay, cedar, oak, hickory, gum, magnolia, and all such timbers. These island fastnesses, by-the-way, are the homes of the remnant of the once powerful Seminole Indians. A contract has recently been made, and ratified by the State, for the drainage of this vast region, which, if successfully performed, will open up for settlement millions of acres of the richest and most valuable sugar and cotton lands in the world.

The regions along the coasts generally contain the best soil for the production of vegetables and fruits. It is also in these localities that the sand-fly, gnat, mosquito, and such pestiferous insects are most abundant. But even here there are months when they are not troublesome : it is during the midsummer months when they are worst, and it is the fact that right in those localities there are places perfectly free from all the insects that infest other places. The coasts, especially on the Atlantic, are very rocky, and the scenery is in general exceedingly tropical and interesting. The woods, fields, air, lakes, bays, and rivers are filled with fur, fin, and feather, flesh and fowl, oysters, turtles, and fruits. The metropolis of all this region is Key West, itself on an island just off the southern extremity of the peninsula ; and other prominent places are Indian River, Lake Worth, Key Biscayne Bay, Florida Bay, Cape Sable, Whitewater Bay, Oyster Bay, Charlotte Harbor, and Tampa Bay.

` This is the region to go to for purely tropical products and for the benefits of a summer climate in winter ; but as a place for a continued residence the entire year, it will not be desirable until many more settlers move in. It is too lonely, and the means of transportation are too few and irregular ; but all who live in those regions are quite unanimous in asserting that the climate is pleasant all the year, and I have reason to believe life is just as pleasant there in all seasons as anywhere, except for the lack of society and transportation above mentioned. If large settlements, towns, and cities were founded there, and regular communication opened, it would be one of the most delightful regions of America, healthy and agreeable, while the products of its salt-water coast, fresh-water lakes and rivers, fields, gardens, and groves would furnish to mankind, at all seasons, the best and most delicious of all foods that human nature craves.

"Like all other tropical countries, Tropical Florida has its wet and dry seasons.* The wet or rainy season is during midsummer, which has a tendency to cool the atmosphere, and render the summer months cooler than they are in the more northern portions of the State or in other portions of the South. During the rainy season nearly the whole country is flooded, the country being so flat and level that the water does not flow off readily. A great portion of the country requires ditching and draining, and, when some systematic method shall be adopted to let off the surplus water during the rainy season, this portion of the State will prove the most productive part of the South. It has but few swamps or marshes, unless you consider the Everglades a marsh. The Alpativkee Swamp, upon the head-waters of the St. Lucie River, is the only swamp of any magnitude in Tropical Florida, and this part of the State has less swamps than northern Wisconsin or Michigan. The country east and south of the St. John's River has more swamps than any other part of the State through which I have traveled. They are principally covered with cypress-timber, and, being easy of access from the St. Johns and Indian Rivers, are valuable. There are fine lands upon Halifax River and

* The following paragraphs are abridged from a report prepared by a resident at the request of the Commissioner of the Bureau of Immigration.

Mosquito Lagoon, which, at a former period, were under cultivation, but were abandoned during the Indian war by their owners. All that portion of the State which I have denominated Tropical Florida is capable of producing oranges, lemons, limes, arrow-root, cassava, indigo, Sisal-hemp, sugarcane, sea-island cotton, rice, figs, melons of all kinds, as well as the vegetables grown in the more northern States. The country around Charlotte Harbor and Biscayne Bay is susceptible of producing cocoanuts, cacao, pineapples, guavas, coffee, bananas, plantains, alligator pears, and all the fruits and plants of the West Indies. The rich lands which skirt the savannas upon the coast side are covered with rotten limestone, and have mixed with the vegetable matter to that extent that the soil will effervesce as soon as it comes in contact with acids. These savannas are valuable for sugar-plantations, as the sugar-cane requires a large percentage of lime, and the climate is so mild that the cane will not require planting oftener than once in ten or twelve years. The *Palma i Christi*, or castor-bean, is here perennial, and grows to be quite a tree. I saw a number as large as peach-trees twenty feet high. Sea-island cotton seems to be a perennial in this section of the State, and is of a fine quality. Live-oak, yellow pine, cabbage-tree, and mangrove are the most abundant forest-trees, though formerly a good deal of fustic, mahogany, lignum-vitæ, and braziletto was to be met with ; but these valuable species of timber have been so much in demand for ship-building and commerce that trees of any size are rare. The most formidable obstacle the farmer meets in preparing ground for cultivation is the saw-palmetto (*Chamærops serrulata*), with plated palmate fronds and sharply serrate stipes. The roots cover the surface of the ground, and are removed by the slow process of the grubbing-hoe. Several species of this genus of palm afforded the Florida tribes food, wine, sugar, fruit, cabbage, fans, darts, ropes, and cloth. Some have good fruit, like plums ; others austere, like dates. They are now chiefly used to make hats, fans, baskets, and mats, with the leaves.

"The land bordering on the Caloosahatchie River and its tributaries is accessible by vessels drawing not more than six feet, and contains enough live-oak to supply the navy of the United States for a quarter of a century. Other val-

uable timber for ship-building is found in the same locality.
Such being the natural advantages which invite enterprise
to this quarter, there can be no doubt that, when its agricultural resources are more generally understood, southern
Florida will be covered with a dense population of thrifty
farmers. Cuba, with almost a corresponding climate, has
several hundred plants which serve as a basis to her agri-
culture, such as grains, farinaceous roots, edible seeds, vegetables, salads, sauces, and fruits ; the great staples of ex-
portation — sugar, coffee, and tobacco ; plants for dyes,
yielding oil, suitable for cordage or cloth, yielding gums
and resins, good for tanning ; grasses ; and woods employed
in various uses. Now, it is well known that most of the
productions of Cuba are growing in south Florida, and,
with cultivation, might be made to rival those of that celebrated island. Sea-island cotton of a fine quality has been
produced in the very center of the peninsula. Florida sur-
passes Cuba in variety and delicacy of vegetable culture.
At all seasons of the year beets, onions, egg-plants, carrots,
lettuce, celery, etc., are produced with the most indifferent
culture, while everything that grows upon vines is in abundance and in great perfection. Cabbages and Irish potatoes, if planted in October, produce well. The former have
been grown at Fort Myers, a single head weighing forty
pounds. Cattle, hogs, and poultry increase astonishingly.
Besides the above, tobacco, pindars, cow-peas, and Irish
potatoes yield abundantly.

"The prairie lands are immense meadows, clothed with
luxuriant verdure, interspersed with clumps of oak-trees
and palmettoes of from five to ten acres each. These lands
are looked upon as inferior for agricultural purposes, and
are subject to periodical inundations during the summer
season—i. e., from the beginning of June to the 25th of
August. They are the favorite resort of vast herds of cattle and game, which roam and graze upon the fragrant herb-
age. The estimate of the amount of cattle is from 150,-
000 to 200,000 head, thereby forming one of the principal
products of the country. Stock-cattle sell for five dollars
per head, and beef-cattle from nine to thirteen dollars per
head. Hogs also do well, and, when strict attention is paid
to them, pay well. I have known and heard of several
instances in which the common woods-hog, two and a half

years old, weighed from 400 to 500 pounds gross. Sheep
and colts, with the natural advantages that this country
possesses, could be made profitable. The forest abounds in
game, such as bears, panthers, deer, cats, raccoons, squirrels, and turkeys, and the lakes and rivers afford innumerable multitudes of fish and waterfowl. There are also numerous small lakes of pure water, some of which are only
a few rods in extent, while others are from two to ten miles
in length, filled with fish. These prairies are the paradise
of the herdsman and the hunter. The cattle require no
feeding during the winter, and one can hardly travel over
the prairies a whole day without seeing from fifty to one
hundred deer."

CHAPTER III.

In the midwinter of 1879–'80 the Hon. Seth French, State Commissioner of Immigration, decided to make an official tour through the southern and middle regions of the State, for the purpose of better informing himself as to the general character of the people, the soil, the products, and the facilities for transportation. He kindly invited the writer to accompany him, and the invitation was gladly accepted. It was a very extensive tour, and gave us an unusually excellent opportunity to fully acquaint ourselves with a very large section of the State. Mr. French—known to all his friends as Dr. French—is a native of New York, but was for many years a resident of Wisconsin. He is a man of wealth, liberal education, fine presence and address, social disposition, thoroughly interested in his duties, and an enthusiast about Florida—in all respects just the man for the peculiar and responsible position which he then held.

At noon of one rainy day late in January, we took passage at Jacksonville on the old, small, odd-looking but excellent steamer Volusia, commanded by young Captain Lund. It is an up-river steamer, an old-timer, built especially for navigating the narrow, crooked channel of the far-up St. John's. The steamer was crowded with passengers, including an elderly lady and her husband, from New England ; a Massachusetts school-ma'rm ; a lady with

a daughter of about sixteen, from Ohio ; and a lady residing in Jacksonville, with three small children and a nurse.
The latter was on an excursion-trip, up and return ; and
those three children, that is to say, the two oldest boys,
kept the entire party in an uneasy fidget for fear that they
would or wouldn't get drowned.

The morning of the third day found us in Lake Jessup,
and from this point the trip was novel as well as interesting.* The St. John's above Lake Monroe (twelve miles
below Lake Jessup) is little more than a narrow and very
crooked creek. Passing out of Lake Jessup, we at once
entered this narrow stream, and found ourselves in a region differing wholly from any other portion of the St.
John's country. It is a flat, level region of savannas, much
resembling the vast prairies of Illinois. In all directions
the eye ranges to the horizon, with nothing to break the
monotony. But though monotonous, it is not uninteresting. These savannas, or prairies, are everywhere densely
covered with luxuriant growths of marshy grasses and
maiden-cane (the latter a tall, slender, waving growth of
the sugar-cane species, in appearance closely resembling
fields of wheat, ten to fifteen feet high), with occasional
clumps of timber, consisting sometimes of but three or
four trees, and sometimes being several acres in extent.
The trees are nearly or quite all of palmetto, and lend a
distinctively tropical appearance to the scenery. They
much resemble small islands dotted over the surface of a
great lake.

Throughout that entire region were to be seen hundreds of cattle grazing on the rich vegetation, which is
said to be greatly liked by them, and very fattening. One
herd alone, owned by J. M. Lanier, numbers over twenty
thousand head, and there are several other herds fully

---

* The lower St. John's is fully described in another chapter.

as large. The scene, too, was enlivened by hundreds of
storks, cranes, curlews—of all gay colors—pelicans, herons,
flamingoes, and water-turkeys, nearly all varieties being
large, long-legged, long-necked, and long-billed, in gay-
colored or snow-white plumage, all quite strange, and curiously interesting to the Northern visitor. Everywhere
they could be seen standing in motionless meditation ; or,
if the boat approached too close, they would rise in a singularly graceful manner, and wheel off into the distance.
The water everywhere was alive with ducks of several
varieties, and numbering millions, probably, while alligators were very plentiful. This, indeed, is the real home
of these great, hideous, but always interesting saurians ;
here are the largest size, the monsters of the race ; often
of ten to fifteen feet in length. This portion of the river
is, in fact, but little traveled. Only five or six small
steamers ply upon its waters, and it is seldom that more
than two steamers pass a given point in one day ; so the
beasts and reptiles that haunt it are but little disturbed,
and thrive unmolested by mankind.

The stream is so narrow that the little steamer, only
about twenty feet wide, often brushed the tall cane on
both sides as it passed along. Now and then it seemed as
if the boat was traveling on land, as it came to some
sharp bends and pushed its way through the tall grasses
almost overarching above. And the channel is so crooked
that in many places the steamer would have to plow its
nose into the bank, let the stern swing around a little,
while a small boat, rowed by two stout deck-negroes, would
tow the head around the sharp bend. After hours of
travel, we could look back, and within one or two miles'
distance see the outlines of the stream zigzagging across
to the right and left, like a great letter S. At one point
we could see across five of these curves within a distance
of two miles. At intervals the stream widens into broad,

shallow lakes, full of fish and covered with ducks. These lakes are the paradise of alligators, fish, birds, and cattle.

Late in the afternoon—it was supper-time—we arrived at Salt Lake, the end of our journey by the boat, having traveled a distance of three hundred and eleven miles by water, or about one hundred and forty-five miles in a direct line, from Jacksonville.

Salt Lake is a small lake, or series of connected ponds ; prairie on all but the east side, which has a heavy growth of timber, the commencement of a forest that covers the intervening country to the Indian River. On the shore was a solitary cabin, the depot of the mule-power, wooden-railed road over to Titusville. We anchored some distance from the shore, for the water was too shallow for the little steamer to go close in. At once several of the passengers took the small boat and went fishing, having a grand success. In a half-hour, five men caught upward of forty-five fine, large fish. Others continued shooting away at the ducks all around us, killing great numbers, that were brought in by the small boats. Many passengers had been shooting at ducks (and alligators) all day ; most of the ducks were picked up by a little Mexican, a member of the crew, who followed along behind in the row-boat, for the steamer goes slowly there, and he took advantage of short cuts.

The next morning was beautiful ; all were up early, and soon the car was seen at the shore cabin. Then two or three negro laborers poled a large lighter out to the steamer, and we were soon seated in the curious vehicle. We met here a party of several tourist-sportsmen returning from a fishing, turtling, hunting-trip on Indian River ; also on the lighter was a cargo of about eighty monster sea-green turtles, their weight marked on their backs. These were on their way to the leading hotels of the North. "Turtle-soup to-day" was their final epitaph.

The journey on this primitive sort of railroad was

through a flat or slightly rolling country, timbered with pine, palmetto, and oak, and it was enlivened by the car getting off the track two or three times, caused by the breaking of the old wooden rails. On such occasions the male passengers would cheerfully assist the very good-natured conductor to replace the car and hunt up and lay a fresh rail. All were in good-humor, and seemed to consider it a part of the business of the trip—a sort of side-show entertainment. Titusville, eight miles from the boat-landing on Salt Lake, was reached early in the forenoon, and we were at last on the Indian River. The town, or settlement, is the county-seat of Brevard County, and has about one hundred and fifty inhabitants. It contains two very neat, well-kept hotels (the Lund House and the Titus House), two or three small stores or shops, a warehouse, and about fifty dwelling-houses. The land thereabout is flat, and appears to be rather poor, although we saw excellent vegetables, and a great abundance of flowers, growing in the gardens of its vicinity. Across the river—it is really a sound, for it has no current, and has a slight tidal action—about a mile wide here, is a strip of land, and beyond this is the ocean. This strip of land varies from a half-mile to two miles in width, alternates in poorest sand-tracts and richest hammocks, where the most prolific crops grow, and is alive with game. Here, without much looking, may be found bears, deer, cougars, wild-cats, panthers, and the wily lynx.

The town with its surroundings is quite tropical in appearance. The Titus Hotel in particular is built in what may be called the tropical style—a large main building with two long wings, all one story high, forming three sides of a square neatly laid out in a garden, and with the rooms opening off of the wide verandas like a row of houses in a city block. The table at once convinces the guest that he is in a tropical region, the meats being principally oysters, clams, fish, shark-steaks, turtle-steaks, etc., with many strange and familiar fruits and vegetables, all tropical, and fresh in January. Colonel H. T. Titus is a noted character, once of great notoriety all over the country, as the fiercest antagonist of old John Brown, the Harper's Ferry Brown. These two, with their followers, had many desperate conflicts in the early days of "bleeding Kansas" history. Colonel Titus is now old, a helpless invalid, and, curiously enough, is an uncompromising partisan of the political party which he so desperately fought in its earlier history.*

Early the next forenoon, Dr. French, Mr. Churchill, and myself, embarked on the trim yacht Mist for a trip to the sugar-plantation of Mr. Perry E. Wager, situated on a lagoon on Banana Creek, six miles southeast of Titusville. It was a delightful day, and the scenery was beautiful, with clear waters and myriads of ducks and strange birds—pelicans, storks, herons, etc.

About noon we arrived at the plantation, and as Mr. Wager and the Doctor were old friends, we were all soon discussing an abundant dinner, after which we walked over the sugar-cane patch of ten acres. It was located in a clearing of gigantic oaks, magnolias, etc., interspersed with wild-orange trees laden with fruit, palmettoes, and the like, and covered with great vines—a jungle-scene of the most tropical kind. The soil was jet-black, and evidently of great fertility. Mr. Wager remarked that the bears and deer gave him much trouble by getting into his cane, of which they are very fond. A walk through the cane was something like a scramble through an Illinois cornfield, only worse, because the cane-stalks were fifteen to twenty feet tall, large as your wrist, and often curled and bent, making it like climbing through a "snake"

---

* Since this was written Colonel Titus has died.

fence to·proceed. We cut three stalks of the cane, each
twenty-one feet long, and they had fifty-two, fifty-four,
and fifty-five joints respectively. The reader must bear in
mind that each joint represents an increased value of the
cane for sugar, and that on the famous sugar-plantations
of Louisiana a stalk ten feet in height, or even eight, with
fifteen joints, is regarded as something to boast of.

Here the planter is not obliged, by fear of frost, to cut
all the crop at one date, thus requiring a large, hastily
collected force and much expense ; but he can employ
three or four hands, one at the mill, one at the sirup-
kettle, and two to cut and haul, and with this small force
can make sugar all the year round. Nor does the cane
require annual planting or cultivation, hoeing, etc., but
they cut the stalks close to the ground, strip off the leaves
(which are much like corn-blades), and thickly cover the
ground with them, thus keeping down the weeds, and
securing, as they decay, a rich compost. The roots soon
"rattoon," and no fresh planting is needed for ten or twenty years.

The sirup of fresh cane is very sweet (to me it was
slightly sickish)—and how the bears, hogs, and darkeys
do love it ! It is very fattening, and a darkey on a sugar-
plantation is always noticeable for his fat, oily appearance.
Mr. Wager grinds his cane in a mill of three iron rollers,
worked by a mule, and boils the extracted juice into sirup
in a large, shallow kettle, the same as is used in making
maple-sugar. With the labor of three negroes, he is able
to net about sixteen hundred dollars from ten acres.

Returning to Titusville, we embarked next day on the
same yacht for a journey down the Indian River. It
was a hazy, soft, dreamy, delicious sort of day, and, as
the boat bowled along with a pleasant breeze, we quietly and indolently enjoyed it. At noon we landed at the
home of Captain W. H. Sharpe, a very agreeable gentle-

man from Georgia, with a Yankee wife, who entertained us hospitably, and showed us his thrifty young orange-grove and cane-field. After an excellent dinner, Captain Sharpe and Dr. Holmes, an Ohio gentleman, now residing here, joined our party ; and, a bushel of oranges being put on board, we continued on our journey, reaching Rock Ledge late in the afternoon of a wonderfully in-teresting day. Here we landed and accepted the warmly proffered hospitalities of Mr. A. L. Hatch. He came here several years ago from Mississippi, in search of health, found it, and in this charming spot is rapidly creating a fine home. He is an enthusiast about Florida, and is a zealous student of the culture of fruits and flowers. We all took an extensive stroll over his lawns, gardens, and fields, and it was like a visit to a botanical or horticult-ural museum, so great is the variety of plants growing there. An evening long to be remembered was enjoyed on his veranda, smoking, hearing of tropical Florida, and watching the full moon rising across the waters, that glittered like silver, while the intervening lawn showed strangely with aloes (or century-plants), palmettoes, oaks festooned with gray mosses, and multitudinous flowers.

Rock Ledge is twenty miles south of Titusville, and two and a half from Lake Winder, where the St. John's River steamers are taken, and freight is shipped to Jack-sonville, four hundred and twenty-three miles distant, or one hundred and sixty on an air-line. Of course the steamers are the diminutive kind, such as I have before described.

From Rock Ledge to New York is about seventy hours' travel. The place derives its name from a formation of coquina-rock along the shore there, and is a very pleas-ant locality, with a good class of settlers, some forty in all. But I think they have placed the price of their lands too high. One hundred dollars per acre for a site on the river is too high for the average immigrant, especially where the land is uncleared and unimproved. It may be worth it—for the soil is undoubtedly rich—to the wealthy, but it will bar out the industrious poor, and retard the growth of the region.

It was here I made my first attempt to eat a fresh-picked guava. I failed miserably then, but have since learned to like the fruit, and think it excellent. As a friend once expressed it, "It's like eating a strawberry inside of an orange, large as a pear," only the seeds are like small shot. The taste for this abundant fruit is like that for tobacco— it must be acquired ; but, as is seldom the case with to- bacco, its acquisition is never regretted.

The next morning Mrs. Hatch served us an excellent breakfast—peculiar in this, that it consisted almost wholly of various kinds of garden fruits and vegetables, cooked in divers ways, to show what an Indian River table can supply. We visited several homes in the neighborhood, everywhere meeting agreeable people, and were shown wonderful gardens. All agreed that snakes and such things were rarely seen, and that flies, gnats, or mosqui- toes were not unusually troublesome in the summer. Poultry, eggs, fish, oysters, turtles, and ducks are too plentiful for special mention. Among other places, we visited the Spratt orange-grove, one of the finest in Flor- ida, with one thousand trees growing on ten acres. The founder, Mr. Spratt, came here about ten years ago, an old man, and with but little means or money. He com- menced clearing the land all by himself, and now has a grove hard to surpass. The land is quite clean, level, and rich ; the trees all very uniform in size and shape, and thrifty, and laden with noticeably fine-looking and richly- flavored fruit. That grove is sure to produce henceforth an income of several thousand dollars annually ; and it is an evidence of what one poor old man can do by living a camping-out sort of life for a few years. Near here also is a fine guava-preserving establishment, recently built by some Massachusetts parties.

After an extended tour of this region—all much alike in one respect, that it presented beautiful scenery and was deeply interesting—one pleasant morning again found us at the little landing on Salt Lake, and we were soon lightered out to another of those curious little upper St. John's River steamers. This was the We-ki-wa, a snug craft, but so very small and so odd; every inch of space being utilized by the bright, active boy, a lad of about fifteen, who acted as steward, assistant engineer, pilot, dish-washer, table-waiter, chambermaid, and general-utility man. There were but five or six passengers, among them an Ohio gentleman, who had with him a fine sporting rifle, which he kindly invited the Doctor and myself to try. The Doctor led off with a splendid shot at a very large alligator, pinning it permanently to the marshy bank where it was sunning itself. Later in the day he killed another. I also had the satisfaction, such as it was, of killing two alligators, big ones. They were very abundant all day; often ten or more could be seen slowly crawling into the water, where they keep their heads up, staring at us, then, their curiosity satisfied, suddenly dropping from sight.

Early the next morning we reached Enterprise, on Lake Monroe, where we staid some time. Our party improved the time by going ashore and visiting a famous sulphur-spring on the estate of Count Frederick de Bary, a wealthy New-Yorker. A fine residence, large orange-grove, pier, and packing-house are here, the spacious grounds all handsomely fenced and improved in neat style, with everything elegant and complete. The spring is circular in form, about fifty feet in diameter, and is located in a pretty nook. The water is green as the greenest paint, and forms quite a good-sized brook. It is slightly warm, tastes strongly of sulphur, but is not unpleasant. Resuming our journey, the boat was soon on her way down the river with our friend, the Ohio man, at the wheel, which he managed with unexpected skill. Blue Spring Landing was reached at noon, and here the Doctor and I left the boat. It was February 1st, and a very warm day. The spring, from which the landing takes its name, covers about an acre, is of very pure, clear water, of a slightly sulphurous flavor, and deep blue in color; it is the fountain-head of quite a large stream that flows into the St. John's. The adjacent grounds are slightly rolling, and the general appearance is picturesque, offering a fine site for a winter hotel. The water looked so cool, clear, and tempting, that we couldn't resist, and, finding a retired nook, we plunged in and enjoyed the agreeable novelty of an open-air bath in midwinter. Afterward a warm walk of about two miles brought us to Orange City, in Volusia County, and we were soon in the cozy, hospitable home of the Doctor, his own Florida abiding-place.

Orange City was founded in 1876 by the Doctor and a number of congenial spirits, mostly from Wisconsin. Already a good deal of land has been cleared, roads and streets have been surveyed and opened in every direction, and lots set off for business and residence purposes, a school, churches, and shops. Several stores and eighty or more residences have been erected, new fences and buildings are constantly being built, and the place is rapidly growing, having a population now of about three hundred, which is increasing every month. One hundred and seventy-five groves, on about one thousand acres of land, are in bloom, and new groves and gardens are being started everywhere in the vicinity. Here I met two young men, brothers, from New York City, who came a short time ago for their health, and now have one of the largest and finest pineapple-fields in the State. The newsy "South Florida Times" is published here. The two following days were spent in short tramps and drives in the surrounding country. The third day, the Doctor, with his son, myself, and Mr. Andrew Jackson, a jeweler from Eau Claire, Wisconsin, a wealthy, shrewd business-man, distributed ourselves in a wagon, and started on a trip through the country. The roads were in good condition, and we trotted along briskly, passing new homes everywhere, the people being all busily engaged in fencing, clearing, building, or setting out trees. At noon we arrived at De Land, another enterprising colony, mostly from western New York. The site was located in 1877 by Mr. H. A. De Land, the celebrated soda-manufacturer of Fairport, New York, and bears his name. The country here consists of rolling, open pine-land, and is quite pretty and home-like in appearance. A fine church and a first-class schoolhouse, one of the best in the State, several stores, and dwellings, had then been erected ; and the buildings were all of noticeably substantial, comfortable construction, while the house-grounds were cleared up and set out with flowers and shrubs. The "Florida Agriculturist" is published here. It has a large circulation, and is considered standard authority on all subjects in its special line.

From De Land we drove to Spring Garden, another of the enterprising colonies of this favorite section. New York and Illinois are mostly represented here. In 1872 Major George H. Norris, a native of western New York, well known in Chicago, came here and purchased an immense Spanish grant, and, having perfected his title, laid out this pretty hamlet. A large amount of land has been cleared in the vicinity, and wide streets have been opened for miles, well fenced, and set out with orange-trees for shade. The "Spring Garden House," quite a cozy, home-like, well-built hotel, is kept by Mr. E. M. Turner, a wide-awake Chicago hotel-man. It stands in a large orange-grove, surrounded by a number of pretty hotel-cottages for invalid guests. A landing-pier and packing-house have been built at Spring Garden Lake, two miles distant, where the St. John's River steamers land goods and passengers. Quite a number of families have their homes here, and form an unusually select and refined community, discrimination being exercised in the sale of lands. Their homes are noticeably well constructed, and have an air of settled improvement, surrounded by lawns, gardens, and groves, grape-arbors, fences, etc. In the evening quite a party of the residents met us at the hotel, and a very pleasant, entertaining time was enjoyed. Accompanying the Major to his hospitable residence near by, I had the pleasure of feasting on a heaping dish of freshly-picked strawberries, and partaking of some excellent samples of orange-wine.

The next morning we drove to the immense orange-groves owned by Major Norris. He has 11,000 trees, mostly on hammock-lands, which are nearly all bearing; in fact, he gathered last winter upward of 460,000, filling 3,100 boxes! In time that grove will produce millions, yielding a princely revenue. The trees were nearly all sour stumps budded with sweet fruit. The Major said, "In a few years I will show the visitor here an avenue five miles long, lined with solid orange-groves all the way," and I think it quite likely that such a spectacle may then be seen. At the house of Mr. B. F. Haynes we were feasted on delicious bananas; and another resident whom we met was Professor Isaac Stone, who was for years United States consul at Singapore. His wife, Mrs. Stone, is the author of a standard work on India—"India and its Princes."

Orange City, De Land, and Spring Garden, are three places that impressed me as favorably as any I have seen in Florida. There are other places that are more interesting for historical reminiscences or scenery, or for some particular enterprise; and others may, very likely, become

THE BANANA.

larger and more active communities, like Sanford, Leesburg, and Charlotte Harbor; but those three places first named will, I think, always be pretty, home-like, prosperous villages, of slow, steady, healthy growth and solid prosperity. The region has a mean elevation of about

seventy feet above tide-water, and is noted for its healthfulness.

From Spring Garden we returned to Orange City, visiting Beresford, Volusia, and Starke's Landing, all on the
lake. They are merely little landing-places, with but three
or four families in the immediate neighborhood, but are
the foci of quite a goodly number of families living back
on the highlands. At Starke's Landing we visited the
famous old grove of Captain Starke, and saw hundreds
of noble orange-trees twenty-five to thirty-five years old,
scattered about irregularly over a grand old lawn. Some
of them are fully thirty feet high, and bear crops of from
two to ten thousand oranges each. This was one of the
grand old English estates of the last century, the property
of Lord Beresford. Remains of his extensive improvements are yet to be seen. Here we saw hogs feeding on
oranges, and it certainly seemed a shame to see them eating such rich fruit. Here also we saw an immense tree
that had just been transplanted with its crop in full fruit,
and showed no signs of injury.

All that region is of hilly pine-land, with open growth
of trees and excellent soil, the exceptions of bad soil being
very few. And it undoubtedly is a very healthy section
and quite free from insects, being high, well drained, pine-
timbered, and open to the pure sea-breeze all along its
eastern coast. Ormond, Port Orange, Daytona, and Smyrna, are all thrifty, enterprising, growing little hamlets, located in the rich hammock-belt of land on the adjacent
ocean-coast, where they have the advantages of good soil
and both fresh and salt water; but the insects in the summer months make a residence there unpleasant except in
some specially favorable locations. Each has from ten
to fifty families of unusually agreeable, select people, the
nucleus of future pleasant communities. In fact, the people of nearly all the villages and settlements throughout

Volusia County are of exactly the right sort of Northern stock, and under their enterprising, law-abiding control, the region is sure to become one of the most prosperous in Florida.

The next morning we bade farewell to the good people of Orange City, and again set out on our travels. At Blue Spring Landing we took the steamer George M. Bird, which in the course of the afternoon carried us to Sanford, where we remained over the following day, a rainy Sunday. Sanford and the adjacent country I have considered important enough to have a chapter to itself; so, to avoid repetition, will say nothing about it here.

Early on Monday morning we resumed our journey in a fine two-horse rig, accompanied by Mr. D. L. Way, editor of the "South Florida Journal," of Sanford. Our route was southwest from the St. John's, and for the first five or six miles the ride was through a flat, uninteresting country, which gradually rises and becomes fairly hilly. Altamonte was reached about noon, and we were invited to the pleasant home of Mr. George E. Wilson, a young man who came here from Maine several years ago, and now has a comfortable house, a large orange-grove, and a grocery, a perfect sample of New England enterprise and thrift. After an excellent dinner, we visited some fine gardens in the neighborhood, and saw ample evidence of good soil and energetic people. It is noted as a pleasant neighborhood, the residents being generally cultured people from the North, and the appearance of the country thereabout is pleasing. It is quite likely that they will have railroad communication with Sanford soon, which will undoubtedly make this a fine locality for either residence or occasional resort.

Late in the afternoon we reached Apopka, where we remained overnight. It is a small place, of about three hundred inhabitants, mostly Southern natives, and the cluster

of cheaply constructed buildings, all of plainest design, un-
painted and weather-beaten, closely huddled together on
the narrow, short streets,
gives it an appearance
much like the backwoods
hamlets of Alabama, Geor-
gia, and the States of that
belt. The soil thereabout
is rolling pine and ham-
mock, and famous for its
fertility. We visited several gardens and groves,
and saw none better any-
where else in the State.
It is an excellent region
for oranges, sugar-cane,
and vegetables, and is exceptionally healthy. The
country is everything that
could be desired, but there
is an evident lack of taste
and enterprise among the
inhabitants. It is the center of a good and growing
trade, has a good average
school, and will, no doubt,
soon have railway connec-
tion with the St. John's at
Sanford. (See Appendix,
note 6.)

A TYPICAL COUNTRY HOTEL IN FLORIDA—"OCKLAWAHA HOUSE," FESDRIVILLE.

Three miles from the
town is Lake Apopka, a
superb body of water—an inland sea, about fifty miles in
circumference, surrounded by a large tract of hammock,
with a rolling black soil, densely covered with forests of

hard-woods, etc. The richness of the soil in this hammock is famous throughout the State. Hon. T. G. Speer, State Senator, is engaged in cutting a series of short canals that will give water communication from Lakes Apopka, Dora, Eustis, and Griffin, into the Ocklawaha, and so to Jacksonville. When this short canal (or a railroad outlet) shall have been secured, this lake will soon be surrounded by a large population.

The next morning we turned northward, and at noon reached Zellwood, on little Lake Maggiore, where we accepted the cordial hospitalities of Colonel T. Elwood Zell, who owns a fine estate and a beautiful home here, and from whom the locality derives its name. The country from Apopka to this place, which we traversed, was all high, rolling pine-land, with frequent lakes and hammocks, evidently very good soil. The vicinity of Zellwood is very attractive, with productive soil and agreeable scenery. The Colonel and his charming wife are Philadelphians, who spend much of their time abroad, but make occasional winter visits to their dainty home on this pretty spot.

It was quite dark when we arrived at Pendryville, on Lake Eustis, where we found very comfortable accommodations at Mr. A. S. Pendry's home—the Ocklawaha Hotel. Mr. Pendry is from Rochester, New York, and has selected a very attractive location for his home. He has cleared a large tract of land, built a good hotel, fenced his lots, and made many improvements. It is generally a rolling pine-land thereabout, with small lakes, and large tracts of hammock bordering on Lake Eustis. Undoubtedly a healthy region of pleasing scenery, it will very likely become in time quite a prosperous place.* Here Mr. Way

---

* This prediction has been verified much sooner than I could then have suspected. Visiting Pendryville in June, 1881, I was struck with astonishment at the progress that had been made in the brief space of a year and a half. The Pendry farm has been laid out in town-lots, which are rapidly

left us to return to his home in Sanford, greatly to our regret, for he proved a most agreeable traveling companion.
He has a fine, thrifty-looking orange-grove, prettily located
on two small lakes, visited by us shortly after leaving Zellwood.

We remained all day at Pendryville, driving about,
viewing the prospects, and forming a very favorable opinion of the locality. The right class of immigrants are settling there, and a railroad is certain to tap that region very
soon. The St. John's and Lake Eustis Railroad is now
within two miles of the hotel. (See Appendix, note 7.)

The next day we drove to Fort Mason, on the opposite
shore of Lake Eustis. On the route we stopped at the home
of the Hon. J. M. Bryan, member of the Legislature, and he
accompanied us to the town, which consists of a hotel, two
well-stocked stores, and a cotton-press. The country and
soil thereabout is rich, low hammock. Here we met Sena-

---

being bought and built upon, numerous orange-groves have been set out in
the vicinity, population is pouring in with unprecedented rapidity, and the
bustle and stir of a prosperous growth are everywhere visible. Owing
largely to the skillful and well-directed efforts of Mr. John A. Macdonald,
editor of the "Florida New-Yorker," attention has been attracted to the
advantages of the locality; and in no portion of the State have I observed
more healthy and pleasing signs of progress—such as neat and tasteful
fences, substantial houses, and lands thoroughly cleared and carefully cultivated. The young orange-groves, too, looked exceptionally well, and remarkably early returns have been obtained in some cases that were called
to my attention. Moreover, as I saw more of the country, I was impressed
much more strikingly with its scenic attractiveness. Rolling hills and undulating slopes are the characteristic features of the region, bold bluffs front
the lakes on almost every side, and from certain points on the northern
shore of Lake Dora (about five miles from Pendryville) views are obtained
that are unlike anything seen elsewhere in Florida. The lake itself nestles
at the foot of wooded bluffs over a hundred feet in height; on the opposite shore still higher hills lift boldly from the water; while farther away
still, beyond Lake Harris, at the distance of twenty-eight miles, a misty
line of heights rises almost mountainously against the horizon.

tor T. G. Speer, who was engaged in constructing his dredging-machine, and he explained his intention of cutting a canal so as to connect the entire series of large lakes in this famous lake-region. This improvement will open up a vast amount of rich soil to transportation conveniences.

The country from this point to Leesburg is all a rolling pine-land, in some places quite hilly, and contains innumerable small lakes and frequent tracts of rich hammocks, in which we saw many wild groves of sour oranges growing, all laden with their deceptive golden fruit. The Doctor pronounced it an excellent region, of rich soil ; but very few houses or improvements were seen. At one of the few houses encountered on the route (a handsome, new building, occupied by a family from Illinois), we stopped and were shown a splendid large orange-grove, yielding the owner an income of several thousand dollars annually. He had come here very poor, had lived cheaply and worked hard, and now is reaping his reward.

Early in the afternoon we crossed the wild head-waters of the Ocklawaha, on a ferry worked by hauling on a rope stretched across on poles. The road on either side was, for a long distance, through a dense jungle, and we were glad to get well through it and reach our destination.

Leesburg, the county-seat of Sumter County, the home of fifteen hundred people, is a quiet, contented, easy-going, rather old-fashioned sort of a place, all the business houses being low, plain, wooden buildings, mostly of one story, ranged along one wide, sandy street. A good winter hotel is badly needed, and would probably be a profitable investment. The town lies in the midst of a rather flat pine and hammock country, the soil of which is nearly all very rich. It has a good school and church, and an orderly society, which includes only one lawyer, who does not make a very large income, although they boast that he can earn double fees by arguing for both parties in the same case. The adjacent region is being rapidly taken up, and already contains many settlers. This is the upper end of navigation on the Ocklawaha River, which furnishes the only outlet of the region. Leesburg has, beyond doubt, a prosperous future before it; within the year, probably, the Peninsular Railroad will reach there. (See Appendix, note 8.)

The whole of the day following our arrival was spent in looking about the town, gathering statistics of its trade, garden and field crops, shipping facilities, etc. The next morning we accepted an invitation to enjoy a sail on Lake Harris, and at an early hour were on board a trim and rapid yacht. The party included Mr. William Fox, once of Chicago, now a prominent citizen of Leesburg; Mr. George Pratt, owner and editor of the "Leesburg Advance"; Mr. Jackson, owner of the yacht, recently of Cincinnati, now residing on Lake Eustis, where he has purchased a fine property; and ourselves.

It was a beautiful day, with a pleasant breeze, and we bowled along over the clear waters of this lovely lake (it is eight miles wide by ten miles long) in exhilarating style. The shore everywhere has much natural beauty, being high, with a rich, dark soil, generally covered with a heavy growth of very large hard-wood trees, oaks, etc., evidently very fertile as well as very picturesque. We passed several fine estates, their lands neatly cleared and fenced, substantial, cozy-appearing houses, surrounded by pretty gardens, flowers, and young groves, presenting perfect pictures as seen from our boat. Among several places at which we stopped was that of Colonel J. W. Marshall, a hearty, genial, intelligent gentleman of the old school, who came here from South Carolina shortly after the war, which so sadly impoverished the planters of that State. Here he has established himself

on a grand estate, containing several large orange-groves
of all varieties and ages, from the tender seedling grove
to the full bearing, and all remarkably thrifty and well
kept. The oldest grove, now in full bearing, yielding immense crops, is one of the finest we saw in all the State,
with the largest-sized trees and the heaviest crops.

The old Colonel showed us all over his extensive estate;
it has a rich soil, carefully cleared, a rolling, hilly surface,
and produces a great variety of plants and fruits, including
teas, coffees, etc., fully demonstrating the fact that everything in the way of fruits, flowers, garden and field products, may be grown on the soil of this lake-region. Taking
us finally into his bearing grove and pausing at a large
tree, the low-hanging branches of which were laden with
easily plucked fruit, he gave us a complete course of in-
struction in the fascinating, divinely refreshing art of "or-
ange-eating and how to do it." And his recipe, while it
may not be of the highest degree of mincing daintiness—
the eating-soup-with-a-fork style—is an exceedingly enjoyable, practical method of getting the juice, the whole juice,
and nothing but the juice, out of an orange. Said he :
"Now, gentlemen, roll up your sleeves, remove your cuffs,
high collars, etc., unbutton your vests and a few other
waist-buttons ; take a sharp knife, pull a dark-shade, heavy
orange, peel it to the quick all around, leave no bitter rind,
shut your eyes and suck ; don't bite—just suck."

The reader hardly needs to be assured that we obeyed
to the letter. I think we each averaged about fifteen oranges in rapid succession—and in silence, sweet silence—
one steady draught of nectar pure and wholesome. Lack
of capacity alone compelled us, one by one, to regretfully
cease this luscious feast ; and repairing to the house, we
were invited, after a short respite, to partake of a fine
dinner, well washed down with select brands from an evidently well-stocked cellar. Soon after dinner we took our

departure from this hospitable home, the old Colonel depositing a huge basketful of oranges in our boat as a remembrancer. We bade him good-by with regret, all hoping that his considerable shadow may never be less.*

A long, circuitous sail was made around the lake that we might view its. beautiful shores, and we reached the hotel in the evening. Early next morning we resumed our journey, and were soon well on our way to Sumterville, west of Leesburg. The route lay through a rather flat, uninteresting belt that appeared generally wet, and, in tracts, marshy, a good sugar-cane region. We crossed one broad body of water, which was much deeper than our driver had counted upon, and, in consequence, we barely escaped the unpleasant incident of a ducking. In some places the road passed through extensive hammocks, always attractive. About five miles from Leesburg we reached the stony belt of Central Florida, the only locality in all the peninsula (except along the coasts and in some of the northern counties) where we found stones. Here they were plentiful, scattered about in all shapes and sizes, and it gave us considerable satisfaction to hear the wheels click along over them, with the music so familiar in more northern regions.

It was noon (Sunday noon) when Sumterville was reached, and our team turned back to its starting-point, while we took quarters at the primitive hostelry that offers scant accommodations to way-bound travelers. Sumterville is an old *ante-bellum* settlement, with large tracts of cleared land—evidently a high level, as it is not wet—with a dark soil, which is undoubtedly very rich and productive. The hamlet contains two or three very rude backwoods sort of stores, and about a dozen dwellings, but has great expectations, that are quite likely to be ful-

* Since our visit, Colonel Marshall has sold this grove for $28,000 cash.

filled, as it is on the present State stage-line and United States mail-route from Ocala to Tampa, and is on the direct line from Leesburg to the latter place, such as a railroad will desire to select. It is a good, healthy, fertile region, needing only settlers.

The next day several of the residents called on us, and we spent the day, a warm one, in visiting a number of gardens and fields and orange-groves in the vicinity. Everywhere the vegetables, crops, and fruits looked finely, growing in great abundance with little care. We also drove to Lake Panasofkee, six miles distant, a large lake surrounded with rich black hammock-land, the region for sugar-cane and all garden and field crops. Also in this neighborhood are numerous large "sinks" of the land, so frequent in all parts of Middle Florida, usually circular in form, the sides quite straight and smooth, varying from twenty-five to one hundred and more feet in depth, and seldom containing any, or but little, water. This, indeed, is the singular feature about them, for often they are close to large lakes whose waters are fifty feet above the bottom of the sink, yet none in the sink. It is as if something had given way in the bowels of the earth, and the soil had fallen in ; but they must all have subterranean outlets, for in no other way can the absence of water be accounted for.

The next morning we took the stage-coach, a little rattle-trap sort of an affair, and were soon on our way to Brooksville. It is a long ride through a decidedly rolling country, mostly pine-land, with very little hammock, and few lakes. The stone belt extends all through this region, ending along the Withlacoochee River. It closely resembles the piny-woods region in Michigan, and the ride became very tedious and monotonous, except that we saw any quantity of feathered and furred game, rabbits, squirrels, quail, etc., and occasionally wild turkeys, large and shy. This is a range where deer and bear also are plentiful.

The entire trip that day was through an unsettled region, the only human beings living anywhere along the road being four or five families of Florida natives, the genuine, unadulterated "cracker"—the clay-eating, gaunt, pale, tallowy, leather-skinned sort—stupid, stolid, staring eyes, dead and lusterless; unkempt hair, generally tow-colored ; and such a shiftless, slouching manner ! simply white savages—or living white mummies would, perhaps, better indicate their dead-alive looks and actions. Who, or what, these "crackers" are, from whom descended, of what nationality, or what becomes of them, is one among the many unsolved mysteries in this State. Stupid and shiftless, yet shy and vindictive, they are a block in the pathway of civilization, settlement, and enterprise wherever they exist. Fortunately, however, they are very few and rapidly decreasing in numbers, for they can not exist near civilized settlements. The four or five cabins we passed of these "crackers" were bare log structures, with low roofs, no doors or windows—merely openings— or fireplaces ; no filling between the logs, and usually no floors ; no out-houses, wells, or fences ; and no gardens or plants, except a sweet-potato patch. A near lake, or spring, supplies their water ; hogs, cattle, and game, their meat ; and the tops of cabbage-palmettoes, sweet-potatoes, and wild fruits, form almost their only diet ; while pellets of clay eaten as a seasoning ingredient take the place of needed salt and pepper.

As the stage was slowly climbing a rise in the road, we were surprised to see four women, seated on a fallen tree close by the roadside ; all were of precisely the same size, with the same features, eyes, and hair, and a vacant, stupid stare ; each wore a light-colored, faded calico dress, of plainest, scantiest possible make, quite clean (a surprising fact), and large, plain, cotton sun-bonnets ; each wore a cheap, bright-hued, cotton handkerchief around her neck ;

A Pair of "Crackers."

and they were all barefooted, carrying their low, thick-soled shoes in their hands. The dress and kerchief appeared to be their only garments—no underwear whatever.

Our driver, a sociable sort of fellow from Ohio, stopped and chatted with this strange feminine quartet, and we learned that they were a mother and three daughters, which was the climax of surprise to us, for the four faces all appeared of the same age. They were going to a dance at a "cracker's," some fifteen miles farther on, and they had already walked about five miles. Think of woman—lovely, tender woman!—walking barefoot twenty miles to dance all night in a close cracker cabin, with whisky-perfumed cracker males, to the scraping of a wheezy violin in the hands of an old darkey; the scene lighted with pine-knots; the feast of hog, hominy, beef, sweet-potatoes, and likely a few villainous compounds of flour, cheapest brown sugar, or sirup, and called *cake* or "risin'-bread." And, perhaps, that cracker ball will be kept up two or three days and nights, until all the stock of eatables and whisky is used up.

The "cracker," when resolved to give a dance, shoots some game and carves a hog, finds a market and sells his game for a little cash, lays in a stock of whisky, a little flour, cheap sugar, sirup, tobacco, hominy, or grits, more whisky, coffee, or cheap tea, goes home, sets the "wimmin-folks" to baking, while he resolves himself into an invitation committee, and sets out on his lean, lank, cracker pony, and invites all the crackers for miles around to "cum raound." And they come. A fight generally ends the dance, and the best man wins the girl, for these dances are usually prolific of "jinin" matches. It should be said, however, *per contra*, that there is very little sexual immorality at these half-civilized gatherings, for the mothers— as in this case—are also on hand, and keep a sharp eye on proceedings; while the men—the fathers—will shoot.

We passed on, and at noon crossed the Withlacoochee River, at Hays's Ferry, where there are two or three cabins. The river is here a wide, deep, dark-colored, swift-running stream. A rope stretched from bank to bank was our means of passage. Just across the river we found the cabin of a cracker, and here we were to get dinner. After a long delay, we were called in and told to "set by"; but, although the table was heaped with food (alleged to be), yet I couldn't eat of it: sweet-potatoes in two styles— baked and fried in slices—but less than half cooked in either shape; bread, merely chunks of yellow, hot, steamy dough, incased in burned crusts; muddy coffee (plenty of grounds for being muddy, if the reader will excuse the pun); and fat pork. There were eggs visible, however; so, under pretense of *not feeling well*, I induced the cook to soft-boil a few, and, having managed to strain off some coffee from its mud basis, worried through a luncheon. The housewife was of indolent, unhealthy, flabby appearance, slattern and unwholesome. Said the driver, who knew them well, "That husband of yours, if he should ever trip up in a mud-puddle, would lie and die there, he is so lazy." And that loving wife replied, with a shallow smile: "Yas, I 'spect that's so; he are mos' droffle, or'nary, lazy-like, sho' enuff, jes' no 'count." The listening husband grinned as if a compliment had been paid him.

Such villainous, disgusting cooking as that found on the tables of the low whites of this region is surely unequaled. The ignorance among the women of this very necessary art is frightful. Living in a region where, almost without solicitation, Nature provides all the daintiest and best of fruits and garden-vegetables, yet their tables seldom have any sauces or fruits of any kind, except occasionally *dried apple-sauce*, bought at the store, or else some wretchedly made guava-jelly. Vegetables are seldom seen on any tables, except those of the land-owner class, or of Northern settlers occupying homes in the neighborhood. No wonder the "crackers" look so unhealthy, or are so stupid, or that the men take to whisky, and like to fight so

vindictively. *Anything* that involves a change must be
agreeable to people fed on such wretched diet. Steam-
engines are great civilizers of nations, but good cooking
beats anything as a civilizer of individuals. I have seen
its beneficial effects among the very worst Indians of the
West.

Resuming our journey, the region passed over in the
afternoon differed somewhat from that of the forenoon,
being more hilly, and involving a constant going up and
down of more or less steep inclines. We were now out
of the stony belt, and the hammocks were more frequent.
No settlers were seen, and game was very abundant. Late
in the afternoon large tracts of cleared land began to be
seen, mostly neglected ; and at supper-time we reached
Brooksville. Standing on the broad, level top of a high
hill, in the midst of many hills—the largest hills we saw
in any part of the State—Brooksville is one of the most
prettily located towns or settlements we saw in Florida,
being equaled only by Tallahassee. It is, in fact, the
most un-Florida-appearing place imaginable, with excellent, rich, dark-brown soils, occasional stones and gravel,
first-class hard country roads in all directions ; forests
of oaks, maple, beech, hickory, and all such hard-wood
growths, rail-fences, and far-viewing hills. All was like
Ohio, Wisconsin, New York—the western part on the Erie
Railway—in fact, anywhere in a hilly but not rocky region. Even the houses, the old and the few (very few)
new ones, somehow do not look Florida-like.

This is one of the most desirable sections of the State.
Although not at all tropical in appearance, yet all the
products of the tropical as well as of the northern climates grow here. Cotton, cane, wheat, oats, bananas,
oranges, peaches, corn, guavas, figs, all thrive as well as in
any of their special regions. Here also we found grass,
a good sod, that seemed refreshing to walk on. Prior to

the war this was a region of large plantations and wealthy planters. All seem to have left, as their slaves left, abandoning everything. The houses decayed and were demolished, fences were destroyed, broad fields have gone to waste, and weeds, underbrush, and tangled vines have everywhere taken the place of cultivated crops.

Next morning we found Mr. Frederick L. Robertson, editor of the "Brooksville Crescent," an old friend of the Doctor's. Horses were procured, and we rode to the resience of State Senator H. T. Lykes, on Spring Hill, six miles distant; then across the country, ten miles, to the large estate of Mr. William Hope, where we found all varieties of vegetables growing finely, and rode through a field of several hundred acres of oats, spreading out over the hills and valleys—Ohio, surely, except for the season (it was February)! Good roads, numerous brooks, hard-wood forests, broad fields (abandoned mostly), plenty of game, was the result of our observations. The town is the county-seat of Hernando County, and contains the court-house—a large, new, wooden building, a good structure, but provokingly plain in design—three groceries, two or three saloons, and about thirty dwellings, nearly all small cottages, generally surrounded by small gardens, and groves of orange and such trees. Everything looks old-fashioned and of out-in-the-country style. Yet in location and soil it is the gem of South Florida; and, if a railroad should ever reach here—which is very likely, for any road to Tampa will surely pass through Brooksville—it will very probably become, in time, the center of a thickly settled, prosperous region.

Late in the afternoon we set out on our journey to Tampa, fifty miles distant. Fort Taylor was reached at twilight. This place, once the site of a military camp, now has but one house, surrounded by a fine grove of old orange-trees. About midnight we reached the hum-

ble cabin of the stage-station, where we obtained lodg-
ings which, though very rough, were acceptable after our
ride of twenty-six miles. The route had been through a
slightly rolling pine-wood region, with a dark soil of
average fertility, few lakes, no settlers, and very little
hammock.

Early next morning we were out looking about the
ranch, a plain little roughly constructed building, surrounded by numerous out-houses, and a garden, where a
variety of tropical plants were thriving. The keeper
was a genuine curiosity, an old regular army veteran,
a native of Maine, who came to this country as a private of the Second Regiment U. S. Artillery to fight
the Seminoles in 1835, and has remained here ever since.
After a breakfast, abundant but rudely prepared, we
resumed our journey, passing through a region similar
in all respects to that traversed on the previous day, lone-
ly and monotonous, rolling pine-land of average fertility,
no settlers, but abundance of game.

At noon we reached the Hillsborough River, a stream
about fifty feet wide and eight or ten feet deep, and
crossed it on a well-constructed toll-bridge. Beyond the
river the appearance of the country changes very much,
being a high, rolling, open-hammock region, with fair
soil and a heavy growth of native wire-grass. Clearings
and houses, gardens and groves, began to appear, and
we were once more in a region of settlers. Late in the
afternoon we at last drove into Tampa, very hot, much
fatigued, dusty, and hungry. The last few miles had
been over very sandy and parched roads, making hard
pulling for the tired horses; and we felt exceedingly
glad when we halted at last in front of a cool, quiet,
inviting-looking hotel, that much resembled a neat and
comfortable village dwelling.

We had completed a long journey seldom taken—a

ride across the heart of South Florida from the Atlantic to the Gulf, a distance of about one hundred and forty miles in a direct line, but about two hundred and fifty as traversed by us, with side-excursions to visit prominent places.

Tampa is an old town, the name being associated with the very earliest Spanish history of the State, and is well known as "a place in Florida" by all school-children throughout the country.

It is quaint and old-fashioned in appearance, contains about fifteen hundred inhabitants, and is situated at the upper end of Tampa Bay. It is laid out with considerable regularity into squares, with streets of usual width, level and clean, but very sandy. Having been designed for a big place, the town is much scattered, the houses average few to the block, and, though the sidewalks are generally good, there is much "cutting across-lots" in going from one point to another. Few of the dwellings are pretentious, but they have a comfortable, home-like appearance, all standing in ample grounds, and nearly all having abundance of tropical fruits, plants, flowers, shrubs and vines, sea-shells, and the like, reminding the visitor that he is in a tropical clime.

The public buildings—court-house, schools, churches, and halls—are all well-built, fair-sized structures, quite creditable to the remote little community. There is no large hotel of the customary hotel style, and such an establishment is greatly needed. The present accommodations for travelers are three small dwellings, neat, clean, and well kept, but not roomy—mere boarding-houses, in fact. The business-houses are all plain, village-like, low-roofed, wooden structures, scattered irregularly along the street leading to the wharf. They generally carry good stocks, and a large business is transacted here.

The United States Government owns a large tract of

land, forming a peninsula which reaches out into the
harbor. It is a lovely spot of about seventy-five acres,
quite like a park, with rolling surface, covered with good
sod of native grasses, while clumps of low-growth bushes
and gigantic oaks and hard-wood trees are scattered about.
The view, looking out over the harbor, is very beautiful.
The barracks, officers' quarters, cavalry-stables, hospital,
and other military buildings, are scattered about the
ground, and are all old, and have a neglected, dilapidated appearance. No troops are permanently stationed
here now; but occasional detachments are sent here for
a few months for sanitary benefit. A walk over these
grounds is quite pleasant, and is one of the " proper
things " for the visitor to do.

Large tracts of land in the suburbs have been cleared
of their pine-woods, laid out into long, wide avenues,
and named after Northern States, the plots comprising
ten or more acres each. Many of these lots have been
sold, and the purchasers have evidently spent much
money and time in improving them. The residences are
unusually well built, tastefully ornamented, and brightly
painted, while neat barns, out-houses, fences, sidewalks,
and the civilized improvements usual in Northern pro-
gressive communities, are everywhere seen—the reason,
perhaps, being that the settlers are nearly all Northern
people. In spite of all this labor, taste, and enterprise,
however, there is a very noticeable number of vacant
houses, showing signs of abandonment.

The appearance of the greater portion of the soil
in the vicinity of Tampa is sandy, with an unhealthy,
ashy-gray color, that promises little for productiveness.
There are occasional tracts of dark, rich soil, but these
are scarce, and very seldom for sale. There is good soil
in that region lying along the coast and on the islands,
but in the immediate neighborhood of Tampa I think it

is mostly poor, and nearly valueless for purposes of fruit or vegetable culture.

The harbor contains numerous islands and is quite pretty. It is alive with fish and ducks. We found the Hon. T. K. Spencer, of the "Sunland Tribune," and enjoyed an agreeable visit with him, looking about the place. The Peninsular Railroad, now in process of construction through the central region of Florida, will doubtless soon place Tampa in direct connection with the commercial centers of the East and North. This will greatly benefit it, besides opening up to settlement a large region. (See Appendix, note 10.)

It was a beautiful morning when we took our departure from Tampa, going aboard the little steamer that carried us down the harbor to the handsome ocean-steamer Lizzie Henderson, one of the fine line of Gulf-steamers (the "Henderson Line") that ply between New Orleans, Pensacola, St. Mark's, Cedar Keys, Key West, and Havana. The boats of this line are large, roomy, well equipped, and well supplied. The freight and passengers were rapidly transferred from the roomy old lighter to the steamer, and we were soon steaming down the broad bay to Manatee, thirty miles distant on Manatee River, which flows into the extreme southern portion of the bay. Immense flocks of ducks of several kinds, innumerable porpoises, and countless fish leaping out of the bright waters, were constantly in sight. The watery pathway of certain shoals could be traced by the sight of hundreds of fish of the six-pound size leaping out of the water in a rapid, direct line.

Late in the afternoon we passed up the broad river several miles to Manatee, where a short stop was made to take on cargo. There was no opportunity to visit the settlement, or to examine the soil thereabout, but the dwellings located along the banks of the river were mostly roomy and neat-looking houses, and several gardeners were at the wharf with vegetables of large variety and excellent quality.

The sun was setting brilliantly as we passed out of the bay into the Gulf; and the islands with their luxuriant vegetation, the solitary, tall, white lighthouse, and the tropical-appearing bar on which it stands, the porpoises disporting in all directions, and the deep-blue waters of the Gulf, all made a scene beautiful to behold and long to be remembered.

At sunrise the next morning we were entering the lovely harbor of Cedar Keys, passing near a number of pretty islands, among them Atsenua Otic Island, where there is a large saw-mill and machine-shop owned by Faber Brothers, of New York, giving employment to a colony of thirty families, mostly Germans, engaged in cutting and preparing the cedar-wood for the famous Faber lead-pencils. At the wharves of the little seaport and railroad terminus we found five large steamers and numerous sailing-vessels, giving it quite an appearance of commercial enterprise.

The Doctor, Professor J. N. Comstock (entomologist of the Agricultural Bureau at Washington, whom we had met on the steamer), and I, enjoyed the day strolling about the streets and limited suburbs, visiting the curious shell-mound—quite a hill, composed of sea-shells of all kinds, such as are found along that coast. It is the scientific supposition that this strange mound was erected by a race of prehistoric dwellers in this region, who resorted here to feast on oysters, clams, etc. It offers a superb position on which to build a large winter hotel, for the scene in all directions, as viewed from that elevation, is beautiful, the whole harbor and the Gulf being visible. We met my old friend Major Parsons here, and had a very agreeable visit and a tramp about the town with him. His reminiscences of Cedar Keys, extend-ing back over a period of forty years since he first came here from the North, a clerk in the Quartermaster's De-partment of the United States Army, under old General Z. Taylor, are very interesting. In the afternoon, while the Doctor dozed, Professor Comstock and I went down to the beach, where the tide was out, and busied ourselves pulling out oysters from the great quantities that solidly line all the shores of the bay, and feasting ourselves to repletion on that luscious bivalve.

Cedar Keys is a port of entry, and has several large mercantile establishments, all carrying extensive stocks, and evidently prosperous. Their patronage is derived from the settlers all along the coast and many goodly rivers that empty into the Gulf there. There is very little, if any, good land on the adjacent mainland. The trade is solely the result of its railroad and shipping ad-vantages. The buildings are mostly constructed of the substantial coquina-stone, and, with its main street (in fact, there is only one street in the place) paved with shells, all white mortary in appearance, it much resembles an old Spanish seaport.

Early on the morning after our arrival, we were again on our travels—the final stage—seated in one of the handsome coaches of the Atlantic, Gulf and West India Transit Company Railroad, better known in its abbrevi-ated and more convenient form of the "Transit," that crosses the State from Cedar Keys to Fernandina. Gaines-ville, Waldo, Santa Fé, Starke, and Lawtey, all thrifty, busy, growing, enterprising places, of which accounts are given elsewhere, were passed. Waldo is an especially pretty place, and the inhabitants show much taste and care, of which they may well feel proud, and for which they deserve much credit. Near the depot is a neat lit-tle park, fenced nicely ; the grounds all about the pretty

town are clean and grassy as a lawn; also, near the depot is a band-stand of neat design, at the base of a ship-
shape, mast-rigged flag-staff, the gift of a jolly old sea-
captain resident. The dwellings, mostly of cottage style,
are neat, tasty, trim, and clean, of generally good design,
surrounded by lawns of grasses and flowers, gardens of
fruits and vegetables, all showing careful labor and attention. The soil thereabout is fertile, and the people
are energetic and industrious. Waldo is a pretty spot, a
good place for either health-seekers or wealth-seekers.

Early in the afternoon we reached Jacksonville, and
the "Tour of Florida with Hon. Seth French, Commissioner of Immigration," was ended.

CHAPTER IV.

It was the middle of March when Captain Samuel Fairbanks, Assistant Commissioner of Immigration, set out on an official pilgrimage through the northern section of the State, in search of information for the use of his bureau. The Captain was peculiarly well adapted for his official position, and especially to investigate this portion of the State, which had in all its parts become familiar to him, through a residence of over forty years. He came originally from central New York, and there are many other people here from that favorite section of the Empire State.

The writer accepted a cordial invitation to join Captain Fairbanks on the proposed trip, and enjoyed a delightful time, for the Captain was a pleasant, entertaining traveling companion, full of interesting information, anecdotes, and reminiscences of the State and the people. The previously described journey in the other portions of the State had given me a fine opportunity to see the wilder and more remote regions, and the present trip gave me an opportunity to learn of the older and more populous sections. Our route lay through the counties of all the northern and western portions of the State, where, in the "piping times of peace," the ante-war days, the true era of Southern prosperity, the planters of Florida lived and flourished and waxed wealthy. In those days

Cotton was King, and the broad rolling acres of the vast plantations that covered the hills and beautiful valleys of the charming region were everywhere white with their great crops of the snowy staple. " Every acre meant another bale, and every bale meant another nigger," was the current saying in regard to it. This was always, from the days of its transfer to American rule, a favorite region with the cotton-planters ; here were obtained the largest yields per acre, of the best quality (the famous sea-island variety), and the earliest in market.

We left Jacksonville late one afternoon, by the Florida Central Railroad, changing at Live Oak (the county-seat of Suwanee County) to the Jacksonville, Pensacola and Mobile Railroad. The early morning hours found us speeding through Ohio, Wisconsin, or central New York ; certainly, it was not Florida in appearance—hilly, with a rich, brown, clayey soil, solid roads, rocks, and fields of grass, just like the Northern States. Early in the forenoon we arrived at Quincy, the county-seat of Gadsden County, and took the stage from the depot to the town, one and a half mile distant by a road which winds prettily over hills and through fine forests.

Quincy is a quaint, old-fashioned town, Southern in appearance (not, however, of the dingy, miserable, "cracker" style), a representative type of once-flourishing industry. It has a large, park-like, well-fenced square, with the court-house standing in the center, one of the old Southern regulation kind of square four-roomed-on-two-floors buildings. Huge oaks and similar trees shade the park, and around it or adjacent to it are the " city " buildings, jail, etc., with plain and rather faded brick stores, the usual number of offices, pumps and water-trough, and the universal Southern hitching-rail on high posts, with always a number of saddle mules and horses attached. Over all is an impalpable but unmistakable mantle of mildewy decay, of neglect rapidly verging on dilapidation. Such is the general appearance of the business portion of Quincy. (See Appendix, note 11.)

The suburbs make an impression altogether more favorable. The residences here are mostly large, well-built structures, with handsome house-grounds, gardens, lawns, out-houses, shade-trees, sidewalks, etc.—in all respects, except that of a few semi-tropical products, closely resembling the usual thrifty appearance of a steady, old, agricultural center in the North. The weather at the time of our visit was lovely (it was March 10th); fruits, flowers, and gardens of thrifty vegetables were everywhere visible; the doors and windows stood wide open, verandas were occupied, croquet-parties dotted the lawns; and "The Pirates of Penzance," and other latest music, was everywhere heard floating through the open windows, from the keys of skillfully played pianos. At the handsome residence of Postmaster Davidson, we were shown some of the finest specimens of the exquisitely beautiful, golden-hued, feathery pampas-grass that I ever saw, and it grows in many other gardens thereabout.

The views across the country in all directions are fine, ranging over broad fields, hills, valleys, hard-wood forests, orchards, good fences, and roomy residences—in all a beautiful region exhibiting unmistakable signs of agricultural prosperity. Nowhere does live-stock grow better. In the near future, when the old (but worthy) class of men and women shall have passed away with their *ante-bellum* ideas of business, crops, social "ranks," education, slave-labor, and their bitter memories of the war, with its defeated hopes and its "lost cause"—when this race, with such memories in their hearts, shall be gone, and the young generation of their offspring, filled with new ideas, new aspirations, new hopes, shall be in full control, then, I believe, Quincy and all the other towns of that fair, fertile region will be among the pleasantest garden-spots in all America. At present the goodly people are "brooding upon memories."

Chattahoochee, which at present is the terminus of the Florida Central and Western Railroad, is merely a little hamlet on the Chattahoochee River, close to the Alabama line, and has stage connection with Marianna, the county-

VIEW ON THE ESCAMBIA RIVER, NEAR PENSACOLA.

seat of Jackson County, another of those old-style, quiet inland towns, a description of one of which answers for all. The State Insane Asylum is located at Chattahoochee, a roomy old structure, clean, and having an air of comfort and adaptation to its purpose, and containing about thirty inmates. The river, in that region, is quite a large, respectable stream, the outlet of an extensive back country—once the water-way of an immense traffic—to the Gulf-port of Appalachicola. The scenery thereabout is very fine, and the atmosphere noticeably soft and clear. This is attributed to the fact that it is due north of the Gulf, and is always tempered by the famous "Gulf-breezes."

From Marianna, a long ride by stage-coach brought us to Pensacola. The ride was tedious and fatiguing, but not really monotonous, for the scenery was very attractive, except in occasional tracts. Vernon, Euchee Anna, and Milton, passed *en route*, are all three county-seats, and are small, drowsy-looking towns, old-fashioned, and in all respects typical specimens of the better class of representative Southern county-seats. A square, an old-fashioned tavern, a court-house, and a few shops, may be said to compose each and all of them.

On every side, in all that region, including Gadsden and adjoining counties, were seen large old plantations, and roomy, old, Southern-style planters' residences, giving evidence of a long-settled region, that had suddenly been arrested in its growth, and was in a state of suspended animation. Yet it is a good country, and has, in fact, a steady growth, though it is of a kind not strikingly perceptible, being in crops and products, instead of houses, factories, and such town improvements, that are more likely to catch the attention.

The great, crying need of all that portion of the State is a railroad, and the series of causes that have prevented the completion of the Jacksonville, Pensacola and Mobile Railroad are disgraceful to all concerned. All the parties—the moneyed cliques, railroad-wreckers, lawyers, and agents—that have for years defeated the construction of that road across this fine region to its natural terminus at Pensacola, deserve the honest execrations of all who reside there ; for they have greatly damaged
4

and retarded the growth and prosperity of what ought to be one of the most flourishing sections of Florida.*

Pensacola is a charming city, clean, nicely laid out,

STREET-SCENE IN PENSACOLA.

with great shade-trees, handsome homes, the houses generally of good architectural taste, with pretty lawns, arbors, gardens, etc. The navy-yard and fortifications, with their garrisons and official staffs of both branches of the service, give it an animated appearance ; and the officers and their families contribute very much to the high reputation for culture and refinement enjoyed by the society there. The city has a large commerce, and is one of the most important lumber-shipping ports in the United States.

In respect to attractions for tourists and visitors, Pensacola is one of the most important places in Florida ; and,

---

* Since the above was written the courts have, after many years of tedious and costly litigation, awarded the railroad to its rightful owners. The road is now known as the Florida Central and Western Railroad, and belongs to the system of the Florida Railway and Navigation Company.

instead of attempting a detailed description of my own, I
will quote the following passages from a well-written and
tastefully printed local hand-book :

" The splendid Bay of Pensacola, unrivaled for its beauty, depth, and security, was discovered by Pamfilo de Narvaez, in 1525. Various adventurers gave it different names,
as Port de Ancluse and St. Mary's Bay, but that of Pensacola, which prevailed, was the true name among the Ind-

VIEW OF BAY FROM SHOT PARK, NAVY-YARD.

ians, the natives of the country. The first settlement was
made by the Spaniards, in 1686. The first Governor was
André Arivola, who constructed a small fort, called San
Carlos, and erected a church upon the present site of Fort
Barrancas. The French took Pensacola in 1719 ; the Span-
iards retook it, and the French again took it in the same

year and kept it until 1722, when it was restored to Spain. In the mean time, Pensacola had been removed to the west end of Santa Rosa Island, near the present site of Fort Pickens, where the Spaniards constructed a fort, which afterward was improved by the English General Haldemand. The settlement remained on the island until 1754, when, the town being partly inundated, the site was removed to the magnificent location which it now occupies. Pensacola was ceded to the English in 1763, by whom it was laid off in regular form in 1765. The town surrendered to the Spanish arms in 1781. On the 7th of November, 1814, General Andrew Jackson, with the American army, entered the town, when the English fleet in the bay destroyed the forts, San Carlos (at Barrancas) and Santa Rosa.

"By consulting the map of Pensacola and its surroundings, the reader will observe the network of water-courses, bays, and bayous centering at that city. The water is clear, bright, and beautiful. Surf-bathing upon Santa Rosa beach, as enjoyable as language can express, the salt-water bathing in the bath-houses of the bay, and bathing in fresh water as clear as crystal, can all be had within a distance of seven miles. The Perdido Bay is one of the loveliest sheets of water in the State, rivaled by the Escambia Bay, with its bluffs and ever-moving fleets. Any attempt to particularize becomes confusing, as the special beauties and attractions of the different bays and bayous are remembered. Escambia River is the 'Ocklawaha' of West Florida. The stranger who wishes to enjoy a short trip will be pleased as the steamer plows through the broad, placid waters of Escambia Bay, and then delighted with the luxuriance of the tropical growth as the vessel winds its way up the narrow and tortuous channel of Escambia River to Molino. At this point the excursionist can take the train and return by rail to Pensacola.

"The fresh-water fishing is superb. The waters literally swarm with all kinds of fish, notably trout, black bass, and pike. All varieties of perch abound, including a special kind, a very game fish, called bream. It is not unusual for a good angler to pull out fifty to sixty of these fish in an hour, weighing from a half to one pound. Both in salt and fresh water, fishing is carried on with pleasure and profit the entire year. In the bay and bayous every description of salt-water fish abounds, and, in the season, fifty cents will purchase half a dozen Spanish mackerel of the size for which the epicure pays seventy-five cents for one half in the

SPECIMENS OF PENSACOLA FISH

restaurants of New York City. These fish, and the salt-water trout, give special excitement to those who love a contest with a very game fish. No one can claim to have seen what fishing is until he has visited the snapper banks off Santa Rosa Island. There the famous red snapper can be caught, two at a time, weighing from five pounds to sixty, as rapidly as the line is thrown in. The limit to the quantity catchable is commensurate with the physical endurance of the catcher.

"The pleasure of boating at Pensacola is not confined to fishing or idly rolling on the mighty wave, or smoothly plowing the placid waters; but added to these charms are the numerous places in the vicinity to go to. The stranger

who may visit it will not wonder at finding first on this list
Santa Rosa Island. Upon its beach, mid-day, in its over-
flowing brilliancy, makes the beholder feel as if, according
to Milton, 'another morn had risen on mid-noon.' The
sunset comes with a splendor and glory unknown to more
northern climes. . . . Santa Rosa Island is a sand-key of
the Gulf, forty miles long, and varying in breadth from a

RUINS OF FORT McRAE, WITH FORT PICKENS IN THE DISTANCE.

fifth of a mile to over a mile across; it is the breakwater
of Pensacola Harbor, and receives the shock of the rolling
seas of the Gulf of Mexico, which often break against it in
fury, while the waters of the bay within are still as a mill-
pond, and scarce a ripple washes the beach of the city front,
seven miles away, though the water at the city is as salt as
that in the center of the Gulf. The sea-beach of the island
is a gently sloping expanse of white sand, back and forth

on which the advancing and receding waves will glide for
hundreds of feet. You can stand where no water is one
moment, and the next be struggling waist-deep against a
surging wave that is climbing up the strand. This beach
is the incubator of the great turtles of the Gulf. Its grad-
ual incline, the easily excavated sand beyond, and the warm
southern exposure, adapt it to their approach, the making
of nests, and hatching of their eggs. So they resort to it
for this purpose, and in due time the young turtles are
hatched, unless the eggs are captured by the various creatures, biped and quadruped, who seek them in the season.
From Pensacola over to the island is about seven miles,
and as the land-breeze of the night sets fair across the bay,
it is a pleasant trip of moonlight nights to run over on a
sail-boat, land on the bay-shore, walk across the island,

FORT BARRANCAS.

which is not a third of a mile
wide opposite the city, and
seek for 'turtle-crawls' on the
Gulf-beach, or bathe luxuri-
ously in the surf. The 'crawl'
shows on the sand where the under-shell has been dragged
along, and, following this up to a point above the wash of
the highest waves, the nest is found, usually about two and
a half feet below the surface. A single nest will contain

from one hundred to three hundred eggs. At Sabine Pass, on Santa Rosa Island, alligators are found by the ten thousand, and are killed in large numbers by hunters who frequent the place.

"While on the island, very few visitors fail to find an interest in collecting shells and sea-beans. Then comes a visit to Fort Pickens. This grand and historic old edifice, though denuded of a portion of the iron dogs of war that used to bay, not 'deep-mouthed welcome home,' but roars of defiance, still possesses a multitude of pleasant and interesting sights and objects that make a visit there both profitable and agreeable. Across the bay is the navy-yard, and just west of the navy-yard is Fort Barrancas. Both are beautiful, and will interest the most indifferent. Added to the novelties to be seen is the delightful society enjoyed by all who know the hospitable and intelligent officers of both the garrisons. Below Barrancas is the Pensacola Lighthouse."

An interesting and agreeable route from Pensacola to Tallahassee is *via* one of the popular Henderson line of steamers to St. Mark's, and thence by the railroad. The pleasures of a Gulf trip are detailed at length in another chapter. St. Mark's is a very ancient port, one of the settlements made by the original Spanish explorers of Florida. Shortly after its settlement a large stone fort and pier were built; but they were long ago permitted to decay, and were finally destroyed by the settlers desiring the cut rock for their own uses. It is now a deserted village, only two or three small and unpretentious buildings marking this famous spot, romantic in historical events, beautiful in scenery, and once a busy mart, the second seaport in all the United States to boast of a railroad terminus. From here to Tallahassee, twenty-one miles distant, runs a railroad, built in 1835–'36. This was, in its early days, a very busy little road, the outlet of all the productive cotton region lying inland. At that time the planters lived in princely style, fairly rolling in wealth; for those were the halcyon days of the slave-owning cotton-planters, and *this* was their paradise. The road is now almost disused, trains only passing over it twice a week, on "steamer-day," connecting with the weekly Henderson steamers.

Tallahassee, the capital of the State, "the floral city of the flowery South," is one of the loveliest places in all America. It is built upon the broad, gently rolling surface of a high hill, surrounded on all sides by other lovely hills and deep valleys, for it is in a region of hills, valleys, and lakes. It is laid out in squares, with Main Street—which is its principal business street—lined mostly on one side with plain, old-fashioned brick stores for a distance of four blocks. This street is fairly level and wide. All the other streets are charmingly irregular and uneven—in fact, many are quite declivitous—and are lined with grand, old, mammoth-sized magnolias, oaks, maples, elms, and other magnificent shade-trees. Broad, roomy, open squares are frequent, all shady, park-like, and inviting.

At one end of the city stands the State-House, a large and very plain brick structure, painted a light color, with a front and rear portico, having each six great two-story columns. It stands in a spacious square on the crest of the hill, and can be seen from a long distance. The grounds are laid out with winding paths and lawns, shaded by many grand old magnolias, oaks, and the like, and the air is redolent with perfume from the many flowers always blooming there.

It is an unpretentious old city, with an air of village-like rustic simplicity; no factories (except one cotton-mill); all is quiet, country life. The residence avenues are mostly lined with cozy little cottages, and comfortable, roomy, substantial mansions of the good old-time style of architecture, and all are surrounded by neatly fenced lawns and gardens, almost all having quite ample grounds, well kept—and flowers, flowers, flowers! Everywhere in the greatest abundance are flowers. A most creditable pride in their lovely home-grounds is exhibited by the citizens, who seem to have a friendly rivalry in this beautiful ornament of nature, that is expressive of culture and a fine taste for the beautiful. Tallahassee is truly a "floral" city.

The suburbs are everywhere lovely, and the views from the streets or house-tops—especially the roof of the State-House—are exceedingly fine. The surrounding country is a vast range of hills, valleys, brooks, lakes, park-like clusters of large trees, broad, well-cultivated fields, large plantation dwellings and cotton-gins, and distant forests—in all, a remarkably beautiful natural panorama of nature, such as is seen nowhere else in Florida.

Here we remained several delightful days at the quaint, old, tavern-like "City Hotel," enjoying numerous drives about the surrounding country. One beautiful day I rode out to "Goodwood," the grand old estate of Major Arvah Hopkins, several miles out of town. This residence was well worth visiting, because it affords a striking evidence of how elegantly the old-time planters enjoyed life. Erected in 1844, it comprises numerous buildings ranged around a large square in the rear, used for laundry, cook-house, milk-house, saddle and harness house, etc., etc.; and the spacious surrounding grounds are laid out in park-like style, with paths, lawns, and innumerable strange plants, ferns, and flowers. Another day a party of us went on a trip to Lake Jackson, a large and long lake, six miles from the city. It closely resembles Cayuga Lake in New York, surrounded by high bluffs, all cleared, and everywhere the broad fields reaching down to the water's edge.

Captain C. E. Dyke, our escort on this trip, and in whose company I enjoyed many other rides and trips, besides evenings at his elegant home, is one of the most notable residents of Florida. A native of New Hampshire, where he long ago learned the printer's trade, he came to this State in 1839, and at once found a "job" in the office of "The Floridian," established in 1828. In 1847 he had worked his way up from the case to the editorial chair, and in that year assumed control of the paper, which he has ever since so ably conducted, without a single failure to "go to press" regularly each week in all that long period of time. Besides being the Nestor of Florida editors, he has for many years been State's printer; and his office, close by the State-House, is a favorite consultation-room for all State officials, who, as a rule, have always placed implicit confidence in his opinions and advice. He is undoubtedly the best informed upon all matters, political and legal, pertaining to Florida, as a Territory and as a State, of any one living. For upward of forty years he has been the intimate friend, confidant, or adviser of nearly all public officials. Knowing all the secret and unwritten history of the State, his stock of historical and personal reminiscences is very great, and, if "written up," would make a volume at once interesting and instructive.

One of the pleasantest resorts in the capital at the time of our visit was the official apartments of Governor W. H. Bloxham, then Secretary of State. An unusually genial, off-hand, sociable gentleman, utterly free from ostentation, he is the favorite of all the State officials, and of a large circle of life-long, intimate friends. Governor Bloxham is a native of Florida, and is the first gentleman elected to that position who has been able to boast of such a distinction. He was born very nearly within sight of the capital, where he now sits as Governor; and his comfortable old home near the city, standing in the midst of an immense plantation of several hundred carefully cleared and cultivated acres, is one of the genuine, old-style cotton-plantations of the most hospitable sort. In the electoral campaign of 1880 he was chosen Governor, and it was unquestionably a good choice, for he is heart and hand in favor of any and all proper efforts to aid the cause of education, of immigration, and development of the State by railroads and similar improvements. He is, in particular, a warm friend of the public-school system, and greatly admires the Northern and Western States for their earnest efforts in this cause. He also believes in extending liberal aid to immigration, hoping to see Florida the home of at least one million people, and covered with a network of railroads and canals. A stanch Democrat, he is not a "Bourbon," but is one who did not believe in the initial secession movement, and is heartily satisfied with the result. So far as he can control or influence the peculiarly retrogressive elements that as yet exert much influence in the political councils of this State, all may be sure that the rights and interests of new-comers will be protected.

An exceedingly pleasant circle of gentlemen to be met in Tallahassee are Chief-Justice E. M. Randall and his Associate Justices, R. B. Van Valkenburg and T. D. Wescott, of the Supreme Court ; also Mr. Charles H. Foster, their Clerk. Judge Randall is from Milwaukee, has lived here many years, and has an elegant home in Jacksonville. Judge Van Valkenburg is from western New York, was a distinguished General in the Union army, and Minister to Japan. He is also a long-time resident here, is warmly attached to the State, and owns a very fine estate on the St. John's River just opposite Jacksonville. Judge Wescott is a resident of Tallahassee, where he dispenses an elegant hospitality. These gentlemen are profoundly respected by all, irrespective of political creeds, and are of great benefit to the State as an encouragement to immigration. They are an unimpeachable guarantee that life and property are and shall be safe in this State, and that lawless desperadoism of the semi-political character—the "Mississippi plan"—will not be permitted or tolerated. The fact that these Northern-born gentlemen are members of the Supreme Court of the State is a greater aid to the cause of immigration than may be supposed, even by the most observing and best-disposed native resident.

Near the city stands the famous Murat estate, once the property of Prince Achille Murat, brother-in-law of the first Napoleon, members of whose family are buried in the beautiful city cemetery. The estate is finely located, and the building-site is unsurpassed, but the house now standing upon it is quite plain and unpretentious. Another local "lion" is the noted Wakulla Spring, which I reached by a pleasant drive of sixteen miles. The spring lies in a rather flat, uninteresting, pine-wooded region, near several cultivated cotton-plantations. It is nearly circular in shape, about four hundred feet in diameter, and the shores are densely wooded to the water's edge. A rude landing has been constructed, and an old darkey is always present with his boat to row the visitor about the glassily smooth surface of the pond. The sides are very nearly perpendicular, and are composed of smooth and solid rock. Sixty-six feet below the surface of the water is the first or upper level, a broad, shelving surface of clean rock ; and through this is a large, irregularly circular opening apparently about one hundred feet in diameter, through which can be seen the lower level or bottom of this wonderful spring, a total depth of one hundred and nine feet. The rock that forms the upper level is evidently not very thick, for in one place there is a perfectly round opening about three feet in diameter, through which can be plainly seen the second bottom, fifty-five feet farther below. It is a great, thin fringe of rock, like a crust, with a vast opening a little to one side of its center.

The water is so marvelously blue that indigo would look pale in comparison with it, and so clear that small gravel and bits of tin one inch square could all be seen plainly on the bottom. Countless fish, some quite large and some very small, could also be seen lazily floating about in the distant depths. While the water is blue, the rocks are of the most intensely brilliant green, over which occasional phosphorescent flashes of shimmering light play fitfully, producing a weird and phantasmal effect. There is neither a ripple nor a motion observable in the water, yet here is a stream that comes pouring up from the bowels of the earth and forms a river (the Wakulla River) sixty feet wide and four feet deep.

This is the spring that Ponce de Leon, the Spanish adventurer and discoverer, romantically supposed to be the long-sought "Fountain of Youth." He and his superstitious soldiers seem to have completely misunderstood their interpreters or the Indians, who probably meant to convey the information that it was a spring of clear, healthy water, that had a beneficial effect upon the bather therein. He and his followers, being where St. Mark's now stands, sought out the Wakulla River and followed it up to this spring, into which they eagerly plunged. It need hardly be said that they came out cleaner, but no younger ; and the lives of many innocent savages were at once sacrificed to appease their disappointed anger. They found, or could see on the distant bottom, the skeletons of two gigantic mastodons, their flesh all gone, but their bare bones perfect and white, their great curling tusks interlocked, evidently fallen in and drowned while engaged in a terrific combat on the brink. There the bones lay until, in 1835, Professor King, of Philadelphia, engaged several men, some of whom are now living in Tallahassee, to recover them. This was successfully accomplished, and they were shipped on board a schooner, to be placed in the museum in Philadelphia ; but, unfortunately, the vessel was lost at sea, in a gale off Cape Hatteras, and these interesting skeletons were finally lost for ever.

Returning home from our visit to this romantic spring, our party visited another smaller but very interesting spring, and also examined a number of the many mysterious " sinks " that are found in that Wakulla region. These sinks are mostly circular in form, about fifty feet in diameter and fifty to one hundred and fifty feet deep, with smooth sides, like great wells, only they are dry, or have but little water in their deep bottoms, while large lakes or rivers may be but a few hundred feet distant, with their waters nearly level with the surface of the ground. The wonder is, how there can be such a difference between the levels of the waters in the lake and in the sink ; how the water of the lake fails to get into the sink, and where the waters of the sink come from and go to. These sinks are found in all portions of Florida, and are a remarkable and characteristic feature of the peninsula.

In Wakulla County is a vast jungle of trees, vines, water, and marsh, that has never yet been fully explored. Neither the United States nor the State Government has ever attempted to survey it (in fact, there has never been a geological survey of this State). Several adventurous gentlemen in Tallahassee have, on various occasions, attempted to penetrate its depths, but found it impossible except at much expense. As far as they penetrated, they found a strange country of volcanic appearance. Everywhere were seen great masses of rocks, often an acre in extent, all cracked and ragged as if upheaved from a great depth. Traces of gold, lead, copper, silver, and iron are said to have been discovered ; and abundant traces of petroleum are found there, and in numerous other localities in that region. It is in this impenetrable jungle that the famous "Florida volcano" is supposed to exist, for a column of light, hazy smoke or vapor may be (and has been for years) seen rising from some portion of it, and provokes the conundrum, "What is it?"

Among other strange freaks of nature in that region is Lost Creek, where a large stream suddenly ends, evidently plunging downward into the earth, in an abyss that is bottomless. Also the Natural Bridge across St. Mark's River, about seventy feet in width and the same in span, over which people pass. A volume could be written about the natural curiosities of Florida that would be deeply interesting and of scientific value. A thorough scientific survey of this State should be ordered by the State authorities ; but, with the present class of able tax-reducers, it is a futile hope to expect any such measure to be authorized.

The people of Tallahassee have a beautiful custom of holding a fair, early each spring, that probably differs from anything in the way of the fair exhibitions held elsewhere in the South. It is a floral fair, held at their spacious fair-grounds, open to all, but of course nearly or quite all the exhibits are made by the Tallahasseeans. The exhibits are vegetables, fruits, and flowers, especially flowers. As might be conjectured, the managers, exhibitors, and patrons generally, are the ladies, who take great interest and pride in this exhibition, so distinctively local, so pleasant, and so indicative of refined taste and culture. I attended the fair of 1880, held in March. Floral Hall was a beautiful sight, with a profuse display of flowers, of all varieties, kinds, forms, colors, and perfumes, all artistically arranged and exhibited to the best advantage.

Nowhere, it may be said in conclusion, is there a more refined and cultured society than in Tallahassee.

Among them are many descendants of the most prominent and aristocratic old families of America, with names that recall old colonial, Revolutionary, and 1812 days in the battle-fields and in State councils; and their large, well-attended schools, numerous, handsome churches, beautiful homes and surroundings, all attest to the high standard of the best society of Tallahassee.

From Tallahassee to Jacksonville the traveler passes over the Jacksonville, Pensacola and Mobile to Live Oak, and thence *via* the Savannah, Florida and Western Railroad. The other important towns in this section, besides those mentioned, may be briefly dealt with.

Monticello, in Jefferson County, thirty-three miles east of Tallahassee, is the terminus of a branch railroad about five miles long, and is a flourishing town of some two thousand inhabitants. It contains two hotels, good schools, a weekly newspaper, and churches of the several denominations, Episcopalian, Presbyterian, Methodist, and Baptist. The climate is almost identical with that of Tallahassee, and the adjacent country is very similar in appearance to that which surrounds the capital. Near Monticello is the Lipona plantation, where Murat resided for some time while in Florida; and in the vicinity is Lake Miccosukee, whose banks figure in history as the camping-ground of De Soto, and as the scene of a bloody battle between General Jackson and the Miccosukee Indians.

Madison is a pretty town of about eight hundred inhabitants, situated on the railway, fifty-five miles east of Tallahassee. It is the capital of Madison County, is built on a plain near a small lake, and contains Presbyterian, Baptist, and Methodist churches. The Suwanee River is near by, and in the county are Lakes Rachel, Francis, Mary, and Cherry.

Live Oak, the county-seat of Suwanee County, is at the junction of the Jacksonville, Pensacola and Mobile

and the Savannah, Florida and Western Railways, and is
the half-way point between Tallahassee and Jacksonville.
The surrounding country is pine-woods with sandy soil,
which looks poor, but which, with a little manure and
good cultivation, produces excellent crops. There are a
number of market-gardens in the vicinity, and great quantities of vegetables are shipped from this point to Northern markets. The town spreads over a good deal of
ground, and contains about eight hundred inhabitants.
A live weekly newspaper, "The Bulletin," is published
here, the schools are good, and there are churches of
several denominations, with some respectable store-build-
ings and a number of pleasant residences. Five miles
south of the town (connected with it by a "tram-road,"
or wooden railway) is Padlock, and four miles north is
the little village of Rixford.

Houston lies six miles east of Live Oak, on the railroad, and is surrounded by a good farming country. Near
the town are some fine springs, and in the vicinity are several beautiful lakes containing an abundance of excellent
fish. Wellborn, twelve miles east of Live Oak, is a much
larger place, and among its population are a number of
settlers who have come thither from Indiana, Illinois, and
Iowa. There are some fine hammock-lands near the town,
and in the neighborhood are Lake Wellborn and other
lakes teeming with fish. Only eight miles away are the
famous Suwanee White Sulphur Springs, attractively situated on the banks of the Suwanee River.

Lake City, the most important place in this region,
is on the railroad about fifty miles west of Jacksonville.
It is a prosperous and substantially built town of some
twenty-five hundred inhabitants, with a number of brick
stores, well-kept hotels, seven or eight churches, good
schools, tasteful private residences, and a large trade in
vegetables and other products of the surrounding coun-

try, including lumber and turpentine. Its climate, being drier than that of Jacksonville, is thought to be more favorable to those consumptives who are in advanced stages of the disease, and the place is a favorite winter retreat for such invalids. Lakes almost surround the town, hence its name. Three miles south is Alligator Lake, which has no visible outlet. In the wet season it is three or four miles across, but in winter it retires into a deep sink-hole, and the former bottom is transformed into a grassy meadow.

The following description of Suwanee County is from a letter written by Mr. N. C. Rippey to the Tallahassee "Floridian." We quote it because it is applicable to all this portion of the State, and contains information of value to immigrants :

"The county lies in a big bend of the Suwanee River, or at least the river forms the boundary-line on three sides. There is a high ridge extending across the county east and west, or nearly so, near the center north and south, some four miles or so in width. It is covered with the finest growth of pine-timber in the county. In it is an abundance of stone, in ledges and in bowlders. It is of a gray color, very soft ; can be easily cut with a knife or saw, and, on being exposed to the air for some time, it becomes as hard and durable as granite, and makes a very fine material for building purposes.

"The country north of the ridge is pine-woods with sandy soil. Here and there are to be found tracts of hammock-lands, varying in size from a few acres to several hundred. These lands contain a rich, loamy soil, and a great variety of excellent hard-wood timber, suitable for all kinds of building and manufacturing purposes. There are a number of beautiful lakes scattered over the country, containing an abundance of excellent fish. There are numerous springs, some of them white sulphur, famed for their medical virtues. There are branches or creeks gushing out of the earth, and after flowing a few miles entirely disappear. The country south of 'The Ridge' is more rolling and fertile, and is underlaid with limestone that frequently comes within a few inches of the surface. There are no lakes or streams of running water. There are a great number of natural wells that appear as though they were cut by the hand of man through solid rock; they are round, or nearly so, varying in size from a few inches to forty feet or more in diameter, and from a few feet to forty or more to the edge of the water; fish are frequently found in the largest; the water is clear and cool. There are a number of caves of considerable size, but they have never been explored to see how far they extend under the earth.

"The pine-lands produce about fifteen bushels of corn per acre. A little manure and good cultivation will yield more than double that; cotton, about a bale to two acres, sometimes three; upland rice, from forty to sixty bushels per acre; oats and rye are raised in considerable quantities, but I was unable to learn the yield per acre; sugar-cane does well, and is a very profitable crop; a great variety of fine vegetables are raised and shipped to Northern markets; there are a number of small vineyards in the county, and some excellent wine is made from the grapes; there are quite a number of small orange-groves, and, strange to say, they are nearly all planted by the hands of women; it is a fine country for peaches and pears. The people are just beginning to find out what a great variety of fruits and vegetables they can raise, and everybody seems determined to have an orchard of all kinds of fruit. 'Turpentining' has become quite an industry, and there are several large turpentine farms in the county that are reported to be very profitable.

"The Suwanee River is navigable for small steamboats to the crossing of the Jacksonville, Pensacola and Mobile Railroad, and for large steamers to Rowland's Bluff, near the southeast corner of the county. The river frequently has rocky bluffs and bottoms, and many fine springs are to be seen along the banks, and some rich lands.

"The population of the county in 1880 was 7,379, of which 4,166 were white and 3,213 were black. Judging from the number of immigrants that have gone into the county this past fall and winter, the white population must now be about five thousand."

Dr. D. G. Brinton says : "The climate of this part of Florida is dry and equable. Many invalids would find it a very pleasant and beneficial change from the seacoast or the river-side, and immigrants would do well to visit it. Game and fish are abundant, and the sportsman need never be at a loss for occupation."

Several new towns have been projected on the route to Jacksonville, and are showing some good results from persistent effort. The names of two are Glen St. Mary and McClenny. The first is near the south branch of the St. Mary's River, in Baker County ; the other is farther east, nearer Baldwin, in the same county.

CHAPTER V.

JACKSONVILLE, the commercial metropolis and social center of the State, is likely to be the first point at which the visitor to Florida will make anything of a stay—the place where he will get his first impressions of the "Land of Flowers." It is a handsome and prosperous-looking city, covering a good deal of ground, and, particularly during the winter season, when all the hotels are thrown open to the thronging guests, it presents an animated and picturesque appearance that is quite exceptional at the South. The streets are remarkably wide, and are nearly all shaded by long rows of mammoth live-oaks, forming arcades of embowering green in winter as well as in summer. Good sidewalks of brick or planks contribute greatly to the comfort of pedestrians, but the streets themselves are too sandy for rapid or pleasant driving, and are "heavy" for all vehicles.

Bay Street is the principal business thoroughfare, and runs parallel to and one block distant from the river. For a distance of about a mile it is lined on both sides with stores, offices, and other mercantile buildings, including several of the leading hotels. The Astor Building, at the corner of Bay and Hogan Streets, is the finest in the city, and in it, besides several stores and a number of offices, is the United States Signal-Service station. Horse-cars, connecting the railroad-depots, run along Bay Street, up

Catherine to Duval Street to the St. James Hotel, down Hogan Street and back to the starting-point, making a very convenient circuit. On the river at the foot of Ocean

STREET-SCENE IN JACKSONVILLE.

Street is a fine public market, and there is a smaller one up-town at the corner of Hogan and Church Streets. Many of the shops make a specialty of "Florida curiosities" (the majority of them manufactured in New York), and con-

nected with that of Damon Greenleaf, on Bay Street, is a
"Museumenagerie," which will prove interesting to visitors, and the admission to which is free.

There is in the city a quite remarkable number of handsome residences, and with very few exceptions they are
surrounded by ample grounds laid out in tasteful gardens
and lawns. Sometimes these gardens are perfect little
parks, and the fruits, flowers, and shrubs all indicate a
semi-tropical region. The society of Jacksonville is universally admitted to be unusually select, cultured, and refined; and the reasons are not far to seek. Many of the
most prominent citizens have been drawn thither from all
parts of the country on account of its climatic advantages,
and are in general the picked men of their several localities. At any gathering of the best society there will be
found gentlemen who have occupied high positions in all
portions of the United States, and in nearly all professions
and occupations—in the army, the navy, the judicial, the
political, literary, artistic, and commercial world. As examples, I may mention that General Spinner, he of the
famous greenback autograph, owns a beautiful home here,
whither he has retired to enjoy the well-deserved comforts
of an honored old age; and that Judge Thomas Settle, of
the United States Circuit Court, the original of Judge
Denton in "The Fool's Errand," has another fine residence.
During the winter season the great hotels (the St. James,
the Windsor, the Carleton, the National, etc.) are thronged
with wealthy tourists from all parts of the world, and the
place has then all the gayety and animation of a leading
summer resort at the North.

Situated on the left bank of the St. John's, at the point
where that noble river makes a sharp bend to the east, the
city presents a very attractive appearance from the water,
and from its higher points commands a pleasing outlook
upon the stream and its low-lying opposite shore. Its situ-

ation is a very favorable one for commerce, and its trade is very extensive, particularly in lumber, the preparation of which gives employment to a number of large saw-mills. Nearly all the railroad and steamer lines of the State center at Jacksonville, and immense quantities of fruit and early vegetables, as well as of cotton and sugar, are shipped thence to Northern and foreign ports.

With what are known as the "modern conveniences" the city is well supplied. It is lighted with gas, has an excellent system of water-works drawing the water from artesian wells, and has recently been provided with an effective system of sewers. The public schools are well organized and in successful operation ; there are a circu-lating library and a free reading-room ; Episcopalian, Pres-byterian, Methodist, Baptist, and Catholic churches ; banks, public halls, newspapers, and telegraphic connection with all parts of the United States. According to the census of 1880, the resident population was 14,500, and the rate of growth has been and is very rapid. When Florida shall have achieved what now appears to be her "manifest des-tiny," Jacksonville will be one of the great commercial and industrial centers of the country.

FERNANDINA.—This picturesque old city, one of the most interesting in Florida, lies on the Atlantic coast, about fifty miles northeast of Jacksonville, close to the Georgia line, being the northernmost point in the State. It is built on the west shore of Amelia Island, overlooking a broad bay which affords the finest harbor on the coast south of the Chesapeake Bay, and which gives it important commer-cial advantages. Vessels drawing twenty feet of water can cross the bar at high tide, and the largest ships can un-load at the wharves. The Mallory Line of Direct Florida Steamers has its southern terminus at Fernandina, and the steamers of the Charleston and Savannah lines call here on

5

their way to and from Jacksonville. One of the most important railroads of Florida—the Atlantic, Gulf and West India Transit Railroad — begins at Fernandina and runs southwest across the State to Cedar Keys; and the Fernandina and Jacksonville Railroad, recently completed, affords a short air-line route between these two cities. With such advantages, it is not surprising that the commerce of Fernandina is large and increasing. Immense quantities of fruits and vegetables are brought thither by the railways for shipment north ; and there is an important export trade in lumber, cotton, and sugar. (See Appendix, note 13.)

Fernandina was founded by the Spaniards in 1632, and has an interesting history, over which, however, I have not time to linger. It is now a busy and prosperous place of about two thousand inhabitants, whose numbers are largely augmented by visitors during the winter season. It is built on a broad plain that rises gently from the shores of the bay, showing to fine advantage from the harbor. The streets are laid out at right angles, are wide and generally well kept, and are everywhere densely shaded with great oaks, magnolias, and similar evergreen trees. The business portion of the city contains some substantial structures; but the largest and finest buildings are the hotels. The Egmont Hotel is one of the finest in the South, and the Mansion and Riddell Houses are spacious and well kept, all being crowded during the season. The suburbs are very beautiful, the houses being for the most part tastefully constructed, and nearly always surrounded by ample grounds laid out in lawns and gardens, and covered with a tropical luxuriance of flowers and shrubbery. Quite a number of orange-groves are found in the vicinity, and opposite the Egmont House is an interesting grove of palmettoes.

Crossing the island in a direction due east from the city, an attractive drive two miles long leads to the famous Amelia Island Beach, one of the finest in America, and af-

A Cluster of Palmettoes.

fording an unsurpassed beach-drive of twenty miles. The beach is as smooth, as hard, and as level as a floor; and during the season it presents an enlivening sight, with its long lines of carriages and other equipages. Another charming ride may be enjoyed to Fort Clinch, a romantic old fortification situated on the extreme northern point of the island.

But of all the attractions of Fernandina and its vicinity the chiefest is "Dungeness," once the home of General Nathanael Greene, of Revolutionary fame, and now the property of General W. G. M. Davis. This noble estate was granted to General Greene by the State of Georgia, in recognition of his splendid services to the South, and is situated on Cumberland Island, about an hour's sail from Fernandina in a small steamer. Cumberland Island lies along the coast of Georgia, close to . the Florida line, and is some eighteen miles long by about a mile in average width. On one side lies the broad Atlantic, and on the other is the sound, across which, at the distance of about a mile, is the mainland. Dungeness, so named by General Greene's wife, is situated at the southern end of the island, and includes about one third of its total area. The magnificent mansion was burned in the early part of the civil war, but the ruins still stand firm as a rock, the massive old coquina-stone walls having actually been hardened by the fire. In the quaint old burying-ground, some distance from the house, lie a number of the relatives of General Greene and his wife ; and here is the tomb of "Light-Horse Harry" Lee, father of General Robert E. Lee.

On a charming morning in January, 1880, I visited Dungeness, and spent a couple of hours in wandering about the beautiful grounds, with their curious old gardens and fruit-groves. It was my second visit to the place, and I felt that I could exist there as a modern

Robinson Crusoe, if need be, and never tire of its loveliness. Such teeming gardens ; such brilliant flowers ;
such wide fields ; such noble groves of grand old live-
oaks and magnolias ; such a tropical luxuriance of tangled vines ; such broad, winding avenues, leading from
the water to the house-park ; such delightfully perplex-
ing walks ; such a glorious sea-beach, the twin of that
on Amelia Island ; such oysters, lining the sound-shore
in millions ; such game and fish ; and such a clear, pure
air—no, never could I tire of Dungeness!—dreamy, romantic, delicious, entrancing old Dungeness !

St. Augustine.—The visitor to St. Augustine may enjoy the consciousness that the spot on which he then stands
has behind it a longer stretch of authentic history than any
other within the limits of the United States. It is, indeed,
the oldest European settlement in our country, having been
founded by the Spaniards under Menendez in 1565, forty-
two years prior to the settlement of Jamestown in Virginia,
and fifty-five years before the landing of the Pilgrims at
Plymouth Rock. Its history has been checkered and romantic in the highest degree ; it was from the very first a
place of considerable note, and the theatre of interesting
events ; and it still possesses a curious aspect and flavor of
antiquity. Coming to it from bustling, active, Northern-
like Jacksonville or Fernandina, one is conscious of a complete and sudden change of time and place—as if the brief
ride on steamer and railway had produced magic results,
and landed him in some quaint, old, dead-alive Spanish town
of the middle ages. The large influx of wealthy settlers
from the North has greatly altered the character of the
place within the past few years ; but the smart modern vil-
las still have the air of foreign intruders, and the quaint,
romantic old city retains at once its individuality and its
unlikeness to anything else in America.

STREET IN ST. AUGUSTINE.

The site of St. Augustine is a flat, sandy, narrow peninsula, formed by the Matanzas River on the east and the St. Sebastian on the south and west. It is separated from the Atlantic Ocean by Anastasia Island, which lies directly in front of the harbor, and for miles around it is encompassed by a tangled undergrowth of palmetto - scrub and other bushes. From Jacksonville it is about thirty miles distant in a southeasterly direction, and it is about forty miles south of the mouth of the St. John's River.

The very streets of St. Augustine are romantic and characteristic, being crooked and narrow — seldom more than ten to twenty feet in width — and all paved with shells. The older houses are built mostly of coquina (or shell-stone, quarried on Anastasia Island), and the prevailing style of architecture is very quaint and ancient, the verandas frequently hanging out over the streets and almost touching each other across the narrow way. The principal streets running parallel to the river are Bay, Charlotte, St. George's, Spanish, and Tolomato. Those running at right angles (east and west) are Orange, Cuna, Hypolita, Treasury, King, Bridge, and St. Francis. Bay Street is the main business street, and commands a fine view of the harbor, Anastasia Island, and the ocean. St. George's is the Fifth Avenue of the place, and contains some of the finest buildings and residences. At the head of this street stands the famous City Gate, once a part of the old Spanish wall that extended across the peninsula from shore to shore, and protected the city on the north. The last traces of the wall have long since vanished, but the City Gate is in a fair state of preservation, and, with its lofty ornamented towers and sentry-boxes, it is a picturesque and imposing structure.

Near the center of the city is the Plaza de la Constitucion, comprising about an acre of ground inclosed with a substantial fence. In the center of the Plaza stands a

monument erected in 1812 to commemorate the adoption
of the Spanish Liberal Constitution; and on the eastern
side is a Soldiers' Monument erected in 1872 by the Ladies'
Memorial Association "in memory of our loved ones who

St. Augustine Cathedral.

THE CONVENT-GATE.

gave their lives in defense of the Confederate States."
Fronting on the Plaza are several noteworthy buildings,
among them the dilapidated old cathedral with its quaint
Moorish belfry, forming one of the "sights" of St. Augus-

tine. The cathedral was built in 1793, and one of the bells
bears the date of 1682. Also fronting on the Plaza is
the Governor's Palace, formerly the residence of the Spanish governors, but now used for the post-office and court-
rooms. Next to this building on the north is the old Convent of St. Mary's, and the Convent of the Sisters of St.
Joseph is a tasteful coquina building on St. George's Street,
south of the Plaza.

Perhaps the most interesting features of old St. Augustine are the Sea Wall and Fort Marion (formerly Fort San
Marco). The Sea Wall is built of coquina, with a granite
coping four feet wide, and is nearly a mile in length, protecting the entire ocean-front of the city. It furnishes a
delightful promenade, and is usually thronged on moonlight evenings. Near its south end are the United States
Barracks, occupying a building which was formerly a Franciscan monastery. At its north end, commanding the sea-
front, is old Fort Marion, probably the most picturesque
structure in America. Like the Sea Wall and most of the
older edifices in St. Augustine, it is built of the coquina
quarried on Anastasia Island, and the construction of it
occupied one hundred and sixty-four years, having been
commenced in 1592 and completed in 1756. The labor of
building it was performed almost entirely by negro slaves,
Indians, and prisoners of war; and every stone of it was
cemented with the sweat of toiling sufferers. While in the
possession of the British, this was said to be the prettiest
fort in the king's dominions; and with its esplanade, moats,
barbicans, drawbridges, massive arched entrance, dark passages, vaulted casemates, ornate sentry-boxes, frowning
bastions, and mysterious dungeons—in which were found
in 1835 two skeletons in cages, victims probably of some
inquisitorial cruelty—it is still a strangely attractive and
interesting spot. For modern warfare, of course, it is quite
useless, and not being kept up for military purposes, it is

quietly crumbling into decay. At present it is simply a favorite place of resort for sight-seers and curiosity-hunters. It is especially popular with romantic, newly-married tour-

ENTRANCE TO FORT MARION.

ists, and with marriageable maidens and their escorts; and it is reputed to have no rival in the number of lovers' vows and marriage-promises that have been exchanged within its recesses.

Of the modern buildings at St. Augustine, the largest and finest are the hotels—the St. Augustine, fronting on the Plaza and Charlotte Street, and the Magnolia, in St. George Street, near the Plaza, being the principal ones. There are also quite a number of fine modern villa residences erected by Northern settlers, and in the environs are many beautiful orange-groves and gardens. The harbor affords unsurpassed opportunities for boating and fishing; and pleasant excursions may be made to the light-houses and coquina-quarries on Anastasia Island, and to the North and South Beaches. Salt-water bathing may be enjoyed in suitable bath-houses, but sharks render open sea-bathing dangerous. The officers of the garrison and a number of wealthy gentlemen who visit St. Augustine regularly each season, have built and maintain a cozy little yacht club-house, which is one of the leading attractions of the place. It is built out over the water of the harbor, just opposite the St. Augustine Hotel, and its hall, richly furnished in the Eastlake style and decorated with pictures, is equipped with leading papers and periodicals from all parts of the world. To the army officers, some dozen or more in number, is due much of the social animation of St. Augustine.

In the matter of healthfulness St. Augustine takes a high place among Florida resorts. Malaria is almost unknown, and the constant sea-breezes moderate the cold of winter and mitigate the heat of summer. Frosts seldom occur, and the mean winter temperature is 58·08°. Nevertheless, cold northeasters are liable to make themselves felt in January and February, and this renders the place less desirable for consumptives than some of the inland resorts. The summer climate is delightful.

CHAPTER VI.

THIS famous river, from its mouth to its head-waters in the far-off regions of Southern Florida, is purely tropical; its waters, shores, scenery, vegetation, all animate objects, the birds in the air and on the water, the fish and reptiles within its depths, are mostly strange, attractive, and intensely interesting, especially to the Northern traveler. It is the only really tropical stream in the United States navigable its entire length, and is different from all others in that it reverses the usual order of the water-courses of America and flows due north. A sluggish, slow current, its entire length lies parallel with, and is only separated by a narrow belt of land from, the Atlantic Ocean, into which it empties at a point eighteen miles east of Jacksonville, close to the Georgia State line.

From its source to its mouth it embraces three varieties of streams, each entirely distinct in form, width, depth, scenery, shores, soils, and vegetation; and these strange transformations not only add greatly to the interest of the river, but relieve it of the monotony characteristic of long rivers. The first stretch of the river, from its mouth to a point shortly above Welaka, a total distance of ninety-seven miles, is a vast lagoon, averaging from one to six miles in width, deep, with a slow current, the shores a series of bold bluffs and declivities, everywhere covered with extensive forests of great live-oaks, sweet-gums, cypresses, willows, and occasional magnolias. These forests tower up grandly, their wide-spreading branches loaded with waving festoons of soft gray Spanish moss and interlaced with gigantic vines, while the soil beneath is mostly free of heavy underbrush, presenting a romantic, park-like appearance as viewed from the deck of the passing steamer.

The settlements are frequent, and are usually attractive-appearing villages, with noticeably large, well-built, bright-looking homes, neat grounds and fences, cozy-looking little stores, fine long piers—everything wearing an air of long-established prosperity. Large estates, having commodious residences, with wide, roomy verandas, standing in the midst of neatly cleared house-grounds, and surrounded by broad fields and thrifty, green-leaved orange-groves, the home pier projecting into the river (for every one residing on the St. John's River *must* have a pier and a fleet of boats to complete his happiness), are everywhere in sight, lining the shores on either hand and charming the traveler with their manifest evidences of comfort and content. This region is regarded as healthy, and is not infested by insects to any unusually annoying degree. No portion of the State is more desirable for the health-seeker, or for the traveler in search of repose, desiring only a quiet, cozy retreat for a summer-like home in mid-winter months, where all the choicest vegetables, daintiest fruits, and most brilliant-hued flowers, excellent fishing, and the pleasures of small-game hunting, may be enjoyed all the year round. For the settler, too, its only drawback is the liability to frosts in occasional years, damaging to the prospects of fruit-culture on a large scale for positive revenue ; but this is not an altogether bad feature, since it enhances the healthfulness of the region. Nowhere do figs, grapes, strawberries, pears, peaches, and all kinds of vegetables, grow to better advantage or produce more abundantly. Oranges also do well on the east side, where ample water protection is secured ; but lemons, limes, pineapples, and bananas are uncertain, though they are unusually nutritious if ripened without injury by frost. (See Appendix, 15.)

Nearly all tourists in Florida "do the St. John's" up to Sanford, but comparatively few take a trip on that portion of the river below Jacksonville; yet those who do not, miss a view which equals in picturesque strangeness any river scenery in America. Here the river is a broad estuary, with no perceptible current, stretching spaciously between low-lying shores, which close it in on either hand with serried ranks of evergreen forest-trees. No town or hamlet breaks in upon the primitive simplicity and wildness of the scene, and the few houses that are here and there seen appear to be lapped and in-

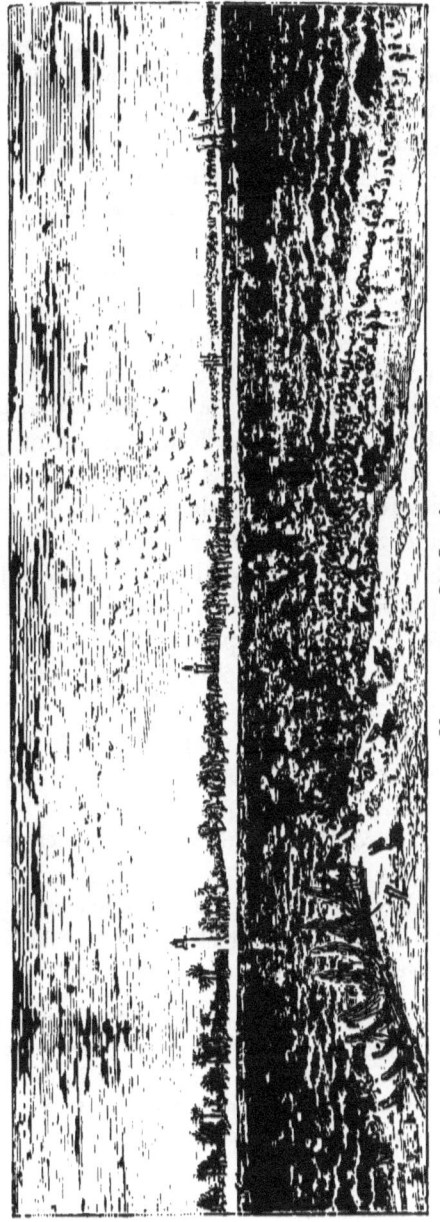

MOUTH OF THE ST. JOHN'S.

wrapped in a soft, dreamy, delicious quiet. Yet there is no sense of loneliness. On the broad bosom of the stream at all hours may be seen the beautiful, swan-like steamers as they come and go to and from New York, Savannah, Charleston, and other ports ; and the countless sailing-vessels that "go down to the sea" lend a perpetual animation and interest to the scene. A winter home here, with a well-kept garden, fruit-grove, and flower-decked lawn, a horse, dog, gun, fishing-rod, and yacht, is as near an approach to the original Eden as one can reasonably expect in this world.

As is the case with nearly all the Southern rivers, the mouth of the St. John's is obstructed by a sand-bar, which interferes seriously with navigation, and which is now being dealt with on the Eads system of jetties. Near the entrance is the famous Pelican Bank, the resort of myriads of sea-fowl ; and a little north is Fort George Island, which is a favorite summer resort of inland Floridians, and which has an hotel, several handsome residences, an observatory, a lighthouse, a quaint old Pilot Town, and some fine shell-roads.* (See Appendix, note 16.)

The round trip up the St. John's River from Jacksonville and return involves about eight hundred miles of travel, and every mile is deeply interesting, with its rapidly shifting scenes of tropical vegetation and life. Always on the steamers will the passengers be seen clustered on the decks, forward and aft, all intently observing the novel and ever-changing panorama, admiring the numerous strange birds, of several varieties, as they gracefully wheel off in the distance, or curiously studying the hideous attractions of the alligators that may be discovered basking in the sunshine

---

* A good view of the lower St. John's is obtained from the steamers which run from Charleston and Savannah to Jacksonville. A better plan, however, affording an opportunity for a short visit to Fort George Island, is to take the little steamer which runs down the river from Jacksonville every afternoon, returning next morning.

along the banks. Alligators are quite wise in their generation, know the universal propensity of mankind to kill something, and are aware of their own very tempting qualities as a target when exposed to a boat-load of travelers, of whom the masculine members are nearly all armed with deadly weapons ; so they do not offer any very extended opportunity to study their physiognomies, but always rush for deep water, the principal impression they convey being that of a scurrying, splashing monster with a great tail curled upward, plunging head-foremost into the water. Above Lake Monroe, in the savanna region, alligators are very plentiful and not shy, but below Lake George they are very rare, and none are seen from the steamers.

Ten miles above Jacksonville, on the west shore, is Orange Park, a neat village of broad gardens, wide streets, a handsome winter hotel, numerous pretty cottages, a river-road lined with large oaks (in one of these is built a lattice summer-house reached by easy ascending stairs), a long pier, and a stylish wharf-house. Five miles farther, on the east shore, is Mandarin, a cozy and prosperous village of roomy, airy, neat homes ; the orange-groves, gardens, lawns, roads, fences, and pier all giving unmistakable evidences of comfort and good taste. Here, showing prominently from the river, is the home of Mrs. Harriet Beecher Stowe. Six miles above, on the western shore, is Hibernia, a pretty hamlet, much resembling Mandarin. Indeed, the same description answers for both, and also for Magnolia, six miles farther up, on the western shore, equally pretty and thrifty.

Green Cove Springs is three miles above (thirty miles from Jacksonville), on a broad, deep bay on the western shore. This is a charming village of several stores, two large, well-furnished and finely appointed winter hotels, and numerous pretty homes. The streets are shady and neat, making it an attractive resort. The springs, from which the village takes its name, are the principal attraction, located in the center of the place and arranged for drinking and bathing. The water is slightly sulphurous and remarkably clear, sparkling, and copious.

Picolata, a pretty locality on the eastern shore, nine miles above, is a small hamlet of four or five houses, with orange-

Mrs. Stowe's Residence.

groves; and on the same shore, four miles above, is Tocoi (forty-three miles from Jacksonville). Here the traveler takes the cars for St. Augustine, fourteen miles distant, across a monotonous, flat, pine-timbered country. Tocoi is entirely uninteresting, merely a railway-depot, with freight-warehouse, car-shed, water-tank, and two small dwellings.

There is a moss curing and packing house near by, where the Spanish moss is prepared for mattresses for Northern markets. This will probably become an important business in Florida in the future. Federal Point, six miles above, is a small hamlet on the eastern shore, with three or four cottages, a store, and numerous young orange-groves. It is noted for the great quantity of strawberries grown there, upward of fifty thousand quarts having been shipped in the winter and spring of 1881. Here are two of the finest orange-groves in the State, curiously noticeable because, contrary to all theories, arguments, or practical trials attempted elsewhere, they are located on low, flat, inferior-looking pine-land, the surface being very little above water. Orange Mills, five miles above, on the eastern shore, is in all respects similar to Federal Point.

Palatka, the county-seat of Putnam County, is seven miles above (sixty-one miles from Jacksonville). This beautiful young city is located at the head of a large bay on the western shore of the river, on a high, broad plateau, affording a grand view up and down the river. The soil thereabout is rich, susceptible of easy cultivation, and yields abundant crops. Hundreds of market-gardeners are settled in the surrounding country, and vast quantities of all kinds of garden-vegetables and small fruits are annually shipped North. In the vicinity are many old, productive, and valuable orange-groves ; and on the opposite side of the river (reached by ferry) is the grove of Colonel Hart, one of the most famous in the State.

Palatka is the second city in size on the St. John's River, and is rapidly growing. It contains numerous large, well-stocked stores, packing-houses, warehouses, hotels, several handsome churches, public schools, and public buildings. The streets are wide, neatly kept, and are generally shaded with large oaks and orange-trees, and lined with many tastefully constructed residences, and neat cottages with ample house-grounds. Thrift, prosperity, good taste, and enterprise are everywhere manifest. The Florida Southern Railway Company (narrow-gauge line), one of the most extensive corporations in the State, has its headquarters here, the car-shops, storehouses, depots, wharf, and general offices being all established. Also the general offices

ENTRANCE TO HART'S ORANGE-GROVE.

of the Ocklawaha River and the Crescent Lake lines of steamers are here, and the Charleston and Savannah lines of ocean-steamers make this place their up-river terminus. It will be seen that its shipping and transportation facilities are quite important. The population is about two thousand, mostly energetic, Northern and Southern-born people.

San Mateo, on the eastern shore, four miles above Palatka, is a very attractive place, situated on a high bluff, with numerous large and thrifty old orange-groves, and many vegetable-gardens. It has a telegraph-office, express-office, and one of the largest orange-packing houses in the State, a church, public hall, school, stores, etc. The society is excellent, the dwellings are neat and attractive, and no place has a better reputation for healthfulness.

A short distance above is Dunn's Creek, leading into the famous Crescent Lake, about two miles wide and six miles long, a beautiful sheet of water lying between St. John's and Volusia Counties. It is surrounded by a fine region, with pleasing scenery and excellent soil. Crescent City, Owasco, and Oakwood, are pretty little hamlets on its shores, the first-named being the largest and most flourishing, with churches, schools, stores, hotel, etc. There are several other little settlements—rapidly increasing—on the lake, which is said to be quite healthy and to have noticeably few insects. A steamer connects this region with Palatka.

Returning to the St. John's, and journeying up-stream, next comes Buffalo Bluff, on the east shore, six miles above San Mateo. This is a pretty little settlement, with numerous thrifty young orange-groves and gardens. Three miles above, on the east shore, is Nashua, very similar in appearance to Buffalo Bluff. Saratoga, a little community, where the steamers occasionally stop, lies between the last-mentioned places, on the same shore. It has good soil, and will likely become a thriving town in time.

Three miles more brings us to Welaka, one of the most charming localities on the St. John's River, and one of the healthiest and prettiest settlements in the State. The location is on a high bluff, crested with an extensive grove of peculiarly beautiful and majestic live-oaks, and the soil, generally free from underbrush, looks clean and park-like.

Here are a number of the best orange-groves in the State. The residents exhibit much good taste in the construction of their homes, and their gardens, lawns, flowers, and fences are noticeably neat. Nearly opposite Welaka is the mouth of the famous Ocklawaha River.

❧ Norwalk is three miles above, on the western shore, the settlement being located about a mile back from the river, in a region of good soil and attractive surroundings. It has schools, churches, stores, etc., and is noted for the excellence of its society and the great amount of vegetables and garden-fruits produced, annually shipping large quantities. It contains many fine orange-groves.

Just below this landing the character of the St. John's River changes. Here the lower St. John's practically ends, and the middle St. John's begins; the broad, clear-water, bay-like form abruptly terminates, and the steamer passes into a narrow channel, fifty to three hundred feet in width, and remarkably crooked. The water is darker, with a coffee-colored appearance which is attributed to the rank vegetation of the region. This is the tropical jungle region of the river, and continues, with occasional exceptions in the shape of pine or high-soil clearings, on up to Lake Monroe, eighty miles above Norwalk. The shores are mostly flat, very little above the surface of the river, which frequently spreads out over the low boundaries of the channel proper, and forms vast, shallow lakelets, where game resorts in great numbers. Everywhere the shores are covered with a dense growth of oaks, cypress, sweet-gum, willow, and the like, all interlaced with gigantic vines in greatest abundance; great clusters of gray Spanish moss hang from the branches, and the ground is covered to the water's edge with an impenetrable jungle of tropical grasses, reeds, brambles, and bushes. Brilliant-hued flowers—some varieties are very large—are everywhere, in the water, on the bushes, the vines, and the trees, and add a novel beauty to the scenery. Occasionally a glimpse may be had of that mysterious and infrequent air-plant known as *woman's-hair*, a mossy growth very closely resembling the long, soft, golden-hued hair of a young woman, and the clusters when seen have an appearance of being thrown carelessly into a tree or bush. Mistletoe-boughs, with their bright-red berries, are also everywhere seen. Here is the haunt of the alligator, where the traveler has a first sight of these famous saurians. They are not plentiful, and must be seen *quickly*, if seen at all, for they are very shy and have a dis-trust of steamers. The managers of the steamer-lines have recently issued strict orders forbidding any shooting from their steamers, a wise and timely regulation, for, by their insane shooting at everything, the tourists were driving all birds, alligators, and animals from this portion of the river. The scene is also enlivened by the bright plumage—snowy white or brilliant red predominating—of the many birds and water-fowls as they gracefully skim through the air, especially the large, long-legged, long-necked, long-billed white herons, which are very plentiful, and present a fine sight as they majestically wheel in slow curves through the air. This dense jungle scenery frequently impresses the traveler with an idea that the adjacent country is uninhabit-able, but such an impression is erroneous, for this is merely a valley region ; there is excellent country lying back at distances varying from a few hundred feet to two miles.

Resuming the journey up the river, from Norwalk it is two miles to Mount Royal, on the eastern shore, a pretty situation with several neat homes and thrifty orange-groves. Just beyond is Fruitland, a little settlement famous for large production of vegetables. (See Appendix, note 17.) To Fort Gates, a small hamlet on the west shore, it is three quarters of a mile. Three miles above, on the eastern shore, is Georgetown, situated at the north end of Lake George. This is a small trading-place, but is one of the most attrac-

tive localities on the river, owing to the excellent taste shown
by the people living near the landing. Their dwellings,
lawns, fences, and gardens are extremely neat as seen from
the steamer. Several fine, large orange-groves are near by,
that bear heavy crops.

The steamer here enters Lake George, one of the largest
and most attractive of the inland lakes of Florida. It is six
miles wide and thirteen and a half miles long, famous for
the variety and excellence of its fish, and as being the resort of myriads of wild ducks and all kinds of water-fowls.
Many parties of sportsmen annually visit the lake for the
shooting and fishing, and always are delighted with their
success. Lake George Post-Office is the first landing on
the lake, two miles above Georgetown, a trim little place on
good soil. One and a half mile farther is Drayton Island
Landing, the port of this famous island, remarkable for its
fertility, abundant crops, and health. Seville, on the east
shore of the lake, is five miles distant, an attractive place,
with a number of fine orange-groves ; and six miles above
is Spring Grove, a small but flourishing settlement on the
western shore. Four miles more and the steamer is at the
famous Volusia Bar, that hides itself beneath the water at
the upper end of the lake, causing endless delay and annoyance to the steamers of the river—often so low for weeks,
falling to three and a half feet, that none but the lightest-
draught boats can cross. An appropriation has recently
been made by the national Government, and a force is at
work removing the obstruction, on the Eads jetty system.

Again entering the river, which is here much narrower
and shallower, five miles from the bar is Volusia, on the
eastern shore, an unattractive landing, the port of a thrifty
back country. On the opposite shore, a quarter of a mile
above, is Astor, merely a well-constructed, large warehouse
and wharf, the river terminus of the St. John's and Lake
Eustis Railroad, a narrow-gauge road leading to Fort Mason

(twenty-six miles distant), where it opens up the famous
Lake Eustis and Lake Dora region, the equal—even the superior—of any region in Florida for superb scenery, excellent soil, rapid growth, and healthy enterprise.

From Astor it is three miles up to Bluffton, a commonplace post-office landing ; and two miles above is the entrance to Lake Dexter, on the east shore, a fine little lake
containing a number of pretty islands, and affording an outlet for Spring Garden and a good back country. From the
entrance it is twelve miles up to St. Francis, an unattractive
landing on an elevated site, once the location of an old-time
Spanish settlement. Six miles above is Hawkinsville, on
the west shore, a mail-landing with two or three houses on
a level clearing of evidently fertile soil, judging from the
thrifty appearance of the oranges and bananas growing there.
It is remarkable for an extensive quarry or bed of coquina,
or shell-rock, the only formation of the kind in this section
of the State or along the entire river.

De Land Landing is one mile above, a solitary, neatly
constructed storehouse on the east shore, the port of De
Land village, which lies four and a half miles in the interior.
It is three miles more to Lake Beresford, a pretty sheet of
water lying on and adjoining the river on the east side.
Here the steamer enters and crosses the small lake to Ros-
siter's, and Alexander's, two landings near each other, small
settlements of three or four cheap, rude little buildings,
the ports of the Spring Garden and De Land villages and
an excellent adjacent region of fertile soil and numerous
settlers.

Again passing up the river, from the entrance of the
lake it is five miles to Blue Springs on the east shore, a
rather interesting landing-place, a wharf, roadway, one residence on a little hill surrounded by a number of exceedingly
large orange-trees that annually bear a thousand and more
oranges each. The spring, that gives the name, is just

6

below—a large pond of remarkably blue, sparkling water of slightly sulphurous flavor, and full of large fish (here for their health, probably (?)). It is the port for Orange City village, on the high lands two miles in the interior.

Eight miles above is We-ki-va, a mere solitary rude log shanty on the east shore just opposite the mouth of the We-ki-va Creek, a dismal location. Here passengers and freights for Altamont and Apopka are transferred to the little craft that ascends to those enterprising towns. Six miles above, passing through a broad, level, open prairie belt—the first on the river—the steamer enters Lake Monroe at its western end (the lake lies east and west), and in four miles more the steamer is at Sanford, a total distance of one hundred miles, by mail-line steamer route, above Palatka, and one hundred and sixty-one miles above Jacksonville.

Lake Monroe is four and a half miles wide and ten miles long, and well stocked with excellent fish. It is practically the head of the middle St. John's River, and the lower terminus of the upper St. John's; and at Sanford, on the south shore, freights and passengers for the interior of Orange County (Maitland, Osceola, Interlaken, Orlando, some portions of Altamont and Apopka) are transferred to the South Florida Railroad at its fine wharf. Also goods and passengers for far-off tropical Lake Worth, Indian River, and the cattle-prairies of the south, are transferred to the curious little steamers specially constructed for the shallow, crooked channel of the upper St. John's.

One mile east of Sanford is Mellonville, merely a pier, an old hotel, and a few dwellings. Everything here was once well constructed, and this was at one time the only settlement on the lake, and quite an important place. It was established in 1835 as a military post during the wars with the Seminole Indians, the landing for the town and garrison of Fort Reed, two miles in the interior, where is now quite an attractive little village and several of the oldest, best, and most productive orange-groves in the State.

Directly opposite, on the north shore of the lake, is Enterprise, the county-seat of Volusia County. It is located on a plateau that rises to a considerable height back some distance from the lake. The soil is excellent and very fertile. The town contains a court-house and county buildings, a spacious winter hotel, three or four stores, and a large saw-mill. It is a neat, pleasant-appearing place and a famous resort for tourists in the winter season. In the vicinity, or suburbs, are several fine residences, the winter homes of Northern families. Much taste is shown in these dwellings, their lawns, gardens, and surroundings. Here is the famous estate of De Bary (the wine-importer of New York City), quite worth a visit to see the extensive groves, packing-house, piers, and such improvements established. A spring of sulphur-water gushes from the earth in the center of a large field on the lake-shore on the De Bary estate. The spring is about fifty feet in diameter, very deep, and the waters remarkably green and strongly impregnated with sulphur. A large hotel, to eclipse anything of the kind in the South as a winter resort, is being constructed there, for which the locality is peculiarly adapted. In this vicinity are a number of the largest and oldest bearing orange-groves in the State.*

* The question of distances on the St. John's River from Jacksonville to Sanford is very puzzling to the tourist, and even to old residents, owing to the differences in the tables of distances given in the innumerable little advertising hand-books, so-called guide-books, railway-charts, etc., varying from one hundred and forty-four to two hundred and thirteen miles, including many intermediate quantities. Some quote " per United States survey," which is erroneous, as there has been no United States survey, except a mere visit known officially as a " preliminary reconnaissance." The figures as given in this article were obtained from Captain William Shaw, an officer who has navigated the St. John's twelve years as captain of several steamers, and who at present commands the steamer Fred De Bary, the

From Lake Monroe to the extreme southern head-waters of the St. John's River, in Lake Washington, is a journey of two hundred and fourteen miles, following the river-channel, which is remarkably crooked, narrow, and shallow. The region above Lake Monroe (the upper St. John's region), the third section of this strange stream, is a total change from the two lower sections already described. It is a vast prairie region, with occasional clusters, or small groves, of palmetto, sometimes a solitary tree, or half a dozen in a group. Here are seen great herds of cattle, for it is an excellent grazing region, and here the lazy, hideous, but cowardly alligators are found in all their glory. Being seldom disturbed by man, they thrive in all this region in great numbers, attain their fullest size, and are not so timid; can be approached nearer than in the northern sections of the State. The entire region is literally alive with game, the rivers and numerous lakes being full of fish of many varieties, the prairie-grasses and the groves filled with all kinds of small game, while bear and deer are abundant, and in all directions may be seen ducks, geese, loons, coots, pelicans, storks, cranes, herons—all kinds of birds and fowls for food or plumage. It is a paradise for hunters and anglers. The journey through this region is always deeply interesting to the traveler (if properly provided with sportsmen's outfits, mosquito-nettings, etc.), who is usually impressed with a feeling of being far away, out of the country, in a strange clime and land.

The lower St. John's presents an attractive *Southern* scene ; the middle St. John's presents a semi-tropical scene of jungles and orange-groves ; but the upper St. John's is the truly tropical region, deeply impressive, more easily re-

finest of the river-boats. The figures can be decreased somewhat by passing over the route direct, without stops, or increased by making stops at all private landings. The distances here given are accurate, as made by the mail-boats.

membered than described. (An extended description of a journey in this region is given in the chapter on the French trip.)

THE ST. JOHN'S RIVER FLEET.—One of the most conclusive evidences of the rapid growth of Florida, especially of South Florida, is the numerous and constantly increasing fleet of steamers that traverse the waters of the St. John's River. It is but three or four years since two or three old and slow-going boats performed all the service upon this great artery of commerce, where now upward of a dozen swift and commodious steamers are barely adequate to the requirements of travel and traffic. Of the several steamer lines now in operation, the "De Bary Line" is the most important and popular. It carries the United States mails, and runs daily to Sanford, stopping at all mail-stations. At the general office of the line in Jacksonville (on their own wharf) will be found Captain William Watson, the manager, and Mr. C. B. Fenwick, the highly popular and genial general passenger agent. The steamers of the line are the Fred De Bary (Captain Shaw), the largest and most elegant on the river, the George M. Bird (Captain Amazeen), the Rosa (Captain Smith), the Florence (Captain Brock), and the Sylvan Glen, a swift boat formerly running on the New York and Harlem line.—The "Pioneer Line," the oldest on the river, comprises four steamers, of which the Arrow (Captain Payne) runs twice weekly between Jacksonville and Sanford, while the little craft Volusia (Captain Lund) runs weekly to Salt Lake and other points on the extreme upper St. John's. The other steamers of this line, the Fox and Daylight, ply between Sanford and all points above.—The "Independent Line" consists at present of the City of Sanford (Captain Rhodes), which runs twice weekly between Jacksonville and Sanford. A fine new boat is shortly to be added to its service.

—The We-ki-wa (Captain Jones) "goes it alone," plying
between Jacksonville and the remote upper regions of the
river.   It is a small and old-fashioned boat.—A small
steamer leaves Jacksonville every afternoon for Fort George
Island, at the mouth of the St. John's, returning next morning, and affording a delightful excursion.—Several small
steamers ply at frequent intervals between Jacksonville
and the various villages and private landings on the river
as far up as Palatka.*

* There are such frequent changes in the steamboat service on the St.
John's River, that the foregoing statement can not be accurately relied on in
every detail.   The tourist, of course, will inform himself at Jacksonville.
More precise information, too, will be found in the chapter "Routes to and
through Florida."

CHAPTER VII.

THE head-waters of the Ocklawaha are formed by a series of springs rising to the surface in the central sections of Orange and Sumter Counties, and by tributary streams from the several large lakes of that region, including Lakes Eustis, Harris, Griffin, and Dora. Some of these springs are remarkable for their size, purity, clearness, and mineral qualities, particularly Clay Spring, near Apopka. The river flows through portions of four counties, with a course almost due north until it touches the northern boundary of Marion County, when it turns due east, and empties into the St. John's at Welaka, twenty-five miles south of Pilatka. Its total length is about three hundred and forty miles, and it is navigable throughout by the little steamers, which also traverse many of its tributaries to their fountain-heads, thus penetrating to all portions of that rich interior region lying in the center of the peninsula. The steamers of the well-known "Hart Line" are a species of craft peculiar to the Ocklawaha, and for many years they afforded the only means of access and transportation for all that vast region. Railroads are now penetrating it, and in a few years the whistle of the locomotive will be heard in every hamlet.*

---

* The St. John's and Lake Eustis Railroad, as before stated, has been extended as far as Tavares, and is projected to a river connection from that point southeast to the St. John's River. The Lake Region is also penetrated by the "Peninsular" and "Tropical" branches of the Transit Rail-

The river, as it is termed, is quite an indefinite body of water. It is more properly a series of lagoons, overflowed swamps, long narrow lakes, and great springs—all connected and interlinked—the water-basin of the western portion of

FOREST ON THE OCKLAWAHA.

the St. John's River Valley. It is an extensive region of dense jungle, lying low and flat, undrainable, and impossi-

road from Waldo, thence southwardly. These roads are being pushed rapidly, and there is a bright prospect that they will soon open one of the most picturesque regions of Florida to easy access.

ble to improve for human use ; and will always remain wild
and unmolested, a paradise for all the strange reptiles, insects, birds, and fish that seek its innermost recesses. To
the pleasure-seeking tourist and the sportsman it affords an
inexhaustible field of interest, but to the invalid, health-
seeker, or practical settler it offers no attractions. As the
steamer follows the vaguely defined course of the channel,
there are frequent landings, localities where points of the
mainland extend like a peninsula into this watery jungle,
affording access and outlets to the more profitable and
healthy regions lying inland. (See Appendix, note 18.)

The writer, as has already been explained, accompanied
the Grant party on their tour through Florida in January,
1880. Returning from a visit to the upper St. John's, at
Welaka, we changed steamers, and were soon snugly quar-
tered on the strange little steamer Osceola, which started
off at once for a night-journey up the Ocklawaha.

The steamers that thread the very narrow and wonderfully crooked waters of that stream are each an aquatic
curiosity. Built especially for the route, they are altogether unique ; there are none others anywhere like them.
They are particularly curious in that they have an appearance of having been placed in service just before completion. Constructed with two decks—quite low between—a
snug little square-shaped wheel-house high up forward, and
a tiny little lobby deck aft, with the row of three or four
little state-rooms ranged between, they are unexcelled for
the accommodations which they afford in the scanty space
at command ; and are a much more comfortable and serviceable craft than their appearance would indicate.*

Upon the roof of the wheel-house of our special steamer
was a large iron box where a bonfire of pitch-pine knots
lighted up the scenery by night. A huge stern-wheel fur-

* For specific information about steamers, hours of departure, fares, etc.,
see chapter on " Routes to and through Florida."

nished the propelling power. The cabin was quite neat,
but a perfect little doll's house in size and furnishing. The
"seclusion that a cabin grants" was not included on this

A RIVER POST-OFFICE.

boat, but it was big enough to afford accommodation for all,
there being but four or five passengers other than our party.
It was but a few moments after leaving the pier at We-

laka that the valiant little steamer suddenly turned, plunged
boldly into a dense thicket, and we were in the very mouth
of the Ocklawaha. The first query on board was, "How
did the pilot find the entrance to the stream?" for it resembled a little brook pouring out from a jungle of over-
hanging trees. Another problem was, "as to how he managed to keep in the right channel on the route"; for it

THE LOOKOUT.

would be difficult to imagine anything short of a bow-knot
more crooked, and there were many places where half a
dozen apparent streams would be found all converging upon
one point, and all exactly alike. The wonderful ability of
that pilot, his foresight, or eyesight, inspired us all with
profound admiration, not to say awe.

The steamer began its journey late in the afternoon,

to give us a night view of the river, and we all spent the evening, night, and morning on deck, deeply interested in watching the scenery, which begins its strangeness at the very outset, and is worth the seeing every rod of the route. It is grand, impressive, strange, tropical—now gloomy and awe-inspiring, now fairy-like and charming, and again weird and wild. The great forest-trees of that region are all of immense size, oaks, gums, magnolias, cypress, etc., interspersed with the more tropical palmetto and palm, all laden and interlocked with a perfect network of immense vines, too tangled for description, brilliant with vegetation—leaves of all colors, flowers of all shapes, sizes, and hues, and loaded with great clusters of mosses. The most conspicuous and abundant of these mosses is the Spanish moss, with its delicate, silvery-gray shade ; but clusters of the popular, pretty mistletoe, with its bright berries, are also seen, and occasional masses of that handsomest of all mosses, the famous woman's-hair. This strange air-growth has a rich, glistening, golden color, is long and fibrous in texture, wavy, and closely resembling a mass of blonde hair. It is a rare moss, and when seen hanging from some bough gives one the impression that three or four bushels of golden locks have been shorn from fair heads and hung thereon for adornment.

The scene is enlivened with birds of many kinds, nearly all strange to the Northern eye—snowy-white storks, cranes, herons, water-turkeys, hell-divers, curlews, etc.—many having brilliant plumage. The waters teem with large turtles and alligators, that quickly disappear as they catch a glimpse of the puffing, chuffing little steamer as it comes around a bend.

The stream is generally very narrow ; in many places, often for quite a long distance, the branches of the great trees interlock across the channel, forming vast arched avenues, paved with a floor of intensely black water, roofed with dense, dark foliage decorated with great fringes of moss. These covered passages are solemn and impressive at any time; but in the night, when lighted up by the blaze of the brilliant bonfire burning on the roof of the wheel-house, then the scene is quite indescribable. The inky water, the lights and shadows of the foliage, the disturbed birds as they wheel gracefully out of sight, all leave an impression never to be forgotten.

Early the next morning, Silver Spring was reached, and after an excellent breakfast all went ashore. There is nothing especially interesting about the locality except the spring. Boats were in readiness, and all enjoyed a row over its translucent surface, and wondered at its marvelous clearness—so clear are the waters, that small pebbles lying on the bottom, sixty-five feet below, can easily be distinguished. We dropped in several small pieces of tin about the size of a silver dime, and could plainly see them at the bottom; and a tenpenny nail, dropped in and closely watched as it descended, could be distinctly traced to its resting-place far below.

The spring has a surface area of about three acres, and the very commonplace, flat, circular shore is mostly covered with a growth of heavy pine and thickets of underbrush. The sides beneath the surface of the water are nearly vertical; in fact, the spring is very like a great punch-bowl sunk in the earth. The water boils up from invisible sources in the bottom, so evenly and quietly, that not a motion is observable on the surface, and so copiously that a deep and navigable river about one hundred feet wide is formed at the start, and in seven miles reaches a junction with the Ocklawaha. (See Appendix, note 19.)

After a thorough inspection of this wonder of nature, we rode over to Ocala, six miles distant, arriving there in season to enjoy a dinner at the comfortable, old-fashioned tavern. The drive from the spring was mostly through

a nearly level pine-wood country, not particularly interesting ; but in the immediate vicinity of the town the soil is

SILVER SPRING.

generally good, and under careful cultivation that is rapidly
improving its value.

A SUDDEN TURN.

Ocala numbers about one thousand inhabitants, is the county-seat of Marion County, and was a flourishing place in *ante-bellum* days, the center of a large neighborhood of wealthy planter society. A railroad has just been completed there from Waldo, on the Transit Railroad, and another road, now building, will soon reach there, giving Ocala at last the much-needed quick steam communication with the commercial centers of the country. Its population is enterprising and energetic, and Ocala is evidently destined to be an important railroad center in the near future, for it is in the direct pathway of other railroads necessary to develop that portion of the State. (See Appendix, note 20.)

The return voyage down the Ocklawaha was without special incident, but repetition can not wither nor custom stale the infinite variety and interest of that unique scenery. Every visitor to Florida should make the famous excursion "up the Ocklawaha," and no one who has once made it will be likely ever to forget a night-journey upon what has been well called "The Mysterious River."

Until recently Silver Spring was the end of the ordinary tourist journey on the Ocklawaha, but the little steamers go far beyond that, threading the upper river, and making the circuit of Lakes Eustis, Harris, and Griffin. These three lakes are among the largest in Florida, and the trip upon them enables the tourist to see some of the most striking and picturesque scenery in the State. Just south of Lake Eustis, with which it is connected by a channel that has not yet been opened to navigation, lies Lake Dora, another large lake, whose high and bluff-like shores remind one rather of the lake region of western New York than of the low and sandy levels that usually characterize Florida. From the summits of several of the headlands on its northern side may be obtained views far and near that will prove memorable in their loveliness—that will haunt the mind long after the vision of them has vanished.

The following table will prove useful, as showing the principal landings on the river and lakes, and the distances from the mouth of the river, which is twenty-five miles south of Pilatka, and nearly opposite Welaka :

TABLE OF DISTANCES ON THE OCKLAWAHA.

	MILES.		MILES.
Davenport	8	Lake Ware Landing	125
Fort Brook	35	Moss Bluff	128
Orange Spring	37	Stark	162
Iola	50	Orange Hope	164
Forty-foot Bluff	54	Slighville	168
Eureka	68	Leesburg	178
Sunday Bluff	70	Lake Griffin Post-Office	183
Palmetto	76	Lovell's	195
Gore's	82	Fort Mason	205
Deurisosa	88	Pendryville	208
Grahamville	92	Esperance	229
Limpkin Bluff	96	Yalaha	234
Silver Springs Run	101	Helena	247
Silver Spring	110	Okahumkee	249

Fair hotel accommodations can be obtained at Leesburg, at Pendryville, and at Fort Mason ; but the latter is a most unattractive place. What is greatly needed in the interest of tourists is a cross-cut railroad from the Lake Eustis region to Sanford on the St. John's, affording the opportunity for a " round trip " up one river and down the other. When this is constructed, as it should be soon, commodious hotels will spring up in all this region.

CHAPTER VIII.

THE INDIAN RIVER REGION AND THE INLAND LAKES.

THE Indian River region is the most widely known of any portion of all South Florida, but it is visited by very few tourists and travelers, owing mostly to its general inaccessibility. The shortest distance from Jacksonville by the usual—and at present only—method of transportation (the St. John's River route) is upward of two hundred miles, and this long journey ends at Titusville, located almost on the head-waters of the famous river. A detailed description of the journey from Jacksonville, also a description of the various places which I visited on the Indian River, is given elsewhere, in the chapter containing an account of the writer's tour of the State with Hon. Seth French. The purpose of this chapter is to give a more comprehensive description of the resources and advantages of the region regarded as a whole.

Indian River runs parallel with the Atlantic coast, northwest and southeast, extending south of latitude 27°, and running north of 28½°, measuring from one and a half to seven miles in width, and from four to sixteen feet in depth of channel, though in many places one may wade more than half a mile from shore.

It abounds in every variety of fish, but is distinguished for its superb mullet, the general weight of which is from two to five pounds, but in many instances they weigh from six to nine pounds, measuring twenty or twenty-two inches in length. The sheep's-head, sea-trout, cavalier, and bass are

LOOKING ACROSS INDIAN RIVER.

large and fine. There are very extensive beds of oysters in the southern portion of the river, of the largest size and most superior flavor ; and these are so accessible that the canning of them would prove a profitable occupation. Turtling is carried on to some extent and proves quite lucrative. The river is separated from the Atlantic by a narrow strip of land from one to three-fourths of a mile in width, the majority of which is poor sand-scrub, though it contains bodies of very rich hammock. Approximating thus near the Atlantic, it has the benefit of the sea-breeze in its pure state, and this, combined with the mild, genial climate of a southern latitude, is what renders it so famous for health —such a thing as sickness being scarcely known upon the river.

The pine-lands largely predominate, some of very fair productive quality, with beautiful sites immediately upon the river having an altitude of eight to sixteen feet above the water. There are also fine bodies of the most splendid hammocks peculiarly adapted to the growth of tropical fruits, the leading varieties of which are the orange, lemon, lime, citron, banana, plantain, pineapple, guava, pomegranate, tamarind, sapodilla, avocado-pear, French lime, mama-apple, sugar-apple, mango, papaw, cacao, date, cocoanut, English walnut, pecan-nut, yam, ginger, cassava, etc. The orange is the leading crop. It requires three years from transplanting to commence bearing, then pays hundreds of dollars per acre, and soon runs to thousands, there having been four to six thousand dollars per acre realized in one season. Bananas grow considerably north of this, and pay from twelve hundred to two thousand dollars per acre. Pineapples promise from eight to twelve hundred dollars per acre. Sugar-cane grows astonishingly, attaining a height of twelve to sixteen feet, single stalks yielding more than a gallon of juice, which, being boiled down, makes over a quart of thick sirup, and produces five or six hundred gallons of sirup per acre. Of peas and pumpkins two crops from the same vine are raised in abundance, and potatoes

flourish the year round. The natural growth of the hammock is the sturdy live-oak, measuring from two to six feet
in diameter; the stately hickory, two to three feet in diameter, and twenty to forty feet to the first limbs; the red elm,
mulberry, wahoo, cabbage-palmetto, with an undergrowth
of hack-bush, torch-wood, marl-bush and vines. There are
also the iron-wood and crab-wood, approximating in weight
to the lignum-vitæ, and susceptible of the finest polish.

There are numerous springs of good water just under
the bluff, and by sinking wells twelve to sixteen feet water is obtained almost anywhere. The water in the hammocks is more or less impregnated with lime, there being a
stratum of coquina-rock underlying the surface, forming
an inexhaustible supply of the most valuable fertilizer. The
woods abound in small game and in deer, bears, and an occasional panther, with the most superior range for every kind
of stock. Four-year-old steers weigh from four to five
hundred pounds, two-year-old heifers from two hundred
and fifty to three hundred pounds, and they calve at that
age. Hogs are raised, with but little attention, to weigh one
hundred and fifty to two hundred pounds at two years old.

The labor of one man, when once properly established, may make his thousands. The great need is transportation. By referring to the State map, it will be per-
ceived that a canal eight miles in length will connect the
Halifax and Mantanzas Rivers; then a little work upon the
Haulover, between Halifax and Indian Rivers, puts it in
connection with St. Augustine. So that a line of light-
draught steamers plying through these rivers, a distance
of over two hundred miles, connecting at St. Augustine
with large-class steamers outside, and by railroad to Jacksonville, gives a direct communication with the world. A
canal is now being opened between these points, the result
of the energy and enterprise of Dr. John Westcott, and the
railroad completed between Jacksonville and St. Augustine

direct, is chartered and projected to run to the Halifax
River, and will soon be built. The Kissimee country bordering on Indian River has an outlet by railroad. With
increased facilities for transit and transportation the future
of this region will be grand.

With these connections, the Indian River will come into
repute for vegetables. It can supply even New York in the
months of January, February, and March with the most
delicate varieties—tomatoes, peas, beans, green corn, cabbages, melons, etc. I have reason to believe that varieties
of grapes can be grown here with success—the Scuppernong
to perfection. The base of all Southern Florida is limestone ; this it is that prevents miasma, and it is this decom-
posed limestone that makes the soils of that region so fertile.

In describing this Indian River region it is appropriate
to include the regions about Lake Worth and Key Biscayne
Bay, both places being in fact a continuation of that special class of soil and products. It is hardly necessary to
mention that all this region, including the Indian River, is
mostly below the frost-line. The thermometer throughout
the year shows a temperature of about 75°, the extremes
being 49° and 92°.

THE INLAND LAKES.

Another delightful variety of country found in Florida
is the central lake region. There are no mountains in the
State, and but few hills worthy of mention, and these few
are usually in more or less unfavorable localities ; but the
absence of these pleasant topographical features is com-
pensated by the great number of lakes, scattered thickly all
through the central regions away from the seacoasts and
large rivers. They are of all shapes and sizes, from ponds
of an acre area in extent to spacious lakes of thirty by fifty
miles dimensions, with flat, pine-clad shores, or bold bluffs,
or rolling banks, or jungle-clad outlines, all pretty, and

filled with remarkably pure, clear water which teems with fish.

In the northern counties are many of these lakes, mostly of large size, with high, rolling shores, and in some respects closely resembling the famous lakes of central New York or Wisconsin. In the vicinity of Tallahassee are several, all beautiful, particularly Lake Jackson, a large sheet of water that is deservedly one of the choice attractions shown the visitor. Lakes Iamonia, Lafayette, Bradford, and Miccosukie, also in the vicinity of Tallahassee, are all beautiful and interesting.

Farther south, in Alachua and Putnam Counties, and lying southeast of the Florida Transit Railroad, is another particularly attractive cluster of lakes. These include Lakes George, Brooklyn, Waldo, Santa Fé, and Deep Lake, all of considerable size, with from three hundred to ten thousand acres area. Lake Santa Fé is the largest of this cluster, and probably the prettiest. On a bold bluff of its fertile shore the Santa Fé Hotel has recently been built, a fine, roomy structure, in the midst of a large, park-like garden, with a charming lawn sloping down to the water's edge. It is only a short drive thither from Waldo Station, on the Transit Railroad. Recently a party of enterprising local capitalists have excavated a series of short canals, thus establishing communication between all the lakes in this chain, and now they have steam transportation from all points on the lakes to Waldo Station.

Farther south again is the famous Orange Lake region, in Alachua and Marion Counties, lying a short distance south of the Transit Railroad. Orange Lake is the principal of these, and is quite a large sheet of water. The famous orange-groves owned by Dr. Bishop and Mr. Harris are located on the shores of this lake, which is skirted by the branch of the Transit Railroad that runs south to Ocala.

Still farther south is found the Lake Harris region, situated in Sumter and Orange Counties, principally in Sumter.
These lakes include Harris, Eustis, Griffin, and Dora, all
large lakes of four to ten miles in length and width. There
are numerous other smaller lakes in their vicinity, but these
named are the principal. These lakes, as explained in the
preceding chapter, form the head-waters of the Ocklawaha
River, and are surrounded by the richest lands of the most
fertile region of Florida. Their shores are everywhere remarkably beautiful, and the land would be highly productive under cultivation. There are already many splendid
orange-groves growing on their shores, and settlers are fast
flowing in.

Lake Panasofkee, situated a considerable distance west
of the Harris cluster, in the same county, is a noticeably
large lake surrounded by rich hammock-lands. (This lake
is fully described in the chapter on the tour of the State
with Mr. French.)

Lake Apopka, just to the south of the Harris group,
is a lake region by itself, so to speak, for all that section
is known to the people of the State as the Lake Apopka
region. It is a large lake, with a coast-line of fifty miles.
The surrounding country is quite beautiful in scenery and
of rich soil. A number of the best orange-groves in the
State are in this region, entirely beyond danger of frosts.

Again passing south and east, the famous inland lake
region of Orange County is reached. It is in the vicinity
of Maitland, Osceola, Interlaken, and Orlando, that these
lakes are most numerous. Looking in any direction from
those places, several of these pretty little lakelets can be
seen. From a certain standpoint in Maitland nine lakes are
in plain sight.

Their sizes vary from ten acres to three thousand acres;
their shores are, generally speaking, slightly rolling. The
land of that region is covered with a heavy growth of pine,

interspersed with occasional tracts of hammock, and the
surface is mostly flat and not very attractive to the eye, nor
very fertile in productive quality, except by fertilizing ; but
an offset to these objections lies in the fact that it is undoubtedly the healthiest portion of Florida.

This lake region is penetrated by the South Florida
Railroad, which extends from Sanford on Lake Monroe to
Orlando, the county-seat of Orange County, and passes the
already-mentioned villages of Maitland, Osceola, and Interlaken. In my tour of the State with Mr. French (Chapter
III), I have already described it at considerable length, and
it is also described in the chapter on "The Sanford Grant."
I may add that the soil directly around Orlando is probably
the best in the region. (See Appendix, note 24.)

Farther south are numerous lakes, many of them quite
large, like Lakes Butler, Conway, Tohopekaliga, Cypress,
Kissimmee, and Marianna, all situated in the center of the
peninsula, and surrounded by a rich hammock-soil. As yet
there are scarcely any settlers in all that extensive region,
which is quite beyond the confines of civilization at this
writing. The country is mostly of a prairie-like character,
resembling portions of Illinois, excepting that the vegetation is purely tropical, including many scattered groves of
stately palmettoes.

Lake Okeechobee, still farther south, is the largest in
the State, covering an area of upward of six hundred
square miles, and extending fairly into the region of the
Everglades. The "Everglades" occupy nearly the whole
southern extremity of the peninsula, and are, as I have
elsewhere said, not so much a marsh as an extensive lake,
which is so shallow as to be overgrown with grasses and
other vegetation. In the rainy season, in particular, its
lake-like character is clearly apparent.

A company of Philadelphia capitalists are proposing to
drain a large portion of this Everglade region, by cutting

7

a series of canals connecting it with both the Gulf and the Atlantic. The enterprise is one of considerable magnitude, and, if fully successful, will be of immense value to themselves, to the State, and indeed to the entire country, as it will open to profitable cultivation millions of acres of the richest soil in the world, especially and peculiarly adapted to the production of sugar.*

In this cursory glance at the inland lakes which constitute a characteristic feature of the Floridian Peninsula, I have not mentioned the innumerable smaller and detached ones that dot the surface nearly everywhere, nor have I attempted even to name the countless "springs" found in all portions of the State, and attaining in many cases to the dimensions of lakes. A volume would be required in order to do justice to them all ; and even then, probably, that more thorough exploration and survey of the State, that is sure to come soon, would reveal the existence of many more.

They are a great boon to the State, not only for their beauty and picturesque effect, but for the facilities they offer to transportation, and the fertility they impart to the soil. Lands on their shores are everywhere eagerly sought by the settler, it being the ambition of all to own a home nestling on a lovely lawn bordering upon some pretty lake. And surely nowhere can there be found more attractive scenes of picturesque domesticity than is afforded by a lake-side home in Florida.

* Since the first edition was published, the Okeechobee Drainage Company have been at work several years, and practically and successfully reclaimed hundreds of thousands of acres of lands in this region.

CHAPTER IX.

THE waters of the Gulf of Mexico wash the entire west and south coast-line of Florida, a stretch of about seven hundred miles.

Commencing about one hundred miles northeast along the Atlantic coast side, a series of islands forms a continuous chain around the southern extremity of the State, and extends in a line bearing south of west from the mainland out into the Gulf.

These islands are generally small, averaging about one hundred acres, excepting Largo and Key West, which are from one to two miles in width and seven to ten miles in length. All are quite rocky, but the sparse sandy soil is very fertile, and everywhere covered with an abundant vegetation. These islands are called keys, and the cluster at the western extremity is the famous Dry Tortugas, where the United States Government has extensive fortifications, storehouses, and military supplies.

South of this long chain of keys, and separated from them by a navigable channel, is the great Florida Reef, a long, narrow ledge of coral, of great danger to the navigation of these waters, being hidden beneath the surface of the ocean, and only exposed to view in severe gales.

All this great line of mainland and island coast presents but few harbors, owing to the shallow soundings. Commencing at the extreme western end of the coast, the harbors are Pensacola, Appalachicola, St. Marks, Cedar Keys,

Tampa Bay, Charlotte Harbor, and Key West. The three ports first named, together with Tampa Bay, have been described in previous chapters.

Cedar Keys is the Gulf terminus of the Florida Transit Railway from Fernandina (one hundred and fifty-four miles), and is also the port of the Henderson Gulf Line of steamers and of the New Orleans, Havana and Gulf Line, both lines having excellent steamers, well equipped and supplied, and scheduled so as to connect daily at Cedar Keys with any of the Gulf and West India ports. Cedar Keys is a dreamy, cleanly kept, irregular little village of orderly and thrifty people. It is built on an island (as its name suggests), and faces to the northeast, quite confusing to the traveler, who usually expects to look west for the Gulf waters. The railroad enters the place across a long bridge that spans the lagoon. The general appearance of the town is pleasing, the one business street being lined with substantial structures, mostly built of coquina-stone, and in design and material having a Spanish, tropical appearance quite in keeping with the surrounding scenery. The trade is mostly wholesale, and amounts annually to several hundred thousand dollars, supplying the retail dealers of all the little hamlets along the coast and rivers of a large portion of that region. To the hunter, fisherman, or health-seeker, it offers attractions equal to any portion of Florida.

Under the guidance of Major Parsons, who has resided here forty-three years, the writer visited all the various points of interest, and enjoyed a pleasant visit in this delightful old place. Late one brilliant afternoon we were on board the splendid new steamship Admiral, that makes two trips weekly between Cedar Keys, Key West, and Havana, and soon all were enjoying the soft, refreshing salt-water breeze and viewing the beautiful scenery of the islands, with their wealth of tropical vegetation, the large, comfortable-appearing dwellings standing in the midst of flower-laden gardens

and broad, bright green lawns. On we sped, passing the
graceful lighthouse and picturesque home of the old light-
keeper, out into the warm blue waters of the Gulf. It was
a lovely, warm evening. After partaking of an excellent
supper, all assembled on the after-deck in the deep enjoyment of cigars, listening to anecdotes, and inhaling the
pure, balmy breeze, observing the clear sky, the brilliant
stars, and bright full moon that lighted the calm waters
like a vast sheet of glittering silver. It was a charming
scene of great beauty, deeply enjoyed and long to be remembered by all the participants, none retiring until a late
hour.

Early the following morning all were on deck, sniffing
the invigorating breeze and watching the many dolphins,
porpoises, and occasional sharks, as they plunged through
the waters in every direction.

To our left, quite plainly in sight, was the coast of Florida, the islands of very tropical appearance forming exceedingly pretty pictures as the bright sun rose behind them.
The coast is for the most part low and sandy, edged by
shoals and bars, and broken here and there by beautiful
bays and indentations. All the larger inlets are filled with
islands, most of which are sandy and arid, though some are
covered with a tropical luxuriance of vegetation.

All along the coast at convenient points are little farming or lumbering settlements; the principal being Crystal
River, Hamosassa, Bayport, Anclote River, Clear-Water
Harbor, Law's Store, McMullen's Store, Philippi's Grove,
Point Penales, Alafia, Terrasea Bay, Little Manatee, Manatee, Sarasota, Charlotte Harbor, and Punta Rassa. Manatee, which is something of a village, is not directly on the
coast, but about eight miles up the Manatee River, in a
pleasant situation, where game is abundant.

Charlotte Harbor, however, possesses greater natural advantages than any other on the Gulf coast, and has been

pronounced by competent authority to be the best harbor
between Port Royal and Pensacola. It is a grand sheet of
water, about thirty miles in length by ten in width, easily
accessible from the Gulf, and studded with hundreds of
beautiful tropical islands, of which the most important are
Pine, Sanibal, Captira, Lacosta, and Gasparilla. The locality has of late begun to attract much attention, and nearly
all the projected railroads of the State have fixed upon
Charlotte Harbor as a southern terminus—among them the
South Florida Railroad, which, as explained in another
chapter, has already set out on the route thither. Indeed,
the geographical, commercial, and climatic advantages of
the place are too apparent to escape notice, and I believe
that some locality on that noble harbor is destined to become a great trade and shipping center, and one of the
most popular winter resorts in the State. All the lands in
the vicinity are good ; and crops of everything that can be
produced elsewhere in the semi-tropical portions of Florida
will grow there and produce abundantly. The scenery is
beautiful, the climate is wonderfully bland and equable,
and game and fish, oysters, turtles, and the like, are found
in inexhaustible quantities. The islands, great and small,
that are so numerous on that beautiful coast, are wonderfully pretty, perfect gems of tropical scenery.

Considering how numerous are the summer resorts, inland and seaside hotels all through the north and west,
and how few are the winter resorts—the hotels specially
for winter tourists numbering scarcely two dozen in all—
and they not in the really tropical region of the State ; and
considering how limited is the tropical region ; how the
number of hotel residents, of tourists, wandering to all sections of the country, summer and winter, in search of health
and pleasure, is increasing to such a vast multitude each
year ; and that the hotels of Florida, even at highest
prices, are scarcely able to accommodate the visitors to the

State—it is apparent that the time is near at hand when a vast winter "Coney Island," with Newport and Long Branch combined, must be established at some point in the southern part of the peninsula, beyond any possible danger of cold, frosts, or extreme changes ; where a sea-beach drive, islands for pleasure-yachts, a race-course, polo-ground, base-ball park, etc., etc., can be established, and where the health-seeker, the hunter, and the fisher, as well as the lover of strange scenes and excitement, may each find special attractions. Charlotte Harbor, with a railroad, would present just such a location ; and railroads must go there. Each season the army of tourists to Florida is increasing, and the farther south they can get the better they like it. And this spot offers attractions not possessed by any other in the whole country for such a resort. As I sat on an elevated spot on the shore of that harbor, and looked over its broad, beautiful expanse, watching the sun sinking behind the lovely islands, and saw many dolphins gamboling in the bright waves, and thought of the myriads of fish and oysters so easy to be obtained, and the soil, so prolific of all dainty fruits, I reflected that it only needed the genius of a Corbin, a Breslin, or a Lorillard, to wake up this dreamy, delicious locality, and make it a spot that would rival any pleasure resort in the world. With competing lines of railroads and steamers, and consequent low fares, all the United States would soon wish to enjoy the novelty of seeing a horse-race, or a game of base-ball, or a yacht-race, or to try a swim, pick a banana, or wear a white suit, in January.

"On Pease Creek, a tributary of Charlotte Harbor, a large amount of elevated and rich lands is open to settlement. The mainland, between the head of Charlotte Harbor, Meyakka River, and Little Sarasota Bay, also offers a fine field for settlement. Between the Haulover and the head of Little Sarasota Bay a high bluff extends along the

Gulf coast, and to those who wish to pitch their tents within sight and sound of the waves this would prove a desirable spot.

"At the southern extremity of Charlotte Harbor is situated Punta Rassa. The improvements consist of the signal and telegraph station—a large wooden structure—a large storehouse, a superior dock, and a fish-ranche. This is the great point for the shipment of cattle to Key West and Cuba. The Caloosa entrance, leading from the Gulf to this point, is comparatively shallow, affording but nine feet of water at low tide at the shallowest points. Leaving the dock and proceeding in a northerly direction for three miles, the mouth of the Caloosahatchie River opens up. Unfortunately for the navigation of this stream, there is but seven feet of water in the channel at the mouth, at low tide. However, this depth would prove ample for river-steamers, and, if it should ever be required, a small expenditure would deepen the channel so as to allow of the passage of any vessel that could enter the port. Soon after entering the river it widens out and becomes a beautiful stream, from one and a quarter to three miles in width, for a distance of thirty miles. The land gradually rises from the river for a mile, or a mile and a half, and I have been assured that it is good, productive pine-land, in many places mixed with shell. (See Appendix, note 21.)

"Fort Myers, distant twenty-five miles from Punta Rassa, is an old military post, which was abandoned after the last Indian war. At present it contains a population of about two hundred persons, the majority of whom are engaged in cattle-raising. Here I found several small orange-groves, and the trees appeared vigorous and healthy. Large patches of bananas flourished with a luxuriance unknown in the more northern portions of the State. But what gratified me most was the existence of eleven cocoanut-trees, seventeen years old, with their pendent fruit and luxuriant leaves. The cocoanut is very susceptible to the influence of frost, and the presence of these trees convinced me that the locality had not suffered from it for seventeen years. At this point the river is much narrower than lower down the stream, but measures one mile and eleven chains from bank to bank. (See Appendix, note 22.)

"By the course of the river the Caloosahatchie telegraph

station and crossing is distant fifteen miles. From the fort to within a short distance of the station the banks of the river are low, and in many places swampy. Near the station the banks are high and the soil excellent. The operator pointed out a lemon-tree near the house, not five years old, that had produced about one thousand lemons. A few of them were hanging on the tree, and I found them thin-skinned and very juicy. We are satisfied that the time is not far distant when the lemons of Southern Florida will drive the diminutive, and, to a certain extent, juiceless lemons of the Mediterranean from the American markets.

"From the telegraph station to Fort Donand, distant twenty miles in a direct line, but more than twice as many by the course of the river, the stream is narrow, varying from one hundred and fifty to four hundred feet in width, but very deep. Between these points the banks of the river are high, and, in some places, almost perpendicular. In many of the reaches, to make a land-

THE CABBAGE-PALM.

ing without a ladder would be a troublesome undertaking. Along the river rich hammocks exist, clothed with a growth of small live-oaks and cabbage-palms ; back of this a belt of pine-timber, and then the open prairie, covered with luxuriant and nutritive grass. From our own observations, and information obtained, the belt of timber on the line of the river is narrow in its whole course. The prairie on each side of the stream is very extensive, and dotted with what is known as 'islands'—patches of live-oak and palm, and belts of pine of limited extent. These oases of foliage furnish protection to cattle and herds. The grasses in this section are more tender and succulent than in the northern and western portions of the State.

"For the production of sugar-cane this section possesses an advantage over Mississippi and Louisiana, where cane has to be cut before it has attained its full saccharine development, in order to avoid the injurious influence of frosts. In Southern Florida the cane will tassel and perfect itself."

Key West was reached about noon on the day after leaving Cedar Keys, and we were soon enjoying the comforts of the Russell House, a large and well-kept hotel. Afterward we rode about the city and island, visiting the extensive water-batteries, the park, and the lighthouse. Everything in and about Key West is strange, foreign, and interesting. The business houses and public buildings, the dwellings, the gardens, lawns, flowers, trees, soil, and vegetation, the appearance of the people, their costumes, and even their names, all are so un-American and suggestive of a foreign clime, that it is difficult indeed to realize it as one of the busy, enterprising cities of our United States. Nevertheless, in this far-off, isolated community of Uncle Sam's family are found the same social sentiments and the same interests as among all American citizens.

Key West has a steady business of exchange and supply for all the settlers and retail dealers of that section of the State. It is not of the intensely active, Chicago sort of business, but it is steady, easy-going, and quiet, as if it were fully established and entirely safe and reliable—and knew it. Cigar-making is the principal industry, exceeding all other interests, employing hundreds of people, mostly Cubans, occupying numerous large establishments, and paying to Uncle Sam an annual revenue of upward of three hundred and twenty thousand dollars. A stroll about the place at once makes it apparent where the famous Key West cigars come from; everywhere are tobacco-dealers

KEY WEST.

and cigar-manufactories, and upward of thirty million cigars were manufactured there in 1880.

The United States has erected several large, substantial
structures here, and the public buildings of the county and

city, also the churches—four—the public schools, opera-house, etc., are all creditable structures. The Government dock, barracks, and forts are all large and costly, this being regarded as one of the most important points in the defensive system of the United States. An unpleasant feature is the impossibility of obtaining cool well or spring water. Wells can not be sunk, and there are no springs, and the inhabitants are obliged to depend on rain-water cisterns or condensed supply. Turtling, sponging, mullet-fishing, and shell-hunting are important industries. A large number of men are engaged in wrecking on the reefs. The population is about ten thousand.

CHAPTER X.

THE SANFORD GRANT AND ORANGE COUNTY.

THE Sanford grant is probably the most extensive land enterprise in the State, and is very likely to become the center of a most flourishing region, unlike anything else of the kind attempted in the United States ; for nowhere else is there any tract of land with a situation so peculiarly advantageous for commercial enterprises, for settlement, and for variety of products.

In 1870 General Henry S. Sanford, of Connecticut, made an extensive tour through Florida, closely examining her many resources and most advantageous localities, and was so impressed with the tract which now bears his name that he effected a purchase of it. It was one of the Spanish grants, so frequent wherever Spanish authority existed, and so famous for uncertain surveying and legal complications.

The tract embraces twenty-two square miles, comprising about thirteen thousand acres, nearly all of good quality and susceptible of profitable cultivation. It lies on the south shore of Lake Monroe, a pretty little inland sea, about ten miles long by five miles wide, into which the upper St. John's empties, and out of which the larger St. John's flows. It is practically at the head of the river navigation—that is, for the larger and better class of steamers. It is one hundred and sixty-five miles from Jacksonville by water route, as shown by the United States Coast Survey, or about one hundred and ten miles on an air-line. The

St. John's River extends for many miles above, but is a small, shallow stream, very narrow, and too crooked for description—a winding brook in a flat prairie-land, except where it widens out into one of the many lakes of that region. None but little steamers of lightest draught attempt its navigation, and even these can ascend but a short distance above Sanford.

Having carefully considered, as I have said, the many advantages which he believed existed there, the General completed its purchase, and at once commenced improvements on a grand scale, clearing off the dense growth of timber from a large acreage on the lake-front ; cutting out and clearing up a number of broad avenues ; and opening up the surrounding country. He also built a fine pier, six hundred feet long, in the lake ; erected spacious storehouses, and an extensive saw-mill and machine-shop—this being one of the largest in the State ; surveyed and located the present city of Sanford, deservedly bearing his name ; erected the elegant Sanford Hotel, standing in ample and well-kept and neatly fenced grounds, its clean, grassy surface laid out with walks and ornamented with flowers and shrubs ; and established a telegraphic line of communication with the outside world.

Everything, except the characteristically tropical fruits, thrives exceedingly well here, especially oranges, lemons, grapes, and garden-vegetables ; also live-stock. The famous Speer grove of oranges is only one and a half mile south of Sanford. It contains five hundred and fifty trees, standing on a little less than six acres of land. The trees are about thirty-five years old, and yield annually from four to five hundred thousand oranges. Upward of six hundred thousand have been gathered in specially favorable seasons. The crop of the season of 1880–'81 was sold on the trees for seventeen dollars per thousand, and netted the owner upward of six thousand dollars. (See Appendix.) An object of special interest in this grove is a lemon-tree of great size that produces annually from twelve to twenty thousand lemons of an excellent quality. Other noted groves of the vicinity are those of Markham, Ginn, French, and others.

Sanford is the northern terminus of the Florida Railroad, now extending twenty-two miles to Orlando, the county-seat, and its freight-houses, car-shops, and fine pier are completed. The pier, built of palmetto and pitch pine, is not excelled by any in the whole country. From one to four steamers—several of which are elegant boats—arrive at the piers daily. (See Appendix, note 24.)

Several enterprises are now under consideration that will add greatly to the importance of the city. Among them are a banking-house, a factory for curing Spanish moss for upholstery purposes, and an establishment for canning, curing, packing, and preserving the delicate fruits of this region. The bank is much needed, and the other schemes are sure to be of great benefit, offering a near and trustworthy market for all fruit-crops.

The city has good schools, two good halls, and about thirty well-established commercial houses, and transacted a business of nearly eight hundred thousand dollars in 1880. The Episcopalians have a very attractive church-edifice, built through the efforts of Mrs. General Sanford.

There is a demand for labor in Sanford, especially skilled labor, such as that of carpenters; in fact, one of the drawbacks has been scarcity of mechanics—and I happen to know of several parties who are now delayed in the prosecution of their intended improvements by the lack of labor. (See Appendix, note 25.)

From the beginning of his enterprise, this has been a serious trouble to the General in his improvements. At first, he attempted to employ colored labor; but in those days, about the years 1874-'74, the "cracker" natives that lived scattered about this region were bitterly opposed to the "niggers," and made it difficult to keep that class of labor ; for the "crackers" were vicious and ignorant, and law was practically an unknown and repudiated quantity. In 1871 the General decided to try foreign labor on the colonization system, sent an agent to Upsala, in Sweden, and at his sole expense brought over a colony of one hundred of these people, for whom he erected cabins, giving to each a homestead of five acres of good land. This answered very well for a time, but there were restless and turbulent members in the party, and one day, incited by up-country politicians, some of them deserted and went to seek higher wages at Jacksonville. By great efforts, the agent of the General succeeded in inducing them to return to their homes and vocations, and to-day, after seven years, they are among the thriftiest, happiest, and most prosperous people in all Florida. It is an incident worthy of mention, perhaps, that one of them a short time ago sold his little property for five thousand five hundred dollars, for the purpose of entering another line of business. Yet he had less than nothing (for he owed for his passage) when he arrived in Sanford seven years since, and was one of the leading opponents of the General's scheme for their benefit. Recently the General has brought over more Swedes, and also some Poles and Italians. All are busily at work, and apparently contented.

The population of Sanford and the closely adjacent country is now about one thousand, and the healthiness of the region is sufficiently demonstrated by the fact that the number of deaths in 1880 was *five*, of which *two* were from accidental causes.

Hunting and fishing are excellent all through this region. One day in February of the present year, Mr. Knowlton, a guest at the hotel, went out fishing on Lake Monroe, and in the afternoon caught one hundred and forty pounds of fine black bass, the most delicious of eating. It excited no particular comment, for others, so I was assured, have frequently beaten that score.

Three miles from Sanford is Belair, the special grove of the General, a fine estate of one hundred and twenty-five acres, all fenced and under the highest cultivation. Here are thousands of orange, lemon, and lime trees, and pineapple-plants, including nearly every known variety of these, and hundreds of other foreign and native tropical plants, fruits, and shrubs. A visit thither is very interesting, and a cordial welcome is extended to all.

Indian-corn, sugar-cane, cotton, tobacco, rice, strawberries, cabbages, tomatoes, watermelons, and all garden products, yield immense crops in the soil around Sanford. During last February—an exceptionally cold month for the season—I visited a number of gardens, where the vegetables were growing just as finely, as rapidly, as prolifically, and with as little requirement of labor, as in any soil, anywhere, at any season. From one garden, comprising three quarters of an acre, four crops had been taken, during the preceding twelve months, by using a moderate amount of fertilizer. Think of that—*four crops in one year!*

The "South Florida Journal," a well-conducted sheet, owned and edited by two live newspaper-men from Ohio, is published weekly at Sanford. The climate is pleasant, and enjoyable all the year ; there is no month that is specially uncomfortable by reason of cold or heat ; nor are mosquitoes and gnats more aggravating than wherever they exist in other regions.

The settlers on this grant are mostly recent arrivals, who come from all parts of the country. Besides the foreign colonies, there are colonies from New York, Ohio, and Wisconsin. The Hon. Thurlow Weed, General O. H. Babcock, Senator H. B. Anthony, and several other prominently known gentlemen, own fine groves on the grant.

General Sanford lives much abroad, and the management

of his vast estate, with its multiplied interests, devolves upon the resident agent, Mr. J. E. Ingraham, a native of Milwaukee, Wisconsin. It is not many years since Mr. Ingraham came to Florida in what was supposed to be the final stage of consumption ; yet no one, to see him now, would suppose that he had not always been in the enjoyment of vigorous health. He is also the President of the South Florida Railroad.

Another energetic and enterprising citizen of Sanford, to whom the people of the city and of the grant—in fact, of all Orange County—are much indebted, is Mr. George H. Sawyer, of Massachusetts (a resident of Sanford since 1875), proprietor of the "City Hotel" and owner of one of the finest gardens in the State. This garden alone, demonstrating as it does the feasibility of a first-rate vegetable-garden in South Florida, entitles him to special mention. During the entire winter his hotel tables are loaded with the best of squashes, cabbages, celery, cauliflower, peas, string-beans, tomatoes, potatoes, radishes, beets, etc., daily culled from the garden. His efforts in displaying Orange County resources at the recent State Fair in Jacksonville (season of 1880–'81) had great effect in directing thither the tide of immigration that is now flowing in ; and he is a prominent mover in all local enterprises.

On the 22d of February, 1881, a county fair was held at Sanford, which was peculiarly interesting as a display of what this portion of Florida can do in the way of midwinter products. Instead of describing it myself, I will quote some passages from a report prepared by Dr. J. L. Richardson, who spent the winter in Orange County, for the Mount Sterling (Kentucky) "Democrat." He says :

"This exhibition was projected as a county fair, to exhibit to the country the actual products of Orange County, in the midst of the severest and most protracted winter the States have ever experienced, and place upon record such facts as demonstrate the possibilities of cheap, comfortable, and profitable living.

"On entering the grounds, the first thing that attracted attention was the line of coops containing poultry in their glossy and peculiar costumes. They were all unexceptionable specimens of their respective species, and their handsome and healthful appearance gives evidence of climatic adaptation. Considering the domestic convenience and the aggregate value of this department, it deserves a large share of the public attention. The geese were worthy of notice for their size and fine development. Their feathers were evidently finer, although, perhaps, not affording so large a yield as in a northern climate. The turkeys, being in their native latitude, were enabled to entertain their admirers with unsurpassed domestic accomplishments, while the Muscovy ducks were equal to the best of their kind. The fantail pigeons were beautifully attractive, and showed that South Florida might become quite as noted and financially valuable in her dove-cotes as old Spain herself.

"The sugar-cane and its products, as exhibited by Mr. G. W. Crawford, of his own growth and manufacture, were of a superior quality, and develops a very interesting and important department of industry. Mr. Crawford, who lives a few miles south of Orlando, is one of the most enterprising and successful farmers in Orange County, and besides the preceding he exhibited green peas, turnips, tropical yams, sweet-potatoes, corn, cabbages, etc., all of mammoth growth. This tropical yam produces enormous tubers of a black color, and equal to the Irish potato in every respect, but of finer flavor. It grows rapidly from any small section of the root, and continues to grow as long as it is in the ground.

"There were turnips measuring three feet in circumference; cabbages weighing from twelve to fifteen pounds, and radishes as much as nine pounds, solid and brittle. The *Rean luxurians*, or Te-o-siu-te—grass of the gods—exhibited by Dr. Kenworthy, is eight or nine feet long, and resembles corn-fodder, and is said to be very prolific, yielding from fifty to one hundred tons per acre. Heads of lettuce that would cover a dinner-plate looked fresh and crisp ; while onions, leeks, kale, parsnips, etc., lay around in rich profusion. Potatoes planted on Christmas-day were of fine size for table use, and altogether it would be difficult to im-

agine a more splendid and attractive show of garden-vegetables, maturing in the open garden while all the other
States lay congealed in the icy chains of winter. The cauliflowers raised near Sanford, for size and beauty, were objects of surprise ; some of the bloom measured fifteen inches
in diameter, being compact and solid. The pineapples were
in every stage of development, while the matured ones
were large and attractive. The cassava, with its products
of beautiful starch and nutritious tapioca manufactured in
the county, demand especial notice as articles of utility and
profitable manufacture. The display of arrow-root from
eighteen inches to two feet long was sufficient evidence that
this part of Florida will produce it in as fine perfection as
Bermuda. The root is tapering at each end—beautifully
white, and jointed like a bamboo.

"Tomatoes hanging on vines recently dug up intruded
their plump and rosy cheeks upon your attention. There
were also pepper-plants with mature fruit upon them grown
without protection, and the tender banana with its purple
and peculiar bloom. All the members of the citrus family
were present, with their aprons full of the yellow and golden
fruits just gathered from the grove. The Japan plum and
fine varieties of strawberries were well represented. These
facts are only stated in justice to show that the inclemency
of the *past* winter—*for it is past here*—has not materially
interrupted the delicate fruit and vegetable crop of Orange
County. Cotton and tobacco were also on exhibition, both
of which can be raised on some lands profitably.

"There was quite a varied and handsome display in the
floral and botanical departments, embracing divers specimens of the coleus, ferns, Brazilian plants, pampas-grass,
jaunty jasmines, etc."

Beginning at Sanford, and bringing to it the products
of the best portion of Orange County, the South Florida
Railroad runs southwest twenty-two miles to Orlando, the
county-seat. The first spadeful of earth in the grading of
the line was turned by General Grant, on the 10th of January, 1880 ; and the road has the further distinction of being
the only "newspaper railroad " in the world—it was built
and is owned by the proprietors of the "Boston Herald,"

who conceived the plan and carried it out with journalistic
promptitude and vigor. It is a narrow-gauge road (three
feet between the rails), is thoroughly well constructed and
equipped, and is the pioneer in what is destined to be a
great railway system when present plans are perfected.

The first station after leaving Sanford (three miles out)
is Belair, the site of General Sanford's famous grove, already described. Two miles beyond is Bent's, a place where
a number of young orange-groves are about to come into
bearing; and two and a half miles beyond Bent's is Sol-
dier Creek. Longwood station is nine and a half miles
from Sanford; Snow's is three miles farther; and three
miles farther still is Maitland, the most important point
on this portion of the line. Maitland is a scattered little hamlet, comprising four or five business houses, and
enjoys the distinction of possessing the finest public hall
in the State (Packwood Hall). Here also is a large hotel, which is open during the winter season. The adjacent region consists of what is called high pine-land, interspersed with occasional tracts of rich hammock, and is
dotted with numerous small lakes, some of which are perfect gems of landscape beauty, while all abound in fish.
In the neighborhood are many improved homes and large
orange-groves. Among the latter is one owned by Bishop
H. B. Whipple, of the Diocese of Minnesota; and a very
fine one, seen on the left from the cars, is the property of
Mr. B. R. Swoope, superintendent and general manager of
the railroad. One of the pleasantest places in the vicinity
is that of Mr. George H. Packwood, crowning a crest which
slopes up gently from the shore of the lovely Lake Sybelia.
He has a large orange-grove and one of the most extensive
grape-arbors in the State, together with pineapples and
other semi-tropical fruits.

The next station south of Maitland (two miles distant)
is Osceola. This also is a pretty region of high pine-lands,

comprising many fine orange-groves, and settled for the most
part by Northern people. Up to this point the country
traversed is level or but slightly undulating, with far-stretch-
ing pine-woods, and a light, sandy soil. Near Orlando the
character of the country changes, the surface becomes more
rolling and hilly, the soil is darker and richer, the lakes are
surrounded by what in this section are called "bluffs," and
the scenery is more picturesque and pleasing. Here is the
high table-land of Central Florida, the natural water-shed
—for an examination of the map will show the streams
flowing east, west, north, and south from this high plateau.
(For description of Winter Park, see Appendix, note 26.)

Two miles this side of Orlando (twenty miles from Sanford) is Interlaken, formerly Wilcox, a place which is
growing with great rapidity, and which seems destined to
become the home of an unusually estimable class of residents, many of them of the cultivated and thrifty New
England type. Among the settlers here are such men as
ex-Governor Pilsbury, of Maine, and the Hon. John G.
Sinclair, of New Hampshire, the latter of whom has thrown
himself with ardor into the development of the place, and
now has, besides a growing orange-grove, a cassava starch-
factory, a saw-mill, and a cotton-gin. Here, also, is the
home ("Waverley Hall") of Major M. R. Marks, one of the
most famous characters of this region, and in fact one of
the best-known men in the entire State—for every one who
does not know him personally knows some of the innumerable anecdotes about him. Originally from Georgia, he
has lived in Florida for nearly twenty years, has contributed
greatly to the development of Orange County, is considered
perfect authority on land-values, and is always loaded with
"a big bargain." Nearly all the real-estate transactions of
the entire region are consummated through him, or through
Mr. Sinclair, who also does an extensive business as a land-
agent. Some of the prettiest lakes in the State surround

Interlaken on nearly all sides, and there is one connected chain upon which a boat-ride of at least twenty miles can be enjoyed. The scenery of these lakes is exquisite, and one is constantly tempted to exclaim, " What a lovely place that is, on that knoll, for a home ! " A good hotel here would be sure to attract many visitors, and there is a probability that such a one will be erected soon.

Orlando, the county-seat, is an old place, typical of the South, a genuine native community of the kind that the traveler finds in all sections of the State, almost always located in a beautiful, bountiful region, where Nature has done everything to aid and please, and where man seems indisposed to do anything. The " boom " that has enlivened every other spot in Orange County seems to have left Orlando comparatively untouched ; yet there is no other locality that offers greater attractions, for the soil is exceptionally fertile and productive, plenty of timber is convenient, and the surrounding country, studded with little lakes, is remarkably pleasing. A court-house and a jail are among the most conspicuous features of the place, but neither these nor the residences are kept in that trim and neat condition that in Florida, as elsewhere, marks the presence of the Northern settler. The hotel is charmingly located in the midst of an orange-grove ; and the entire region, on account of its elevation, perhaps, enjoys a remarkable exemption from mosquitoes, sand-flies, and the other insect-pests. The " Orange County Reporter " is published here by an energetic Western man, and is one of the best local papers in the State.

For the present, the South Florida Railroad ends at Orlando, but this is only temporary, and preparations are being made for its extension southwest. Its ultimate destination is Charlotte Harbor, on the Gulf-coast, of which a description is given in a previous chapter. Several branch lines are also projected, and the one to Lake Tohopekaliga will probably be completed by the time this book appears.   (See Appendix, note 24.)

ORANGE COUNTY, which comprises all the above-mentioned places, and which extends westward to the beautiful Lake Eustis region described in another chapter, is better known than any other portion of the interior of the State, and has succeeded in securing a larger share of the immigration that has lately set in from the North and West. More activity and public spirit are exhibited there than elsewhere, and more pains are taken to collect and disseminate information as to its resources and advantages.   Partly for these reasons, and partly because it is a typical county of the central portion of South Florida, I shall quote somewhat extensively from an article descriptive of its resources and advantages, which appeared recently in the "Orange County Reporter," and which is understood to have been written jointly by Major Marks and the Hon. John G. Sinclair :

"Orange County lies in the very heart of the Peninsula of Florida, and on the highlands of the narrowest portion of the peninsula.   From this county flow streams to the north, south, east, and west, showing at a glance that it is the highest region lying between the ocean and the Gulf. It is thus exposed to both east and west winds, which effectually drive away malaria.   Except in the low and heavily timbered lands on lakes and rivers, fevers are almost unknown.   There are no prevailing diseases common to this portion of the State ; and, semi-tropical as it is, no case of yellow fever or cholera has ever been known here.   Even the vaunted health resorts of Colorado show a death-rate among the resident population of double that of Orange County ; while, of the invalid and tourist class, the death-rate in that much-advertised region is fully ten times as great as among the same class here.   The late Government census shows but thirty-one deaths in a population of 6,618 in Orange County for the year ending June 1, 1880.   This includes all classes and all causes.   This immunity from

sickness is due first to pure water, and secondly to the prevailing winds which carry away all malarial poisons, and at
the same time modify the temperature to so great an extent, during both summer and winter months. A record
kept by a careful observer, for the past year, shows that
the highest point recorded by the mercury last summer was
97° ; the lowest the present winter 34°—a less variation of
temperature in a whole year than is frequently experienced
in higher latitudes in twenty-four hours. The residents of
Orange County are free from those sudden climatic changes
which are so severe a tax upon the vital energies of residents
of the Northern States. Colds are therefore rare and never
severe, and catarrh among old residents is rarely found.

"Orange County lies on the west side of the St. John's
River, that stream forming the eastern boundary of the county. It contains about sixty-one Congressional townships.
Its northern extremity touches Lake George ; its southern reaches and includes Lake Tahopekaliga. Lying upon
both the eastern and western borders are chains of large
lakes ; the largest, Lake Apopka, upon the west, covering
an area of fifty-six square miles. The interior is thickly
dotted with lakes of smaller size, ranging from an acre to a
thousand acres in extent. The water in these lakes is pure
and soft. The bottoms and shores are sandy and hard. In
all of them fish abound, and the angler can find plenty of
sport. Upon the high pine-lands surrounding these little
lakes, beautiful building-sites can be found, where a home
can be made and embellished with all the shrubs and flowers
that can be grown in a semi-tropical region. It is here that
semi-tropical fruits flourish and reach a degree of development not surpassed in any part of the world. Oranges,
lemons, limes, citrons, guavas, figs, bananas, and pineapples
reach perfection here, and their culture, for either profit or
personal gratification, is attended with the most satisfactory
results. . . . Strawberries and grapes also do well. The
former fruit begins ripening in January and continues until
May. With the full development of the resources of the
county, the culture of this fruit will receive attention. It
ripens at a season of the year when there is little danger of
loss in transportation, and when people in the larger cities
in the North would be willing to pay exorbitant prices for
the fresh fruit. . . .

8

"Nine tenths of the failures in orange-culture that have occurred up to this date are due to indolence and mismanagement. Intelligent industry has always been rewarded with success. The orange has natural enemies in the scale and other insects, but good care will overcome all of these. The only enemy to the citrus family that can not be successfully combated by man is the frost, and it is here that Orange County has an advantage over any region lying to the north of us. Its elevated position and numerous lakes afford a protection from frosts that, in spite of all claims to the contrary, is not possessed by any portion of the State north of Lake George. The recent cold weather—the coldest with one exception in forty-eight years, and in some localities the coldest since 1833—did not damage the trees or fruit in Orange County. This statement is made in the teeth of all contrary assertions, and in proof of the claim we invite an inspection of the groves of Orange County just at this time, before there has been time for trees to recover from the effects of the cold. We do not claim that we had no frost. It is not even pretended that no injury was done in this county. Tender vegetables in the garden were killed or damaged, and those who were engaged in vegetable-gardening were subjected to loss. But neither trees nor fruit were injured, with the exception of the guavas in a few exposed situations, as there is abundant evidence here to show. . . .

"Cotton, sugar, and rice can be successfully and profitably grown upon a large portion of the lands of Orange County. Where an attempt has been made, upland rice has proved a successful crop on the high pine-lands. The cotton-crop of the present year has in most cases proved a profitable one, and the sugar and sirup crop, just now being marketed, has amply repaid all effort. The sugar-crop has received but little attention for years, owing to the difficulties attending the marketing of the product, and the consequent low prices offered by local buyers. The present year shows a little improvement in prices, and there is reason to believe that coming years will give a marked improvement in this respect. Upon the margins of these beautiful lakes there are large areas of land adapted, both by character and situation, to the production of sugar. And it is a significant and suggestive fact that while envious portions of the State and the South are claiming that old Orange County was as severely injured by the late cold weather as any other region, our planters are now, three weeks after the cold wave, engaged in grinding cane and making sugar, and the quality is not affected. . . .

"Winter gardening will pay a larger per cent. on the capital and labor invested than the most successful agricultural operations in the North. It is not claimed that a larger yield per acre can be secured in Florida than in the fertile valleys of the Mississippi and Missouri. But a reasonably good crop can be grown here at a season of the year when the farmers of the North are ice-bound and can raise nothing. A bushel of tomatoes grown in the North will net the producer one dollar. The crop comes into market just at a time when every farmer and gardener has produce to sell. The market is soon overdone, and the price gets so low that it will not pay for picking and marketing. One dollar per bushel for the season would be a good average price. A bushel of tomatoes grown in Florida and put into the New York market from December to February, will frequently net the grower ten dollars. Five dollars could always be depended upon, and thus the Florida truck-grower has an advantage over his Northern competitor in being able to get his products into market at a season of the year when he can find a ready sale at fancy prices, instead of seeing them go begging in an overstocked market at a starvation price. The fruit-growing industry will always be the chief attraction of this region. But, while the fruit-grower is waiting for his trees to come into bearing, he must manage to live. To do this he can engage in market-gardening, sugar-growing, or raising cassava for the starch-mills, and thus secure a fair income and a good living from the start. Any of these he can do without in any way interfering with the culture of his grove; and, indeed, while the trees are small, vegetables can be grown among them to advantage. The cost of living is light. Fuel costs nothing, and the family clothing will not exceed one half what is necessary in the North. . . .

"Orange County is to-day attracting more attention and increasing faster in population than any other county in the State. Its rolling, high pine-lands, lying along the heights

which divide the waters of the ocean and the Gulf, are undoubtedly the best drained and as well adapted to the culture of the orange and all semi-tropical fruits as any in the
State, and to these advantages in this respect may be added
absolute exemption from damaging frost. Here, too, the
water is as pure and as sweet as in New England, and there
is entire exemption from fever and ague and other malarious diseases found in lower sections of the State. From
September to April the climate is much like the finest
Indian-summer days of the North, while from April to
September the mercury rarely registers more than 96°.
Situated on the narrow part of the peninsula, alternate
breezes from the Gulf and the ocean modify the heat and
render the nights cool and comfortable ; and the universal
expression of people settled here from the North and West
is, that while the heat is more uniform and longer continued, it never reaches the extreme heat of the places from
which they came, and that their summers spent here have,
on the whole, been quite as comfortable as those of their
former homes. National official statistics show that the
death-rate of the State of Florida is two and three fourths
per cent., while that of New Hampshire is three per cent.,
and in other New England States and in the West the percentage is still larger. In Orange County, in a population
of upward of seven thousand, the late census returns show
only thirty-one deaths for the year ending June 1, 1880.

"How does the summer heat affect a Northern man ? is a
question frequently asked. The best reply is the fact that
sunstroke is unknown, and that with reasonable precautions
there is no more inconvenience from heat here than in the
North. The writer came from the North last May, just at
the unfavorable time of the year. For the first time in five
years he was able to follow his business through the entire
summer ; and was free from that general letting down of
the nervous forces experienced for years while following
his profession in Iowa.

"The highest point recorded by the mercury last summer
was 97° ; the lowest reached the present winter—and this
has been the coldest since 1857, and with one exception
since 1835—is 34°, showing a total annual range of 63°.
In the boasted health-resorts of Colorado we have experienced a greater variation than this within twenty-four

hours. It is its equable temperature and absolute freedom from sudden changes that make South Florida so desirable a region for people suffering with throat and lung affections and catarrh. If the latter disease is curable, a residence here will effect a cure.

"An idea prevalent, particularly in the North, is that our State swarms with reptile and insect life, while the fact is that in this locality at least we are as exempt from both as any in the country. The writer of this article has yet to see his first rattlesnake or moccasin, though he has spent much time in hunting and fishing, and traversing the forests, for the last year.

" We have mosquitoes here, but neither so numerous nor troublesome as in the city of Boston. Sand-flies abound in some sections of the State, but not here. Our land is what is called high pine, dotted with hundreds of clear-water lakes, upon the shores of which are the finest orange and fruit lands in the world ; not only the orange, but the lemon, lime, banana, pineapple, grape, guava, citron, fig, strawberry, and all semi-tropical fruits can be produced in abundance and with large profit. Turnips, squashes, beets, cucumbers, cabbages, onions, and all vegetables are raised quite as easily here as elsewhere, and find ready sale in Northern markets at remunerative prices. Cotton, sugar-cane, tobacco, cassava, arrow-root, etc., can be profitably raised. Transportation to and from the cities of New York and Boston is cheaper from this point than from either of those cities to the interior of Maine, New Hampshire, or Vermont. For instance, the freight on oranges per box, from Sanford to Boston, is sixty-five cents ; barrels of starch, eighty cents per barrel, and other merchandise proportionately low. The St. John's River, navigable by large steamers with which we are connected by twenty miles of rail, opens to us, by water communication and cheapest rates of transportation, the best markets of the world.

"Much valuable land is now open to the actual settler, and may be had by others from Government price, at points remote from transportation, to five, ten, twenty, thirty, and up to one hundred dollars or more per acre at points immediately on the railroads, or lakes connecting with the rail. Ten acres of land is amply sufficient for a grove of five hundred trees. Here as elsewhere there is more danger of cultivating too much than too little land, and it is generally better to buy five acres near transportation than fifty acres more remote, for the purpose of fruit-growing, on account of the trouble, expense, and damage to fruit by teaming.

"We are asked if capital can be profitably invested here. There are virgin forests of the finest pine, cedar, cypress, and oak in the Union for sale at low prices. The rapid disappearance of that class of timber in the North and West, and the immense local demand for building and fencing—for here we have no stone for fencing—and the material for boxes for fruit and vegetables will give a sure and more rapid advance to these timber-lands than has been witnessed in any State in the Union. Here, too, money can be loaned on security as safe as United States bonds, at from ten to fifteen per cent. per annum. Here, too, are gigantic unimproved water-powers, surrounded by the finest cotton-growing lands in the Union. We need tanneries, boot and shoe and furniture manufactories, carriage-builders, etc.

"The State laws exempt to every head of a family a homestead of one hundred and sixty acres in the country, or half an acre in town, together with one thousand dollars' worth of such personal property as the owner may select. The legal rate of interest is eight per cent., but contracts may be made for any rate. Taxes are rather high, the present rate of assessment in this county for all purposes being one dollar and fifty-five cents per hundred dollars. But this is on a valuation entirely too low. The State Treasury is solvent, paying cash on all warrants drawn against it, and the bonded debts of the State are gradually being reduced, and interest is paid thereon promptly."*

* The above-quoted article was written in 1880, and while its facts are in the main correct now, some statements relating to freight and transportation would have to be modified. It is fair to add that other counties than Orange have shown a surprising degree of development during the last four years, and much that is said of it would apply to them as well.

CHAPTER XI.

An Ocean Voyage in Winter.

ONE of the pleasantest incidents of a visit to Florida, if the journey be made by water, as it should be, if possible, is the sea-voyage thither. To the resident of New York and the Eastern section of the North the opportunity thus to go to the tropics by sea is afforded weekly by the Mallory Steamship Line (Pier 20, East River), the only ocean-route to Florida from the North which involves no change or transfer. The steamships of this line that make the Florida trip direct from New York to Jacksonville, stopping at Port Royal and Fernandina, are the Western Texas, of twelve hundred and ten tons, Captain Hines, and the City of San Antonio, fifteen hundred and forty-seven tons, Captain Risk ; and it is sufficient to say of them that they are first-class sea-going passenger-steamers, built of iron on the most approved models, provided with all known appliances for safety and comfort, and fitted up with elegance and taste.

In making the journey by this sea-route the contrast between the two regions and climates is much more marked and noticeable than in going by land. Leaving New York in the midst of winter, the tourist sees pass by him in glistening panorama the snow-clad hills and shores of Long Island and Staten Island, feels the chilling blasts, and gladly seeks the warm and cozy cabin to escape the discomfort

of the cold. Slippers and easy coats are donned, pipes and
papers are produced, cards and dominoes are called for ;
and soon, without formal introductions, the passengers are
rapidly becoming friends (and what friendships are so
warm and unreserved as those formed on a sea-voyage ?).

Next morning land is nowhere to be seen ; you are out
on the vasty deep, and quite likely it is a surprise to you to
find that it is so smooth and calm. Very many people on
their first sea-voyage allow their imaginations to be stimu-
lated and their apprehensions aroused by the accounts which
they then recall of terrible storms and waves " mountain-
high," of plunging and straining ships, of iron-bound and
dangerous coasts, and the like ; but while all these things
are possible, yet, like the possible frightful railway accident,
they are seldom seen or experienced. In spite of the general
impression to the contrary, the weather along the Atlantic
coast of America is nearly always fair and agreeable. The
writer has made several passages around the famous Cape
Hatteras, and each time had the good fortune to find it
like a journey on an inland lake. Each time the waters
were mirror-like in their smoothness, and this experience,
by no means a rare one, has produced a skeptical feeling
in regard to that cape of so many disagreeable stories.
Moreover, even should "rough weather" be encountered,
the worst to be feared is an acute attack of the *mal-de-mer*,
and a prolongation of the time consumed by the voyage.
Of downright danger there may be said to be none, such a
thing as a serious accident to one of these stanch coast-
wise steamers being among the rarest of occurrences.

The second day, schools of porpoises begin to appear,
flying-fish and jelly-fish are often to be seen, occasional
glimpses of the coast to the west are obtained, and the
polite officers are kept busy pointing out and giving the
names of the tall, warning lighthouses that are almost constantly in sight. At Port Royal a short stay is made, the

passengers flock on shore, and here you first begin to realize that you have left the dreary regions of winter behind. As he nears the wharf, the tourist will begin to think that, in the number of smells at least, it resembles the city of Cologne. This, however, is due to the vast quantity of fertilizers which is constantly on storage near by.

Next day—the fourth from New York—Fernandina is reached, a lovely island city of broad streets, and ample flower-gardens surrounding handsome houses. Here we get our first near view of the palmetto and the orange-tree, and of that teeming luxuriance of vegetation which marks a semi-tropical clime. Again on board, and seven hours later the steamer is passing swiftly up the broad and beautiful St. John's River, affording on either hand a continuous panorama of the most pleasing and novel scenery. Soon the mighty screw ceases to revolve, we round gracefully up to the pier, good-bys are hastily exchanged, and the tourist is in Jacksonville,* the social headquarters in winter, and the chief commercial center of the Land of Flowers. Here at last he finds June in January; and, as he discards his overcoat and takes his farewell glance at the steamer which brought him thither, he will be apt to recall Thomas Buchanan Read's suggestive and graceful lines :

> " Yon deep bark goes
> Where traffic blows
> From lands of sun to lands of snows;
> This happier one
> Its race is run
> From lands of snow to lands of sun."

* Since the foregoing was written, a change of plan has occurred, by which the steamers of the Mallory Line stop at Fernandina, and passengers are carried to Jacksonville in one and a half hour by the new short-cut railroad. It is understood that this arrangement is only temporary, and the steamers will, in the near future, resume their through trips direct to Jacksonville.

The Atlantic Coast of Florida.

On its Atlantic seaboard Florida presents some curious physical features. Along its entire extent there are no good harbors, except at Fernandina and St. Augustine, and the soundings are shoal for some distance out ; yet just back of the coast-line, for a distance of over three hundred miles south of the mouth of the St. John's River, there is a succession of streams and lakes and lagoons which afford almost uninterrupted inland water communication along more than two thirds of the total length of the peninsula. The most important link in this chain of waters—the Indian River— is fully described elsewhere. At the northern extremity of Indian River a canal, two thousand feet long, known as the Haulover, leads into the Mosquito Lagoon, which extends northward about twelve miles to Oak Hill, and then, through the Devil's Elbow, connects with the Hillsboro River. The latter extends northward about fifteen miles, and then becomes known as the Halifax River, which begins about twenty-four miles south of St. Augustine. All this portion of the State is exceptionally attractive, with a fine climate, excellent sea-beaches, rich soil, and a varied capacity for production. Its chief need at present is easy and certain connection with the natural markets for its products ; and this is likely to be afforded by a canal which the Lake Okechobee Land Company propose to include in the great system of public improvements which they have undertaken to carry out. (See Appendix, note 28.)

Their plan is to construct a continuous line of canal, suitable for commodious steamers of light draught, beginning at a point at or near the confluence of Pablo Creek and the St. John's River, and extending thence in a southerly direction to and including Lake Worth, a total distance of about three hundred and thirty miles. In this connection the following passages from a "Report to the Company," by the civil engineer (Mr. James E. Kreamer), who examined the proposed route in the spring of 1881, will prove interesting :

" In constructing the Coast Canal from the St. John's River south, advantage may be taken of the waters of Pablo Creek, North River, Mantanzas River, Mata Compra, and Smith's or Haulover Creek, Halifax and Hillsboro Rivers, Mosquito Lagoon, Indian River, St. Lucie Sound, Jupiter Narrows, Lake Worth Creek, and Lake Worth. All of the above-named waters are adjacent to, and generally parallel with, the east coast of Florida, being separated from the ocean by peninsulas and extended narrow islands, varying in width from a few yards to several miles. These inland waters, affording an almost unbroken line of communication, may, at a reasonably moderate expenditure in systematic construction presenting no embarrassing engineering problems, be developed into a great canal, possessing features peculiarly its own. Merely where the artificial work of joining river to river is performed can it be regarded as a canal proper, as from these points it develops into those majestic arms of the sea, from thirty to one hundred miles in length, varying from one to six miles in width, bordered on either side by a country enjoying unbounded agricultural resources, a semi-tropical luxuriance in beauty of foliage, scenery of an exceedingly varied and picturesque character, and blessed with a climate throughout the entire year the most equable and salubrious enjoyed by any State in the Union.

" From St. Augustine the Mantanzas River extends in a southerly direction a distance of twenty-five miles, with an average width of one half mile. Its waters are salt and tidal, and with the exception of isolated bars, and a rapid shoaling for a distance of three miles from the head of the river, there is a fair channel for light-draught boats. Anastasia Island, which acts as a breakwater for the harbor of St. Augustine, forms the eastern shore-line for a distance of eighteen miles to Mantanzas Inlet. The natural surface is not so elevated as on the west shore, and is composed in part of shell-land and black, loamy sand, capable of producing profitable crops. On the mainland are beautiful groves of pine, red cedar, and oak. Desirable cleared land is worth from fifty to one hundred dollars per acre, depending on location and richness of soil. South of Mantanzas Inlet the river rapidly contracts in width and depth to its junction with Pellicers Creek, at which point the work of constructing that portion of the canal connecting the Halifax River properly begins, consisting of a cut eighteen miles in length. In this operation advantage may be taken of the Mantanzas to its junction with the Mata Compra Creek, thence generally following this stream to its head, from which, for a distance of six miles, the route crosses the country to the source of Smith's Creek, which will have to be deepened and straightened to within four miles of the head of the Halifax. The country to the west of this portion of the line consists of flat woods, prairie, savannas, high and low hammock of oak, palmetto, wild-orange, etc.; the surface undulating, soil sandy, and, judging from the topography and general indications, the opening of this section of the canal can be readily accomplished.

"That interesting arm of the sea, whose several divisions are known respectively as Halifax River, Hillsboro River, and Mosquito Lagoon, forming a common channel, with an outwatering at Mosquito Inlet (latitude 29° north), continues to the south and parallel with the ocean-beach a distance of fifty-five miles, and is separated from it by a narrow strip of land about three fourths of a mile in width. The hamlets and towns of Holly Hill, New Britain, Daytona, Halifax City, Port Orange, Blake Post-Office, and New Smyrna, on the margin of the river, are desirably located, principally on rich, high hammock-lands of palmetto, oak, and other forest-trees. The inhabitants are from all sections of the Union, generally prosperous and anxiously awaiting the opening of the canal, and the consequent impetus to the general industries of the country. Daytona is the most important town on the river, possesses a good hotel, stores, etc. New Smyrna, in the year 1770, was the seat of a large and profitable trade in indigo, immense crops of which were cultivated by a colony of Minorcans, under the guidance of Andrew Turnbull; the dense hammocks, old canals, and turnpikes are silent monuments attesting to the vast extent of the plantations devoted to this enterprise. The river varies in width from one half to two and a half miles, possessing a fairly direct channel, intercepted by sand and oyster bars, rendering portions of the route very tortuous ; beautiful islands dot its surface, and the shore-lines are covered with verdure to the water's edge. A low belt of sand about seven hundred yards in width, pierced by a narrow canal, known as the Haulover, separates this system from Indian River, whose coralline bed and generally well-defined shore-line extends a distance of one hundred and twenty miles to the south, a narrow fringe of sand protecting it from the ocean, the only communication therewith being at Indian River Inlet, latitude 27° 30′ north. At the respective distances of ten, twenty-one, and thirty-six miles from the Haulover, Titusville, Rock Ledge, and Eau Gallie are located ; the first-named, the county-seat of Brevard County, being the most prominent. It possesses a good hotel, and is the general headquarters for business on the river. Rock Ledge is the center of a large section of country devoted to the cultivation of the orange. One thousand acres of land in this vicinity will, when set in trees, give an output of over three hundred thousand boxes per annum. Merritt's Island, extending from the head of the river to a point opposite Eau Gallie, is noted for its valuable lands, tropical fruits, and rich yield from the sugar-cane. The St. Sebastian River partially drains the northern portion of the Halpatiokee Flats, and is the most prominent of several streams joining the lagoon north of Indian River Narrows, which are due to a number of islands contracting the channel at this point. Fort Capron, fifty-six miles south of Eau Gallie, and opposite Indian River Inlet, is the site of a military post, established in 1849. Meteorological observations, extending over a series of years, show an equable temperature, with comparative dryness, mild and salubrious climate, and absolute immunity from epidemic disease. An abundance of fruit, vegetables, game, fish, oysters, etc., would certainly commend this as a site for a commodious hotel. Twenty-five miles south the St. Lucie River, which is the principal outlet for the drainage of a vast territory lying east of Lake Okeechobee, is confluent with the Indian River ; it has a wide and deep channel branching off into a north and south prong, and in constructing a drainage canal from Lake Okeechobee to the forks of the St. Lucie, opposite the mouth of the latter, it will be necessary to open an inlet connecting Indian River with the ocean. The inlet at Gilbert's Bar, just south, has been opened on several occasions, and as often, due to its natural features, closed. On the east side of Indian River, just north of the mouth of the St. Lucie, a large bay extends toward the ocean, and is separated therefrom by a sandy ridge not over three hundred feet wide, with a possible underlying stratum of coquina. The ocean-beach forms a slight cove at this point, beyond which is a reef exposed at low tide and concave to the shore-line. These conditions are very favorable to the maintenance of an inlet, the opening of which I would recommend at this point ; and if once formed due to the action of tidal waters, its permanence is assured. Indian River, for a distance of one hundred and twenty miles, will average one and a half mile in width, widening at points to five miles, with a generally direct channel, requiring dredging at intervals in order to render it safely navigable.

"The land bordering the river is generally high and low hammock, interspersed with scrub palmetto, with some marsh adjacent the narrows. The soil is very productive, sugar-cane and tropical fruits maturing to perfection. Three miles south of the St. Lucie we enter Jupiter Narrows, which are very tortuous, necessitating the labor of straightening and deepening at several points. They extend south, measured by the channel, a distance of twenty miles to Jupiter Inlet, intercepting Peck's Lake and Hope Sound ; a dense growth of mangrove covers the low borders ; and from general observations afforded by the openings, I inferred the land for the entire distance to be of good quality, and the same character as that farther north.

"A continuation of Jupiter Inlet to the west for a distance of eight miles, forms the Loocahachee, a broad river, from which are several branches, bordered by cypress, oak, etc., leading into the prairies and flats. From the inlet to Lake Worth, by the windings of Lake Worth Creek, the distance is about thirteen miles ; in a direct line, not over seven. A single cut of one hundred yards in length will make a saving of one and a half mile in distance ; this same feature is noticeable in a marked degree at other points. There is a depth of five feet of water in the channel from its mouth to the rapids ; from this point to the canal and Haulover at Lake Worth the water is comparatively shallow, and at its head is about eight feet above the level of the surface of the lake. A direct cut from the rapids to Little Lake Worth, which is immediately north of Lake Worth proper, would shorten the distance materially. It is not necessary to comment on the favorable character of the land in the vicinity of Lake Worth, as, even with its present development, semi-weekly cargoes of vegetables and tropical fruits in their respective seasons could be provided."

THE SOUTHEAST AND SOUTHWEST COASTS.

The following passages are from an interesting article which appeared in a recent number of the "Semi-Tropical Magazine," written by M. A. Williams, a civil engineer of Jacksonville :

"The climate upon this coast is exceedingly pleasant and healthy, being fanned almost continually by the sea-breezes, and the lands are adapted to general cultivation, but particularly to semi-tropical fruits. The orange grows there to great perfection. These inland waters are more properly speaking *sounds* rather than rivers, and upon their borders there are localities of great beauty. The waters abound in the finest variety of fish. Indeed, the fisheries at particular places on these waters can not be excelled as to quantity, quality, and variety of the fish, and the same can be said of Charlotte Harbor, Sarasota, and other points upon the Gulf. So far a portion only of these fisheries have been used, chiefly for the West India market, but, with population and increased facilities for shipment, they must become of great value at no distant day.

"The coral formation of the peninsula crops out upon the surface in the neighborhood of Biscayne Bay, and, although the land is exceedingly rocky, yet it is productive and well adapted to the cultivation of tropical fruits. Upon the islands lying off the southeast coast of Florida—Elliot's, Key Largo, and the islands farther south—is where the pineapples for the United States are produced. There were more than one hundred thousand pineapples produced upon Key Largo the present year. This fruit produced upon these islands is said to be of better flavor and of superior quality to that produced upon the Bahamas, and sells for a much better price in the New York market. All other tropical fruits grow here to perfection. The surface of the lands is rocky almost beyond description. In surveying upon them, I had frequently to pile up rocks around my Jacob's staff to make it stand upright. In fact, the entire cultivation is done with the hands and the use of a wooden stick ; a common hoe or plow can not be used. The woods growing upon these islands differ from those of any other portion of the State ; they are mostly exceedingly hard, heavy, and when dressed very beautiful.

"The Caloosahatchie and Pease Creek, upon the Gulf-coast, are large and beautiful rivers, and have upon their borders a very large amount of excellent land ; and upon these waters the cocoanut, banana, pineapple, guava, and other tender tropical fruits grow to perfection. It is also well adapted to the culture of sugar-cane. The Caloosahatchie River, from its entrance into Charlotte Harbor for forty miles up, is more than a mile wide ; it then narrows into a deep channel with precipitous banks, and is from one hundred and fifty to two hundred feet wide. It so continues to the falls at Fort Thompson. All the streams that flow from the Everglades, both on the Atlantic and Gulf, have falls, thus proving the practicability of draining this immense area of submerged lands. In my judgment the Caloosahatchie is the best tropical region of this State ; indeed, it would be hard to excel it for beauty of location and adaptation of soil for tropical fruit-culture anywhere. Besides, it commands a large area of country south of it, embracing the best cattle-range in the State. The propriety of connecting this with the Okechobee Lake and the Kissimmee River by canal, thus giving an inland navigation for several hundred miles in the center of the peninsula, is a matter that has been ably stated by other persons.

"The country around Forts Meade and Bartow, upon the head-waters of Pease Creek, is in many respects one of the most desirable portions of Florida. It is a region of clear, open-water lakes, with beautiful running streams of limpid water. The land is generally first-rate pine, with clay subsoil, and is very productive. This is an exceedingly healthy region, and is almost entirely free from mosquitoes. The lands on the head-waters of the Alafia are similar in all respects to those just mentioned.

"There are good lands upon the Manatee River and Sarasota Bay, and in other portions of Manatee County, with locations of great beauty and value. Previous to the war the largest sugar-planting interest in Florida was upon the Manatee River."*

* The growth of all the tropical fruits mentioned above has increased immensely in this section since the article was written. This is specially the case with pineapples and cocoanuts.

CHAPTER XII.

PERHAPS I can not begin this chapter in a better way than by quoting the following passage from the official and carefully prepared pamphlet of the State Bureau of Immigration :

"The climate of Florida is not a *hot* climate in summer, but mild, and not subject to great changes of temperature. The winters are not *cold* and *freezing*, but uniformly *cool* and *bracing*. Throughout the whole twelve months, the rainy, cloudy, disagreeable days are the exception ; fair, bright, sunny days the rule. The thermometer seldom goes below 30° in winter, and rarely above 90° in summer. The official records show the average for summer, 78° ; for winter, 60°. The daily constant ocean-breezes in summer modify the heat (the Gulf-breeze, coming with the setting sun, cools the air at night) ; a warm or sultry night is almost unknown. Official sanitary reports, both of scientific bodies and the army, show that Florida stands first in health, although in the reports are included the transient or recent population, many of whom take refuge here as invalids, some in the lowest stages of disease. In the greater portion of the State, frost is rarely known. The summer is longer, but the heat less oppressive, than midsummer at the North ; this results from its peculiar peninsular shape and the ever-recurring breezes which pass over the State. For days together, New York, Boston, and Chicago show, in summer, temperature as high as 100° ; it is very rare that it reaches that degree in Florida for a single day, generally ranging below 90° : not oppressive, modified by the ever-changing air ;

not sultry, close, or humid ; mornings and evenings always cool and bracing. Natives and old residents, if asked, would say they preferred the summer to the winter months for climate. This climate is peculiarly adapted for vegetation. There are years when in some localities there is a drought, and years when portions of the State have had excessive rains, but they do not extend far. In the early spring, when most of the planting season occurs, there are frequent showers ; from the first to the middle of July, the rainy season commences, continuing till the middle of September ; the rain falls almost every day, commencing in the early afternoon, lasting from a few minutes to a few hours, rarely as long as the last period, often heavy with thunder and sharp lightning, then ceasing, leaving the air cool and sweet, the sky clear and bright ; the porous soil quickly absorbs the water and leaves the footway dry. These rains fill up the low, flat lands and ponds, and are injurious to crops when planted on such lands, underlaid by hard-pan. But on the high pine-lands and high hammocks the rains are of advantage, making crops grow rank and heavy. The 'rainy season' is not of regular annual occurrence.

"We take from Dr. A. S. Baldwin's tables, kept for the Smithsonian Institute, as follows :

"'Jacksonville, latitude 30° 15', longitude 82°—mean of three daily observations for twenty years, 1844–'67. Thermometer :

January	55°	July	82°
February	58°	August	82°
March	64°	September	78°
April	70°	October	70°
May	76°	November	62°
June	80°	December	52°

"'The army records show for twenty years, variation at St. Augustine, Florida, 23°.

"Rainfall at Jacksonville, average for ten years, 54·5 inches ; the largest quantity in August and September, and the least in November.'"

From my personal experience, I can indorse the above opinions. The winter of 1879–'80, in all portions of Florida,

was about as delightful a season as can be imagined ; but,
as that winter was an exceptionally fine one, perhaps it
should not be taken as a criterion. The summer of 1880
was the hottest known in years, in this State. In a few
localities the thermometer attained 102° on several occasions. Yet I spent the entire summer and autumn in South
Florida, engaged in a vocation that required me to be out-
of-doors nearly all the time. I rode about on horseback
through the woods at all hours of the day, but on no occasion did I really suffer from the heat or feel it in any way
unbearable. In fact, I thought it a pleasant, agreeable
summer, and never enjoyed better health. I was frequently
caught out in the sudden showers—often regular drenches—
in the rainy season, and was as wet as though I had been
under a shower-bath ; but I always remained out and dried
by the wind or sun as the case might be. I saw on three occasions the thermometer register 102°, but we were all prepared for warm weather, and did not find it so oppressive
as such a temperature would indicate. The winter of 1880
–'81 was considered the coldest and stormiest of many
years, yet we probably enjoyed two thirds of the evenings,
sitting out on the verandas as in May weather. Three times
the thermometer went below 40° ; once, December 30th,
it touched 32°, damaging tomatoes and such garden-vegetables—also bananas, guavas, and pineapples. On most of
the evenings and early mornings in January we had fires
in our rooms, but it was not cold of the Northern kind,
neither unhealthy nor disagreeable, simply chilly. We com-
plained loudly at 55° above zero.

This was my experience of the weather in Orange County, which is situated considerably north of the center of
the State. In the counties farther north, up to the Georgia
line, it was several degrees colder but not freezing—except
the cold snaps in December and March—nor bitter, only
much colder than is usual in Florida. It was in this sec-

tion that the disastrous cold snaps occurred December 30th and March 29th, when the thermometer registered about 20° above zero for a few hours, and ice formed in Jacksonville and damaged fruits, flowers, and crops. It caused no personal suffering, and was damaging to fruits and crops only of the tenderest kind, because unexpected like any climatic calamity. Such severe cold weather is not usual in this State, and should not be regarded as an evil liable to occur frequently. It was an exception. Its damage was less than from a drought, wet season, or locust-plague, so frequently occurring in other States. The rainy, cloudy days of December and January were so unexpected and un-Florida-like, that all felt disgusted.

I must say, however, that we were somewhat reconciled to our disasters and discomfort, as we read of the actual and widespread suffering at the North and in the great Northwest. I recollect that in February we were reading almost daily in the newspapers of great storms of snow and sleet, of delays and dangers on railways, of interruptions to telegraphic communication, of loss of life and property, of terrible suffering from cold and hunger, of whole regions devastated by floods, and of the entire machinery of business and transportation brought to a standstill. At the same time, in many parts of the North, diphtheria, small-pox, and similar scourges, were causing the death of many thousands, involving doctors' bills (if no worse) for hundreds of poor families whose resources were already strained in procuring fuel and clothes for the necessary warmth. Now, it is the plain unvarnished truth that that same month of February, 1881, in every part of Florida, was as warm, as sunny, as genial, and as healthy, as any May month ever seen in the North. Fruits and flowers were growing every-where, crops were being planted or gathered, straw-hats and light clothes were common, and—in the more southern regions—swimming and bathing in the ponds and in the

sea were enjoyed. Oranges were being gathered in every
section where the frost had not damaged them, and among
the out-door attractions were fishing, hunting, riding, boating, and yachting. Open doors and windows were the universal rule, the evenings were usually spent on the broad
'verandas, and fresh garden-vegetables were on the tables.
By reference to the files of the "South Florida Journal,"
I find that on the 22d of January Mr. George E. Sawyer,
of Sanford, started for the State Fair at Jacksonville, with
an exhibit of oranges, lemons, limes, guavas, bananas,
lemon and banana blooms, cabbages, cauliflowers, lettuce,
turnips, radishes, and carrots, all just plucked in the open
air.

In the matter of healthfulness, too, the contrast was
equally great. Probably not two people in the thousand
died during that February in all Florida ; certainly none
died from the effects of cold, or from those frightful epidemics that are the terror of the North. Pneumonia is unknown in Florida ; so are diphtheria and small-pox. Even
the summers are remarkably healthy, except for the malarious fevers which are due to local conditions that are easily
recognized and guarded against. There was never known
a case of sunstroke or of hydrophobia in Florida. Yellow
fever has been known to occur in the State, and there are
five localities that have acquired the bad reputation always
inflicted upon a place that has been visited by this terrible
epidemic ; but in each place, on each occasion, the disease
was brought there by infected vessels ; in no case was it
of local or spontaneous origin.

The question of climate and health, however, is peculiarly one in which the opinions of specialists are all-impor-
tant ; and, having now offered my own testimony in the
matter, I propose to cite the confirmatory evidence of those
who have given most attention to the matter, and whose
conclusions are most entitled to respect. Dr. Joseph P.

Logan, one of the most distinguished physicians in Atlanta, Georgia, contributed a valuable article on " Climate-Cure " to " Gaillard's Medical Journal," for March, 1881, and from it I make (by permission) the following extracts :

"Without undertaking to cover the whole ground embraced in the subject under consideration, or to engage for the present in the discussion of the speculative theories now so rife in regard to the details of special influences of climate upon disease, I propose as a rule, in general terms, that the best climate for the invalid suffering from any disease is that which furnishes the largest opportunity for interesting, comfortable, and healthful out-door exercise, thoroughly ventilated sleeping-rooms, and in which there is the least necessity for burdensome clothing.

"While for many years the weight of evidence in favor of the State of Florida, as furnishing these conditions to a higher degree than any other portion of the United States, has been very decided, yet, owing largely to a want of careful discrimination upon the part of medical advisers in sending persons in the fully developed or advanced stage of consumption to that State, and the natural anxiety of even the most hopeless sufferers to exhaust every possible resource in the effort to prolong life, doubts as to the real advantages of that region have arisen, and repeated efforts have been made by enthusiastic members of the medical profession to establish a climatic sanitarium elsewhere. At various times it was to be found among the snow and ice of Minnesota, the great elevations of Colorado, the plains of western Texas, or the sand-hills and uplands of South and North Carolina, or Georgia ; but the writer is strongly impressed with the conviction, after a number of years' consideration of this subject, and such opportunities of observation as in his judgment authorize him to put upon record the opinion, that all these attempts will in a large majority of cases of tubercular disease, and more strikingly so with reference to the other diseases to which reference has been made, prove illusive.

"His testimony is, that while from the causes mentioned, and the want of judgment in various ways upon the part of sufferers from these diseases who have made the experiment, and we regret to say the want of moral courage (to which the writer pleads personally guilty) in facing and presenting the inevitable to our patients, respectable professional and popular doubts as to the efficiency of the climate of Florida as a remedy for consumption have arisen ; yet the drift of the sentiment of both classes, within the scope of his observation, is more marked at the present hour in favor of the idea that nowhere else in this country is to be found the same reliable evidence as to the value of climate-cure in disease, and specially in consumption, as that which has been accumulating for many years in regard to the State of Florida. That there is a decided exemption from tubercular consumption, as originating in Georgia and other Southern States in the same latitude, as compared with the northern sections of the United States, and that many persons in the incipient stage of the disease, or with a proclivity in that direction, in the North, have been greatly benefited by a removal to the milder and more genial climate of almost every portion of the Southern States, and especially in Georgia and the Carolinas, is doubtless true ; but that this advantage has been mainly due in this region to the greater opportunity for exercising in comfort and safety in the open air, and to the escape from the noxious influences of a long winter residence in close and heated rooms, rather than to any specific curative influence of the climate, there is no doubt.

"That thousands and tens of thousands of delicate people with an inherited or acquired proclivity to consumption, and many cases even of the actual incipient development of the disease in the more northern sections of the United States, and to a more limited yet appreciable extent even in this section (where our winters are characterized by frequent northeastern storms of rain, alternating with sharp northwestern winds), may have their terms of life greatly prolonged, and in a large proportion of cases escape a fatal result from the disease, by a permanent removal to, or a residence for the entire cold season in, the State of Florida, upon the principle already alluded to, and to a much greater degree, and possibly to some extent to an additional curative influence in the climate, is established by many well-authenticated instances of such results, some of which the writer may undertake to put upon record, at some future time, if they can be gathered up in proper professional form.

"As to the result, however, of the plan adopted by most persons of spending a few weeks or months in Florida, and especially of deferring their departure from inhospitable climates for a winter residence in this more genial region until they have been subjected to an attack of cold or bronchitis, as the result of the inclement weather of the early winter, and then returning in the months of spring, when the climatic changes are greater and more trying than at any other period of the year, I have nothing favorable to say, and believe that the only fair test of the influences of the climate can be realized by spending the entire cold season, say from the first of November to the last of May, or by residing there the entire year in some readily-found locality free from malaria.

"And, now that the wonderful success of semi-tropical fruit-culture is established beyond controversy, and a most pleasant, profitable, and suitable occupation is found, even for the invalid, who is not entirely disabled, and with the admirable attractions afforded by the abounding game for hunting, and the charming small lakes teeming with fish for boating and angling, and with the opportunity to almost literally live out-doors (the desideratum for the consumptive invalid), with something constantly to interest, and with no time hanging heavily upon the hands or for brooding over disabilities, it would seem that a very bonanza of health, pleasure, and wealth, even for the invalids, has been found.

"After visiting Florida a number of times, and regarding the whole State as more or less favorable in the climatic advantages offered, I would state that these are combined to a greater degree than in any other accessible and improved section, in that portion of the peninsula known as *South Florida*, and especially in the county of Orange, with parallel and more southern counties to the region of Tampa upon the Gulf-coast, extending far into the interior, embracing hill and dale and large bodies of rolling, majestic pine, oak, and magnolia forests, and many beautiful, sparkling lakes, which, in that region where evaporation from

9

and percolation through the soil is very extreme, furnish, in connection with the soft and charming breezes from the Gulf or ocean, a desirable humidity in the long intervals between the rains, characteristic of that section during a large part of the year, and to such extent, specially in the winter, as to constitute it the 'dry season' as compared to the 'wet season' from July to September. . . . Without, then, intending to ignore the advantages of the winter climate of the Southern States generally, and especially the piny and sandy sections of Georgia, the Carolinas, and Northern and Middle Florida, and in some exceptional seasons of the San Antonio regions of Texas, my advice to the invalid seeking a reliable and genial climate for the cold season is, to ship from Jacksonville (the point of steamboat departure from the upper or lower St. John's River, as you may prefer to term it), two hundred miles by water, for Sanford, or Enterprise, on that magnificent expansion of the St. John's called Lake Monroe, at the head of large-steamboat navigation. And, as the invalid will not go where he can not find comfortable accommodations, it is well to state that here and in the adjacent sections of park-like, rolling pines in the counties of Orange and Volusia, good hotels and boarding-houses have already sprung up where but a few years ago was a primeval forest. . . .

"But, however necessary, attractive, and useful such public-houses are, it is not in luxurious and crowded hotels that the highest conditions for health anywhere, and especially for 'climate-cure,' are found ; and, instead of lounging in the hotels of Jacksonville, St. Augustine, and many other points of interest to the mere pleasure-seeker upon the St. John's or in this region, I would advise, as an important factor in a thorough test of this climate, at least in diseases of the lungs, that the invalid should be as much segregated as possible, and where practicable that he should have his own house, however simple and inexpensive it may be, and that it should be surrounded by groves, gardens, and vineyards, as an interesting and valuable resource for both pleasure and profit to the health, even if there should be no occasion for it to the pocket."

For more specific details and tabulated data, I am permitted to draw largely upon an address on the " Climatology of Florida," which Dr. Charles J. Kenworthy, President of the Florida Medical Association, delivered at a recent meeting of that Society. The address has since been published in pamphlet form, and should be read in its entirety by those who would obtain precise and statistical information as to the climate and hygienic conditions of Florida ; but the following somewhat copious extracts will serve to indicate the general conclusions which Dr. Kenworthy has reached, and the evidence upon which those conclusions are based. He says :

"Difference of opinion exists in the profession regarding the effects of climate in the treatment of pulmonary and other diseases. Having been a member of the profession for over the third of a century, and having treated disease in private practice, as well as in several hospitals in the United States and in other lands, I have reason to believe that I am justified in expressing mine. My reason for settling in this State was my wife's health. She was a sufferer from phthisis, aggravated by a Northern climate. From my personal knowledge of the climatic advantages of this State, acquired by frequent visits, the first in 1844, I resolved upon settling in Jacksonville. As a result of change of climate, combined with rational medication, my wife was restored to health. In 1849 I was connected with Bellevue and Blackwell's Island Hospitals, New York, and contracted typhoid fever and cholera, followed by *postmortem* poisoning ; and impaired health was the result. Tracing my family history, I found that my mother and fourteen of her brothers and sisters had died of phthisis. With impaired health, a laryngeal affection, and an hereditary predisposition to tuberculosis, I had anything but a bright prospect before me. I looked to climate as my sheet-anchor, and sailed for Australia, and a dry and warm climate improved my health ; and to-day, as you can all perceive, I am in the enjoyment of as good health as usually falls to the lot of men of my age. After a permanent residence in this State of nearly six years, I am convinced of its healthfulness and the superiority of its climate, and deem myself warranted in expressing an opinion. . . .

"In this age of rapid, cheap, and comfortable traveling, the advantages to health of a change of climate should be considered by every person suffering from pulmonary or chronic disease, or broken health. It is a pleasant, and in many cases a valuable, remedy if judiciously advised. 'It would be difficult,' says Sir James Clark, the standard authority on climate, 'to point out the chronic complaint, or even disordered state of health, which is not benefited by a timely and judicious change of climate.' The diseases most likely to be benefited or cured by change of climate are phthisis, laryngeal and bronchial affections, asthma, disorder of the digestive organs, chronic gout and rheumatism, affections of the kidneys, and broken health. A change of climate is beneficial to strumous children, is invaluable during convalescence from acute and chronic disease, and more especially is it one of the chief resources of restorative medicine.

"A large majority of patients require a moderately warm, dry, and bracing atmosphere, and the few demand a warm, sedative climate, where the atmosphere is not alone warm, but humid ; and here steps in that knowledge that should be possessed by medical men who recommend climatic change as a remedial agent. A moderately warm, dry, and bracing air, with but few sudden and great atmospheric changes, is especially adapted to tuberculous disease in its early stages, catarrh, chronic bronchitis, chronic rheumatism, debilitating mucous discharges, renal diseases, dyspepsia, and some cases of asthma. A moist, warm, and sedative climate is best adapted to many cases of advanced phthisis, dry asthma, chronic bronchitis, accompanied with great irritability of the pulmonary mucous membrane, and a hard, dry cough. The particular locality, or what climate shall be chosen for a winter resort in any given case, is a matter of great importance, and should not be based on this or that letter or publication. Facts, figures, experience, and favorable factors of climate should determine the question. An error in this direction may be fatal, and, before a physician advises a patient to resort to any particular locality, he should carefully investigate each particular case, arrive at a correct diagnosis, and familiarize himself with the factors of each winter resort. Many an invalid who would be restored to comparative health, or at least survive

for years, if he wintered in a temperate climate, is sent to
a region where zero is frequently reached, where atmospheric changes are frequent and great, and where the patient is confined to heated rooms for days together, and
debarred from taking exercise and enjoying the health-
giving influence of sunlight and pure air. Others are
sent to a warm and relaxing climate, when they require
a temperate, dry, and bracing one. Fashion and the
influence of some leading physician have much to do with
this.

"In this active business country, we find many persons
who have been overworked, and present a breach in the
chain of those vital processes whose continuity constitutes
health—a condition popularly known as 'broken health.'
. . . In Florida, the worn-out man of business, suffering
from 'broken health,' will find the necessary relaxation from
'brain-fag,' opportunities to take out-door exercise, plenty
of sunshine, pure and bracing air, and other necessary ad-
juncts to relieve a condition affecting the many. In this
connection, I can not refrain from referring to what I consider an important fact. From my observations in the
United States and in foreign lands, and in hospital as well
as private practice, I have been forced to notice the infre-
quency of chronic disease and broken health in Florida.
In my visits to various portions of this State, I have met
with many persons, old and young, who live from year to
year on improper food, and who drink water from shallow
holes, near marshes, and yet, singular to say (although such
persons are somewhat anæmic), they do not present any
manifest diseased condition. In cities, towns, villages, and
rural districts, where residents are supplied with proper
food and drink pure water, a case of chronic disease or
broken health is seldom met with. And if we have a climate in which these conditions rarely occur, are we not justified in concluding that it will exert a powerful influence
in restoring the invalid to health? As most of you are
aware, I have, at various times, visited many portions of
the State, and have been surprised to meet so many persons
who have settled in it as invalids and have been restored to
health or comparative comfort by the climate—a large proportion of them having been sufferers from pulmonary diseases. And what surprised me most was the fact that none

of their offspring manifested any constitutional predisposition to pulmonary disease. Independent of uterine diseases among females, so common in every civilized country, and constitutional syphilis among colored people, I will ask you if your experience will not bear out my statement, and if your practice among residents is not almost exclusively confined to acute and not chronic disease and broken health? If this is a fact, it would appear that the climate is peculiarly adapted to the cure of such conditions, and have we not a potent agent to use, and, if used aright, to benefit suffering humanity? . . .

"The word climate, in its common signification, indicates a region bounded by certain arbitrary lines, but in medicine it possesses a wider meaning. The effect of climate upon the human system is the sum of the influences which are connected with many factors. The climate of any locality, professionally speaking, depends upon its temperature, atmospheric vicissitudes, prevailing winds, humidity, its elevation above the sea-level, its proximity to the ocean or oceanic currents, its contiguity to mountains, lakes, rivers, arid areas, soil, drainage, vegetable productions, malaria, general sanitation, and other factors, which we shall briefly consider. . . .

"Temperature is an important factor in climate, and a very large proportion of the profession, who have made a special study of pulmonary diseases, advocate a dry, sunny, and temperate climate for their successful treatment. In view of the great dissemination of phthisis throughout all zones, and the marked percentage of mortality ('nearly two sevenths of all deaths resulting from this disease'), it is exceedingly important that correct opinions should prevail with regard to its treatment. The importance of laboring to check this disease and limit its mortality is an urgent necessity, more especially when there is a growing demand for more attention to the preservation of health, and when the conviction is gaining ground that this is an important function of medical science.

"The modern professional view that a *temperate, dry, and sunny clime* is best adapted to the treatment of a large proportion of pulmonary diseases is one of the most valuable contributions that modern science has made in the treatment of such diseases. It may be stated, as a general rule, that pulmonary diseases are more frequent in cold and changeable climates than in those that are moderately warm and dry. The climatological distribution of pulmonary diseases in the United States is illustrated by the following table from Blodgett's 'Climatology' :

STATES.	Deaths by phthisis.	Per cent. of entire mortality.	Deaths by disease of respiratory organs.	Per cent. of entire mortality.
Maine...................	1,702	22·4	2,074	27·35
New Hampshire..........	924	21·84	1,092	25·82
Vermont................	751	24·09	884	28·24
Massachusetts...........	3,426	17·65	4,418	22·77
Connecticut	968	16·75	1,280	22·31
Rhode Island............	470	20·92	572	25·52
New York...............	7,890	17·04	10,846	23·42
New Jersey	915	14·15	1,176	18·19
Pennsylvania............	3,520	12·33	4,821	16·80
Delaware...............	118	9·76	185	15·30
Maryland...............	1,101	11·44	1,679	17·34
Virginia................	1,616	8·48	3,540	18·56
North Carolina...........	562	5·83	1,688	16·60
South Carolina...........	269	3·34	1,343	16·69
Georgia.................	279	2·80	1,334	13·44
Florida.................	43	4·61	108	11·60

" The above figures do not properly represent the mortality from phthisis originating in this State, for they do not indicate the number of deaths occurring among invalids who came to the State in the last and incurable stages of phthisis. 'From the United States census tables and other statistics, the fact is developed that phthisis in the United States progressively decreases from Maine to Florida. Dr. Lawson, Surgeon-General United States Army, sets down the mortality from tubercular consumption as three times greater in the Northern than in the Southern States.'

" To illustrate one important factor of climate—temperature—I shall quote from the official records of the Signal Service of the United States Army for the months of November, December, January, February, and March, regarding the temperature of certain points recommended as health resorts :

LOCALITY.	Years.	November.	December.	January.	February.	March.	Mean for five months.
Cannes, Mediterranean	3	54·6°	48·8°	48·5°	49·4°	52·8°	50·8°
Nice, Mediterranean	3	53·8	48·5	47·0	48·4	51·8	49·9
Mentone, Mediterranean	3	55·2	50·5	48·8	50·4	53·4	51·6
Nervi, Mediterranean	3	55·2	47·8	46·2	47·8	49·0	49·2
Nassau, New Providence	1	75·7	72·3	72·2	71·9	74·4	73·3
Atlantic City, New Jersey	4	45·3	35·3	32·2	33·2	37·1	36·6
Augusta, northern Georgia	4	54·9	47·6	48·1	49·6	57·0	51·4
Breckenridge, Minnesota	5	17·3	13·4	6·8	13·1	18·9	13·9
Duluth, Minnesota	4	28·8	21·6	12·4	19·2	25·7	21·5
St. Paul, Minnesota	5	28·3	20·0	13·0	19·4	27·6	21·7
Key West, Florida	5	74·5	70·5	70·5	71·7	73·8	72·2
Punta Rassa, Florida	5	69·7	64·8	65·5	65·9	69·8	67·1
Jacksonville, Florida	4	62·1	55·8	56·2	56·9	62·7	58·7
Aiken, South Carolina	5	54·7	46·7	46·4	47·5	56·4	50·3
Los Angeles, California	1	62·1	55·3	54·1	51·6	55·8	56·3

"As thermometric range is a matter of great importance in the causation and treatment of disease, more especially pulmonary affections, we will give the ranges for the cold months at a few points recommended as winter resorts :

LOCALITY.	Years.	November.	December.	January.	February.	March.	Mean for five months.
Atlantic City, New Jersey	4	45°	48°	48°	48°	46°	47°
Augusta, Georgia	4	49	49	51	48	50	49
Minnesota, three stations	4	70	63	57	58	58	61
Florida, three stations	4	35	37	35	33	35	35
Colorado, two stations	4 & 2	68	70	72	58	66	67
Los Angeles, California	1	41	44	35	30	35	37

"To illustrate thermal ranges for one year, we shall quote from the work of Dr. Denison, and add ranges for Florida obtained from Signal Service Reports for corresponding period :

LOCALITY.	Mean monthly range.	Range of monthly means.	Annual means.	Annual range.
Atlantic City, New Jersey..........	41·0°	44·1°	49·7°	89·5°
Norfolk, Virginia.................	44·0	40·7	57·3	89·5
St. Louis, Missouri...............	53·0	57·4	54·2	117·0
Cheyenne, Wyoming........	61·5	48·9	43·6	136·0
Denver, Colorado...............	60·5	53·7	49·2	131·0
Colorado Springs.................	63·5	47·7	46·8	123·0
Florida Peninsula................	20·7	19·2	73·4	50·0

"In forming an opinion regarding climates, many factors must be considered, and altitude is of less importance than temperature, prevailing winds, dry soil, and a low mean relative humidity. 'With regard to the temperature of the air, it is absolutely certain,' says Professor Buhl, 'that it is not the mean temperature of a place which regulates the frequency of catarrh or phthisis, but only the *larger, sudden, and oft-recurring vacillations of temperature,* which the compensatory power of our body is unable to resist. Therefore the temperature of the air and its rapid vacillations must be regarded as exciting causes of inflammatory phthisis.' Atmospheric changes in the North and West are sudden and great; but in Florida they are infrequent and not extreme. At times, what are called 'cold snaps' occur, but their visits are infrequent, and they seldom last over one, two, or three days; and at any time the invalid can take exercise out-of-doors in the middle of the day. Owing to the low level of the land, the absence of snow and ice, and the warmth of the soil for a long distance to the north and west of this State, and the influence of the winds from the Gulf, the northerly and westerly winds are modified and robbed of their harshness and refrigerating effects before they reach Florida, and as a consequence they do not exert the same injurious influence that they do at points to the north and west of this State. In reply to my circular letter, that accomplished observer and meteorologist, Dr. Baldwin, who has been in practice in this city for over forty years, remarks: 'Stormy weather here is comparatively rare, sustaining a proportion of about one storm here to ten at the North and Northwest. The air here is remarkable for its purity, and the temperature renders it possible for the patients to take out-door exercise, so as to inspire the pure air.'

"The subject of winds is a matter of importance in estimating the adaptability of any climate as a health resort. The prevailing winds for the five cold months in Minnesota are from the north, northwest, and west. A reference to the Signal Service Reports shows that four hundred and fifty-three observations were taken during November, December, January, February, and March, at three stations in Minnesota, and north, northwest, and west winds were found blowing from these points one hundred and ninety times. During the same period, and as a result of a similar number of observations at three stations in East Florida, the wind was found blowing from the east, southeast, and northeast, two hundred and twenty-three times. All are aware of the refrigerating effects of northerly and westerly winds in the North and West, and that during their continuance a majority of invalids must of necessity be confined to the house. The Appalachians interfere, to a great extent, with the course of northerly and westerly winds, and by the time they reach this favored land they are robbed of their injurious influences. At times these winds affect the northern and western portions of the State, and several times during the winter slight frosts may occur. During some winters the mercury does not reach 32° Fahr.; as evidence of this, I need but refer to the fact that the lowest temperature in this locality during the past winter was 34°.

"Easterly winds have a bad reputation. . . . In one section of the world, at least, easterly winds are not objectionable, and this is in Florida. On the peninsula, easterly winds are the prevailing ones in the cold months. During November, December, January, February, and March, at three stations in East Florida, easterly winds, east, northeast, and southeast, were found blowing at two hundred and twenty-four observations. Owing to the proximity of the Gulf Stream, with its vast volume of heated water to the east of the coast, the easterly winds are robbed of the harsh and searching properties which characterize them in most localities. As an evidence of the influence of the Gulf Stream, thousands of miles from Florida, even after it has parted with much of its warmth, we need but refer to its effects in modifying the climate of the south of England and France. However objectionable easterly winds may be in other sections, in this evergreen State they are the opposite.

"Precipitation of moisture, in the form of snow and rain, is a subject worth consideration by the invalid. In the North and Northwest the presence of snow renders the taking of exercise a laborious and unpleasant occupation ; and when it melts, and assumes the form of slush, walking entails the risk of wet feet, colds, and inflammatory affections of the lungs. In Florida, the winter is the dry season, and rains are infrequent. Owing to the character of the soil in a majority of places, the rain is absorbed as rapidly as it falls, and within a few minutes after a shower an invalid can walk out without incurring the danger of wetting the soles of his shoes.

"One of the most important factors of climate in the treatment of disease, and more especially affections of the respiratory organs, is a dry climate ; and, under the bare supposition that this or that is a dry climate, invalids are frequently consigned to an unsuitable locality. By some peculiar process of reasoning, the masses have arrived at the conclusion that all cold or elevated localities possess dry climates. But an unprejudiced examination of the subject will soon dispel the illusion. . . .

MEAN RELATIVE HUMIDITY.

LOCALITY.	Year.	November.	December.	January.	February.	March.	Mean for five months.	Mean for five months.
		per ct.	per ct.	per ct.	per ct.	per ct.	per ct.	per ct.
Mentone and Cannes.....	3	71·8	74·2	72·0	70·7	73·3	72·4	
Nassau, New Providence..	1	76·1	72·0	77·0	72·5	68·4	73·2	
Atlantic City, New Jersey.	5	76·9	73·1	80·6	77·3	76·8	78·1	
Breckenridge, Minnesota..	5	76·9	83·2	76·8	81·8	79·5	79·6	74·5
Duluth, Minnesota.......	5	74·0	72·1	72·7	73·3	71·0	72·6	
St. Paul, Minnesota......	5	70·3	73·5	75·2	70·7	67·1	71·3	
Punta Rassa, Florida.....	5	72·7	73·2	74·2	73·7	69·9	72·7	
Key West, Florida.......	5	77·1	78·7	78·9	77·2	72·2	76·8	72·7
Jacksonville, Florida.....	5	71·9	69·3	70·2	68·5	63·9	68·8	
Augusta, Georgia........	5	71·8	72·6	73·0	64·7	62·8	68·9	
Bismarck, Dakota	1	76·6	76·4	77·4	81·6	70·6	76·5	
Boston, Massachusetts....	1	68·0	61·8	66·6	68·2	63·7	65·6	

"To place the subject of mean relative humidity in a clear and unmistakable light, we shall freely use the material furnished by the Signal Service Reports, and not use data of private individuals, which are not always reliable. I will simply remark that, when the atmosphere is saturated with moisture, it is said to contain one hundred per cent., when one-half or one-quarter saturated, fifty or twenty-five per cent., and, when absolutely dry, 0.

". . . Among the factors on which the development and progress of pulmonary diseases certainly depend, dampness of soil is an important one, and merits the consideration of physician and patient. . . . Dry, sandy, or gravelly soils, at a sufficient elevation to insure perfect drainage, will be, *cæteris paribus*, more healthy than a cold, clayey soil, or even a sandy soil, with water near the surface at a higher elevation. And, before a physician advises a patient to visit a given winter resort, he should acquaint himself with the peculiarities of the locality as regards soil and moisture ; for if a cold, moist soil is productive of disease, a locality where such soil exists can not be favorable for the invalid, and should be avoided. Dr. Jones, of St. Paul, Minnesota, says that 'those localities only should be recommended where the soil is sandy, or highly pervious to water, and where rainfall is rapidly absorbed.' These conditions exist to a marked degree in a large portion of this State ; hence its advantages as a climatic resort.

"Malaria is a subject which enters into the discussion of all southern climes, and we unhesitatingly assert that Florida has been misrepresented in this respect. 'It is the custom,' remarks Dr. Lente (page 21), 'of many persons living at Florida resorts, off the St. John's River, to represent for obvious reasons that fever prevails there the year round, and that it is dangerous to resort to it at any time. In this manner they have excited senseless alarm in the minds of those proposing to come to Florida, and have diverted them to other Southern resorts, thus in the end injuring themselves as well as others.' Unprincipled hotel-keepers and runners, and the agents of steamboat and railroad lines leading to other localities, aid more or less in this fraudulent attempt to gain patronage. The bugbear malaria is, in my humble opinion, a prolific source of disease among visitors to Florida. By misrepresentations (to use a mild term) tourists and invalids have been led to believe that the entire water-supply is productive of disease, and as a consequence they refrain from drinking a sufficient quantity of water, or dilute it with poor whisky or brandy, to counteract its bad effects. Interested parties have expatiated so much with regard to the air being charged with malaria in winter, that invalids and patients become alarmed, and as a sequence they daily swallow quinine, and thereby produce nervous or functional derangements. They keep the pure air out of their rooms, breathe an air contaminated with their own breaths and exhalations, and at night assemble in halls and parlors and inhale vitiated air poisoned by their own breaths, and the elements resulting from the combustion of coal-gas and kerosene. They inhale, for hours at a time, air charged with carbonic acid, and shun the pure night air as they would the emanations of the deadly upas-tree. Visitors act imprudently, and as a consequence suffer from nervous derangements, colds, and diarrhœas, which they attribute to malaria or the climate. The cause of slight indispositions affecting visitors, is not malaria, but indulgence at table, change of drinking-water, eating excessive quantities of fruit, or the inhalation of air poisoned by human breaths, or the resultants of the combustion of coal-gas and kerosene, and a deficiency of the pure air that a beneficent Creator has placed everywhere within their reach. If visitors would let quinine and arsenical pills alone, control their appetites, eat moderately, inhale plenty of the salubrious air of the State, and not swelter in heated halls, parlors, and unventilated bedrooms, we should hear less of the bugbear malaria. At various times since 1844, I have navigated the larger streams of this State, visited the Everglades and Lake Okechobee, and almost every bay, inlet, and river, from Cape Sable to the Suwanee River, and for over two months at a time slept in an open boat, with nothing but a simple awning stretched over the boat's boom, and in no instance did my companions or self suffer from malaria or a chill. Before I became a resident of the State, my companions and self were unacclimated, and in no instance were we so foolish as to swallow quinine, arsenic, or alcoholic liquors as antidotes to malaria or chills. I speak from personal observation, experience, and extended inquiry in various portions of the State, and I unhesitatingly assert that the opinion entertained with regard to the prevalence of malaria during the cold months in Florida is unfounded. . . .

"From my observations from Canada to the Gulf of Mexico, I am convinced that febrile diseases assume a milder form, and are more easily cured, in Florida than in States to the north of it. I shall no doubt be met with the reply, 'Look at the waxy complexions and gaunt forms of many Floridians, met with at some of the landings and depots.' I admit the mild impeachment, and can attribute their cachectic condition to bad water, insufficient clothing, unsuitable and uncomfortable habitations, and the improper food they eat from childhood to the grave. In any other State but Florida, they would be the victims of enlarged spleens, cardiac dilatation, chronic gastritis, tuberculosis, dropsical effusions, or albuminuria. But contrast the natives referred to with those who have comfortable homes, sufficient clothing, and who drink pure water and use good and nutritious food ; or with Northern and Western people who have been in the State for years, and the latter will be found to be pictures of health. I admit that in Florida, as everywhere else, there are insalubrious localities, but they should be avoided by strangers. But, to avoid them, interested parties should not listen to the senseless twaddle of irresponsible hotel-keepers, hotel, steamboat, and railroad runners, or strangers suffering from a severe attack of aërophobia. A majority of the cases of illness occurring among visitors in this State, are referable to indulgence at table, drinking impure water, the inhalation of impure air, the American weakness of rushing hither and thither, occupation of unventilated rooms, and a ridiculous system of senseless drugging indulged in by strangers, as a consequence of the advice given by physicians who are ignorant of the climate and its diseases. . . .

"Considering climatic factors, as a result of experience, observation, investigation, and study, we are convinced that Florida presents more attractions and advantages as a winter resort for invalids than any State in the Union. The temperature is favorable, the mean relative humidity is peculiarly adapted to the treatment of all forms of pulmonary disease, the air is salubrious, and in a large portion of the

State dry and bracing ; atmospheric changes are infrequent, and not so great as in other sections east of the Rocky Mountains. Rains are infrequent, and sunshine and fine weather the rule. The State possesses insular, interior, dry, and moist localities, semi-tropical and cooler sections ; and if the nature of any given case should necessitate a change of base, a suitable climate can be reached in a few hours and at a trifling expense.

"For fear of being accused of painting Florida in too bright colors, we shall use the language of others :

"Dr. Charles A. Lee, the learned editor of Copeland's 'Medical Dictionary,' remarks : 'Proceeding south from Canada to Florida, the seasons become more uniform in proportion as their annual temperature increases, and they glide imperceptibly into each other, exhibiting no great extremes. Compared with the other regions of the United States, the Peninsula of Florida has a climate wholly peculiar. The climate is so *exceedingly mild and uniform*, that besides the vegetable productions of the Northern States generally, many of a tropical character are produced. We have already spoken of the mildness of the climate of this region ; it appears to possess an insular temperature not less equable and salubrious in winter than that afforded by the south of Europe, and is, therefore, well adapted to those forms of pulmonary disease, as bronchitis and incipient phthisis, as are benefited by a mild climate. *Mildness and uniformity* are the two distinguishing characteristics of the Florida Peninsula. If we compare the climate of East Florida with the most favored situations on the Continent of Europe, and the islands held in the highest estimation for mildness and equability of temperature, in regard to the mean temperature of winter and summer, that of the warmest and coldest months, and that of successive seasons, we shall find the results generally in favor of the former.' After citing the mean difference of successive months and annual range of a number of climatic resorts in comparison with stations in Florida, he remarks : 'Thus it is easily demonstrated that invalids requiring a mild winter residence have gone to foreign lands in search of what might be found at home—an evergreen land, in which wild flowers never cease to unfold their petals.'

"In discussing the most suitable climates for invalids,

Dr. Wilson, late Medical Inspector of Camps and Hospitals, United States Army, remarks : 'Neither upon the southern coast of France, nor anywhere under the bright Italian skies, can a winter climate be found so equable and so genial to the delicate nerves of most invalids as can be enjoyed in our sanitary stations in Florida.'

"Dr. H. A. Johnson, of Chicago, states : 'I had about fifty patients last winter in Florida and Georgia, and they came back better. Even those in whose lungs cavities existed, were better than they would have been had they staid in Illinois. I will, therefore, advise patients in the latter stages of consumption to go to Florida.' "

To this cumulation of evidence and facts it would seem that nothing more need be added ; but the following suggestions, by Dr. D. H. Jacques, of Fernandina, are inserted because of their great practical value to invalids, and to all those who visit Florida primarily from considerations of health :

"The error into which invalids generally fall lies in supposing that the benefit to the health to be looked for in the South, and especially in Florida, comes directly from the *warmth*. Now, while the warmth is, in itself, a great benefit to a large class of invalids, it is not necessary to come South for that alone, when it can be got at home by artificial means. There are two things, however, which the invalid can not get at the North in winter—at least not in their fullness—in connection with the artificial warmth suggested, *fresh air and sunshine*. These are the things to come South for, and coming for these there will be no disappointment. The fresh air you will get every hour of the day and night. You can not shut it out if you would. As for the sunshine, one bathes in it, breathes it, drinks it in at every pore, till it permeates the whole system ; and there is no medicine like it. It is the invalid's own fault if he does not get enough of it ; and to what end is the South "sunny" if one will shut himself up in a darkened room? An open-air life is easy and pleasant here, the year round. The invalid should, according to his strength, take daily exercise in the open air. Horseback-riding (and Southern saddle-horses are excellent), walking, boating, hunting, and fishing offer, in Florida particularly, diversified recreation, and the evergreen forests of live-oak and magnolia, or of the majestic long-leaved pine, furnish attractive meandering roads and bridle-paths. Our gardens, too, if properly kept, are always attractive, and there is no day in the year in which some flower may not be gathered. That must be a lazy person indeed, who, having the strength to get out, will shut himself up in the house in such a charming climate ; and if one, by reason of weakness, can not take the exercise recommended, let him at least bask in the glorious light of the Southern skies, which floods the broad veranda of every Southern house and penetrates even the most shaded garden-walk.

"Another mistake very generally made by invalids who spend the winter in the South is in returning to the North too early in the spring. When the weather begins to get pretty warm here, and they see the peas in bloom in the garden, and the Irish potatoes up and growing, they get impatient to be at home ; but at home the peas are still in the seed-box, and the potatoes are safe only in the cellar. The cold winds and rains, or the snow and sleet, of a Northern March are terribly trying to one who has spent the winter in a warm climate, and even April is often far too chilly for the invalid's health and comfort.

"With those who are afflicted with diseases of the lungs and bronchial tubes, or are strongly predisposed to consumption, the best and only safe way is to *come here to stay ;* and they must not wait too long before making up their minds and putting their good resolutions into practice. Delays are generally dangerous. In all cases like these they are fatal.

"'But the summers are so hot, and malarial fevers so prevalent and dangerous,' the reader may say. The remark suggests another point. Here are two more popular errors, and they are the complements of those noted in another part of this article. The winter climate is supposed to be uniformly warm and delightful, and to possess some mysterious, hidden healing virtue. Neither of these assumptions is correct. There are always brief periods in winter, even in Florida, in which the weather is anything but lovely, and, as for the mysterious hygienic influences prevailing here, they are, after all, merely pure air and bright sunshine. The supposed extreme heat and unhealthfulness of the summer are equally imaginary. Our summers, particularly in Florida, are long and warm, but instead of being less comfortable and pleasant than those of the North, they are more so, and in the main fully as delightful as the winters. The thermometer often marks a higher temperature in New York or Boston than in Fernandina or Jacksonville, and its variations are much greater there than here. Our nights, even in midsummer, are invariably cool. We never swelter in our bedchambers, through the long dark hours, but sleep sweetly under our blankets, with the cool, fresh air circulating all around us.

"We have chills and fever during the summer and autumn in many localities, on the borders of some of our rivers, creeks, and swamps, and sometimes bilious remittent fevers. They prevail in similar situations at the North and West, and are there of a severer type. We do not advise the invalid to make a permanent home in these malarious localities; and, with these exceptions, the South generally is as salubrious in summer as in winter, and as much so, to say the least, as any Northern region. Florida affords localities without number perfectly free from fevers and all other diseases of local origin. These are found on her numerous sea-islands and along the Atlantic and Gulf coasts, as well as on the more elevated and naturally drained pine-lands of the interior."

CHAPTER XIII.

THE discovery of Florida carries us back almost to the middle ages, and its first permanent settlement antedates that of Jamestown by forty-two years and that of Plymouth by fifty-five years. No other portion of the North American Continent has had so long and so varied a history; and for this reason it will be impossible for me to do more here than give a rapid outline or summary of the principal events.*

According to some authorities, Sebastian Cabot visited the coast of Florida in 1497, only five years after the discovery of America by Columbus; but this is very doubtful, and the received opinion among geographers is that Cape Hatteras was the southern limit of Cabot's voyage. The actual discovery of Florida is generally credited to Ponce de Leon, who, after subjugating the Island of Porto Rico, set out in search of a certain Fountain of Youth which was at first said to be located on the Island of Bimini, and then, not being found there, on another island farther away to the northwest. He left Porto Rico early in 1512, and on the 27th of March reached the coast of Florida at a point a little north of the present site of St. Augustine. It was Easter-Sunday (called *Pascua Florida* in Spanish) when he made land, and partly on this account,

* It need hardly be said that the chief authority for this chapter is the excellent "History of Florida" by George R. Fairbanks, published by the Lippincotts, of Philadelphia.

partly because of the green and flowery appearance of the
country, he gave it the name of FLORIDA, and took possession of it in the name of their Catholic Majesties of Spain.
About two months were spent by Ponce de Leon in visiting different portions of the shores of what he supposed to
be an island, and in exploration of the interior ; but he
found neither the Fountain of Youth nor any indications
of the expected riches ; and finally, discouraged by his ill
success and by the fierce hostility of the natives, he abandoned the quest and returned to Porto Rico, where, in
order to magnify his discovery, he made a flattering report
of its beauty and richness, and obtained the title and privi-
leges of Adelantado of Florida, on condition that he should
conquer and colonize the land.

Following in the track of Ponce de Leon, a pilot named
Diego Miruelo visited Florida in 1516, and, having obtained
some pieces of gold from the natives, spread glowing accounts of the country among his comrades in Cuba. In
1517 Fernandez de Cordova landed upon the coast, but was
so vigorously attacked by a large body of natives that,
after losing a number of his men, he returned to Cuba to
die of his own wounds. Shortly afterward one Alaminos,
who had accompanied the previous expedition, made a descent with three ships, but was beaten off by the vigilant
natives in two attempts to land. These disastrous experi-
ences appear to have dampened for several years the ardor
of the Spanish adventurers, but in 1520 a rich official named
De Ayllon, wishing to capture slaves from among the Indians, landed at a point now in South Carolina but then included in the limits of Florida, and having inveigled a
hundred and thirty of the natives on board his ships, set
sail with them for Hispaniola, and thus won for the Spaniards the implacable hatred of all the Floridian tribes. In
the following year (1521) Ponce de Leon, aroused by the
exploits of Cortes in Mexico, set out to conquer a new em-

pire in Florida ; but he greatly underestimated the power of the natives, who killed large numbers of his followers, drove the rest to their ships, and gave Ponce de Leon himself a wound of which he died shortly afterward in Cuba. Three years later (1524), De Ayllon made another slave-hunting expedition to "Chicora," but this time the natives beat him at his own game, and having lured his party into an ambuscade, massacred two hundred of them and compelled the rest to seek safety in flight.

For several years after these untoward events the attention of Spanish adventurers was absorbed by the splendid achievements of Cortes ; but in 1528 Pamfilo de Narvaez, commissioned to conquer and govern the country, set out from Spain with a great expedition of nearly five hundred men-at-arms and landed a little north of what is now known as Tampa Bay. Aiming at once to explore the interior and to find the stores of precious metals which he was convinced existed somewhere, he left the ships and set out with three hundred men ; but the natives were relentlessly hostile, the long-sought gold was never found, provisions were wholly unobtainable, and after weary wanderings and unspeakable sufferings the expedition perished almost to a man, Narvaez himself having been blown to sea during the night in a boat in which he was sleeping. The chief result of this expedition was the narrative of Cabeça da Vaca, who with three other survivors (all who escaped) became famous "medicine-men" among the Indians, and after seven years made their way westward by land to their countrymen in Mexico. They were the first Europeans whose eyes ever beheld the Mississippi River, and Mr. Fairbanks points out that the credit of this great discovery should be given to Da Vaca rather than to De Soto.

After the ill-fated expedition of Narvaez, Florida enjoyed eleven years of quiet, and then came that expedition of Hernando de Soto which is one of the most famous in the early annals of America. Fresh from the laurels which he had acquired under Pizarro, and laden with his share of the plunder of the Incas, De Soto easily obtained a commission to conquer and govern Florida, and with equal ease secured a numerous company to aid him in the enterprise. On the 25th of May, 1539, his fleet entered a bay which he named Espiritu Santo (now Tampa Bay), and disembarked one thousand men-at-arms and three hundred and fifty horses. Fired by stories which the wily natives here told him of the rich cities and "a great store of christal, gold, and rubies, and diamonds" that lay to the northward, De Soto sent his vessels back, and started boldly forth with his followers upon those painful wanderings which ended only when half a continent had been traversed, and his worn-out body had been anchored to its final resting-place beneath the turbid waters of the Mississippi. The story of those wanderings is one of the most romantic in history or fiction, but it has been so often told as to need no newer version, and limitation of space would prevent anything like justice being done to it here. Hither and thither through that vast territory which borders the Gulf of Mexico, but always bearing westward, the ever-dwindling array accompanied its indomitable leader during three long and weary years, and then, leaving him in his watery grave, the remainder coasted the Gulf in improvised boats, and finally reached the Spanish settlements in Mexico—only three hundred and eleven persons surviving of the thousand who four years before had landed at the harbor of Espiritu Santo.

Religious zeal originated the next attempts to effect a lodgment in Florida. In 1549 four Franciscan friars landed at Espiritu Santo Bay, and tried to penetrate the country; but three of them were incontinently slain by the natives, and the other one abandoned in discouragement the attempt to Christianize unbelievers who backed up their heresy with the hatchet. Ten years later, in 1559, Don Tristan de

Luna sailed from Vera Cruz with a great expedition comprising fifteen hundred soldiers, and a large number of friars burning with zeal for the conversion of the Indians, and landed at the Bay of Pensacola (then called Santa Maria Bay). Almost at the outset a great storm wrecked the entire fleet and destroyed a large part of the provisions; but De Luna sent back for more, marched into the interior, encountered the usual opposition from the natives, lost hundreds of his men by disease, hunger, and fatigue, quarreled bitterly with his subordinate officers, returned discouraged to the Bay of Santa Maria, and was finally ordered home by the Viceroy of Mexico, under whose auspices the expedition had been undertaken.

This abortive enterprise of De Luna's is noteworthy as the last of the Spanish exploring expeditions that visited Florida. Two years after its disastrous end a party of French Huguenots under Jean Ribault came over, and after making land near St. Augustine, coasted northward, entered the St. John's River (which they named the May), and established a short-lived colony at what is now Port Royal. In 1564 a larger party of Huguenots under René de Laudounière landed at the present site of St. Augustine, had a friendly interview with the Indians, and then proceeded northward to the St. John's, where they built Fort Caroline on what is now St. John's Bluff. As was usually the case with the French colonists in America, the Huguenots succeeded in establishing amicable relations with the Indians; but Laudounière's men were soldiers rather than workmen; they were not prudent in the management of their supplies, and in 1565 they would have been compelled to abandon their undertaking but for the timely arrival of an English fleet under Sir John Hawkins, who not only generously supplied their more pressing wants but sold them a small vessel, and a good store of powder and ball. Even this timely aid, however, did not dissuade the colonists

from their fixed determination to return to France ; but on
the very day fixed for their departure (August 28, 1565) an
expedition that had been sent out under Ribault for their
relief arrived in the St. John's with five hundred men,
besides some families of artisans.

In the mean time, stirred to fresh endeavor by what
they regarded as the intrusion of the French, the Spaniards
had determined to make one more effort to secure the possessions that had already cost them so dear ; and a great
expedition under the command of Menendez, a naval officer
of considerable distinction, set sail from Cadiz on the 1st
of July, 1565. This expedition comprised in all about
twenty-six hundred persons, and about two thirds of
them reached the coast of Florida, a little south of St. Augustine, on the 28th of August, the same day that Ribault's
fleet came to anchor off the mouth of the St. John's.
Learning from the Indians of the presence of the French,
Menendez coasted northward, and on the 4th of September
came in sight of Ribault's vessels, which immediately put
to sea and escaped their assailants. After a fruitless chase
of the flying enemy, Menendez returned to St. Augustine
(which he named in honor of the day of his arrival upon
the coast), disembarked his forces, and commenced fortify-
ing. These proceedings being reported to Ribault, the latter gathered all his available force, including most of the
garrison of Fort Caroline, and set sail on September 10th
with the idea of attacking Menendez before he could complete his defenses ; but a terrible tempest overtook him,
drove his vessels far down the coast, and wrecked them
between Mantanzas and Mosquito Inlet.

Suspecting that the French fleet had put to sea, and
that even if it had escaped shipwreck several days must
elapse before it could make harbor again, Menendez determined to attack Fort Caroline, and on September 17th set
out overland at the head of five hundred men. His success

was only too complete. The French were taken by surprise, and almost without resistance the Spaniards rushed into the fort and began an indiscriminate massacre which, for a time, spared not even women and children. Only seventy persons in all escaped, and some of the prisoners were hung upon the neighboring trees with the cynical inscription over them, "Not as Frenchmen, but as Lutherans."

Having repaired and strengthened the fort (which he named San Mateo), and garrisoned it with three hundred men, Menendez returned in triumph to St. Augustine, and there learned of the unfortunate position of the shipwrecked Ribault. Proceeding to Mantanzas Inlet with a party of his men, he compelled the French to surrender, partly by promises and partly by threats, and then when they were helplessly at his mercy had them cruelly massacred to a man, not even sparing the gallant Ribault. "The atrocity of the deed," says Mr. Fairbanks, "struck all Europe with horror, even in that day ; and the shocking story has been perpetuated over three hundred years, giving the name of Menendez a stain of infamy which time can not wipe out."

Thus ended in one of the bloodiest tragedies of history the efforts of the French to establish a colony on the southern coast of America, and for many years the Spaniards were left in undisputed possession of their territory. Not quite undisturbed, however, for they soon quarreled with the natives, and found the latter very different antagonists from those more effeminate races whom their countrymen had encountered in Mexico and Peru. Even at this early date the Florida Indians exhibited the hardy and obstinate courage which distinguished them at a later period, and they kept the soldiers of Menendez everywhere close shut up in their forts. Harassed by these troubles and by disaffection among his own men, Menendez exhibited an indomitable perseverance, and, besides gradually enlarging and strengthening St. Augustine, established other posts at

10

various points, sent out several exploring parties, and secured a foothold in Florida which was never afterward lost. Finally, in the spring of 1567, believing that the interests of the settlements would be advanced by his going to Spain, he set sail in a small vessel of twenty tons burden which he had caused to be built.

During his absence occurred one of the most notable of all known instances of that law of retributive justice which is said to operate in human affairs. The leaders of the French nation had exhibited a singular indifference to the sad fate of Ribault and his comrades, and the event appeared to have been forgotten if not forgiven ; but in the breast of an obscure captain named Dominic de Gourgues an insatiable thirst for revenge was aroused, and he devoted himself to its gratification. Supplementing his own resources by borrowing money from his friends, he procured three small vessels, enlisted one hundred and eighty-four men, and set sail on the 22d of August, 1567. Good fortune appeared to wait upon his enterprise in its every stage. He secured the hearty coöperation of the Indians, completely surprised Fort San Mateo, and captured it with even greater ease than Menendez had captured its predecessor, Fort Caroline. Most of the garrison fell under the swords of the Frenchmen or the clubs of the Indians ; and the prisoners, being led to the spot where Menendez had caused the Huguenots to be hung in 1565, were suspended beneath an inscription which De Gourgues had caused to be burned with a red-hot iron upon a tablet of pine : "I do this, not as unto Spaniards, nor as to outcasts, but as to traitors, thieves, and murderers ! "

For a period of about a hundred years after this dramatic achievement, the history of Florida offers scarcely a single event over which the chronicler finds it worth while to linger. Menendez returned to his colony in the spring of 1568 and reëstablished the confidence that had been impaired by De Gourgues's inroad ; but he soon tired of his profitless position, and going again to Spain he was in 1574 appointed captain-general of the Spanish fleet. Little progress was made in the settlement of the country, and the importance of Florida greatly diminished in the public estimation. In 1586 Sir Francis Drake, returning from a freebooting expedition in the Spanish Main, captured and burned St. Augustine ; but it was speedily reoccupied and rebuilt, though its growth was so slow that as late as 1647 it only contained three hundred families. In 1665 a noted buccaneer captain named John Davis made a descent on St. Augustine with seven small vessels, and again pillaged and burned the unfortunate town.

Toward the end of the seventeenth century began those hostile demonstrations between the Spanish colonists in Florida and the adjacent English colonists in South Carolina and Georgia which furnish one of the most dismal chapters in American history. According to the claim of Spain, Florida embraced the entire territory as far north as Virginia, and westward to the Mississippi. When, therefore, the English began to settle in the Carolinas the Spaniards looked upon it as an unwarrantable intrusion, and, moreover, believed that these settlers aided and abetted the pirates who preyed upon Spanish commerce in all these seas. The ill feeling gradually deepened until, in the year 1670, the Spaniards sent an expedition to attack the settlements on the Ashley River, which, however, returned without having accomplished anything. Two years later another expedition was sent which inflicted great damage upon the infant settlements and perpetrated atrocities that aroused the bitterest indignation. For a time, however, the Carolinians were too feeble to retaliate, and the Spaniards took advantage of the lull to begin colonizing the western coast of Florida. In 1696 a fort was built and a settlement established at Pensacola, and a little later St. Mark's was founded.

But by this time the English colonists had become conscious of increased strength, and the ambitious Moore having succeeded the cautious Archdale in the government of Carolina, advantage was taken of a rupture between England and Spain, and in 1702 a sea and land expedition was organized whose object was nothing less than the complete conquest of Florida. After capturing and burning St. Augustine, Governor Moore failed to capture the fort, and was compelled to retreat without achieving any of the objects with which he had set out. His abortive expedition cost the colony of Carolina six thousand pounds, and led to the issue of the first paper money ever circulated in America. The Indians were now introduced into the conflict on both sides, the Florida tribes making an unsuccessful incursion into Carolina in 1702, while in the following year, with the aid of the Creeks, Governor Moore attacked and almost destroyed the Indian towns under Spanish protection in what is now known as Middle Florida.

From this time on a state of affairs prevailed something like that which used to exist on the Scottish border—forays and counter-forays occurring at brief intervals, and the hostilities on both sides being carried on with all the atrocities of savage warfare. The year 1706 saw a joint French-Spanish descent on Carolina which was thwarted by the skill of the Governor of the latter province; in 1708 the Carolinians made a devastating raid through all Northern Florida; in the year 1714 there was a general outbreak of the Indian tribes in Carolina, which was said to have been instigated by Spanish emissaries; and when driven out of Carolina several powerful tribes of these Indians took refuge in Florida, whence they maintained a constant and harassing warfare upon the Carolina settlements.

In the mean time hostilities had begun between the Spanish colonists in West Florida and the French colonists, in what was then called Louisiana. In 1718 the

French capture the Spanish fort at Pensacola ; the Spaniards straightway retake it ; the French capture it again in the following year, and, thinking to put an end to the matter, destroy the fort and burn the town. Nothing daunted, the Spaniards begin another settlement on Santa Rosa Island in 1722, and a few years later rebuild Pensacola.

Added to the other sources of ill feeling between the Spanish and English colonists, was the fact that the former afforded a refuge and protection to the fugitive slaves of the latter. This had been a fruitful cause of complaint from the beginning, and soon a further grievance was found in the fact that absconding debtors and other criminals found a convenient asylum in Florida. In 1725 an unsuccessful attempt was made to settle these difficulties amicably ; and in 1727 Colonel Palmer, with a body of three hundred militia and some friendly Indians, carried fire and sword over the entire province up to the very gates of St. Augustine.

The settlement of the new colony of Georgia by General Oglethorpe in 1732 was resented by the Spaniards as a further encroachment upon their territory, but, as it increased very materially the strength of the English colonists, the latter were not likely to yield to remonstrances. Continual bickerings ensued, negotiations between England and Spain led to no result, and finally, in 1740, Oglethorpe gathered a force of regulars and militia, marched to St. Augustine, and, after bombarding the fort uselessly, returned to his own province. Now came the turn of the Spanish Governor, Monteano ; so, gathering a force of some three thousand men and thirty-six vessels, he set out from St. Augustine with the determination to strike a decisive blow at the new English colony. At first he was successful, but before he had done much damage he was baffled by a neat stratagem on the part of Oglethorpe, and retreated in deep chagrin. The next year (1743) Oglethorpe again invaded Florida, and offered battle under the very walls of St. Augustine, but, having no ordnance, and the Spanish refusing to fight in the open, he was compelled to retire without accomplishing anything. Fortunately, in 1748 a treaty of peace between England and Spain caused a suspension of these chronic hostilities between the rival colonies. Upon the renewal of the war in 1762, Havana fell into the hands of the English ; and as Spain wanted Cuba and England wanted Florida, an exchange was effected by which on the 10th of February, 1763, the provinces of East and West Florida passed into the possession of the British crown.

Under British rule Florida enjoyed a period of peace and growth and prosperity such as it had never before known. At the time of the cession, the Spaniards had held the country for upward of two hundred and fifty years, yet the interior was still almost wholly unexplored, the settlements were little more than forts, and the entire population amounted to only six or seven thousand, of whom many left the country on the change of flags. The first English Governor (General James Grant) took immediate steps to promote the settlement of the province and to develop its resources, and his efforts were cordially seconded by the public-spirited gentlemen who had been induced to settle there. Roads were laid out, bounties were offered for indigo and other productions, immigration was encouraged in every possible way, and peace was made with the Indians. Sir William Duncan and Dr. Turnbull brought out fifteen hundred Greeks and Minorcans and settled them at New Smyrna ; and, though the enterprise ended disastrously, it had a good effect in calling attention to the industrial opportunities afforded by the country.

In the War of the Revolution Florida took no part, but it afforded an asylum for many thousand loyalists from Carolina and Georgia, and the British used it as the base for their operations against Savannah. Upon the breaking out of hostilities between England and Spain in 1779, De Galvez, the Spanish Governor of Louisiana, captured Baton Rouge, which was then within the limits of West Florida, and in 1781 attacked and captured Pensacola. At the conclusion of the general peace in 1783, England, feeling that Florida thus isolated was no longer worth retaining, exchanged it for the Bahama Islands, and the Spanish flag once more floated over the peninsula.

With the passage of the country under foreign domination most of the English settlers abandoned their homes and went to the " States "; and a truly Spanish lethargy settled down over the land, broken only by Indian wars, and by the occasional attempts of " filibusters " to get possession of the country and erect a " republic." In 1795 Spain ceded to France all that portion of Florida lying west of the Perdido River ; and when, in 1803, Louisiana was sold to the United States, all this valuable territory passed into the possession of the latter power. In 1812 Fernandina was captured by a band of " patriots " whose actions are thought to have been connived at by the United States Government ; and in 1814, the British having sent a fleet to Pensacola and manned the forts, General Jackson stormed the town and destroyed the fortifications. Again, in 1818, General Jackson invaded Florida in order to chastise the troublesome Seminole Indians ; and finally, by a treaty concluded on the 22d of February, 1819, and ratified on the 19th of February, 1821, the Floridas were ceded to the United States.

Upon the change of flags the administration of affairs devolved for a time upon the military authorities ; but on March 3, 1822, Congress passed an act establishing the Territory of Florida, and the machinery of free representative government was soon in regular working order. Several counties were organized, the capital was located at the former Indian settlement of Tallahassee, and immigration began to move in.

The settling of the country would have proceeded much more rapidly but for the difficulties presented by the Indians, who were in possession of the best lands, and extremely jealous of their rights. It was the desire of the whites that the Indians should be removed, like the Creeks, to some reservation west of the Mississippi, and negotiations to this end were begun in 1828. Several of the chiefs, including Osceola, were bitterly opposed to such a change ; but the majority were willing at least to consider it, and a delegation was appointed to visit and report upon the proposed reservation. Owing to procrastination and delays, this delegation did not set out upon their journey until September, 1832, and upon their return in March, 1833, their report was favorable. But in the mean time the opposition among the Indians had become more violent, and many of them refused to accept the recommendation of the delegated chiefs. The United States authorities, holding that the Indians were bound under the terms of the treaty to accept this recommendation, determined to force them to do so ; and thereupon began the longest, bloodiest, and costliest war that was ever waged between whites and Indians in America.

This war—known in history as the Seminole War—was too complex in its operations and too varied in its vicissitudes to be dealt with in detail here. An admirably clear and minute account of it will be found in the closing chapters of Fairbanks's " History of Florida," and with less space than is there devoted to it justice can not be done to the subject. Beginning with the appalling massacre of Major Dade's command on the 28th of December, 1835, the war raged unceasingly until August, 1842. The Indians fought with amazing pertinacity and courage, and the result of the campaigns of 1835 and 1836 was decidedly in their favor. After that they gradually lost ground ; but not until General

Worth took command in 1841, and inaugurated the policy of pushing the campaign in summer as well as winter, and of tracking them to their swamp fastnesses, was their spirit quenched or the vigor of their resistance broken. When the deadly conflict at length ended, most of the Indians who had escaped death had been transported beyond the Mississippi, and only an insignificant remnant of the once powerful Seminole tribe was left in a reservation at the southern end of the peninsula, where their descendants still support themselves frugally by hunting, fishing, and the raising of cattle.

But, though triumphant in the end, the United States had paid dearly for the victory. Six or seven generals had been employed with varying degrees of ill fortune, the lives of fourteen hundred and sixty-six regular soldiers, of whom two hundred and fifteen were officers, had been lost, and the expenditures had amounted to upward of nineteen million dollars, a vastly larger sum then than now. And worse than all, perhaps, the growth of Florida had been set back fully a generation. Plantations that dated from the earliest settlement of the country had been broken up, agricultural occupations had been almost completely suspended, hundreds of families had been either butchered or driven off, and immigrants were deterred from venturing where the conditions of life were so precarious. Of the many cruel misfortunes to which Florida has been subjected, the Seminole War was probably the most disastrous in its effects.

For the later history of Florida—that which has occurred within our own remembrance—we must content ourselves with a few dates which may be useful for reference, and for which the last edition of Appletons' " Cyclopædia " is our authority.

Florida was admitted into the Union as a State on the 3d of March, 1845. An ordinance of secession from the Union was passed on the 10th of January, 1861, by a con-

vention which had assembled on the 3d.   On the 7th Fort
Marion, the arsenal at St. Augustine, and the Chattahoochee
arsenal were seized by order of the State authorities ; and
on the 12th, the navy-yards and forts at Pensacola were
taken.   Early in the following year (1862) Fernandina,
Jacksonville, St. Augustine, and other places on the east
coast, were retaken by the national forces, and held to the
close of the war.   Restrictions on commercial intercourse
with Florida were removed by a proclamation of President
Johnson dated April 29, 1865, and on July 13th William
Marvin was appointed provisional Governor.   On October
10th was held an election of delegates to a State Conven-
tion, which assembled in Tallahassee on the 25th, and on
the 28th repealed the ordinance of secession.   Subsequently
a Legislature and State officers were elected, to whom the
civil authority was transferred in January, 1866.   Under
the reconstruction measures of Congress in 1867 Florida
was made a part of the Third Military District, of which
Major-General Pope was appointed commander.   A conven-
tion to reorganize the State government was authorized by
vote of the people in November, 1867.   It assembled at
Tallahassee on the 20th of January, 1868, and subsequently
framed a new Constitution, which was ratified by the people
in May.   At the same election State officers and a Legislature were chosen.   The Legislature convened on June 1st,
and adopted the fourteenth amendment to the Federal
Constitution, in consequence of which Florida was recognized as a State by the General Government.   On July 4th
of that year the government was transferred to the State
authorities.

   The growth of the population of Florida has been as
follows : in 1830, 34,730 ; in 1840, 54,477 ; in 1850, 87,445 ;
in 1860, 140,424 ; in 1870, 187,748 ; in 1880, 271,864.

CHAPTER XIV

FLORIDA FOLKS AND FAMILIES.

FLORIDA is rapidly becoming a Northern colony. The tide of immigration to this State is large and steadily increasing, and is beyond doubt soon to assume immense proportions, and the immigrants as a class are unusually intelligent people. Nearly all of native American birth, the foreign-born element is of insignificant dimensions at this date. (See Appendix, note 29.)

Generally described, they are people who read—and continue to read—and are well posted on the resources and advantages of the various sections of the United States, and know exactly what they desire. They come here with a fixed purpose, that only requires a short period of local observation and examination of the precise soil and climate for their proposed special enterprise. It is no mining-excitement attraction here, with visions of gold to be picked up in lumps, but a healthy feeling of hope of a genial climate, and a slow but steadily increasing wealth made from the soil. There is a total absence of the wild, anxious, eager class of excited, young, single men arrayed in flannel shirts, broad felt hats, top-boots, armed with knives and immense navy revolvers, their brains filled with visionary ideas of suddenly acquired wealth, that are so plentiful in Western countries and mining regions.

The immigrants to this section are the extreme opposite; they are, as a class, middle-aged men, mostly with families, evidently of good average education, well dressed, of quiet, deliberate demeanor and a fixed purpose ; just the class that establish the very best of peaceable, healthy, sound, safe, and in every way desirable communities. Such people seldom emigrate, and always improve themselves and their community wherever they reside.

All States and sections are represented in this stream of immigrants. There are colonies from Wisconsin, Michigan, western New York, New Hampshire, Connecticut, Indiana, and Ohio. The latter State appears to have the largest representation here ; they are largest in numbers, and more of them are to be found occupying positions of trust, influence, and general confidence, than of any other State. New England as a region is largely represented—quite a New England winter garden—and it is mainly New England energy, brains, and solid capital that are now developing the State. Nearly all the railroads, steamboats, mills, factories, and the like, are directly or indirectly the product of New England or New York brain-work and capital.

One very noticeable feature of the population here is the small number of foreign-born people, especially of the Irish race. I have met but about a dozen of the latter in all parts of the State, and but one of them was of the regulation typical "son of the sod," having the pure brogue. All whom I met were occupying good positions, and appeared to be in prosperous circumstances—far better than the average of Irish people in the North. Germans are also few in actual numbers, but there are more of them than of any other class of foreign birth, probably more than of all other foreign-born combined ; and, as is the rule with that excellent, industrious, thrifty, frugal, peaceable race, they are all doing well, and generally own good homes, shops, stores, saloons, or gardens. The Swedes, of whom there is a colony in Upsala, near Sanford, are a very prosperous, industrious, healthy, and enterprising class, and make excellent colonists.

There are many natives of Old England residing in all portions of the State. Hale, hearty, thrifty, and industrious, their families and homes are pleasing evidences of prosperity and the sound judgment typical of the solid English land-owner the world over.

Of Chinese there are very few, though there ought to be many of them in Florida. I believe in the "heathen Chinee"; his neatness, thrift, and excellent unobtrusiveness, always quiet and orderly, are in every way commendable; and everywhere I found the people favoring Chinese immigration—in fact, a general desire to replace the colored labor with Chinese labor. Colored labor for the house, field, grove, or garden, while easy to control, is very far from satisfactory. It is always uncertain, indolent, and negligent, unless closely and incessantly watched. As a class, the colored servants are given to falsehood and petty theft, are liable to leave you without a word of warning just when badly needed, and are wasteful of your stores and provender. There are exceptions, but such are few, and can not be relied on; their only praiseworthy quality is their easy good-nature. The silent, neat, careful, polite Chinese are far preferable. (See Appendix, note 30.)

The least desirable of American immigrants are, as a class, from "Alabawma." They are the real and ideal "cracker," mostly very poor, ignorant, shiftless, improvident, conceited, and lazy; and they are about the only class of immigrants to Florida that are useless. They are to this State what the low class of Europeans are to the Northern States—a damage and a hindrance. There are excellent people in Alabama, and some very worthy families come here from there, but the lower class of them as a rule are not very beneficial to any State. The best immigrants from the Southern States are from Georgia; in fact, the average Georgian is a shrewd, thrifty, sober, industrious individual —a regular Southern Yankee. They are good citizens if at all educated, and are nearly always on the side of law, order, and progress.

The native Florida "crackers" are few in numbers, and are rapidly becoming fewer. They have but little influence in the affairs of the counties or in the several communities; but, singularly enough, they have a preponderance in the

A Country Cart.

State Legislature, owing to the manner in which the representatives are chosen, and their influence there is not very beneficial, to say the least. Time and immigration, however, will change all this condition of things. The best class of these "crackers" are the cattle-herders, a tough, rough, and dare-devil, good-natured crowd, to be sure, but active, and more wide-awake than that class generally are, especially those found near the settlements.

In the northern counties dwell the old-time aristocracy of the State, the class who were the intelligent, fashionable society of the South. They are, however, few in numbers at present, are exclusive and proud, and yet at heart are very worthy, kind-hearted, and truly good people. Their only fault is that they were born, reared, and trained under absolutely different social conditions from those which now obtain, and they can not learn to fully accustom themselves to their new life and surroundings. They mean well, and deserve respectful sympathy. They can not learn the Chicago-New England spirit of progression, and it is useless to expect it of them—that is, of that generation now passing its latter day of prime. It is to be hoped that the generation now growing into manhood may better understand, and be more disposed to take, an active part in the "manifest destiny" of the State. It must realize that in Florida, as elsewhere, "the old order of things passes away, giving place to the new."

It is entirely useless—notwithstanding all arguments to the contrary—for the Northern immigrant to expect to become an intimately familiar guest and neighbor of the old residents and aristocrats of the South. They will tell you they "welcome you," and if you are a gentlemanly, peaceable, respectable citizen, they *do* welcome you, after a fashion ; but it is the welcome extended to a polite stranger—sincere but cool, honest but always formal. It is vastly different from the state of society at the West, and for vastly different reasons. In the West is found no former "old-time" society ; the settlers there are themselves the original and only society ; and, as is always the case with sensible people when they meet in far-off places, they are sociable, hearty, and cordial toward one another. There all are deemed respectable members of society until convicted of crime or misdeed. Here in the South, the older residents do not, and I believe can not, understand that sentiment of social intercourse and bluff, hearty good-fellowship which is felt among the peoples of the East, North, and West ; and the new-comer might as well give up any hope or resentment in the matter. It is caused by the laws of human nature that make the Esquimau, the Chinese, the Russian,

the Turk, the Frenchman, the Englishman, the New-England-
lander, and the Southerner, each believe his country, people,
and customs to be the best. It can not be changed in one
generation. The immigrant from other regions must simply wait patiently until there is a sufficient number of other
immigrants settled near him to form a congenial circle of
intimates. In the mean time, one thing is sure : in health
or sickness, in trouble or disaster, you will always receive
kindly attention, care, and assistance from these excellent
people, if you at all deserve it.

The rush of immigration is to the semi-tropical central
Florida regions along the Transit Railroad, the St. John's
River, and the coasts ; these are the localities where the
new settlers are pouring in, clearing lands, fencing, building
homes, setting out groves, planting gardens, building railroads, mills, factories, etc. Putnam, Sumter, Volusia, Orange, Brevard, Marion, Alachua, Manatee, and all the counties of that extensive section, are the chosen spots of the
new-comers ; and that section will soon be the most populous and powerful portion of the State. In none of these
counties will the new-comer find himself far away from
congenial companionship and friendly associations.

Churches are being built in all the new towns and hamlets, and nowhere is religion more strictly observed than in
Florida. In all the older towns and communities they have
as attractive and as well-attended churches as anywhere in
our country. Schools are scarce, but are increasing. The
State has a good school law, and the school system is
gradually developing into a strong and vigorous condition ;
but it will take time, more settlers, and care to make it
anything like Indiana, Illinois, or such States of special
educational facilities. ' The State Legislature, too, must
pass under the control of a class of law-makers who have
lived under and seen the effect of a liberal support of public schools. Even if they were excellent legislators on gen-

eral questions and requirements, most of the present law-makers of both political parties know little or nothing of the perfect educational systems of the North and West. It is not at all a question of their political views. (See Appendix, note 31.)

But there are other drawbacks, for which the Legislature or people can not be held to blame. In the first place, the number of children is so small, and the territory of the districts necessarily so large, that the schools are lightly attended. In the next place, the wages paid the teachers are too low to make it an object for first-class instructors to seek positions here, except an occasional person who has come here for health and light employment; and even these soon find more lucrative occupations. In the older, larger cities, like Tallahassee, Tampa, Key West, Pensacola, and all old-settled places, especially Jacksonville, there are very good schoolhouses, good teachers, and good methods; but the terms should be made longer, and the pay to all teachers considerably increased.

There is comparatively little crime in Florida; property and life are nowhere safer than here. This is very noticeable where the homes are few and far between, and of such light construction that they might easily be entered by the burglar or more desperate villain. Such scoundrels are remarkably few. The laws are generally well enforced on all such evil-doers; and where these fail or are too dilatory, a rough-and-ready popular justice is apt to perform their work. The judges and justices as a class compare favorably with those of other States.

Much has been said and written about crimes committed in this State as the result of color and politics. It is stoutly asserted by some that many lives have been lost and much property destroyed from these causes; and it is as stoutly denied by others that such things have been done. I believe there have been such crimes committed, and that politics has been the cause of much trouble, loss of life, and damage to property ; but I have not included any of these acts in my views about scarcity of crime, for I do not regard political outrages, however atrocious, as belonging to the common-law class of crimes, great or small. They are different, resulting from entirely different causes, in which it is fair to suppose the followers of both political beliefs were in some degree in fault, and that the remedy and total avoidance can only be brought about by intelligent, friendly understanding of the rights of all. Time, education, and commercial prosperity only will prevent these political misunderstandings and crimes. And it must be remembered that it is but a few years since a great war, with its embittering, desolating effects, was raging, and that this region was a battle-ground, and the participants in these disgraceful political quarrels were engaged on the two sides of that great struggle. But happily such animosities, such disturbances, and such unhappy influences are rapidly passing away, and everywhere the political is giving way to the enterprising commercial interest. The elections of 1880 were undoubtedly as peaceably conducted in Florida as in any other State of our Union. The misdoings, if any, were such as time, better laws, and sound common-sense will eradicate and effectually put an end to.

The negroes, who form so prominent an element in the other Southern States, are less numerous and less conspicuous in Florida than elsewhere ; though of course, as they perform most of the manual labor and are almost the only attainable domestic help, they are found everywhere in greater or smaller numbers. Here, as always, they are a picturesque and amusing class, and one of the most interesting episodes of my life in Florida is connected with a period of several months during which I was in continual and close contact with large numbers of them in the construction of the South Florida Railroad. Holding official relations with this enterprise in several capacities, I was at one time commissary, and this, of course, involved almost constant relations with the laborers. These laborers, who were all negroes, except the mechanics, numbered about six hundred, and were mostly Georgians, who came in gangs especially for the railway service.

They were a strange set of beings. The pleasure-seeker who visits a minstrel entertainment in the North may suppose he is seeing a comical creature of the imagination, but it is not so ; in fact, the most grotesque acting or the most distorted lingual expressions that the " nigger delineator " ever perpetrated on the stage is far from equaling the reality as seen and heard in a camp of negro laborers. Such wonderful jokes, such crushing retorts, such verbal pyrotechnics, and such uproarious shouts of laughter, can never be heard elsewhere ; and the accompanying gestures and pantomime are often more original and characteristic than the language itself. The only drawback to the amusement of listening at these gatherings is the shocking profanity and disgustingly vile language in which the negroes indulge. The most simple remarks in their social conversation are commonly interlarded with a number of oaths and foul words that is positively startling. They seem to think that it strengthens and emphasizes their conversation ; and there can be no doubt that the practice is partly due to their association with low whites, and to a desire to " talk as big as the white folks."

The camp reached, after a day's labor, all hands would speedily bring out their stowed-away " grub-boxes." Fires were quickly burning, and soon a multitude of skillets were ranged over the coals, in each a chunk of fat side-pork ; this, and a cupful of boiled " grits " or hominy, with molasses for sauce, and a cup of coffee, is their usual meal. Sometimes they vary this with a can of salmon, or a fresh fish caught in the innumerable lakes, or a gopher caught in the woods, and made into soup. (This last is a species of large land-turtle ten to twenty inches across its back-shell, living in deep holes which it burrows in the ground. They are very plentiful, and their cavernous-looking retreats are everywhere seen here. They are incorrectly called "gophers" by the negroes and natives.) They also frequently make up batches of corn or wheat-flour cake, to be eaten with molasses. Pork, however, is their chief article of food ; they ate it three times a day, and averaged about five pounds each in seven days.

Meals over, the fun began. Musical instruments, consisting mainly of banjoes, fiddles, and guitars, began thrumming everywhere ; soon a jig would strike up, all the feet (such feet !) would begin beating time, and before very long some dancer would bound forward and commence a shuffle, perhaps two or three others joining in, and keep it up until they dropped from sheer exhaustion. And the singing, especially after sunset, was always a noticeable feature, frequently quite fine. When two or three voices start— joined in one of their countless melodies, like nothing heard elsewhere—it is very attractive. Generally all hands in camp would join in the chorus ; and when heard a little distance off through the pine-woods, it was strangely beautiful and often solemnly sweet.

As a class, the genuine, pure blacks are always the best laborers ; they work hardest, most willingly, honestly, and efficiently, always performing the most labor in a day, and making least trouble to the foremen and officers. The genuine African is an excellent, worthy worker. But it is different with "them yeller fellers." These are always more dainty, more quarrelsome ; they are the class that carry watches and revolvers, always shirk, always do things a trifle different from the way ordered, always quarrel with their foremen about their time, about their rations, about their pay, and about everything. They are up to all manner of tricks, giving their names differently to their foremen, the commissary clerk, and the paymaster, creating all sorts of unexpected confusion and disputes, requiring close care and watching, greatly increasing the duties of the overseers. If there was any mischief or deviltry in the camp, we nearly always discovered that a mulatto was at the bottom of it.

The 10th of each month was pay-day, the great day' with the darkeys, and a busy day at the pay-table. It was a regulation holiday with the gangs ; not a bit of work would they perform, but at an early hour they would gather at the pay-office—scuffling, dancing, shouting, singing—a happy crowd indeed. One dollar per day was the regular standard price ; the colored "spikers" (men who drive the track-spikes) and sub-foremen received a dollar and twenty-five to a dollar and forty cents per day. The older darkeys of about forty or fifty years, especially the genuine blacks, were, as I have said, by far the best laborers ; they usually kept records to "tallies" of their labor, and always were correct. But the young darkeys, especially the "yeller fellers," the class that loves to dance and sing, never averaged over fifteen days' labor in the month, and were always disputing their time-accounts.

After pay-day they would strangely be missing—that is, the younger class—but a hunt through the woods would reveal their whereabouts ; under the trees and in out-of-the-way thickets they were to be found in small, quiet, earnest-faced little groups—gambling ! The darkey is a most inveterate gambler, the equal of the Chinaman or Indian in this vice. The Chinaman will gamble himself away—that, is he will bind himself to work for his winning opponent for certain lengths of time ; the Indian will gamble away his horses, tepees (or wigwams), squaws, and papooses ; but the darkey will gamble all he has earned by months of hard labor, and all he can steal from his hard-working fellow-laborers.

After two or three days the gangs would begin to return to work, silent for a day or two, dispirited, disgusted, dead-broke—in fact, "played out."

Two or three of them wouldn't return to work—no, sir ! *They* put on airs, joked, smoked cigars, ate melons, 'bananas, etc., and went on a trip down the river to Jacksonville, bought watches, canes, etc. *They* were the winning gamblers.

The pay-rolls exhibited a lamentable condition of ignorance among them, less than ten per cent. signing their names. About thirty or forty whites of the poorer class of natives were employed on the gangs, and the lack of edu-

OUT FOR A DRIVE.

cation was even greater among this class, for less than four per cent. could sign their names. In reply to the request to "sign your name," the old darkeys always politely replied, "I can't write, sir "; but the whites would, in a shamed manner and low tone, say, "You jest put it down, please, my hand is hurted and sort o' weak like—ahem!" or they would remark that their hand was "so dirty." I have seen them slyly wrap a bit of cloth or a handkerchief about their hand while awaiting their turn, so as have an excuse for not signing.

As a rule, the young blacks can read and write, and are very proud of the accomplishment. They seize the pen and delight to attach their autographs (generally of three or four names, the Williams and Johnsons greatly in the majority) in an airy, rapid, careless sort of style ; it always profoundly impresses the assembled lookers-on, and adds a dignity to labor that is quite overpowering to witness. The blacks are always solid friends to all educational improvements. In all their camps were individuals who did the reading and writing ; read the newspapers aloud, read the letters received by their less intelligent companions, and wrote the letter and postal-card replies—this class are "immense" on letters. Frequently these scribes (always young) make a pretty good thing of it in this amanuensis service.

It was often a group quite worth seeing to visit one of their camps in the evening. There the large fire of pitch-pine knots was blazing brightly, lighting up their small collection of queer little huts built of railroad-ties, in the tall pine-woods, making a good picture indeed, with the entire party all grouped about one of their number—all intently listening to him reading the latest newspaper ; they always insisted that he should read it *all*. Such intense attention, eager eyes, and various attitudes, such quiet, earnest facial expressions, and such costumes—or lack of costumes—all frequently formed pictures that would delight an artist.

And after the reading was completed, then to hear the Babel of arguments, opinions, and comicalities, was another source of interest to the observer. Often their jokes and puns were quite original and good.

It is always something of an astonishment to find how well posted these otherwise ignorant negroes are on political matters, local events, or any important occurrences ; they seem to have a secret sort of freemasonry by which they learn everything going on. Ignorant, but very cunning and unscrupulous, they would be a terribly dangerous element of society, were it not for their well-known fear of fire-arms, and their naturally peaceful disposition. As a rule, all negroes go armed ; razors are their characteristic and specially favorite weapon ; but they are very fond of revolvers also, and many of them carry one. Give the ordinary negro a cheap shiny watch, a revolver, and a cane, and he is "happy as a lord."

The negro, I think, will not play a permanent or prominent part in Florida. In moderate numbers, no doubt, he will always be found there, but his shiftless, incompetent, and indolent ways will not long be endured by the class of vigorous and thoroughgoing Northern and Western men who constitute the bulk of the immigration to Florida at present. The better class of foreign laborers will gradually supersede him, and should John Chinaman ever be introduced in any considerable numbers, as I have suggested, the days of "Sambo" and "Cuffee" would speedily be numbered.

CHAPTER XV.

ORANGE-CULTURE.

THE orange is by far the most important of the semi-tropical fruits grown in Florida, and its culture is rapidly becoming the leading industry of the State. In nearly all sections it is found growing either in fields or house-gardens, as common and as natural to the climate and locality as the apple in the colder States. Whether or not it is indigenous is as yet an unsettled question, but the weight of evidence seems to be in favor of the idea that it was first introduced by the Spaniards, and that the many wild groves of " sour " oranges that are now found in various localities are simply the result of that deterioration which all the cultivated fruits undergo when left for long periods to run riot in a state of nature. It is well known that the apple, left to itself for a sufficient period, will ultimately revert to the " crab " ; and the difference between the " crab " and the choice varieties of the eating apple is about the same as the difference between the wild " sour " orange and the cultivated " sweet."

Since the earliest settlement, apparently, oranges have been grown in Florida, but in a very careless and desultory way. It is only since the war that any special attention has been given to their production, or any effort made to cultivate them for profit ; and what is sometimes called the " orange craze " has developed within the past six or eight years. The financial panic of 1873 caused many people

11

who were educated and shrewd to seek other and less precarious opportunities for investment than are afforded by ordinary "business." Many of these, gathering together the wrecks of their fortunes, came to Florida ; and, quickly perceiving the commercial value of this and similar fruits, set the "boom" going that has already attained immense proportions, and is increasing annually with gigantic strides. At present, the orange is undoubtedly the staple product

ORANGE-TREES.

of the State : it is to Florida what cattle are to Texas, corn and pork to Illinois, wheat to Iowa, and peaches to Delaware.

An orange-tree is a very attractive sight at all seasons of the year—with a straight, symmetrical, upright trunk covered with a smooth, sleek, pale-gray bark, and graceful curving branches which spread in all directions and are always clothed with an abundant foliage of rich, glossy, dark-green leaves—that is, if the tree is well cared for. Its regular blossoming season is the spring, but trees may be seen in blossom at all seasons, and sometimes one may see on the same tree blossoms, and green and mature fruit. The blossom is a small star-shaped flower, snow-white, and of a waxy look. The oranges ripen from late in November until early in March, depending somewhat upon the variety and the season ; and it would be difficult to imagine a more fascinating spectacle than a grove, or even a single tree, when fully laden with its ripe, golden-hued, luscious fruit.

The orange is a very hardy tree in its own natural habitat and under the right conditions—cold being its chief enemy. It is sociable, too, and appears to like human companionship ; it being a noticeable fact that those trees that are nearest inhabited dwellings are usually the largest and most prolific. It continues to grow until thirty to forty years of age, and is estimated to afford a productive yield for at least a hundred years. In a famous grove in the northern part of the State stands a tree known to be upward of eighty years old, yet it has every appearance of youthful vigor, and bears enormous crops. Orange-trees are hardly in what can be called their prime until after they are twenty years old, and then they increase in value for at least twenty years more.

It is surprising under how much neglect the orange will live and even thrive, but, in order to be made a reliable source of profit, it must be constantly and intelligently cared for. The remainder of this chapter will be devoted to pointing out a few of the essential conditions of successful orange-culture—such as will enable the beginner to avoid the mistakes that are most commonly made ; but, for more specific and minute details, the proposed fruit-grower must provide himself with a trustworthy and comprehensive treatise.*

LOCATION.—This is the most important consideration in starting a grove. With proper care oranges will grow in almost any part of Florida, but it is wise to select a location which combines the largest possible number of favorable conditions. As I have already said, cold is the greatest enemy of the orange-grower, and a fierce controversy has been raging for several years between different sections of the State as to what is called a "frost-line," above which, so it is said, orange-culture can not be pursued with any confidence in the returns, while below it the danger from frost is very slight. This line is usually placed at the twenty-eighth or twenty-ninth degree of latitude. Those living south of the "frost-line" direct attention to the fact that during the severe winters of 1876–'77 and 1880–'81 nearly all the fruit in the section north of it was irremediably spoiled and lost. On the other hand, those living north of the line call attention to the undeniable fact that a large majority of the old and productive groves are located *above* the supposed line, and that immensely the larger portion of the "Florida oranges" have been for many years, and are still, furnished by this section. It is difficult to reach any definite conclusions regarding the matter,† as

---

* Much the best work on the subject is Rev. T. W. Moore's "Treatise and Handbook on Orange-Culture in Florida," of which a new, revised, and enlarged edition has just been published by E. R. Pelton & Co., 25 Bond Street, New York.

† My own personal opinion is that it is, to say the least, *prudent* to get as far south as possible. There can be no doubt that killing frosts are rarer in the more southern portions of the peninsula, and it is well to avoid as many risks as possible, even if it be admitted that no portion of the State is wholly exempt from frost. Moreover, there are other tropical and semi-tropical fruits the culture of which may be profitably combined with

both views are advocated with equal ardor and sincerity by equally able and experienced men. There are two or three points, however, that may be regarded as settled. The industry can not be entered upon with any certainty in the northern or northwestern portions of the State. Most of the old and valuable groves in the upper division are located on the *east* side of the St. John's River, and their comparative immunity from the effects of cold is attributed to the extensive water-protection on the northwest. Mr. Moore considers that the water-protection afforded by the St. John's is equivalent to at least one hundred miles of southerly distance ; and throughout the peninsula it is considered desirable to secure the protection of a body of water on the northwest, the direction whence the cold winds come. In the absence of water, a protection of forest-trees is valuable, but these should shelter the trees on the southeast. Another important consideration in locating an orange-grove is accessibility to market : one should be sure to locate himself either near some established line of transportation or in the immediate vicinity of some line that is sure to be established in the near future. To haul oranges even ten miles over such roads as those of Florida is no slight task, and the fruit is very liable to be damaged in the process and thus rendered worthless.

Soil, etc.—Says Mr. Moore : " The orange will grow in a variety of soils—in clayey, sandy, shelly, or loamy soils, in hammocks black or gray, on pine-lands or black-jack ridges. It does well on soil underlaid with clay or sand. It will even do well on a light soil underlaid with white sand if fertilizers are applied annually. But whoever wishes to plant an orange-grove should be careful to select the best available soil. Perhaps the poorest soil suitable for orange-growing is that underlaid with a white sand, as

that of the orange, and these can not be grown with profit north of Lake George.—G. M. B.

such a soil leaches very readily the soluble manure. Perhaps the best soil is found in our dark-gray hammock with deep soil underlaid with a yellow clay or yellow sand subsoil. The natural growth should be tall and large with an abundance of live-oak and hickory, as such a growth would indicate an abundance of lime. Of our pine-land, that on which the hickory is found mixed with the pine, with yellow subsoil, should rank first. Such a soil is really a mixed hammock and pine. Next to this is the pine mixed with willow, oak, and black-jack. Considering the ease with which such lands as the last two classes are cleared and planted, the readiness with which the orange grows on them, they deserve a high rank, and especially if fertilizers are close at hand. In selecting a location in the purely pine-lands, select that which is thickly set with tall trees, well drained, and with a yellow subsoil. Such soils, if occasionally dressed with alkaline manures, grow the orange admirably." Low pine-lands, called " flat woods," should be avoided, and all lands which have a subsoil of "hard-pan" or quicksand. The trees grow more vigorously on the low, rich hammocks, but it is thought that they do not attain such great age as on the high lands, and the fruit is less adapted for transportation. Mr. Davis says, "Where high, hard-wood hammock-lands can be had, they should be preferred, other things being equal." No wet land—no soil not susceptible of thorough drainage—will do for orange-culture.

PRICES OF LAND, CLEARING, ETC.—There is still much land to be had in Florida at the Government price (one dollar and twenty-five cents per acre), but these are rarely so situated in respect to transportation facilities that it is wise to put an orange-grove upon them. The price of land held for sale by private parties ranges from five to one hundred and twenty-five dollars per acre, the difference being due mainly to greater or less nearness to settlements or to lines of transportation. Choice "lake-fronts" are

usually the most costly. The cost of clearing pine-land
is from ten to thirty dollars per acre, according to the
amount of undergrowth and the amount of "grubbing"
required ; of clearing hammock-lands, from thirty to one
hundred dollars per acre. The cost of plowing the land
and preparing it for the trees is from three to five dollars
per acre. It is very important to have the soil properly
prepared. Orange-trees will not thrive on new, "sour"
land, and it is desirable to have the soil thoroughly broken
up and pulverized some time before the trees are planted.
The best plan of all is first to raise a crop of cow-peas on
the land, and, when these have been turned under, then set
out the trees.

SELECTING THE TREES.—In their serviceable little
"Guide to Orange-Culture" the Manville Brothers say :
"Young, transplanted trees from the nursery should be
selected ; they have well-developed fibrous roots, are little
retarded by moving, and easily adapt themselves to the
various circumstances of soil, location, etc. The orange
does not reproduce itself with certainty from the seed.
Seedling trees are much longer in attaining maturity than
budded trees, and have no advantages over the latter.
Budded trees should therefore be selected in all cases. So-
called 'sour stocks' are more hardy and vigorous than the
sweet ; they are especially adapted to low land, where the
latter do not thrive. Sweet stocks are admissible on the
high lands, and are preferred by some. A bud of one or
two years' growth on a stock three or four years old, is the
most profitable and convenient size and age." It used to
be represented, probably by interested parties, that sweet
seedlings grow larger and ultimately produce more abundantly than budded trees ; but experiment has disproved
this, and it is now admitted that the budded trees not only
bear several years earlier than the seedlings, but make
quite as productive and vigorous trees. In choosing the

young trees in the nursery, choose those that have the largest trunks.

VARIETIES OF THE ORANGE.—These are very numerous—in fact, I have never met any one, even among those regarded as high authority, who could tell just how many kinds there are. Upward of sixty varieties are mentioned in some publications, yet the growers say there are many more, and every grower has one or two special varieties of his own. In Mr. Moore's treatise there is a comprehensive chapter on the different varieties, which the reader would do well to consult, as it is not possible here to do more than name a few of those which form the staple of an orange-grove. Of the common native sweet orange, always good and reliable, good varieties are the Nonpareil, the Homosassa, the Magnum Bonum, the Peerless, and the sweet Seville. The Navel orange, so named because the bloom - end bears a striking resemblance to the human navel, is excellent and popular. Of the imported varieties, the Jaffa has the reputation of being a remarkably early bearer, and the Mediterranean Sweet ranks high. The Mandarin or Tangierine orange is of small size, but very dainty and clean in appearance, and of a peculiar fruity flavor. It is sometimes called the "kid-glove orange," because you can break the skin and peel it without using a knife or staining the fingers. The "sour " orange has the flavor of the lemon, and makes a good orangeade and a wine that resembles sherry. The "bitter-sweet" has a skin bitter as gall, but the pulp is sweet, and an excellent wine is made from it. The "myrtle" is a small variety which grows in clusters and has a very sour taste; it is quite a favorite with housewives, for it makes delicious wine, orangeade, or preserves.

DISTANCES APART OF THE TREES. — Some growers recommend twenty feet as the proper distance, some twenty-five, and some thirty. The closer they are to-

gether, of course the less is the expense of land and cultivation, but on the other hand the trees are stunted ultimately if placed too close to each other. Twenty-five feet
is probably a good medium. At twenty feet apart, there
will be one hundred trees to the acre ; at twenty-five feet
apart, seventy-two trees to the acre ; at thirty feet apart,
fifty-six trees to the acre.

PLANTING.—Under favorable circumstances trees may
be transplanted with success during any month of the year,
but the best time is when the sap is dormant, from December to March. If planted in summer, watering, mulching,
and shading will probably be necessary. In removing the
trees from the nursery, as many roots as possible should be
taken up, and great care should be exercised to avoid
breaking or bruising them. Whenever they are thus injured, they should be trimmed with a sharp knife. The
tap-root should be left about twelve or eighteen inches
long ; if too long it will double up on being reset. The
holes for the trees should be freshly dug, and must not be
too deep ; more trees are lost by too deep planting than
from any other cause. As the trees always settle a little
after being set out, they should be raised three or four
inches above the surface, to allow for this. The upper or
brace roots must not be covered up at the collar ; and
under no circumstances should the tree be set deeper than
it stood in the nursery. The earth should be pressed carefully and firmly about the roots with the hand, giving
them as nearly as possible their original position. It is
better to select a cool, wet time for planting, but, if the
ground is dry, water should be plentifully supplied when
the work is finished. Manville Brothers recommend that
the newly-planted trees be mulched, whether the season
be wet or dry ; Mr. Moore recommends it only in case
the planting is done in hot summer weather. Before
the tree is left, its upper part should be trimmed in pro-

portion to the trimming which the roots have been subjected to.

CULTIVATION.—Contrary to what used to be the prevalent idea, the orange requires careful cultivation, and will
not really flourish without it. During the growing season
(spring and summer) the more frequently the soil is stirred
the better ; during the winter the cultivation may be suspended, though some think it best to keep the ground free
from grass and weeds the year round. Mr. Moore favors
the latter policy, but in this matter something depends upon
the character of the soil. For the first two or three years
vegetables may be grown among the young trees, but they
should never be planted nearer than four or five feet from
the tree. Moreover, no crop should be raised without first
applying an ample quantity of fertilizers to the soil, and
the area plowed each year must be gradually narrowed.
If the roots are injured, the trees suffer seriously ; hence,
among older trees, where the roots have extended themselves over a considerable part of the surface, the best
implement for cultivating is the " sweep," which keeps
down the grass and weeds without going deep enough to
damage the roots. Particular care must be taken in cultivating not to allow the soil to pile up around the trunks
of the trees.

FERTILIZING.—The orange-tree is a ravenous feeder, and
requires a soil rich in plant-food ; and if the locality chosen
for the grove does not contain this in the requisite quantity,
the want will have to be supplied. According to Dr. G. W.
Davis, the best fertilizer for the young growing orange-tree
is well-rotted stable-manure. Manville Brothers recommend
muck composted with animal manures, or with lime. Commercial fertilizers designed especially for the orange-tree
are numerous, and some are doubtless valuable. Mr. Moore
recommends the muck found in rivers, creeks, lakes, and
ponds ; and remarks that green crops turned under are high-

ly beneficial to young trees. "Rye, oats, and barley sown in the fall and turned under in the spring, and followed by one or two crops of cow-peas during the summer, help forward a grove of trees wonderfully. It is still better if this be accompanied by a dressing of wood-ashes ; one ton to the acre is not too much." Of course, in applying fertilizers the orange-grower must be guided by the special qualities of his soil, supplying those elements which are lacking. When the leaves of a tree are yellowish in hue, there is probably a deficiency of nitrogenous manures, while leaves of a dark, vivid green indicate an abundance. In general, it may be said that young and growing trees require nitrogenous manures, while bearing trees require abundance of potash. Owing to the porosity of most of the Florida soils, it is better to give the grove a light annual dressing than to apply a large quantity at once.

Pruning.—Judicious pruning is highly important in an orange-grove. The tree should be encouraged to form a low head, so as to protect the trunk and roots from sun and frost ; and the interior of the tree should be kept open by cutting out all except the most vigorous lateral branches. Dead wood should be cut away ; also all diseased or unshapely branches. "Water-shoots" on the trunk should be cut or pulled off. The principal pruning should be done in the spring and with a sharp knife. It may be slackened when the trees come into bearing.

Insects and Diseases.—As a rule, the orange-tree is not subject to many diseases, particularly if the trees are kept in a healthy, vigorous condition, with the ground well cultivated. The most formidable insect enemy is the scale-insect, but it seldom attacks any but feeble trees. For removing them, apply a strong solution of whale-oil soap ; and if this fails, Dr. Davis recommends the following : Dissolve five pounds of any hard soap in a small quantity of boiling water, put it into a forty-gallon cask, add ten pounds of carbonate of soda, broken into small lumps, fill the cask with soft water, and stir until it is thoroughly dissolved ; scrub the trunk and branches with a brush dipped in this solution, and shower the tops and foliage with it by means of a rose-nibbed syringe. Against other insects the best protection is a good flock of fowls. The cause of "rust" is not yet fully made out, some claiming that it is due to an insect, others to a fungus. Slaked lime from burned oyster-shells sown broadcast over the grove and allowed to sift lightly through the branches and leaves of the trees, is a good corrective. The most serious disease is that known as the "die-back." If this is confined to a few branches, it may be due to the sting of an insect. If, on the other hand, it is general, it shows either that the trees have been planted too deeply (and the remedy is to dig away the soil or to reset the tree), or that the roots have struck a "hard-pan" subsoil (and for this there is no remedy but removal to another site).

In conclusion, it must be said that orange-groves do not make themselves ; their value, indeed, consists in the very fact that it takes years of hard labor and a very considerable expenditure of money in the mean while to raise them. As to the returns that may be expected, one is generally told that in three years from the setting, if budded trees are put out, the grove will be in bearing. While this is true in the sense that some oranges may then be found upon the trees, it is also true that no paying crop can be looked for in so brief a period. As a general thing, if the grove has been properly cared for, it ought to be self-supporting by the fifth year, after which its returns should gradually increase year by year, until at the end of ten or twelve years the crop, at a cent an orange on the tree (the price is now much higher), should yield ten dollars per tree. Estimates are usually made much higher than this ; and, indeed, there are trees in Florida the fruit from which will annually bring upward of a hundred dollars each ; but these are very rare exceptions, and I believe the estimate I have given to be a fair one. At least, if one expects no more than that, he may be reasonably sure of not being disappointed.

CHAPTER XVI.

THE extent of the subject properly belonging to this chapter, and the variety of products that must be dealt with, are so great that it would be impossible for any one to treat it adequately from individual knowledge of all the facts. The knowledge and the experience of others must be relied upon in large measure, and fortunately the fruits of this knowledge and experience are readily obtainable. Within the past fifteen years much attention has been given to the procurement of accurate data concerning the resources of the State ; the State Bureau of Immigration, and nearly all the counties, besides many special associations and societies—horticultural, agricultural, and stock—having expended large sums in the investigation. Persons of known competency and trustworthiness have generally made these investigations ; and the results have been given to the public in various pamphlets, circulars, reports, addresses, and newspaper articles. I have collected many of these pamphlets, etc., especially those the authors of which are known to be able and intelligent persons, fully acquainted with the topic written of, not only from observation but from practical experience, often of many years. In the following statements and suggestions I have supplemented my own knowledge and observations with the information thus acquired ; and as the chapter has been submitted, since it was written, to the scrutiny of several competent persons, it is believed that, as far as it goes, it can be relied upon.

After the orange, which is fully treated of in the previous chapter, the most important of the semi-tropical fruits is—

THE LEMON.—The lemon is produced in the orange-belt of Florida to a degree of perfection far surpassing anything of the kind in any other part of the world.

The tree grows more rapidly, produces fruit sooner, bears a larger crop, and has larger and better-flavored lemons, than are found anywhere else. I have seen and picked lemons of one and a half to two pounds' weight, and at the State Fair saw lemons weighing two and a half pounds! In many respects the lemon-tree resembles the orange, and its cultivation is the same, except that it *does not* require such rich soil ; it does best on a light, sandy soil. It is a tenderer plant, however, requiring care to protect it from the cold, which it can not bear as well as the orange. Below the frost-line, of course, there is no danger, and it may be left to itself. It is a rapid and rampant grower, not so smooth and graceful as an orange-tree, but spreading out its branches wildly in all directions up and down. It commences bearing fruit about two or three years sooner than the orange-tree, and bears much larger crops. An orange-tree may be expected to bear in its sixth year two hundred oranges and one thousand in its tenth year ; the lemon-tree will bear in its third year two hundred lemons and five thousand in its tenth year, on the average. The first two or three crops are usually a coarse, spongy fruit, but the succeeding crops improve each year in delicacy and excellence.

The fruit bears handling and transportation remarkably well, and it is generally thought by competent observers that it will prove quite as profitable a crop as the orange, with the advantage of producing returns two to three years sooner. It is destined to become a very important product.

THE LIME.—This is a very dainty and delicious fruit, smaller in size but otherwise closely resembling the lemon. The juice is more agreeably acid and makes a very pleasant drink ; a glass of limeonade is sure to be remembered with pleasure. It grows very rapidly, like a small lemon-tree, bears in its third year, and produces large crops. The culture is precisely the same.

THE CITRON.—This is the chief of the citric family of fruits. It is in all respects like the orange, in appearance of the tree as well as in the care required. The fruit closely resembles the orange, except that it is larger and more yellow in color. Plucked from the tree, it is not a pleasant fruit to eat. Heretofore but little attention has been paid to the cultivation of this fruit in Florida, except for variety and ornament, and it is not usual to observe more than one or two trees in a large garden of several acres in extent, though it is grown here with the greatest ease and perfection, frequently producing fruit weighing ten pounds, and there is no doubt but that it may be cultivated, preserved, and introduced into our home-markets as an article of commerce, with great profit to the producer. There is no other variety of this species so easily propagated, and none more hardy, or that yields its fruit so quickly, or produces more abundantly ; and the circumstance that both the fruit and the sugar for preserving it are produced in the same field, with equal facility, gives to the American cultivator a great advantage over the foreign producer in our market. The citron prepared and preserved by private families in Florida for home use is of much finer quality, lighter colored, and more transparent, than the imported.

BERGAMOT.—This is a hybrid of the orange and the lemon, is small, yellow in color, has a thick skin, is juicy, with a sour-sweet, flavorless taste. It is cultivated chiefly for the oil which is distilled from the rind, and known to chemists and in the trade as " oil of bergamot."

THE FIG.—This delicious fruit grows with remarkable vigor and thrift in all portions of the State. It is quite hardy, bears in the third year, produces large crops, and is a profitable fruit, requiring little care or expense. It

THE FIG.

very closely resembles the quince-tree of the North, in appearance. A simple preparation of figs by boiling in sirup furnishes a most palatable and wholesome preserve that only needs to be known to become a universal favorite. If figs can be prepared for a lucrative market by drying anywhere on earth, it can be done in Florida ; and though it has been done but little as yet, it is certain to be one of the industries of the future.

THE OLIVE.—With the exception of a few trees grown for ornament, this most valuable tree has not been cultivated in Florida. That it will succeed and produce large crops is undoubted, judging from the few specimens now growing ; and attention having been directed to it recently, it will probably be extensively planted. It begins to bear about ten years from the seed, bears annually, and increases in the amount of product to the age of thirty years. It is very long-lived, some trees in Southern Europe being known to be eight hundred years old and showing no signs of decay. The fruit and the oil made from it are valuable as food, and in demand for commercial purposes.

THE PINEAPPLE.—This delicious plant produces remarkably fine large fruit in all portions of South Florida. It is the king of tropical fruits. It is planted from the

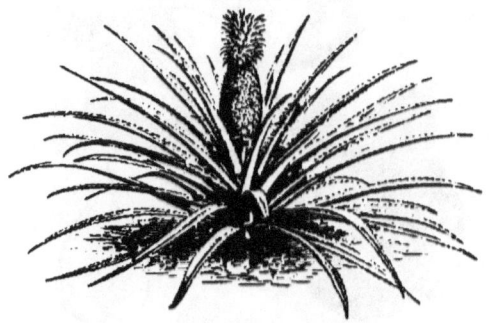

A PINEAPPLE-PLANT.

suckers or shoots taken from the matured fruit and stock. These can be purchased at from one and a half to two and a half cents each ; and about twelve thousand can be planted on one acre, placed twenty to twenty-four inches apart. They bear fruit in the twentieth month, and continue bearing all the year.

The owner of a pineapple patch can have fruit every day of the year. They require little or no care, nor very rich soil, nor fertilizing ; but they can not bear cold, and care must be taken to protect them from frosts. An acre is certain to produce six to ten thousand pineapples, which sell readily at prices which make them a very profitable crop.

The Banana.—This fruit is planted like a field of gigantic corn, which it much resembles in the care required and young growth, but it attains vast size with immense leaves. Each stalk produces one bunch in from fifteen to eighteen months, which sells for one and a half to two and a half dollars. After the fruit ripens, the large leaves fall off, the top dies down, and new suckers start out from the roots. One of these suckers is sufficient to perpetuate the old stock, and the rest may be replanted in new places, to any extent desired. No fruit is more healthy and nutritious than ripe bananas, and few are more esteemed. In South American countries they are also cooked while green, and are said to be very palatable.

The Cocoanut.—This tropical product grows vigorously in the keys and mainland of the extreme southern portion of the State. It much resembles a palm or palmetto tree in generally appearance. It requires no care after setting out, and produces fruit after the sixth year. It does well in Florida, producing extrasized fruit of excellent quality. A tree will bear from one hundred to five hundred nuts annually, in monthly bunches.

The Date, etc., etc.—The date, tamarind, sapodilla, papaw, sugar-apple, custard-apple, and all similar tropical fruits, grow abundantly in all portions of tropical Florida, with little or no labor, and produce large crops of the best quality of fruits of their kind.

Date-Palm.—This excellent and valuable fruit is cultivated with entire success south of 28° north latitude, and the tree often perfects its fruit as far north as 30° north latitude. Numerous large and beautiful specimens of this tree may be seen in the gardens at St. Augustine. It is one of the most beautiful trees of the vegetable kingdom. Its long, graceful, ever-verdant, ever-waving, ever-changing branches make it the most picturesque of all plants for landscape-gardening, and should adorn the grounds of every homestead in Florida.

The fruit is greatly and justly esteemed by the inhabitants of Egypt, Arabia, and Persia, on account of its concentrated and nutritious properties : large numbers subsist almost entirely upon it. It is generally the sole food of

THE DATE-PALM.

the Arabs and their camels on their long and tedious journeys over the desert, the men feeding upon the fruit and the animals upon the stones. The inhabitants of these countries also boast of the medicinal qualities of the date-fruit, and of the numerous uses to which the different productions of this tree may be applied. From the leaves they make couches, baskets, bags, mats, and brushes; from the branches or stalks, cages for their poultry and fences for their gardens; from the fibers of the trunk, thread, ropes, and rigging; from the sap, a spirituous liquor; and the body of the trees furnishes fuel.

The date-palm is propagated from the seeds and suckers, but more successfully from the former. The cultivation of this fruit should be greatly extended, as it may become an important and profitable resource of the inhabitants of Southern Florida. The bunches or clusters of this fruit often attain a weight of fifteen pounds.

THE SHADDOCK (sometimes called mock-orange, or forbidden fruit).—This was brought from China to the West Indies by Captain Shaddock, from whom it derives its present name. There are at least six varieties, only one of which is useful or desirable as a fruit. Some of these attain a very large size, frequently weighing ten to fourteen pounds. It is chiefly used for ornament or show, and where several sorts of oranges are presented at dessert it forms a striking addition to the varieties in the way of contrast. The most desirable variety of this fruit is sometimes called grape-fruit. It possesses a reddish pulp, with most agreeable sub-acid sweetness, and is excellent for quenching thirst; and from the thickness of its rind will keep longer than the fruit of any other of the citrus family. This variety is well worth cultivating for the excellence of its solid, vinous pulp, which furnishes a substitute for other acid fruits in pies, tarts, jellies, etc.

LOQUAT.—This fruit is known in the South as the Japan plum. The tree is an evergreen, and grows ten to twelve feet high, and is desirable in every Southern garden on account of its hardiness, withstanding a greater degree of cold than any of the semi-tropical fruits. It ripens its fruit in February and March, when most other fruits are gone ; is a profuse bearer, and is readily propagated by seeds and cuttings.

PEACHES, NECTARINES, PEARS, PLUMS, ETC.—When peaches begin to bloom in Delaware and New Jersey, they are one half grown in Florida, and no better peach country can or need be found than along the line of the Florida Railroad. At one year's growth from the pit, peaches often attain, even in West Florida, the height of ten feet. Care, selection, and attention can place in the Northern market the choicest peaches from Waldo and Starke, several weeks before they can be raised North. There is no country where the marketing of peaches, whether fresh or dried, can be made more lucrative, or where they can be more profitably canned. This tree is long-lived, healthy, and vigorous throughout Florida, and is never subject to injuries from the peach-worm or the diseases which so universally afflict the fruit in the Northern States. The most delicious peaches may be raised almost without care by every family, and in abundance sufficient even for the economical feeding of swine. The early varieties of this fruit ripen in the beginning of June, and the latest sorts continue until late in August. The earliest and the latest varieties should be chosen for cultivation in Florida, as the rainy season commences in July and continues throughout that month, causing much of the maturing fruit to crack.

The nectarine, the apricot, and the almond, are all at home in Florida, and not less vigorous, healthy, or productive than the peach ; and all who will take the trouble to plant and care for the trees may be assured of an abundant reward.

The plum and the prune are also healthy and productive, being entirely exempt from the ravages of the curculio so prevalent at the North. All the varieties of the wild plum are indigenous and abundant in nearly every part of the State. Many of the varieties are of excellent quality, and, when cooked, form a delicious preserve for family use or for canning.

Pears and quinces are worthy of more attention than they have heretofore received. It is believed that some varieties of the former will do well, but as yet their cultivation has not been sufficiently tested to fix their *status* among the fruits of Florida. Experiments that have been made seem to show that the Lecomte pears can be made a highly profitable crop. They are nearly as attractive in appearance as the Bartlett, are but little inferior in flavor, and can be put into the New York market at a time when no other pear can be found.

The Persimmon.—The persimmon is found wild in every section of the State. The fruit, at least to the natives, is agreeable to the taste, and, ripe or dry, is used largely for the table and for home-made beer. Some Japan varieties are now being introduced, which are said to be of very large size, and seedless. The Japanese esteem the persimmon as their most valuable fruit.

The Pomegranate.—Pomegranates are of two kinds, the sweet and sour. The bush is large, graceful in foliage, and beautiful in pendent crimson flowers and fruit. As an ornamental tree it is one of the best. The fleshy covering of the seed is a beautiful pink, and has a pleasant, subacid taste, in flavor not unlike the red currant. The rind is bitter, and often used medicinally ; also for domestic coloring and ink.

The Pecan.—This tree is valuable as a forest-tree for its lumber, and profitable for its fruit. It is now being extensively planted, requiring only the ordinary care of indigenous trees. The cost is trifling. It bears in about ten years from the seed, growing straight, tall, and graceful.

It need not occupy land used for cultivation. Some cultivators have set the pecan out so as to make a permanent boundary line of their land.

GRAPES AND CHERRIES.—Most of the American and foreign varieties are easily grown, ripening from June to November. The St. Augustine grape, so called, is a choice grape for eating or wine. The Scuppernong in all its varieties is cultivated largely, being a rapid grower, an abundant bearer, long-lived, and needing but little pruning or care. It is found most profitable as a table-grape or for wine. Much attention is being given to the growing of grapes and the making of wine.

The black cherry is found wild, but the tame or cultivated cherry does not seem to succeed, though we see no reason why it should not, where fruits of similar habit grow well.

BLACKBERRIES AND HUCKLEBERRIES.—The low, creeping blackberry, or dewberry, abounds in old fields and roadsides, and ripens in April. The high-bush, also found in the same localities, ripens in June and July; the huckleberry about the same time. All bear well, and can be had for the picking. The improved kinds do well where tried.

STRAWBERRIES.—This queen of small fruits nowhere in the world finds a better location for culture; plants put out in September fruit often in January, frequently in February, and may be counted in full bearing and ripening in March and April. The growers about Jacksonville and up the St. John's River are many, and shipments have been made largely and profitably. In size, color, bouquet, and taste they are superior to most, equal to the best, and surpassed by none; the best varieties only are grown. The cultivators pick carefully, select and pack honestly; and Florida strawberries, like Florida oranges, have earned a name. By using refrigerators the fruit reaches

New York and other Northern cities, fresh and cool, only about four days from picking. Being always in advance of any other locality by some weeks, the first shipments bring large prices, and the demand keeps pace with the supply.

12

CHAPTER XVII.

FIELD AND FARM PRODUCTS.

ALL the crops of all portions of America can be grown in Florida. Some produce better here than anywhere else, others no better, a few not so well, but they will all grow and produce fair yields. And in all cases they require less care or labor than elsewhere; there is not an exception to this assertion known of in the long list of productions. Besides, in many cases the same soil can be replanted with the same or some other product within the same year.

Of the various field-crops cotton has by custom ranked as the staple product in this State; however, it is one of the least productive, although it pays as well here as in any other State or country where it can be grown. Sugar is the "king" field-product of Florida, and it can hardly be doubted that ere many years have elapsed a considerable portion of the sugar and molasses that are now imported at the cost of millions of dollars from Cuba and elsewhere will be drawn from the soil of the Peninsular State.

SUGAR-CANE.—In both climate and soil, Florida is peculiarly well adapted for the growth of sugar-cane, the long period of warm weather and the absence of cold affording a longer period for the cane to mature. In Louisiana, owing to the frosts, the cane never tassels, and has to be ground as soon as mature; in South Florida it always tassels, and can be worked at leisure through a period covering several months. What is known in Louisiana as "fair land" will produce from fifteen hundred to two thousand pounds of sugar to the acre ; rich land, thoroughly fertilized, will produce from two to four thousand pounds. The black hammock or "sugar-lands" of Florida will produce at least equally large crops, and it is believed by many planters that, with fertilizing, the pine-lands will produce as well, and of a better quality. The soils of Central and South Florida are, in general, peculiarly adapted for the cane. Here the cane matures and perfects its seed, and often attains a height of from ten to fifteen feet, even when grown for a number of years on the same land without manure.

Sugar-cane grows in joints of from three to six or nine inches in length, like the reeds used for fishing-poles, with a sort of partition between each two joints of a hard, vegetable substance. At or near each of these partitions, on one side of the cane, is an eye, which is always exactly opposite to the eye attached to the next joint above or below ; so that the eyes on a perfect cane together form two rows of eyes on opposite sides of the cane. From each of those eyes, when covered with earth to the proper depth, proceed the sprouts and roots which constitute in time the complete cane. Cane does not of necessity require replanting every year, the stalks being cut in the fall. From the same roots, in the next year, unless the root is injured by cold, drought, or excess of moisture, there springs a second growth of sprouts similar to the first. This subsequent repeated growth from the same root is called ratooning, and may be repeated from year to year for several years. The value of these succeeding or ratooning crops is variously estimated, some asserting that it continually deteriorates after the second year, and others maintaining that with care it may be ratooned indefinitely. The common opinion is that replanting is necessary once in three or four years. But Judge Dupont, of Quincy, in Gadsden County, one of the northern counties in this State, told me that he had raised cane from the ratoon six successive years without either diminution or deterioration. I am informed that on the lands of Indian River has been raised the nineteenth crop of cane from the same planting, and on the shore of Lake Worth cane is now growing which has not been replanted since the early Indian wars. The probability is, that the character of the ratoons and the extent of their repetition depend upon the quality of the original seed, the cultivation, and the fertilization it has received.

SUGAR-MILL.

While cane is one of the hardiest and most certain of all known crops, and will thrive under neglect that would be fatal to almost anything else, yet it as certainly responds to deep and frequent cultivation and generous fertilizing as any crop that can be specified, and its varying yield of from five hundred to five thousand pounds to the acre bears unmistakable testimony to the degree of care bestowed upon it. Good cultivation, indeed, will accomplish wonders with the cane ; and though only the rudest processes of manufacture are as yet employed in Florida—the home-made wooden cylinders are the usual type of mill—the results obtained are sometimes fabulous. It is known that one small planter near Picolata, during the past year, with no help except that of his own little boy, made from two acres of land forty barrels of sugar and five hundred gallons of sirup ; and I have already told of the planter on Indian River who, with the assistance of one negro man, netted sixteen hundred dollars for five acres. When the attention of capitalists shall have been drawn to the opportunity, and improved processes of manufacture introduced, there can hardly be a doubt that the production of sugar will be the leading industry of the State.

Cotton.—Generally speaking, cotton is a safer crop in Florida than anywhere else ; but it is subject to some risks from drought, rain, cold, and caterpillars, and other crops which require less attention and are less dependent upon negro labor are superseding it. Sea-island or long cotton is raised mostly from the Suwanee River to the ocean, and south of latitude 30°. The average product per acre is from one hundred and fifty to two hundred pounds, though it often exceeds double that. This species of cotton is only raised on the sea-islands bordering South Carolina, Georgia, and in Florida, the latter State raising over half the total crop. Short cotton is grown west of the Suwanee to the western and northern boundaries of the State ; it will average from two to five hundred pounds to the acre. In grade, Florida cotton rates with the best.

Corn.—This great food-staple is grown in all portions

of Florida, and the produce here as elsewhere varies according to fertility of soil and cultivation. Ordinary pine-land
will produce, say, ten bushels ; good hammock-land, twenty
to twenty-five bushels. Governor Drew, in 1878, on common pine-land, which had been cultivated only six years,
raised one hundred and thirty bushels to the acre. Of
course, the land was thoroughly prepared, well manured,
and well cultivated. Corn here is planted from February
to April, plowed at intervals, laid by in June and July ;
blades stripped for fodder, and stalks with ears left in field
to be harvested at leisure. It may be cribbed in field in
the shuck, suffering no damage from weather, or housed in
corn-crib near the dwelling ; shucked and shelled if for
sale or food. When fed to stock, it is fed in shuck. ·One
person with one mule can easily cultivate from thirty to
forty acres, and, as the time from planting to final plowing
is only from four to five months, it leaves ample time to
cultivate another crop of peas or sweet-potatoes, with same
labor on same land. The corn usually raised is the white
variety, largely used in meal and hominy for food, especially at the South. The Northern farmer, who has been used to
see forty to sixty bushels ordinarily raised on the old homestead, should, in comparing the relative production South
and North, take into consideration cheapness of land, number of acres which can be cultivated, time taken to produce
crop, expense of gathering, saving, housing, and also value,
transportation, and its quality. White is best for food.
All things considered, corn is one of the most useful and
profitable crops to raise in Florida.

WHEAT, RYE, AND OATS.—In the northern and northwestern section of the State wheat is grown to some extent,
but it is not generally raised as a regular crop. Sown early
in the fall, rye and oats do well, affording a good winter
pasturage. They mature in the early spring, and are not
thrashed, being cured and fed to stock in the straw.

Rice.—There are thousands of acres in every section of the State that are peculiarly adapted to the production of rice, but it has not been cultivated as yet to any extent, except for domestic use. The cultivation is as simple as that of any cereal, and twenty-five to seventy-five bushels of rough rice to the acre is a fair yield. The idea that rice can only be successfully grown on low lands that can be overflowed at certain seasons has proved to be mistaken. What is known as "upland" rice can be grown on any fairly good and well-irrigated soil; and the success with which this has been cultivated in Florida seems to indicate that in future, when rice-cleaning machinery has been introduced, this will be one of the great staples of the State. Maturing earlier than in other States, new Florida rice has a proportionate advantage.

Sweet-Potatoes.—This article of food is as indispensable in all Southern households as rice is to the Chinese, macaroni to the Italian, or the Irish potato to the Irishman. White or black, no family is so poor but it has a potato-patch. It yields all the way from one to four hundred bushels to the acre, according to soil, cultivation, and season; is grown from root, drawer, and slips; is planted from June to August, and matures from July to November. It is of easy cultivation, and may be dug and safely banked in field and yard, or housed.

Irish Potatoes.—The common Irish potato grows fairly well in all parts of Florida, but does best in the northern and middle sections. The yield is not so large as in the North, but will average from one to two hundred bushels per acre, and in choice locations along the St. John's and in North Florida the product is sometimes upward of four hundred bushels per acre.

Tobacco.—Tobacco will grow anywhere in Florida. A superior quality of Cuba tobacco, from imported seed, is mostly grown in Gadsden and adjoining counties, and fully equals the best imported. Before the war it was extensively and profitably cultivated, and mostly sold to Germany, agents visiting the State to purchase. It requires careful attention, will yield from five to seven hundred pounds to the acre, and sells for from twenty to thirty cents a pound. Latterly there is an increasing home and State demand by cigar-manufacturers, and the area of cultivation is extending.

PEANUTS.—The peanuts grown in Florida rank with the best in quantity of production and also in quality. They are largely used on the farm as food for swine, and are remarkably fattening. Almost any soil is suitable for the . crop, the cultivation is simple and inexpensive, and the yield is liberal.

MELONS.—"The Northern man," says the writer of the "Bureau of Immigration" pamphlet, "who has only seen the prize melon, pumpkin, squash, and other fruits of similar kind, is astounded at the size of Florida growth. It is no rare thing to see watermelons as large as a nail-keg, weighing seventy pounds, muskmelons twenty to thirty pounds, and pumpkins and squashes will often weigh one hundred pounds. A watermelon which does not weigh, at the least, twenty-five pounds, is considered hardly salable; thirty to thirty-five pounds is about the average of the watermelon brought to market. Those raised are of the best-known varieties, and here the flavor seems more pleasant, and the flesh more crisp and solid, than elsewhere. The raising of them is not a matter of much care; they are mostly found in the corn-patch, where they grow unseen and uncared for. Except where raised for shipment North, in recent years, they are grown by truckmen, who ship by the car-load North and West, the season for sending generally commencing the last of May and continuing until August. Muskmelons also are of large size, and delicious cantaloupes are raised easily; indeed, vines of all kinds succeed well, the long, warm season favoring rapid growth."

JUTE AND RAMIE.—All the fibrous plants grown in warm latitudes do well in Florida, and most of them are indigenous. At one time Sisal hemp was extensively grown, but the Indian war laid waste the country where it was planted, and the cultivation has not been resumed. Recent-ly, the culture of jute and ramie has begun to attract attention ; and, now that machinery for preparing the fiber has been invented, there can be no doubt that both crops are of the highest commercial importance. It is estimated that to move our crops of cotton, wheat, and grain requires an expenditure of about twenty-five million dollars annually for bags and bagging ; and ramie and jute yield fibers equal to the best brought from the East Indies. For the cultivation of them Florida seems especially well adapted, and both grow like weeds. The seed of jute should be sown in March or April, and it may be cut in June, July, or August ; it is estimated that the yield is thirty-five hundred pounds per acre, and the crop is sure and cultivation easy. The prepared fiber is used to make bagging, gunny, coarse cloth, mattings, cheap carpets, and burlaps. The ends of the stems are used for making paper, as are the old sacks and bags. The stems may be used for garden fences and coarse baskets, and they make good charcoal for gunpowder.

Ramie is a permanent crop ; once planted, it reproduces itself indefinitely. It is first produced, not from seeds, but from small shoots or roots, and about three thousand roots (costing twenty to twenty-five dollars per thousand) are required to plant an acre. The crops may be gathered at any season, and four crops may be obtained from the same land each year, averaging five hundred pounds to the acre for each crop. The crude product is worth twenty to twenty-five cents per pound ; prepared properly by machin-

ery, it is nearly as valuable as raw silk. These are the
crops for North Florida.

CASSAVA, ARROW-ROOT, ETC.—The cassava, from which
starch and tapioca are made, does astonishingly well in
Florida, and attains great size. The Hon. John G. Sinclair, of New Hampshire, has erected a cassava starch-mill
at Interlaken, in Orange County, and by experiment on his
own place he has shown that from four to six hundred
bushels to the acre can be raised on high pine-land with
little fertilizing. The starch yielded by it is excellent in
quality, and finds a ready sale to Northern manufacturers.
Here, probably, is the germ of a great industry; for the
cassava can be grown right in the orange-grove without
damaging the trees. Florida arrow-root grades in quality
and price with the best Bermuda, and is easily cultivated.
Comptie, the bread-root of the Indians, grows without any
cultivation.

TIMBER AND LUMBER.—Of all the States Florida has
the largest area of original growth of timber. Excluding
land in cultivation, the area covered by lakes, rivers, savannas, etc., there are probably nearly, if not quite, thirty million acres of land covered with timber, and of this the yellow
pine is fully three quarters. The level and rolling lands
are mostly covered with the yellow and pitch pine, which
attains a great size in girth and length. The lower lands
near rivers, lakes, and swamps abound in valuable timber,
of which live-oak, other species of oak, hickory, ash, birch,
cedar, magnolia, sweet-bay, gum, and cypress constitute a
great proportion. The red cedar is particularly adapted for
lead-pencils, and is largely exported to Europe for the best
manufactures, as also North and East. The magnolia and
bay are fine woods for ornamental furniture; the cypress is
valuable for shingles, sash, doors, blinds, and inside finish,
railroad-ties, etc. The yellow and pitch pines have a world-
wide reputation as being the best for any and all uses where

A CYPRESS-SHINGLE YARD.

strength, elasticity, and durability are desired, and are now being largely used in ornamental and expensive structures. Finished up in its natural grain for inside work, floors, frames, pillars, arches, and roofs, it presents that substantial as well as rich finish not attained with other material. While there are many mills on the Atlantic and Gulf sides, and a few on the railroad, which manufacture pine lumber, as yet the consumption is small, and future supply is assured for years. Recently some cedar mills have been built which prepare the wood of size for pencils. Most of the cedar, however, is shipped in the log, roughly hewed. Some oak and hickory is shipped in rough-hewed sticks, but as yet not much use is made of the hard woods. Lumber of fair quality sells for from five to fifteen dollars per thousand feet at the mill.

VEGETABLE-GARDENING.—In other portions of the book I have already cited a number of instances of the extraordinary success attained in vegetable-gardening, and will therefore content myself here with a few general statements. In Middle and South Florida fresh vegetables may be had during each and every month of the year, and there is no portion of the United States where the ordinary garden-vegetables produce so abundantly or attain such marvelous size. Recently, the raising of early vegetables for the Northern markets has attained the dimensions of a leading industry—rivaling in magnitude and profitableness the production of tropical fruits. Tomatoes, cucumbers, green peas, egg-plants, strawberries, and the like, can readily be placed upon Northern tables at a season when such vegetables have hardly begun to be planted in the New England and Middle States; and the price obtained for them at such times affords an almost incredible profit. Indeed, comparing results for a series of years, it is probable that the vegetable-gardener will be able to show returns surpassing those of even the most successful orange-growers;

and of course the results are secured very much sooner, and with less original outlay.

At present the most successful vegetable-gardening is done along the line of the Transit Railroad and on the lower St. John's, near Jacksonville; but all portions of the State are well adapted for it, and South Florida has a little the advantage in the matter of earliness of season and freedom from frost. Wherever transportation facilities are secured, there "gardening for profit" can be undertaken with confidence; and as most vegetables can be raised in a young orange-grove without injury to the trees—with benefit, if properly attended to—the development of the industry will probably be enormous in the future when the North has come to rely upon Florida for its early vegetables, and when railway and steamer lines have prepared themselves for the expeditious performance of the business.

WHEN AND WHAT TO PLANT.—The following valuable suggestions on this head are copied *verbatim* from the official pamphlet prepared for and published by the State Bureau of Immigration:

"No precise instructions would be strictly applicable for all parts of Florida; we give briefly what may generally be safely adopted for Florida say at and north of latitude 29°; south of 29° a year's experience and information will safely guide. One thing is favorable: the period of planting any special crops covers weeks and months, so that failure from exceptional circumstances need not occur.

"In *January* plant Irish potatoes, peas, beets, turnips, cabbages, and all hardy or semi-hardy vegetables; make hot-beds for pushing the more tender plants, such as melons, tomatoes, okra, egg-plants, etc.; set out fruit and other trees, and shrubbery.

"*February.*—Keep planting for a succession, same as in January; in addition, plant vines of all kinds, shrubbery, and fruit-trees of all kinds, especially of the citrus family, snap-beans, corn; bed sweet-potatoes for draws and slips. Oats may also be still sown, as they are in previous months.

"*March.*—Corn, oats, and planting of February may be continued ; transplant tomatoes, egg-plants, melons, beans, and vines of all kinds ; mulberries and blackberries are now ripening.

"*April.*—Plant as in March, except Irish potatoes, kohl-rabi, turnips ; continue to transplant potatoes, okra, egg-plants ; sow millet, corn, cow-peas, for fodder ; plant the butter-bean, lady-peas ; dig Irish potatoes. Onions, beets, and usual early vegetables should be plenty for table.

"*May.*—Plant sweet-potatoes for draws in beds ; continue planting corn for table ; snap-beans, peas, and cucumbers ought to be well forward for use ; continue planting okra, egg-plants, pepper, and butter-beans.

"*June.*—The heavy planting of sweet-potatoes and cow-peas is now in order ; Irish potatoes, tomatoes, and a great variety of table vegetables are now ready, as also plums, early peaches, and grapes.

"*July.*—Sweet-potatoes and cow-peas are safe to plant, the rainy season being favorable ; grapes, peaches, and figs are in full season. Orange-trees may be set out if the season is wet.

"*August.*—Finish up planting sweet-potatoes and cow-peas ; sow cabbage, cauliflower, turnips for fall planting ; plant kohl-rabi and ruta-bagas ; transplant orange-trees and bud ; last of month plant a few Irish potatoes and beans.

"*September.*—Now is the time to commence for the true winter garden, the garden which is commenced in the North in April and May. Plant the whole range of vegetables except sweet-potatoes ; set out asparagus, onion-sets, and strawberry-plants.

"*October.*—Plant same as last month ; put in garden peas ; set out cabbage-plants ; dig sweet-potatoes ; sow oats, rye, etc.

"*November.*—A good month for garden ; continue to plant and transplant, same as for October ; sow oats, barley, and rye for winter pasturage or crops ; dig sweet-potatoes ; house or bank them ; make sugar and sirup.

"*December.*—Clear up generally ; fence, ditch, manure, and sow and plant hardy vegetables ; plant, set out orange-trees, fruit-trees, and shrubbery ; keep a sharp lookout for an occasional frost ; a slight protection will prevent injury.

"It will be seen from the above that there is no month in the year but what fresh and growing vegetables can be had for sale and domestic use. This latter is a large item in expense of living. The soil is so easily worked, so easily cultivated, that most of garden-work can be performed by even delicate ladies, and young children of both sexes. Indeed, most Florida gardens are so made—no frozen clods to break or rocks to remove. A garden once put in condition, properly managed, will produce abundantly and constantly. The rapid growth assures large and tender vegetables, early and luscious fruit. A single season will afford strawberries from the setting out, ripe figs from two-year-old cuttings, grapes the second year, peaches the second and third years, oranges from the bud in three to five years. At a little cost, a little care, one can literally sit under his own vine and fig-tree, and enjoy fresh-plucked fruit the whole year."

CHAPTER XVIII.

LIVE-STOCK.

THE first sight of a pure in-and-in-bred Florida hog or cow is not calculated to impart to the visitor from northern climes, especially if he be from the stock-regions, a very favorable impression of Florida as a stock-raising State. The hog, the genuine "cracker" hazel-splitter, is a lean, lank, wiry, quick-motioned beast—a deer in hog shape. It is a slander on the portentously fat porkers of Illinois to call the Florida specimen a hog at all. From the snout to the tail he is all of a size, and the head is one third of the total length, the long and thin body being placed on noticeably long and thin legs. And how he can run, or root! The tourist always enjoys a hearty laugh when told "Those are hogs," and innumerable are the puns and jokes at their expense. The well-to-do Northern or Western farmer visiting here is very sure to view them with downright contempt, and to form a very decided opinion about the fitness, or unfitness—mostly the latter—of Florida as a stock State.

But such a hastily formed conclusion would be a great mistake. Florida is a first-class State for live-stock, and no one should feel any confidence in an opinion based on the specimens of wild, uncared-for stock found roaming about the woods.

It should be said, moreover, that the Florida hog, in spite of his looks, has many good points which deserve recognition. In the first place, his meat is always tender and good ; and his lean hams are delicious, either dried, smoked, or salted. And it must be considered that the native hogs are descended from a common, Spanish scrub-breed brought here centuries ago among the droves landed here for the use of the soldiers of De Soto ; that they are never penned, carefully attended to, or well fed. In fact, no care whatever is taken of them by their owners, but they roam about, feeding themselves, which makes them wild and lean. An owner having, probably, as many as two hundred hogs, rarely sees them, but hunts them up from time to time, and shoots one for table-food. If he wishes to sell a number for market, he hunts them up, drives them into a pen, and so disposes of them " in a lump."

Hogs thrive excellently in all parts of the State, especially in the northern tier of counties ; indeed, better hogs can not be found in the United States than those raised in Northern Florida. I have seen as fine, large, fat hogs there as ever were raised out West, especially among the farmers in Leon, Gadsden, Madison, and Jefferson Counties. But all counties are equally good. And those farmers—they are few, however, as yet—who have imported fine-blooded, improved stock can always show as creditable porkers as can be raised anywhere. It is said, too, that no disease has ever appeared among swine in Florida. They are, in all respects, a very profitable property, involving little care or expense, and always sure of finding a good market. There is probably no portion of the United States in which the food that hogs require can be obtained with less expense, or raised with less labor, than in Florida.

In regard to sheep, some of the largest and best flocks in the country are found on the farms in the hilly, well-watered, and grassy sections of Northern Florida. They do best in that part of the State, it being too warm in the southern counties to make it desirable or humane to try to raise them there. Jackson County is preëminent for sheep-raising, but, in any of the twenty-three fine, healthy coun-

FLORIDA PINE-BARRENS.

ties that compose Northern Florida, they do splendidly. Everything is in their favor—climate, food, water, soil, and markets. The northern part of Florida, it should be borne in mind, is not a tropical fruit region, but for stock-raising of the easiest, most profitable kind, it can not be excelled by any section of the United States.

Cattle-raising has long been one of the principal and most profitable of all the many resources of Florida, and strange as it may appear, it is most extensively carried on in the extreme southern portion of the State. There is no doubt that Northern Florida is unexcelled for cattle-raising, although at present, and for many years past, it has been most extensive in the southern part, on the Gulf. Punta Rassa, at the extreme southern end of Charlotte Harbor, is the third port in the United States for cattle-shipments ; and the vast savannas, or prairies, in that region, are grazed by thousands of heads. Cattle-herding is about the easiest occupation in the State, but it takes capital to start in it, and it requires time to develop it. As to the grade of cattle, it is the same as with the hogs—the native breeds are small and extremely unpromising in appearance ; but, as in the case of hogs, this is all for lack of care and breeding, and where high-grade, blooded cattle are introduced, and are attended to with anything like the attention given by Northern stockmen, they do just as well as anywhere, and involve far less expense and labor.

It is often remarked as strange by the visitor to Florida, and is undoubtedly true, that in a State where cattle abound and may be kept almost for nothing, such a thing as fresh milk is almost unprocurable. In the remotest districts, canned milk brought from the North is constantly used ; and in a herd of cattle numbering hundreds there is not a single milch-cow. This, however, is due to the "custom of the country," and not to any difficulty that is encountered in keeping good milch-cows in Florida. There as else-

where, of course, they require attention, and can not be left
to gather all their food in the woods and swamps, as is done
with ordinary stock-cattle; but it has been proved in innumerable instances that cows properly fed and properly
looked after will give milk as good in quality and as abundant in quantity as similar cows will give anywhere. This,
however, is true only of cows that have become acclimated,
and those of the choicer Northern and foreign breeds are
not easily acclimated. The best and surest milch-cow is
what is known as the Georgia cow—one brought from
the neighboring State of Georgia; and next to these are
the native cows that have been separated from the ordinary cattle while heifers, and treated as animals from
whom milk is desired should be treated everywhere. I
am inclined to think that there is nothing to which Florida farmers could more profitably give their attention than
to the production of a good breed of milk-giving cows
adapted to the peculiar local conditions.

Horses, when kept properly stabled out of the sun and
dews, and fed and groomed as any good horse should be,
thrive as well in Florida as in any other portion of the
South. The principal drawback in keeping a horse in
good condition, especially in the towns and cities of Middle and South Florida, is the sandy roads. Out in the
little-traveled country and in the woods, the roads are well
enough, and a horse can trot along as well as anywhere;
but in the towns, where the roads are deeply cut up, it is
very hard upon all draught-animals, and great care should
be taken not to overload or overwork them. In particular,
a good horse should not be intrusted to the care of a colored hostler or driver, if you care much for the horse. A
mule is best adapted to a negro teamster; it being among
the predestinate things of nature that negroes and mules
should come together.

Sandy roads are the worst feature of life in Florida,

and will be for many years, for there is no method of effectually improving them except at great expense. The roads in Northern Florida are free of sand, except in a very few localities, and are as good as any country roads in the whole country, and in some localities in the southern counties there are also good stretches of roads; but in the latter section generally they are sandy to a degree that it is more easy to resent than to describe. This prevents much carriage-riding or walking on the roads, and is the principal cause of the very little visiting among neighbors in the scattered settlements, where it is quite noticeable that the women seldom exchange visits, or indulge in "calls," as is the very popular custom among their Northern sisters.

But in those counties where the roads are sandiest are found the most numerous lakes; indeed, the whole region is a network of lakes, and the settlers' homes are generally bordering on or adjacent to a lake. These lake-side dwellers are sure to have a row-boat, and in such cases visits are more frequently interchanged among the accessible neighbors. Saddles, row-boats, steamers, and railroads will always be the principal methods of travel and intercommunication. Carriages for pleasure, or wagons for labor, will never be so common, or so necessary, as elsewhere.

In the case of horses, as in that of cows, the Northern-raised animals, especially the fancy breeds, do not do well in Florida, particularly if any work is required of them. The Western horses would probably be found better adapted to the climate and other conditions, but they have not yet been introduced in any considerable numbers. The native horse is a small, bony, pot-bellied animal, very shabby-looking and destitute of "style," but capable of more work on a scantier supply of provender than any other creature with which I am acquainted, except a mule. The demand for horses in Florida at present much exceeds the supply, and the prices are consequently disproportionately high, and this is another department of stock-raising to which farmers should give more attention. Specimens that I have seen show that under proper care and treatment the native variety is capable of being made a very presentable as well as serviceable animal.

Barn-yard fowls of every description do remarkably well in all sections of the State. Eggs and chickens are a certainty at all seasons of the year, and the only thing from which they need protection is the pilfering fingers of the negroes. As a flock of fowls is very useful in keeping the insects out of an orange-grove, they may be allowed considerable space for roaming, and under these conditions would require but very little additional feeding. Moreover, it *pays* to raise them, as the demand in the vicinity of towns or settlements nearly always exceeds the supply, and the prices asked and obtained for them are surprisingly high.

CHAPTER XIX.

OPPORTUNITIES for the sportsman are wonderfully abundant in all sections of Florida—the variety of game and fish being undoubtedly greater than in any other region of equal size in the world.

In all parts of the State are large clear-water springs, ponds, lakes, bayous, and rivers. These fresh-water bodies are literally alive with fish, principally black bass, pike, grunts, sheep's-head, all varieties of perch, bream, etc. Along the entire salt - water coast, with all the harbors, bays, sounds, and inlets, the fishing is simply superb, including mackerel, mullet, salt-water trout, sea-bass, whiting, red snapper, pompano, cavalli—in fact, the variety is innumerable. Wherever you find water in all Florida, fresh or salt, you will find inexhaustible opportunity for the exercise of the angler's art.

All along the coasts, too, especially the lower Atlantic and Gulf coasts, green turtles are very plentiful. Some of them are monsters in size, and turtle-hunting (also hunting for their eggs) is very attractive sport. Often one hundred and fifty to three hundred eggs are found in a nest ; they are delicious eating, like the turtle itself, which is so greatly relished by the epicure everywhere. Oysters in countless millions line the shores, and are everywhere cheap and excellent.

They speak of trout-fishing here, but it is a mistake. The trout, the dainty, golden, speckled trout of Northern waters, does not exist in Florida. What is here called the trout is in reality the Oswego black bass, which, as is well known, is a nice, gamy, delicious fish, but not the dainty aristocrat of Northern streams.

Everybody fishes, or at least *can* fish, in Florida, and I have enjoyed many pleasant trips with jolly fishing-parties in various parts of the State. At Cedar Keys I once saw three housewives grouped on the long railroad-pier there, each ensconced under an umbrella, and all comfortably fishing in the most neighborly, sociable, matter-of-fact manner. It was a very common event with them; they were merely out marketing for their dinner—a large, free market, very convenient indeed. One of them showed me two fine, plump, six or seven pounders, her catch in about fifteen minutes.

Fishing is always made additionally interesting in Florida by the great variety of strange and curious creatures that are constantly being captured, and are rarely seen elsewhere.

Of feathered game the variety and quantity are almost as great as of the fish. It is practically unlimited everywhere in the State. At the place where I resided in the summer of 1880—and there were ten men there in the party —I have seen several coveys of quail all at one time feeding about in the yard, or among the orange-trees, often approaching within ten feet of the veranda where we were seated, and glancing up at us without a shade of fear or timidity. Everywhere they feed about in the barn-yards among the common fowls (except, of course, right in the towns and villages); and in a ride of a mile I have frequently seen a dozen coveys scudding across the roadway but a few steps distant.

No other bird is quite so abundant, perhaps, as the quail; but, according to Hallock's "Camp-Life in Florida," the game-birds include the wild-turkey, the Canada goose, the mallard, the canvas-back, the teal, the black duck, the scaup-duck, the red-head duck, the wood-duck, the ruddy duck, the raft-duck, the green wingtail, the blue wingtail, snipe, golden plover, piping plover, black-billed plover, woodcock, yellow-legs, woodpeckers, godwits, curlew, black-necked stilt, larks, rails, herons, cranes, kingfishers, and ibis. There are also eagles, vultures, hawks of several varieties, crows, owls, coots, loons, pelicans, and paroquets. There is hardly a section of the State in which some of these species are not abundant, and there is no season of the year when the sportsman need seek far for his prey.

Of furred game many kinds are found. Among the larger game there are the bear, the panther, the lynx, the gray wolf, the gray fox, and the wild-cat. Deer (of a very small size) are found nearly everywhere, but are most abundant in the southern and western counties, and especially in the larger islands. Hunting them is probably the best sport that Florida affords.

Early one morning in Brooksville, while I was in one of the little groceries there, an old "cracker," one of the genuine native sort, came riding up. He was an interest-ing specimen; his appearance, costume, and language were all "cracker," and his horse, equipments, and gun were curiosities. He dryly remarked, and his language was plain, that he "were gwine arter a de-eer fur dinner, fur the old 'ooman say her war outer meat." About two hours later I was interested to see him again ride up with a fine, fat, two-year-old buck thrown across his nag. He had "found his meat," and the body was yet warm. Evidently deer are plentiful thereabout, and he knew where to find them.

Bears and panthers are somewhat scarce. Their haunts are mostly on the islands and in the southern counties; but they are "scared up" in all parts of the State, usually right where and when least expected, of course. As game they

13

A HUNTER'S CAMP.

are rather difficult to find, except for a party specially hunting them, and prepared to go to the remoter sections of the State, where settlers are few.

Alligator-shooting is too easy to be mentioned among the resources of the genuine sportsman. It may be enjoyed anywhere, especially on the upper St. John's and in the swamps ; but, like buffalo-shooting out West, it is so tame, after the first excitement of seeing this peculiar game, that it becomes rather tiresome. The killing of them has now become a regular occupation, the skins being an article of commerce and exported in large quantities. The smaller game is extremely plentiful everywhere, and includes raccoons, opossums, squirrels (the Southern fox-squirrel and the gray squirrel), and rabbits.

Of Florida, much more accurately than of most other places to which the term is applied, it may be said that it is "a paradise for sportsmen." "In the immediate vicinity even of such centers of population as Jacksonville, St. Augustine, and Tallahassee," says a trustworthy writer, "there is excellent sport for either the angler or the huntsman, and it is only necessary to penetrate a short distance into the country in any direction in order to find game incredible in quantity and variety. One great advantage which Florida offers to sportsmen is that, owing to the extreme mildness of its climate, what is called 'roughing it' is a much less trying process than perhaps anywhere else in America. By taking only the most obvious precautions as to clothing, etc., even invalids may camp out for weeks with substantially no risk ; and, so much of the locomotion being by water, there is comparatively little likelihood of exhausting fatigue. Some of the most ardent of every season's sportsmen belong to the class of 'consumptives' who, before reaching Florida, were afraid to venture out of the house after sunset."

CHAPTER XX.

BECAUSE Florida is a semi-tropical region, it is quite generally the opinion of people in other regions that it is the natural home of all kinds and varieties of hideous, poisonous, troublesome reptiles, insects, and "bugs," that creep, crawl, or fly. Such pests are always supposed to dwell in warm climes, and the name of India, Mexico, or any tropical region, at once suggests tarantulas, boa-constrictors, vampires, and fleas; and doubtless the great majority of people entertain a very similar opinion of Florida, and perhaps firmly believe that on this account human life in midsummer is all but intolerable there. Such an opinion is another of the many erroneous ones about Florida that are current among those who have not seen for themselves. It is a wrong belief, and will require but a short chapter to refute it.

Alligators exist in all portions of the State where there are any marshy, wet, swampy jungles or lakes; but they are not a pest, they are quite cowardly, and the largest of them will run from a child of six years, unless actually cornered, or cut off from their retreat in the nearest water. The exception, of an alligator attacking any one, is as rare as the runaways of an old family horse. It *may* happen, but as a matter of fact very rarely does happen. Instead of a danger, they are merely an object of curiosity to all residents and visitors.

These great reptiles propagate their species from eggs,

which the female deposits in large numbers in the muddy
recesses of the shores of their haunts. She digs out a spacious hole, and depositing the eggs—several hundreds in
number—at one time, proceeds to cover them, and when
she has erected a stout earthwork over them her maternal
duties are entirely finished with *that* brood. After a
lengthy period (the precise time is variously given by different authorities) the little 'gators come forth, and, with
unerring instinct, make a direct line, over all obstacles, to
the water ; while, with equally unerring but cannibalistic
instinct, the big alligators at once proceed to devour the
little ones. (See Appendix, note 32.)

Of snakes there are but ten or eleven species in Florida,
and only five of these are poisonous : the rattlesnake, the
cotton-mouthed moccasin, the water-moccasin, and two
kinds of adders. The king-snake, the bull or gopher snake,
the black snake, the coach-whip, and the common ground-
snake, are the harmless species. Of these last mentioned,
two kinds—the black and the king snakes—are the friends
of humankind, for they wage relentless and usually vic-
torious warfare upon all others of their loathsome species.

But, after all, there are very few snakes in Florida, and
they are rarely found save in dense undergrowth or in sel-
dom-visited regions. I have traveled over many portions
of the State, and been much in the woods and underbrush
in South Florida, and I never saw a deadly snake ; in fact,
I saw but one coach-whip and five or six black snakes.
Nor have I met anybody that has seen more than a very
few deadly snakes. To see two or three in a residence of
half a dozen years seems to be about the average. Their
scarcity is principally due to the numerous hogs, deer, owls,
hawks, coons, and skunks, all of which are deadly enemies
to them, and to the extensive fires that annually burn over
the underbrush of large tracts of land.

There is also a species of centiped that is poisonous, its

sting being about as virulent as that of a mad hornet; but these pests are scarce, and are not considered a danger. The same is the case with a small species of scorpion, and a similar species known as a grampus.

Flies are very few, noticeably so in the case of the common house-fly; there are several varieties of horse-flies that are not especially troublesome to the horses, but are remarkable for their great size—often an inch and three eighths long. There is also a fly of about the same large size, mostly found around horses, and commonly known as the "horse-guard," for it never lights on horses, buzzes in their faces, or worries them in the least, but gobbles in any and all flies that light on the horse, devouring the little flies, but only eating the heads off of the larger ones.

Mosquitoes are as elsewhere a great nuisance, where they exist. Their season is in the months of April, May, June, and July; and they are very few in other months. In many localities none are to be found at any season; and in the greater portions of those localities where they exist, they do not come in "clouds" or "swarms." It is only in some peculiarly low and swampy location that they annoy one as they do in New Jersey and Michigan.

The little black gnat and the tiny sand-fly are the most villainous torments. These, indeed, are perfect pests, but they are only in "full bloom" from August to early November. A thin veil worn like a cap over the head entirely protects you from all annoyance from them, for they do not bite or sting, but are simply possessed with a ravenous desire to explore one's eyes and ears. They are not general to the State, but are found in a few sections only, and are not at all poisonous.

If you walk through the woods, especially among old pine-logs, there is a red-bug, a minute insect, which frequently attacks your ankles and bites, but you are only made aware of it by the pimple or scar; it does not poison the flesh. You can escape their bother by each morning or evening bathing the ankles with ammonia or camphor, or by rubbing them with vaseline—that is, if you *must* be out in the woods. Also, in the autumn, if you are out in the swamps, there is a wood-tick that assaults you, very much like the red-bug, but its effect and the remedy are precisely the same as with the red-bug.

Fleas are undoubtedly a great pest, but as their cause is well understood it is not impossible to keep reasonably free of them. They are due to the innumerable dogs, hogs, and other live-stock that are allowed free range everywhere; and if these are kept at a respectful distance and rigidly excluded from the house, fleas also will be apt to be conspicuous by their absence.

Around dwellings there is a species of cockroach, of mammoth size, which sometimes causes a good deal of annoyance. They are not very numerous, however, are very shy and clumsy, and may easily be got rid of by the means that are found efficient elsewhere.

The foregoing list includes, I believe, all the insect pests and annoyances that are liable to trouble one in Florida. Of these, very few invade the house; that is, if it *is* a house as understood in the Northern States—a neat, clean, wholesome abode; but if you can be brought to inhabit a flimsily constructed, dirty "cracker" cabin, open for everything to enter, they will very probably visit you, and may even be induced to take up a permanent residence.

As a final word I would say that if one lives civilized, keeps clean as to house and person, and uses mosquito-bars and nettings for the beds and screens for windows and doors, just as is done at the North, the insects are no more troublesome here than there.

CHAPTER XXI.

THE first and greatest need of Florida is population. It is beyond all other regions of America the most favored for poor people with little capital but of industrious disposition, able and willing to work. Capital and wealth are always welcome everywhere, but it is an established fact that, wherever labor leads, capital always quickly follows. Look at the history of all our Western States. It was always the case that the poor pioneer emigrant with a rifle, and an axe or spade, hewed the first pathway. It was the "wheelbarrow" emigrant that opened up the great mining regions of the Rocky Mountains; then came the small storekeepers, then the wholesale dealers, then the bankers—the real capitalists—railroads, and telegraphs : and thus were States founded and solid prosperity established.

By all means let the poor people come to Florida, for nowhere can they live so cheaply, and so quickly "earn a living"; while, if they are at all industrious and possessed of common good judgment, they can soon accumulate a competency. If they can bring a little money, sufficient to obtain a few acres of land at cheapest rates or to take up a homestead on the public lands, to build a cheap cottage, and to subsist for six months, so much the better; they are then sure to succeed and gradually better their condition. But even if empty-handed, let them come, for employment can surely be found to preserve life and give the newcomer time to look about for a better chance.

Study the advantages of Florida, with its many and rapidly increasing lines of water and rail communications to all parts of the country, cheap rates, and rapid transit ; then turn to those offered to the poor man in the far-off, bleak, inhospitable West—of vast, treeless, waterless, fruitless plains, or comfortless mountains ; where railroads are the only means of transit, and they are in nearly all cases without competition, have high rates, and, being generally monopolists of the soil of their section, hold the settler in an iron grasp ; where Nature offers nothing but a place to breathe in, and only by hardest labor and through constant struggle can life be sustained.

An important consideration for the settler is that Florida is emphatically a region of health, and of the activities which come from health. There is no such thing as "enervating effects," etc., on the settler in this region. It is not far enough south. I find everywhere, among the people here from colder climes, the same activity of brain and body, the same effort to improve, as among the people of any other locality.

Look about Florida—see the new towns springing up everywhere ; the railroads, steamboat lines, mills, factories, stores, new residences, new appliances for cultivation of the soil, machinery, implements, new schemes for raising, increasing, marketing, shipping, and obtaining profits from all soil products : are not these conclusive evidences of the vigor and activity of the new-comers ?

For, with very few exceptions, it is the Northern people, so rapidly moving in here, that are developing the true resources and capabilities of the State, and who are engaged in all the enterprises of private or public benefit. Everywhere they are planning new improvements, draining swamps, "locating" town-sites, laying out streets and lots, clearing large tracts of fertile soil, setting out orange-groves, experimenting with new crops, opening stores, founding churches and schools, erecting saw-mills, cassava-mills, and fruit-preserving establishments, building new railroads, putting new steamboats on all these waters, hunting out new " springs," building new hotels—in fact, civilizing this entire region. Everywhere the labor, the enterprise, and the money of the Northern-born settler are apparent.

The old slaveholding element, with its aristocratic and exclusive ideas, is very small in Florida, and that small number is only found in a few places in the northern counties. Moreover, the visitor or settler will find these people (I mean the better class of the old-time slaveholding planters) at heart very good, hospitable, and kindly-disposed people. Such has always been my experience, and I have met many of them.

I believe none of these people desire a return to slavery times and customs ; and, leaving out the bitterness natural to humankind when defeated, I believe they honestly wish to see Northern people settle here.

The "cracker" element, the "poor white trash," are too few in number and too insignificant in influence for special attention. They are, as a class, merely white barbarians, rapidly dwindling away ; and, as new settlers move in, the "cracker" moves off.

Capitalists can also find in Florida a broad field for the investment of money. Banks are greatly needed in several of the new towns. The exchange on the sales of the great crops and the vast amount of goods being brought in every week, not by seasons but continuously, and all such commercial transactions, make the need of banking-houses very great. The arrivals of steamers at Sanford and such principal points on the St. John's average about thirty each week, and their cargoes each way, and passenger-lists, are indubitable evidence of healthy commerce and increasing prosperity, where money is plentiful and well employed. The State laws regarding security for cash advanced are of the most favorable kind, giving the money-lender safe and certain aid without entangling delays. No State has more favorable laws. (See Appendix, note 33.)

Another great need is railroads in all parts of the State. If well located, they would pay handsome returns upon their cost. Railroads can be built here with much less expense than anywhere else in the United States ; there being fewer "cuts and fills," the soil being easier to work, right of way freely obtained, and the ties very cheap. The stumpage of the best varieties of timber on the lands that the State so liberally gives would, if judiciously utilized, pay very handsomely.

Paper-mills, to use up the vast quantities of scrub palmetto-tops, cassava-mills, sugar-mills, canning establishments for vegetables, oysters, turtles, etc., preserving-factories for fruits, orange-wine vaults, mattress-factories to use up the abundant Spanish mosses (a splendid article for mattresses), tanneries for the immense number of hides produced in the whole State, turpentine and tar stills, machine-shops for manufacturing furniture, etc., of the palmetto, cedar, cypress, and hard woods of this region—these are but a few of the needs of Florida, and of the opportunities afforded to capitalists. Orange-culture is in a peculiar sense an occupation for men with capital at command ; and few things would pay better than to bring a number of choicely situated orange-groves to the bearing period, and then sell them at the prices which such groves readily bring.

Even if one does not care to risk money in the ordinary business enterprises, there are ways of making it very productive. It can be loaned on perfectly good security at from ten to eighteen per cent. per annum.

CHAPTER XXII.

ONE of the greatest sources of perplexity to the new-comer is the vast amount of contradictory advice sure to be tendered him. If he asks a settler for an opinion about a certain piece of land, or how to select orange-trees, or when to plant or how to plant, or about vegetables, or about transportation, he is certain to receive a lengthy argument completely exhaustive of the subject in question, and every detail *proved* by the settler from his personal experience and observation. This, of course, is encouraging, and the new-comer goes on his way, rejoicing that he now knows all about the matter, and prepared to follow the instructions as given. Unfortunately, he happens to mention the subject to another settler, a discussion ensues, and to the new-comer's profound astonishment he hears all the statements made by his previous informant combated, overthrown, demolished, and their absurdity *demonstrated*. Congratulating himself upon his lucky escape from the bad venture he was about to make, he proceeds to follow the advice of his last authority, when he meets a third, and the same result ensues. The advice of the second informant is proved all wrong, and an entirely new theory is positively asserted to be the right and only true one.

So it goes : and, if the new-comer should consult a dozen different people, he would probably receive from each an explanation totally different and distinct, and each declared by the relator to be the result of personal experience. It is wonderful, it is utterly confusing ; and it very frequently results in causing the new-comer to enter into a bad bargain, to waste much money and labor, and ultimately to give up in disgust, sacrificing his property for a song, and going away, bitter against Florida.

But the truth is, the fault was largely with himself. He should not depend solely upon advice, but should use his own judgment ; and to form a sound judgment he should spend a small amount of extra money, and travel about to different localities, carefully observing and studying for himself. Hasty purchases are very apt to be regretted in Florida as well as elsewhere ; and it is always money well spent that is spent in looking about for the right locality, the right soil, the right class of products, the right opportunity for transportation, and the requisite advantages as to health, markets, neighbors, schools, and the like.

The experiment of a man, especially with a family, transferring all his interests and hopes from a temperate to a semi-tropical region, is necessarily a trying one. The climate, soils, products, seasons of labor and rest, of planting and harvests, are totally different. Indeed, nothing is the same ; even the new-comer and his family change in diet, hours of rest and labor, even in the constituents of their blood. Yet the change is one that involves no insuperable difficulties, provided due care be exercised in the matter of diet, exercise, labor, and habits of life. The abundance of certain fruits that are regarded as luxuries elsewhere is very apt to betray new-comers into over-indulgence in the matter of food, and this, of course, should be guarded against. The water-supply, too, should be carefully scrutinized, and any indications of impurity should cause its use to be discontinued. Moreover, until he becomes thoroughly acclimated, the new-comer should avoid as much as possible long-continued exposure to the summer sun, or to the air of damp localities. In all these respects he would do well to observe and follow the customs of the more intelligent "natives."

A fruitful cause of failure among new-comers to Florida is their greed for vast possessions; they want a hundred-acre grove at an outlay not sufficient for ten acres. Remember, it costs money, labor, and tedious time to produce an orange-grove; and a snug, well-cared-for, thrifty grove of five acres, with say three hundred trees, all brought to quick and prolific bearing, is a far surer and more desirable investment than one three or four times as large which can not be kept in an equally high state of cultivation. Observation has shown that a small grove can be brought to bearing from two to three years sooner, and at much less proportionate expense of money and labor, than a very large one. One reason of this is, that in a large grove the work must all be performed by hired laborers, while in a small one the owner is quite likely to do much of it himself. The fertilizing, too, for a large grove must all be purchased, while on the small grove the barn-yard and stables, the poultry, the dwelling, all contribute—until the amount to be purchased is very small.

If you desire to engage in vegetable-gardening (a very profitable enterprise, if rightly conducted), you must use good judgment: select good black or dark-brown hammock soil, not too wet; shelter it from the east wind, if on the Atlantic coast; and locate close to some established line of transportation. It will be much the wisest policy to pay a high price for five or ten acres located convenient to shipping facilities, than a low price for larger acreage too far from market.

If you desire to engage in the culture of purely tropical fruits, such as bananas, pineapples, etc., there is but one essential direction to be observed—it is to *go south*, beyond the region of frost-visits, select any cultivated soil, pine or hammock, and locate near some convenient and established line of transportation.

One class of persons against whom the new-comer must be on his guard is the "land-shark." There are land agents in Florida who are as trustworthy as the same class anywhere, and whose advice and assistance may be of great service to the settler ; but, on the other hand, almost every locality is infested by one or more "sharks," who prey upon new-comers by offering them "the greatest bargain to be had in the State," the prices asked being usually about twice as much as the property could actually be bought for. Usually very plausible in manners and talk, these men are well calculated to impose upon the inexperienced, but a little inquiry among other parties will usually suffice to expose their true character. One rule should be inflexibly adhered to by the settler, and that is, never to be persuaded into "closing" hastily with a "bargain," and never to buy a piece of land until he has consulted two or three different parties as to its quality and price.

As a general thing, if he has exercised due care in the selection of his land, the settler need have no fear of malaria or "fevers." He will naturally be discouraged by the sallow, tallowy look and listless manner of many of the "natives " ; but whoever, in any place, should live as they live, eating such wretched food, neglecting body and mind, would at the end of a few years find himself in the same condition, which is due not to the locality but to the mode of life. With the right sort of a house, food of good variety and quality and *properly prepared*, cleanly habits, and healthful exercise for the mind as well as the body, people may enjoy as much vigor and activity in Florida as anywhere in the United States.

I have observed in all parts of the State that the women express less liking for Florida than do the men ; in fact, in reply to the question invariably asked of all, " How do you

like the State?" of all the Northern-born women I have
met, but three or four replied in a hearty, convincing manner that they really liked it. This appears somewhat
strange, when we consider the fact that the climate, fruits,
flowers, garden dainties, and the like, such as women usually are fond of and delight in, are so abundant in Florida.
The principal source of their objections is the same as in
all new countries : women seldom enjoy pioneer life, but
prefer old, settled communities, churches, schools, finished
dwellings, society, *sidewalks*, and intimate social intercourse.
The sandy soil, heavy roads, and absence of sidewalks, especially in South Florida regions, are the real cause of the
prevalent discontent of the women. Added to this is the
general neglect of new settlers to provide lawns, grass-plots,
flower-gardens, poultry-yards, etc., to attract and divert the
attention of their female companions. In the towns throughout Northern Florida, where the improvements are more
general, there is most content among the women ; and in
the few homes in Southern Florida where the house is neatly constructed, with wide, cool piazzas, lawns, and flower-
gardens, a poultry-yard well stocked, and *a cow* (thus pro-
viding spring chickens, fresh eggs, fresh milk, and butter,
things always so agreeable to the housewife)—in homes
where these surroundings are found, is always found resig-
nation if not contentment.

Be cautious, look about you, use your own best judgment, avoid land-sharks, begin on a small scale at first, be
scrupulously cleanly of person and house, provide good food
and have it well prepared, and, though you are a "new-
comer," you may enjoy life and prosper in Florida.

CHAPTER XXIII.

JACKSONVILLE is the principal objective point for all Florida visitors. It is the focus where all lines of travel from all parts of the North and West terminate, and where all the local lines of railroads and river-boats have their beginning or chief office; where information concerning all portions of the State can be obtained, and all uncertain routes to interior points of interest decided upon. This supremacy is shared in some degree by Pensacola. That is the chief Floridian city on the Gulf, and is best known to the people of the adjoining Gulf States. In fact, Pensacola belongs, by all natural and geographical laws, to Alabama, and was far more accessible to the people of that and neighboring States than to those of Florida. This difficulty has been remedied by the completion of the Pensacola and Atlantic Railroad, from its initial terminus on the Chattahoochee to its natural and originally proposed terminus, Pensacola.

To the tourist from New England and New York, the West and South, there are several routes open, all accommodating and desirable.

TO FLORIDA BY WATER.

One of the well-appointed steamers of the Mallory Steamship Line sails from Pier 20, East River, at three o'clock P. M. each Friday,* visiting Port Royal *en route*, arriving at Fernandina on the

---

* There are many lines connected for entry into Florida, and no doubt an increase will be made from year to year, and such changes ensue as will render it impossible for the conditions given of prominent routes to be relied on for any series of years from the time of publication in a standard volume. Therefore, we would say, to ascertain the combinations, schedules, and routes of any particular year, reference must be had to Appletons' annually corrected Guide-Books, or the numerous guides for each season always at hand.

morning of the following Tuesday, and connecting at the wharf there with the train to Jacksonville (only thirty-three miles, an hour's pleasant ride over the new railroad). For invalids and all who enjoy the novelty of a short sea-voyage this route offers superior attractions. Returning, a steamer leaves Fernandina each Thursday. The steamers at this time are the Carondelet, State of Texas, and City of San Antonio.

A steamer of the New York and Savannah Steamship Line sails tri-weekly at different hours from Pier 43, North River, direct to Savannah, sixty hours' sea trip, connecting there with the Florida steamers to Fernandina and Jacksonville, some of which follow the channel between the mainland and islands, properly known as the "Sea Island Route," much like a beautiful tropical river journey. Corresponding schedule from Savannah to New York. The Florida trains, of course, connect with these ships.

The steamers from New York to Savannah connect also, by the water route, with trains from Fernandina to Jacksonville, on the new direct coast-line, a run of about one hour and a half. There are now five steamers on the New York and Savannah Line—City of Savannah, Tallahassee, City of Augusta, Chattahoochee, Nacoochee.

Through tickets by all rail between Jacksonville and New York, $31; by rail to Savannah or Charleston, thence by steamship, $25.

Between Jacksonville and New York another line of fine steamers connects at Savannah and Charleston, touching at Fernandina— the City of Palatka and the City of Monticello. This is a late line, with very efficient vessels. They take the outside passage, Charleston and Palatka being the destinations. Through tickets to New York at this time, $23; round, $41.

A line of steamers exists between Fernandina and Savannah, known as the Key Line, the rail connection in Florida being with the coast road to Jacksonville, under the recently formed Florida Railway and Navigation Company. In conjunction with this company the De Bary Line purposes to put steamers on the same route for the season of 1884-'85. For travelers who wish to see the historical inside coast route the facilities promise to be very complete.

Steamship lines exist between Savannah, Baltimore, Philadelphia, and Boston, sailing each way once a week at different hours. Those on the Philadelphia line are the Juniata and the Dessoug.

The New York and Charleston Steamship Line. One of the first-class steamers of this line sails from Pier 27, North River, for Charleston direct, connecting there with the coast line of railroad to Florida, and the steamers outside to Savannah, Fernandina, Jacksonville, and Palatka. Special schedules exist with the steamers City of Palatka and City of Monticello.

The New York and Charleston Steamship Company advertise ships to Boston, Philadelphia, and Providence, Rhode Island. Their present ships to New York are the City of Columbia, City of Atlanta, Delaware, and San Domingo.

The Old Dominion Steamship Line. One of the large and fine steamers of this line sails tri-weekly from Pier 26, North River, for Portsmouth, Virginia, connecting there with the Seaboard Railroad to Weldon, North Carolina, and thence through to Florida by either upper or lower lines. This is the quickest of the water routes to Florida from the North, but of course only about half the journey is performed by boat.

The Lewis Bucki is a fine, safe sail-and-steam vessel which sails about twice a month between Jacksonville and New York city, carrying heavy freights and some passengers. She has been on the line about three years, and has made the passage with great regularity and safety.

Sailing-vessels (regular lines) are constantly plying between the leading ports North and East to Fernandina and Jacksonville.

On the Florida Atlantic coast—from Jacksonville to Port Orange, Daytona, and New Smyrna—sail-vessels make alternate trips about once a week; and they run to meet the demand of commerce as far down as Lake Worth, the extreme point south of the inner range of coast waters, in latitude 26° 35', making this trip at irregular times. A steamer is on also in the winter season for New Smyrna and the adjacent waters. The Greenwich, for the season 1884–1885, leaves St. Augustine for points farther south, making alternate trips weekly in connection with the Jacksonville and St. Augustine Railway. The different agents for the outside sail-boats may be learned on inquiry in Jacksonville. In some cases the captains act as their own agents.

New Boston, Baltimore, and Florida Line.—Very recent arrangements have been made to put on lines of steamships between Boston, Baltimore, and Florida, the nearest heretofore direct ocean communication with Boston and Baltimore being by the Savannah steamship lines with those ports. The present arrangements are made in connection with the Florida Railway and Navigation Company to unite with their railway terminus at Fernandina. The first steamer of these lines will be the Jessie H. Freeman, which is announced to leave Baltimore on the 10th of October, 1884, direct for Fernandina.

These are important ocean lines, showing that every season creates a new demand for communication with the medi-aquean State of the Union. So frequent and much more increased will be the future provision for this demand that, as we have said, the public must depend upon the announcements of our periodical guidebooks to keep pace with the new details of information.

New Florida and Boston Steamship Line.—The "Florida Herald" of the 25th of September, 1884, announces arrangements for the early establishment of a new line of ocean steamships between Boston and Fernandina, to connect with the Florida Railway and Navigation roads.

The company that are to operate these lines is Messrs. Seaverns & Co., fruit importers and merchantmen of Boston. It is understood that arrangements were completed, and the lines will commence operations early in October. The Boston line will be weekly, and operate two large steamers, carrying both freight and passengers.

The nearest direct line of steamers between Boston and Florida has been that for several years in existence to Savannah. Assuming that the new line will be put in operation, it will be the first direct line between Florida and the metropolis of New England.

FROM NEW YORK TO THE GULF PORTS.

Fine steamers always sail from New York to the Gulf ports, stopping at Key West, the extreme South Florida city, *en route* to Havana, New Orleans, and the Texan and Mexican ports. Persons wishing to commence their Florida tour in the southern extreme of the State—in which Audubon lingered a long time in his researches —will find all facilities in thus reversing their point of departure.

GULF WATER ROUTES.

These routes have not been as much in demand heretofore as those on the Atlantic, because the wants of travel and commerce have not been so great on the Gulf side. But there has been regular communication by steamers along the Gulf coast, those ships making the whole trip from New Orleans to Cedar Keys, Key West, and Havana, and also by Messrs. Miller & Henderson's lines to varying points from Tampa, the headquarters of the line. As there has long been railroad communication at Cedar Keys, all these vessels reach there regularly, or as occasion may require. So, also, as there has been accomplished, in the year 1884, the first railway communication between the Atlantic and the classic region of Tampa, and travel and commercial intercourse will take on new life, strongly evinced even at this immediate time, the marine communication at the points named must of necessity be more frequent and imposing. The following are the vessels on the Gulf line:

The *Morgan Line* of ships is expected to be replaced about the 1st of November for the season 1884–'85. (No announcement at this date.) The ships heretofore have been the Morgan and the Hutchison, and it is supposed they will resume their places on the line. The winter schedule is weekly, both ways, between New Orleans and Havana, stopping at Cedar Keys and Key West only. One steamer touches at Cedar Keys, going down, on Friday, and one, coming up, on Saturday. Persons going to Cuba should get passports from the consul at Key West, as customary.

Of the steamers of the *Tampa Steamship Company* (Miller, Henderson & Co.) the steamship T. J. Cochran, between Cedar Keys and Tampa, touching at all Manatee River landings, leaves Tampa every Sunday and Wednesday at 8 A. M., connecting at Cedar Keys with express-train F. R. and N. Co. 7 A. M., Monday and Thursday. Leaves Cedar Keys every Monday and Thursday on arrival of F. R. and N. Co. express train, 6.30 P. M., connecting at Tampa with Tampa and Key West Steamship Company's steamer Dictator for Key West and Punta Rassa every Tuesday and Friday at 3 P. M.

Press communications announce, for the season 1884 '85, as follows:

"A steamboat line will start running this autumn from Cedar Keys—that of the Gulf Steamship Company, calling at the principal shallow harbors along the coast between Cedar Keys and Tampa. Their steamer, the Governor Safford, a thirty-thousand-dollar boat, now being built by the Pusey & Jones Company, of Wilmington, Delaware, will have first-class accommodation for passengers. She will be one hundred and thirty-two feet from stem to stern and her draught only three and a half feet.

"The Plant Investment Company will run a line of steamers from Tampa to Key West and Havana, with full passenger accommodation, connecting with the South Florida Railroad. A small steamer is to make a connection on Tampa Bay and the coast with the numerous shallow harbors as far as Manatee."

The Cincinnati Southern, direct line from Cincinnati to Chattanooga, Tennessee, then by the Georgia system to any point in Florida, *via* the Savannah, Florida and Western Railway, or other route.

The Louisville and Nashville—almost in a direct line to Pensacola, Florida, connected by the Tennessee and Georgia system with all other points in the State. New Orleans and Pensacola are connected by a junction of the Northern line forty miles north of Pensacola; thence to New Orleans by mainly a coast line along the attractive margin of the Gulf. This line connects prominently with Montgomery and Selma, and, as before said, along the whole northern frontier of Florida to Jacksonville, by the Pensacola and Atlantic and the Florida Central and Western roads.

Piedmont Route.—Richmond, Danville, Charlotte, Greenville, and Atlanta; or same from Charlotte to Augusta, Savannah, or Jessup; thence by the Savannah, Florida and Western Railroad to the first connection with Florida at Waycross, or farther west on the same line at Dupont or Climax, Georgia. The name of the line is from the *pied* or mottled slopes of the depressions of the Alleghany chain along which it runs—effects formed by the blue mountain mist and the rich autumn foliage of the distant hills.

Shenandoah Valley—from Shepherdstown, Virginia (on the upper Potomac), to Roanoke, Virginia; thence by the various lines to Florida.

Virginia Midland—from Washington to Lynchburg.

Richmond and Alleghany—to Roanoke; thence uniting with the systems of the Carolinas and Georgia.

East Tennessee, Virginia and Georgia—connecting with the preceding at Roanoke, and running along the eastern border of Tennessee, *via* Bristol, to Atlanta; thence to Florida by the systems of Georgia and Alabama. This may be called the transmontane route, in distinction from the eastern Piedmont, as it courses along the western slopes of the southerly chain of the Alleghanies as far as Cleveland, Tennessee.

The Seaboard—from Portsmouth, Virginia, to Weldon, North Carolina.

The Atlantic Coast Line. — Weldon, Wilmington, Charleston, Savannah, Waycross.

FLORIDA RAILWAY ROUTES PROPER.

The Savannah, Florida and Western (formerly the Atlantic and Gulf, from Savannah to Bainbridge, Georgia) has with the change become a leading branch of what is sometimes called the "Plant System." Its branches into Florida extend from Waycross, Georgia, to Jacksonville, Florida; from Dupont, Georgia, to Live Oak, Florida; thence south to Branford, on the Suwanee; thence southeast to Newmansville and Gainesville, making connection with the other roads in the peninsula. The same system also merges the *South Florida* road, from Sanford on the St. John's, at Lake Monroe, continuing thence south to the Kissimmee country, and completing the long-mooted project of a road to Tampa. Another short branch enters Florida, at the far west of the main Georgia line, at a point a few miles east of Bainbridge, called Climax, connecting with the Florida Central and Western road one mile east of the Chattahoochee River.

The Florida Central and Western is the road from Jacksonville to Chattahoochee, with branches to Monticello and St. Mark's, combined under what is known as the "Florida Railway and Navigation Company," with the old road from Fernandina to Cedar Keys, and the branch from Waldo on the latter line centrally down the peninsula, *via* Orange Lake, Silver Spring, and Ocala, Marion County, thence to Wildwood, Leesburg, and Panasofkee, Sumter County. From Leesburg a branch is projected between Lake Griffin and Lake Harris to Tavares. The objective point of this line is Charlotte Harbor. In that direction, at the date of this revision, the press of South Florida announces that nine miles of grading has been completed, and ten miles of right of way cut. The work now extends south of Dade's battle-ground, and is fast approaching Little Withlacoochee River. The road passes through a very fine country, which only needed railroad transportation to develop it.

Probably a large part of the work will be completed to Tampa by the time this revised work is in the hands of the reader.

The same system includes the coast-road from Fernandina to Jacksonville. This road, though at present not making immediate connections, is but a transfer to the Jacksonville and St. Augustine, by coach and steam-ferry across the St. John's, and to the Waycross and Florida Central depots.

The Plant System, by recent purchase, owns the Brunswick and Albany (Georgia) Railway, which crosses the Savannah and Bainbridge roadway, in the route of the former, westwardly to Albany, Georgia. The intersection of the roads has given the name Waycross to the point; the circumstance and growth of the place have made it widely known, until popular custom has applied it to the whole route between Savannah and Jacksonville. Brunswick, though in Georgia, is almost a Florida port, and no doubt the Plant interest have secured it with reference to holding a diversion from their main line to Florida, in connection with steamers from Brunswick to Fernandina, as a link of the archipelago route to Florida. Brunswick is one of the finest harbors, also, on the coast. By the same way, the "Cumberland route" existed a few years ago to Florida, the main water-way being inside Cumberland Island, well known from its association with the name of General Greene. Brunswick itself is on the mainland of Georgia, opposite St. Simon's Island, on which General Oglethorpe once located his now extinct colonial capital.

The Pensacola and Atlantic Road.—After leaving Chattahoochee (the crossing being made by a fine bridge), this road makes the through westward Florida connection in the northern part of the State. In this vicinity, on the eastern side of the river, botanists find the home of rare members of the forest family (almost the lone denizens of the world of their kind), the Florida yew (*Taxus Floridana*) and the *Torreya taxifolia*, or the species of the fir or spruce named after the honored Professor Torrey.

The tourist who may linger at Chattahoochee will soon learn the traditions of this (General Jackson's) camping-ground, when the smoke was clearing away from the battle of New Orleans, and he was called on to protect our Gulf frontier from the schemes of Indians, and foreign intermeddlers through the coast territory of Spain. Hereabout was his military base toward the sea. The trench of an old fort is still to be seen on the hill at Chattahoochee, and a tree with the mark of a cannon-ball driven clear through it, which it is said Jackson fired to show the Indians the superiority of artillery over bows and arrows. Below, near the river, is the site of the fort in which the hostile elements of Indians, negroes, and whites concentrated to threaten the American frontier, but which was nearly wiped out by General Clinch, of the United States Army. This now silent ground, like many others in Florida, was once the stirring scene of a campaign necessitated by a great emergency, and which the energy of a Jackson made brief and dramatic.

This line to Pensacola runs through the counties of West Florida bordering on Alabama, first through Marianna, the county-seat of Jackson County, about twenty-five miles from Chattahoochee. The other westward counties are notable as the land of the colony of Scots who settled there early in the century, and with whom is associated a remarkable history as the offshoot of the Scotch refugees in the early days of Virginia and North Carolina. The road runs west to Milton and the country around the head of Pensacola Bay, the fine lumber-region which has been so tributary to the wealth of Pensacola. The company has given new life to the route, having created De Funiack, near Pensacola, and other promising places.

The boundary between Georgia and Florida is a direct east and west line from the St. Mary's River to the Chattahoochee. This line runs nearly equidistant between the Georgia road from Waycross to Bainbridge, and the Florida road from Jacksonville to Chattahoochee. The connections of the Georgia with the Florida road, as mentioned, are Waycross, the direct connecting point with Jacksonville; Dupont, the direct link with Live Oak; and Climax, a station near Bainbridge, Georgia, by a short line to Chattahoochee. Climax, as the name implies, is a crest of the subsidence of the Appalachie country, which gives the name to that portion of the Chattahoochee river, from the entrance of the Flint River into it near Bainbridge, to the Gulf—the Appalachicola. The connections with the railroad in Florida, bordering on Alabama, are by the ordinary roads from the Alabama counties.

The Jacksonville, St. Augustine, and Halifax road is in operation between Jacksonville and St. Augustine daily, and surveys have been made to continue it to the Halifax River (one of the upper estuaries on the eastern coast), for which the charter provides. No

14

doubt that extension will soon be made. (A coast water-route is being opened between St. Augustine and the Halifax, by utilizing the Matanzas River, and opening the rest of the distance through the marshy courses and higher lands. Dredges of an effective character have been for several years on this route, and its early completion is promised, through the enterprise and energy of Dr. John Westcott.)

The St. John's Railway, from Tocoi, on the St. John's, to St. Augustine, is in operation, and has been successfully, for many years.

The Jacksonville, Tampa and Key West road runs and is completed to Palatka.   It is

THE FIRST TO BRIDGE THE ST. JOHN'S.

This is done at Buffalo Bluff, a short distance south of Palatka, where the road is to cross to the eastern side of the river to avoid some natural obstacles on the western side. It will then pass between Lake George and Dunn's (Crescent) Lake; thence along the eastern side of Lake Woodruff; thence to the westerly side of Lake Monroe, there crossing again to the west side of the St. John's, by another bridge, making connection with Sanford. A branch is projected from Seville, on the east side of Lake George, to the Halifax River, on the east coast, above Port Orange.

For the present the Tampa connection is complete by the Plant road, and the route to Key West is held under the charter until the times are propitious for the stupendous undertaking. The "isles of the sea" will be joined by rail from the mainland in time.

At West Tocoi (opposite the Tocoi of the St. John's Railway) the J. T. & K. W. touches, and communication is had with East Tocoi by a steam ferry-boat which the St. John's Railway Company have recently put on.

The Lake Jessup and Indian River road is completed from Sanford to Lake Jessup, Orange County. Though this is but a link in the chain, the construction of that much insures the completion of the remainder under the special charter of the work. It is projected to run round the westerly and southerly end of Lake Jessup, eastward to Titusville.

The St. John's and Lake Eustis road commences at Astor (named after William Astor, who owns a large tract in the vicinity), on the west bank of the St. John's, opposite the old army head-quarters of Volusia, on the east side, in Volusia County. The road runs direct southwesterly to the great central lake-region of Sumter and Orange Counties, which is to the State what the Great Lake region of the Northeast is to Canada and the Union.

The road strikes the lakes first on the northern end of Lake Eustis at Fort Mason (many of our growing places in Florida retain the names of the old forts located by the Government during the Indian war, which have spread out as cities have from the ancient *burghs* or castles of Europe); thence touches on the northeast of the lake at Eustis; thence to Tavares, near the west end of Lake Dora, diverging southwest to Lane Park on Lake Harris. A much more extended projection is to Orlando, centrally in Orange County, winding along southeast between Lake Dora and Lake Apopka, in the immediate lacustrine center. From Fort Mason, on the north of Lake Eustis, southwesterly to the south end of Lake Griffin, the road is projected also to Leesburg, there meeting the connection of the Florida Southern from Palatka, and the Railway and Navigation Company's road from Waldo.

The Florida Southern road extends from Palatka to Gainesville (with an incompleted branch north to Lake City); thence from Perry, a station east of Gainesville, southward to Ocala; thence to Leesburg, in Sumter County and is projected southward.

The extension of the Transit (Railway and Navigation Company's) road from Waldo southward, crosses the Palatka road at Hawthorne, about six miles east of Perry, and this and the South Florida (Palatka) road run somewhat parallel with each other, five or six miles apart, to Leesburg.

The South Florida road is opening its way toward Tampa and Charlotte Harbor, its objective point, having located through Hernando County, and the company has constructed buildings for its office purposes in Tampa.

THE INTERIOR WATER-WAYS OF THE STATE.

The St. John's River is the great water thoroughfare of the State, the great river of the "Gulf South," running four hundred miles southward of the coast-line of the north Atlantic.

The De Bary Line, on the St. John's River, now consists of the City of Jacksonville, Rosa, Fannie Dugan, Welaka, Sylvan

Glen, Pastime, Water-Lily, De Bary, Crescent City, Anita, and Magnolia. The last-named two run to Palatka, thence across to Dunn's River and Crescent City. The others run through to Sanford and Enterprise. Boats run daily. Agency foot of Laura Street, Jacksonville. Special wharves there and rear of the center of the block, east of Laura Street.

As mentioned elsewhere, the De Bary Line will unite with the Florida Railway and Navigation Company, the present season of 1884–'85, in putting on boats to run with the road from Fernandina on the delightful inside passage to and from Savannah.

As no exact programme, where there are a number of boats concerned, is likely to be fixed even for a season, there may be changes on the river lines and their detachments, which will always be announced.

The People's Line consists, at the present time, of the H. B. Plant, Chattahoochee, Margaret, and Jennie Lane. These make the usual river trips through. Wharves in rear of block, between Laura and Hogan Streets.

Both lines now carry United States mails.

Independent Line.—Steamer Chesapeake. Agency and wharf at the foot of Hogan Street, same as that of the City of Palatka and the City of Monticello.

These agencies may be more conveniently known to visitors to Jacksonville by saying that Laura is the street running from the east end of the St. James Hotel, and Hogan that running from the west end of the St. James, passing the Windsor and Duval.

The steamers of these lines run from Jacksonville to Sanford and Enterprise daily, excepting those before named running from Jacksonville to Palatka and Crescent City.

Another *Independent Line* on the river consists of the Georgea, Port Royal, Comet, the Harvey Hill, and Mary Draper. These run to points between Jacksonville, Palatka, and Crescent City, daily and tri-weekly, according to the necessary schedules for the season. Agency at the foot of Ocean Street, the first street east of the present city post-office, or more in the neighborhood of the Carleton and Metropolitan Hotels.

The Florida Steamship Company's Line—being now the fine steamers City of Palatka and City of Monticello, duplicates of the St. John's, which formerly ran on the same route (from Charleston to Palatka, *via* Savannah, Fernandina, and Jacksonville, making the outside ocean passage to the St. John's), but which is now running between New York and Long Branch. For the season of 1884-'85 these steamers will make the trip three times a week, touching at all important landings.

Most of the steamers to Tocoi, Palatka, Astor, and Sanford, connect with the trains at those points.

The steamers that navigate the Ocklawaha start mostly from Palatka, according to announced time. Occasionally they start from Jacksonville direct, but it is when they have some special freight or other object for making the trip through.

Improvements have been made on the older railroad connection with St. Augustine *via* Tocoi, on the St. John's, by a large ferry-steamer which has been placed on to cross the St. John's River to the west side opposite Tocoi, the connection being with the J. T. & K. W. Railroad, which runs along near the west bank of the St. John's River, thus forming a rail route west of the river from Jacksonville and Palatka to St. Augustine; as great an event this, in the railroad history of Florida, as was the institution of roads on the Northern rivers, where water communication was before the only mode of travel.

Distances to landings on and from St. John's River :

FROM JACKSONVILLE.

	Miles.		Miles.
To Mulberry Grove *	12	To Fort Gates *	106
" Mandarin	15	" Pelham Park	112
" Hibernia *	23	" Georgetown	113
" Magnolia *	28	" Lake George	115
" Green Cove Springs *	30	" Drayton Island *	116
" Picolata	44	" Seville	120
" Tocoi	49	" Spring Grove	126
" Federal Point	58	" Volusia	134
" Orange Mills	63	" Astor—St. John's & L. E. R. R. *	134
" PALATKA *	75	" Manhattan	136
" San Mateo	79	" Bluffton	140
" Edgewater	80	" Hawkinsville *	160
" Buffalo Bluff	87	" DeLand	162
" Nashua	95	" Beresford	163
" Welaka	100	" Cabbage Bluff	165
" Beecher	101	" Blue Spring	168
" Norwalk	103	" Sanford *	193
" Mount Royal	105	" Mellonville *	195
" Fruitland	105	" Enterprise	198

FROM ASTOR BY ST. JOHN'S AND LAKE EUSTIS RAILROAD.

To Lake Eustis.................25 | To Leesburg.....................51
" Fort Mason.................25 |

FROM SANFORD BY SOUTH FLORIDA RAILROAD.

To Lake Maitland ....20 | To Kissimmee................... 40
" Winter Park.................22 | " Tampa.......................115
" Orlando.....................23 |

FROM ENTERPRISE.

To Smyrna.....................30 To Titusville....................
" Halifax ....35 | " Oak Hill....................50

FROM SANFORD.

To Lake Poinsett........ ....130 To Lake Harney.................30
" Lake Geneva................. 15 |
      Places marked thus * are on the east side of the river.

DOWN THE RIVER.

Kemp's Mail Line consists at present of the steamers Mystic
and Mermaid, one of which leaves for Mayport and Pilot Town daily
at 3.30 P. M.   Mayport is on the south side of the mouth of the St·
John's, Pilot Town on the island opposite.   The steamers pass close
to the bluff, on which was the oldest identified settlement of Europeans north of the Gulf of Mexico.   The same steamers leave Jacksonville for Palatka daily at 6.30 A. M.

The Fox, Captain T. W. Lund, now runs from Jacksonville to Salt
Lake, in near communication with Titusville, carrying passengers
and freight for the Titusville region of Indian River.   Fare, $12
through.

THE UPPER ST. JOHN'S.

The Ashtatula and Marion make trips from Sanford to Lake
Poinsett once a week each, being the highest point on the St.
John's that steamers usually reach.   Occasionally they run to Lake
Winder, still farther south.   Fare, generally $6; round trip, $10.
Hour, 9 A. M. from Sanford.

OTHER ROUTES.

Steamers run on Indian River; on the Sumter and Orange
County Lakes; on Lake Tohopkeliga and the Kissimmee; on the
Suwannee; on Tampa Bay and some of the smaller rivers of the

Gulf; occasionally enter the St. Mark's; on the Choctawhatchee Bay and Pensacola Bay and branches; but no schedules are published for special public use.

The Chattahoochee route is supplied with fine steamers, which ply from Columbus, Georgia, to Appalachicola, touching at Chattahoochee, and generally connecting with the trains when not prevented by the rise or fall of the river. The Appalachicola (Chattahoochee) route is a delightful one for leisure tourists. Steamers touch at towns and landings all along the river.

APPENDIX.

Note 1, page 13.—Florida has the largest area for long-staple cotton, which is almost entirely grown east of the Suwannee River and on the peninsula. It will be essentially a sugar-growing State when the great drainage of South Florida is completed. Many of the Louisiana sugar-planters are now becoming interested in the peninsula for sugar-growing. As a mere incident of the capability of the land for sugar-growing, as much as two hundred hogsheads of sugar were grown on less than two hundred acres, in 1850, by Colonel H. R. Sadler, on the St. John's River, five miles above Jacksonville, on the west side, on high pine-land. In former years sugar was a leading article of commerce on the peninsula; since the civil war, it has been much superseded in public attention by citrous fruits and early vegetables.

Note 2; page 13.—At the time of the present revision of this work new facilities of travel for tourists have been completed. The first railroad connecting the East with Pensacola, westward, is in operation. Tourists are extending their travel along what is termed Mainland Florida, connecting with the oldest American settlements of the State, Monticello, Tallahassee, Quincy, and Marianna, in their order. Railroads also connect with the far-south Gulf-side—one now completed to Tampa, and others pushing in the same direction. So, also, on the Atlantic side, railroads will be in operation from the St. John's to Indian River before the revised edition of this book is fairly in hand. St. Augustine, the oldest city; Pensacola, of historical fame; and Tampa, the landing-place of the New-World adventurers a hundred years before the Pilgrims saw Plymouth Rock, are now in close connection with the rest of the world.

Note 3, page 14.—What Floridians now call, locally, the "Peach Country," is the northerly part of the peninsula, where the branches of the St. Mary's and the Suwannee flow on either side of the geological "ridge" from the mysterious Okefinokee which, it is said, stands upon the crest. Peaches will grow well in any part of the State; but they form "a crop" in the region named.

Note 4, page 23.—Within these latitudes, in the central portion of the peninsula, lies what is specially termed the Lake Region; being that in which are the lakes and connecting streams of Marion, Sumter, and Orange Counties. Its chief connection heretofore has been the famous Ocklawaha from the St. John's, but it is now intersected by several railroads diverging each side southwardly to the Atlantic and Gulf, uniting with the roads from Waycross, Georgia, and Pensacola, Florida.

Note 5, page 43.—There are Ormond, Daytona, Port Orange, New Smyrna, and other important points along the coast; lagoons called the Halifax and Mosquito (parts of the coast-chain of waters which are frequently included in the name Indian River), as well as other growing places in Volusia, the county in which Orange City and the other points named are located. New Smyrna is the old English settlement of Turnbull, broken up and almost obliterated by alleged wrongs done the colonists by the founder. The event forms an interesting episode in the history of St. Augustine. The settlers took refuge in the "ancient city."

Note 6, page 46.—The population and aspect of Apopka, as well as other places referred to, are given as supposed at the time of the first edition of this book. Apopka has, no doubt, largely increased and improved. Eustis and Tavares, towns which may almost be said to have taken their start since, have come to be important places in the county. Other settlements in the county have kept their growth.

Note 7, page 48.—At the time of the present revision the St. John and Lake Eustis Railroad, between Lakes Dora and Eustis, is completed to Tavares. It is projected to Orlando, to connect with the St. John's River. This road will tap this whole section.

Note 8, page 50.—While the Astor Railroad from the St. John's River connects the towns east of the central lakes of Sumter and Orange Counties, Leesburg, on the north side of Lake Harris, in Sumter County, is connected by the Mid-Peninsular system of railroads from Wildwood, on what is called the Tropical road, a part of the new Railway and Navigation Company system.

Note 9, page 58.—The crossing of the Withlacoochee River, just before reaching Brooksville, is the site of a severe action during the early part of the Indian war of 1842-'45. It was here that General Clinch crossed his small command of United States troops, and was surprised and defeated in a severe fight suddenly on the south side of the river. Governor Call, of Florida, was on the north side with his command of State troops. There were no boats —nothing more than a felled tree—on which to cross the narrow river; and from this or other difficulties a large part of the command of Governor Call failed to cross. Crimination and recrimination for a long time existed from this circumstance. General Clinch, however, by the noblest heroism, saved himself and the most of his command. The battle of the Withlacoochee was a thrilling event in the "Florida War."

Note 10, page 63.—During the last four years there has been a great change in Tampa. The South Florida Railroad from Sanford on the St. John's River, *via* Kissimmee City, gives railway connection with the outside world. Other railroads to this point are in progress and will soon be completed. The present population is two thousand, and there has been a notable improvement in the hotels, the appearance of the dwelling-houses, and the amount of business done. The Plant Railway system has been the making of Tampa, and numerous important business-houses have sprung up. The development of the tropical fruit culture, pineapples, bananas, etc., has also been an important fact. Tampa was the spot on which the Spanish *conquestadores* first set foot in their march through North America. Aside from the new commercial interests developed by the railroad connection with the St. John's River, Tampa is the center of a large commerce with the Gulf lines of steamers plying on the coast.

Note 11, page 69.—Several destructive fires have of late years occurred in Quincy; and, being off the tourist's line, it has not until recently entered upon the new era. The through rail connection with Pensacola, and the aroused spirit of its stable and good population, has put the place far in advance of the condition above mentioned. It is one of the very oldest towns in the State, the national spirit of its founders being evinced in the adoption of a name.

Note 12, page 70.—Originally the Chattahoochee (U. S.) Arsenal, erected there from the seeming necessity following the war of General Jackson on the Spanish frontier before the purchase of Florida.

The arsenal was taken and held by Confederate troops during the civil war. After peace it was presented by the Government to the State, and was used until 1877 as a State-prison. It was then changed into a public lunatic asylum, and the contract-labor system was adopted by the State to employ the prisoners. The remains of one of Jackson's old camping-grounds, and of a square earthwork of his creation, are still visible near, on beautiful hills overlooking the Chattahoochee River, and reminiscences of the old leader still linger around the historic precinct.

Note 13, page 96.—The former named road has recently been merged into the Florida Railway and Navigation Company system, including the road from Jacksonville direct to Chattahoochee, the coast road from Fernandina to Jacksonville, and the southerly continuations of the Transit road from Waldo.

Note 14, page 98.—Dungeness has recently been purchased by Mr. Andrew Carnegie, of Pittsburg, who is erecting a magnificent mansion on the old ruins, and otherwise restoring this noble property.

Note 15, page 109.—It is proper to state that, while this expression is current in the varying opinions as to the best place for orange-culture, groves exist by the thousand all along the river on both sides,. and away from the river. They are increasing and flourishing. Mandarin, fifteen miles above Jacksonville, is the oldest fruit settlement in the State, and a place of large export.

Note 16, page 110.—On another smaller island, adjoining Fort George, almost within the mouth of the river on the north side, is "Pilot Town," the residence of most of the pilots. It is only separated from Fort George by a small stream, crossed by a narrow bridge. It is named Baton Island, whether from the shape of an Indian baton, or the painted war-club, from which Baton Rouge—included in the ancient Florida—takes its name, is left to the curious to establish. It is supposed it was from this island that De Gourges crossed to the opposite shore of Mayport, when he destroyed the Spanish forts at the mouth of the river, and thence advanced to his vengeful assault on Fort Caroline, a few miles west.

Note 17, page 117.—The "Fruitland Peninsula" is a name given to the land lying between the St. John's and Dunn's Creek and Lake (modernly called Crescent Lake). It has been extensively settled of late years. It will be seen on the map east of the point called "Fruitland."

Note 18, page 127.—The Lake country, forming a large part of Marion, Sumter, and Orange Counties, is as rapidly filling with population as any part of the State. Though there are many places on the margin of the "Lake-river" undesirable for settlement, like the St. John's, the better sites—and they are numerous—offer fine locations, which are being rapidly taken.

Note 19, page 131.—Silver Spring is entered by a branch of the Ocklawaha running west about the center of Marion County. Boats conveying the commerce of the region lie at ease in the Spring, it being a reservoir amply large for an interior port. The Peninsular Railroad has for several years connected the Spring with the North, so that its water-communication is not now so much depended on. This spring ranks as one of the most entrancing natural spectacles that the mind can contemplate.

Note 20, page 134.—Ocala, six miles from the Spring, experienced a rapid growth in the last ten years. A large part of the town was destroyed by fire in the summer of 1884; but, like the effect of fires frequently, new hotel accommodations, business-houses, and other improvements are arising from the ashes.

Note 21, page 150.—Within the past two years the remarkable achievement has occurred of the opening of the Caloosahatchie to Lake Okeechobee, as part of the great drainage-work. Several steamers have made the passage from the Gulf to the Kissimmee River by this route.

Note 22, page 150.—Over half a million of cocoanut-trees have been planted in South Florida, on the Gulf and Atlantic coast and islands, within the past two years. The growth of the cocoanut is now looked on as one of the surely profitable crop industries of Florida.

Note 23, page 156.—It should be remarked that over the reports of orange-crops given in the text of the first edition of this work, as above, a great increase has occurred in subsequent years. This is especially the case with young groves, the crops of which increase fully up to the age of the Speer grove.

Note 24, pages 143, 157, 166.—The South Florida Railroad has since passed under the control of the Plant Syndicate, and has been completed to the previously unexplored region of the Kissimmee, *via* the new city of Kissimmee at the head of Lake Tchopkeliga, thence to Tampa. It taps the whole of the lake-region, and is already proving of incalculable benefit in developing Southern Florida.

Note 25, page 157.—Since the writing of this book great changes have taken place in Sanford. Several fine churches have been built; fine public buildings have been erected, and there is a new bank. The trade has nearly doubled. Skilled labor has poured in, and there is now but little trouble from the scarcity of good mechanics.

Note 26, page 164.—Winter Park is a finely designed settlement, having special reference to a class of settlers that is desirable, and this is secured by the condition of building a good house on a lot sold. It was projected just as the first edition of this work was in press, and is fulfilling the hopes of its projectors. Winter Park, as a destination, forms a fine drive from Orlando and the other points in order along the railroad.

Note 27, page 171.—The changes on this line demand a word of correction. At present the steamers run only to Fernandina, stopping at Port Royal, South Carolina. New vessels have taken the place of the ones mentioned, and run weekly each way. They are equipped for both passengers and freight, doing a very large business in the latter department.

Note 28, page 176.—A more extended work on the same line is comprehended in the charter of the Okeechobee Canal Company, which is at present in abeyance, because of the immense work of drainage on the Gulf-side of Okeechobee and the Kissimmee Valley previously undertaken. The charter and operations of Dr. Westcott tend to a great extent to accomplish the object of the Okeechobee Company on the east side of the peninsula.

Note 29, page 225.—The first impulse of immigration came from the Northern and Eastern States, but within the last four or five years settlers from the Western and Southern States have poured in, and to-day fully equal the tide of colonization from the other sections, and it may be said are no less thrifty and enterprising. While what is said on page 226 as to the importance of New York and Eastern capital in building railways and carrying on other extensive improvements is largely true, it is also true that many capitalists from other sections have invested successfully and contributed handsomely to the growth of the State.

Note 30, page 227.—Many of the colored people are all that is charged in the way of indolence and shiftlessness. But there has been a steady improvement in their character. Most of them under proper management make good house-servants and field-laborers, and give as satisfactory service as could be reasonably expected.

Note 31, page 231.—Whatever ground there may have been for the charge of legislative indifference to public-schools prior to 1880, it is certain that the State law-makers have recently shown as much intelligence and zeal in furthering the public-school system as can be found in any State. This has cropped out in many ways, proving that both the public and the Legislature are thoroughly alive to the importance of educating the masses, both white and colored.

Note 32, page 291.—The impression that alligators devour their young, though common, is probably an error. Nature provides that the young enter the bodies of the mother for a time as a refuge and protection. The same is the habit of the young saw-fish and other marine creatures and some quadrupeds. It is only an extension of the marsupial provision.

Note 33, page 297.—Ten new banks have been started in Florida during the last four years, but are still insufficient to the demand. The rapid growth of the State and its great industrial and commercial development make this form of investment for the capitalist a very safe and desirable one.

BOOKS OF TRAVEL.

Florida for Tourists, Invalids, and Settlers : containing Practical Information regarding Climate, Soil, and Productions; Cities, Towns, and People; Scenery and Resorts; the Culture of the Orange and other Tropical Fruits; Farming and Gardening; Sports; Routes of Travel, etc. By GEORGE M. BARBOUR. With Map and numerous Illustrations. 12mo. New edition, in red cloth, flexible, $1.50.

TABLE OF CONTENTS : I. Questions and Answers; II. Natural Divisions of Florida; III. A Trip through the State with Commissioner French; IV. A Trip through North Florida with Captain Fairbanks; V. Jacksonville, Fernandina, and St. Augustine; VI. The St. John's River; VII. The Ocklawaha River, Silver Springs, and Ocala; VIII. The Indian River Region and the Inland Lakes; IX. The Gulf Coast and Key West; X. The Sanford Grant and Orange County; XI. Random Sketches: An Ocean Voyage in Winter—the Atlantic Coast of Florida—the Southwest Coast; XII. Climate and Health: Suggestions for Invalids; XIII. Retrospective: An Historical Sketch; XIV. Florida Folks and Families; XV. Orange-Culture; XVI. Other Tropical and Semi-tropical Fruits; XVII. Field and Farm Products: Vegetable-Gardening; XVIII. Live-Stock; XIX. Fur, Fin, and Feather; XX. Insects and Reptiles; XXI. Opportunities for Labor and Capital; XXII. A Word of Friendly Advice to New-comers; XXIII. Routes to and through Florida.

Two Years in Oregon. By WALLIS NASH, author of "Oregon, There and Back in 1877." With Illustrations. 12mo. Cloth, $1.50.

"Mr. Nash presents in a favorable view the agricultural and business prospects of the country, the social and political life of the people, and, while he does not claim that a competence can be secured without persevering industry, he maintains that the inducements offered to the enterprising and energetic are such that, in a few years, the emigrant of moderate means and some experience will be able to acquire a home and pecuniary independence. The book contains a vast amount of information useful to the emigrant, and it is written in a pleasant, chatty style. The descriptions of the varied scenery, the character sketches of the settlers, and the laughable incidents recounted, give an additional pleasure to the volume, which is enriched by several illustrations of Oregon scenery."— *Chicago Journal.*

In the Brush ; or, Old-Time Social, Political, and Religious Life in the Southwest. By the Rev. HAMILTON W. PIERSON, D. D., ex-President of Cumberland College, Kentucky. With Illustrations by W. L. Sheppard. 16mo. Cloth, $1.50. New cheap edition. Paper, 50 cents.

"Here I have drawn word-pictures of many scenes in the social life of a generation and a state of civilization rapidly passing away, never to reappear, that otherwise would have had no memorial except as perpetuated in the traditions of the people. I will only add that I am indebted to no library, to no book, not even to a newspaper, for a single fact presented in this volume. They were all gathered incidentally, while laboriously engaged in the duties of my profession as the general agent of the American Bible Society, and while traveling for years in the interests of the college over which I was called to preside. They all relate to the ante-bellum period in the history of our country."— *The Author.*

For sale by all booksellers; or sent by mail, post-paid, on receipt of price.

New York: D. APPLETON & CO., 1, 3, & 5 Bond Street.

APPLETONS' GUIDE-BOOKS

APPLETONS' GENERAL GUIDE TO THE UNITED STATES AND CANADA.

Revised each Season to date of issue. In three separate forms:

One Volume Complete, pocket-book form, roan, $2.50.

New England and Middle States and Canada, one volume, cloth, $1.25.

Southern and Western States, one volume, cloth, $1.25.

With numerous Maps and Illustrations.

APPLETONS' EUROPEAN GUIDE-BOOK.

Containing Maps of the Various Political Divisions, and Plans of the Principal Cities. Being a Complete Guide to the Continent of Europe, Egypt, Algeria, and the Holy Land. Revised and corrected each Season. In two volumes, morocco, gilt edges, $5.00.

APPLETONS' HAND-BOOK OF SUMMER RESORTS.

Revised each Season to date. With Maps and numerous Illustrations. Large 12mo, paper cover, 50 cents.

APPLETONS' DICTIONARY OF NEW YORK AND VICINITY.

An alphabetically arranged Index to all Places, Societies, Institutions, Amusements, and other features of the Metropolis and Neighborhood, upon which information is needed by the Stranger or the Citizen. Revised and corrected each Season. With Maps of New York and Vicinity. Paper, 30 cents.

NEW YORK ILLUSTRATED.

A Pictorial Delineation of Street Scenes, Buildings, River Views, and other Picturesque Features of the Great Metropolis. With One Hundred and Forty-three Illustrations from drawings made specially for it, engraved in a superior manner. With large Maps of New York and Vicinity. Large 8vo, illustrated cover, 75 cents.

THE HUDSON RIVER ILLUSTRATED.

With 60 Engravings on Wood, from Drawings by J. D. WOODWARD. Royal 8vo. Paper, 50 cents.

APPLETONS' GUIDE TO MEXICO,

Including a Chapter on Guatemala, and an English-Spanish Vocabulary. By ALFRED R. CONKLING, Member of the New York Academy of Sciences, and formerly United States Geologist. With a Railway Map and numerous Illustrations. Second edition, revised. 12mo, cloth, $2.00.

New York: D. APPLETON & CO., 1, 3, & 5 Bond Street.

APPLETONS' HOME BOOKS.

A Series of New Hand-Volumes at low price, devoted to all Subjects pertaining to Home and the Household.

Complete in twelve volumes, handsomely printed, and bound in cloth, flexible, with illuminated design. 12mo. 60 cents each.

The twelve books are also put up in three volumes, four books to the volume, in the following order, handsomely bound in cloth, decorated. Price of each of these volumes, $2.00, or $6.00 the set, in box.

1. Building a Home. By A. F. Oakey. Illustrated.

" Mr. Oakey discusses house-building for the purposes of people of moderate means in the Middle States, and gives plans and elevations of cottages, from the very cheapest to a house to be built at a cost of $9,000. The conditions of building, with reference to the climate and material, are fully set forth, and the class of readers whom the book contemplates will find it of advantage.'—*New York World.*

2. How to Furnish a Home. By Ella Rodman Church. Illustrated.

" Mrs. Church's directions for house-furnishing, while very artistic and cheerful, are adapted to the wants of the great army of limited incomes. What may be done in the way of home decoration and upholstery is pointed out, with advice on the finishing touches that so often go to make a house a home."—*Philadelphia Ledger.*

3. The Home Garden. By Ella Rodman Church. Illustrated.

" We have instructions for gardening and flower-raising, in door and out. Roses and lilies have separate chapters, and there is much valuable information about ferneries, city gardens, miniature greenhouses, and methods of utilizing small spaces for vegetable-raising."—*Albany Argus.*

4. Home Grounds. By A. F. Oakey. Illustrated.

" 'Home Grounds' tells, in a very suggestive way, how the surroundings of a suburban home may be made beautiful at little expense."—*Christian at Work.*

5. Home Decoration : Instructions in and Designs for Embroidery, Panel and Decorative Paintings, Wood-carving, etc. By Janet E. Ruutz-Rees. With numerous Designs, mainly by George Gibson.

Contents: I. Introductory; II. General Remarks; III. Materials and Prices; IV. Stitches and Methods; V. Window-Hangings and Portières; VI. Screens; VII. Lambrequins and Small Panels; VIII. Incidental Decorations; IX. Wood-carving.

6. The Home Needle. By Ella Rodman Church. Illustrated.

Contents: I. "Go Teach the Orphan-Girl to Sew"; II. Beginning Right—Under-Garments; III. Under-Garments (Continued); IV. "The Song of the Shirt"; V. Rudiments of Dress-making; VI. Dress-making in Detail; VII. Sewing and Finishing; VIII. The Milliner's Art; IX. Children's Garments; X. House Linen; XI. The Mending Basket; XII. A Patchwork Chapter.

7. Amenities of Home. By M. E. W. S.

"The author has not spared good sense, right feeling, or sound principle. A better book for the family circle it would be hard to name."—*Literary World*.

8. Household Hints; A Book of Home Receipts and Home Suggestions. By Mrs. EMMA W. BABCOCK.

"The author has evidently been used to the nice economics of life, and her experience is of more than ordinary value. The book is not entirely given up to culinary items; there are talks on various subjects, and happy suggestions on making and ordering a pleasant home, that shall have a 'certain physiognomy of its own.'"—*Boston Courier*.

9. The Home Library. By ARTHUR PENN, editor of "The Rhymester." Illustrated.

CONTENTS: I. A Plea for the Best Books; II. On the Buying and Owning of Books; III. On Reading; IV. On Fiction (*with a List of a Hundred Best Novels*); V. On the Library and its Furniture; VI. On Book-binding; VII. On the Making of Scrap-Books; VIII. On Diaries and Family Records; IX. On the Lending and Marking of Books; X. Hints Here and There; XI. Appendix—List of Authors whose Works should be found in the Home Library.

"A practical, suggestive, serviceable volume, belonging to a series of what may be called domestic guide-books, all useful, instructive, and convenient."—*Saturday Review*.

10. Home Occupations. By JANET E. RUUTZ-REES. Illustrated.

CONTENTS: I. Introductory; II. What can be done with Leather; III. The Possibilities of Tissue-Paper; IV. Modeling in Wax—Flowers; V. Modeling in Wax—Fruits, etc.; VI. The Preservation of Flowers and Grasses; VII. Spatter-Work; VIII. Frame-Making; IX. Collections; X. Making Scrap-Books; XI. The Uses of Card-Board; XII. What can be done with Beads; XIII. Amateur Photography; XIV. Miscellaneous Occupations.

11. Home Amusements. By M. E. W. S., author of "Amenities of Home," etc.

CONTENTS: I. Prefatory; II. The Garret; III. Private Theatricals, etc.; IV. Tableaux Vivants; V. Brain Games; VI. Fortune-Telling; VII. Amusements for a Rainy Day; VIII. Embroidery and other Decorative Arts; IX. Etching; X. Lawn Tennis; XI. Garden Parties; XII. Dancing; XIII. Gardens and Flower-Stands; XIV. Caged Birds and Aviaries; XV. Picnics; XVI. Playing with Fire—Ceramics; XVII. Archery; XVIII. Amusements for the Middle-Aged and the Aged; XIX. The Parlor; XX. The Kitchen; XXI. The Family Horse and other Pets; XXII. In Conclusion.

12. Health at Home. By A. H. GUERNSEY, and I. P. DAVIS, M. D., author of "Hygiene for Girls."

CONTENTS: I. Home Surroundings; II. Privies and Water-Closets; III. The House itself; IV. The Air we Breathe; V. The Water we Drink; VI. The Food we Eat; VII. Lighting and Warming; VIII. Disinfectants; IX. The Bedroom; X. The Clothing we Wear; XI. Personal Habits; XII. Household Practice; XIII. Poisons and Antidotes; XIV. Accidents and Emergencies.

This series covers almost every topic pertaining to the American Home, and makes altogether an invaluable library on the most interesting of all themes. Many of the books are copiously illustrated.

New York: D. APPLETON & CO., 1, 3, & 5 Bond Street.

ERRORS IN THE USE OF ENGLISH. By the late William B. Hodgson, LL. D., Professor of Political Economy in the University of Edinburgh. American revised edition. 12mo, cloth, $1.50.

"This posthumous work of Dr. Hodgson deserves a hearty welcome, for it is sure to do good service for the object it has in view—improved accuracy in the use of the English language. . . . Perhaps its chief use will be in very distinctly proving with what wonderful carelessness or incompetency the English language is generally written. For the examples of error here brought together are not picked from obscure or inferior writings. Among the grammatical sinners whose trespasses are here recorded appear many of our best-known authors and publications."—*The Academy.*

THE ENGLISH GRAMMAR OF WILLIAM COBBETT. Carefully revised and annotated by Alfred Ayres. With Index. 18mo, cloth, extra, $1.00.

"I know it well, and have read it with great admiration."—Richard Grant White.

"Cobbett's Grammar is probably the most readable grammar ever written. For the purposes of self-education it is unrivaled. Persons that studied grammar when at school and failed to comprehend its principles—and there are many such —as well as those that never have studied grammar at all, will find the book specially suited to their needs. Any one of average intelligence that will give it a careful reading will be rewarded with at least a tolerable knowledge of the subject, as nothing could be more simple or more lucid than its expositions."— *From the Preface.*

THE ORTHOEPIST : A Pronouncing Manual, containing about Three Thousand Five Hundred Words, including a Considerable Number of the Names of Foreign Authors, Artists, etc.. that are often mispronounced. By Alfred Ayres. 18mo, cloth, extra, $1.00.

"It gives us pleasure to say that we think the author, in the treat ent of this very difficult and intricate subject, English pronunciation, gives proof of not only an unusual degree of orthoëpical knowledge, but also, for the most part, of rare judgment and taste."—Joseph Thomas, LL. D., *in Literary World.*

THE VERBALIST : A Manual devoted to Brief Discussions of the Right and the Wrong Use of Words, and to some other matters of Interest to those who would Speak and Write with Propriety, including a Treatise on Punctuation. By Alfred Ayres. 18mo, cloth, extra, $1.00.

"This is the best kind of an English grammar. It teaches the right use of our mother-tongue by giving instances of the wrong use of it, and showing why they are wrong."—*The Churchman.*

"Every one can learn something from this volume, and most of us a great deal."—*Springfield Republican.*

A GEOGRAPHICAL READER. A Collection of Geographical Descriptions and Narrations, from the best Writers in English Literature. Classified and arranged to meet the wants of Geographical Students, and the higher grades of reading classes. By JAMES JOHONNOT, author of "Principles and Practice of Teaching." 12mo, cloth, $1.25.

"Mr. Johonnot has made a good book, which, if judiciously used, will stop the immense waste of time now spent in most schools in the study of geography to little purpose. The volume has a good number of appropriate illustrations, and is printed and bound in almost faultless style and taste."—*National Journal of Education.*

It is original and unique in conception and execution. It is varied in style, and treats of every variety of geographical topic. It supplements the geographical text-books, and, by giving additional interest to the study, it leads the pupil to more extensive geographical reading and research. It is not simply a collection of dry statistics and outline descriptions, but vivid narrations of great literary merit, that convey useful information and promote general culture. It conforms to the philosophic ideas upon which the new education is based. Its selections are from the best standard authorities. It is embellished with numerous and appropriate illustrations.

A NATURAL HISTORY READER, for Schools and Homes. Beautifully illustrated. Compiled and edited by JAMES JOHONNOT. 12mo, cloth, $1.25.

"The natural turn that children have for the country, and for birds and beasts, wild and tame, is taken advantage of very wisely by Mr. Johonnot, who has had experience in teaching and in making school-books. His selections are generally excellent. Articles by renowned naturalists, and interesting papers by men who, if not renowned, can put things pointedly, alternate with serious and humorous verse. 'The Popular Science Monthly' has furnished much material. The 'Atlantic' and the works of John Burroughs are contributors also. There are illustrations, and the compiler has some sensible advice to offer teachers in regard to the way in which to interest young people in matters relating to nature."—*New York Times.*

AN HISTORICAL READER, for Classes in Academies, High-Schools, and Grammar-Schools. By HENRY E. SHEPHERD, M. A. 12mo, cloth, $1.25.

"This book is one of the most important text-books issued within our recollection. The preface is a powerful attack upon the common method of teaching history by means of compendiums and abridgments. Professor Shepherd has 'long advocated the beginning of history-teaching by the use of graphic and lively sketches of those illustrious characters around whom the historic interest of each age is concentrated.' This volume is an attempt to embody this idea in a form for practical use. Irving, Motley, Macaulay, Prescott, Greene, Froude, Monumsen, Guizot, and Gibbon are among the authors represented; and the subjects treated cover nearly all the greatest events and greatest characters of time. The book is one of indescribable interest. The boy or girl who is not fascinated by it must be dull indeed. Blessed be the day when it shall be introduced into our high-schools, in the place of the dry and wearisome 'facts and figures' of the 'general history'!"—*Iowa Normal Monthly.*

New York: D. APPLETON & CO., 1, 3, & 5 Bond Street.

www.ingramcontent.com/pod-product-compliance
Lightning Source LLC
Chambersburg PA
CBHW031335070726
47496CB00017B/1128